Photo: Fiona Melder

Kim Lock is an internationally published author of four novels. Her writing has also appeared in *Kill Your Darlings*, *The Guardian*, *Daily Life* and *The Sydney Morning Herald* online, among others. She lives in regional South Australia with her family.

THE OTHER SIDE OF BEAUTIFUL

KIM LOCK

FICTION HQ

First Published 2021
First Australian Paperback Edition 2021
ISBN 9781867214908

THE OTHER SIDE OF BEAUTIFUL
© 2021 by Kim Lock
Australian Copyright 2021
New Zealand Copyright 2021

This is a work of fiction. Names, characters, places, and incidents are either the product of the author's imagination or are used fictitiously, and any resemblance to actual persons, living or dead, business establishments, events, or locales is entirely coincidental.

Published by
HQ Fiction
An imprint of Harlequin Enterprises (Australia) Pty Limited (ABN 47 001 180 918),
a subsidiary of HarperCollins Publishers Australia Pty Limited (ABN 36 009 913 517)
Level 13, 201 Elizabeth St
SYDNEY NSW 2000
AUSTRALIA

A catalogue record for this book is available from the National Library of Australia
www.librariesaustralia.nla.gov.au

Printed and bound in Australia by McPherson's Printing Group

MIX
Paper from
responsible sources
FSC® C001695

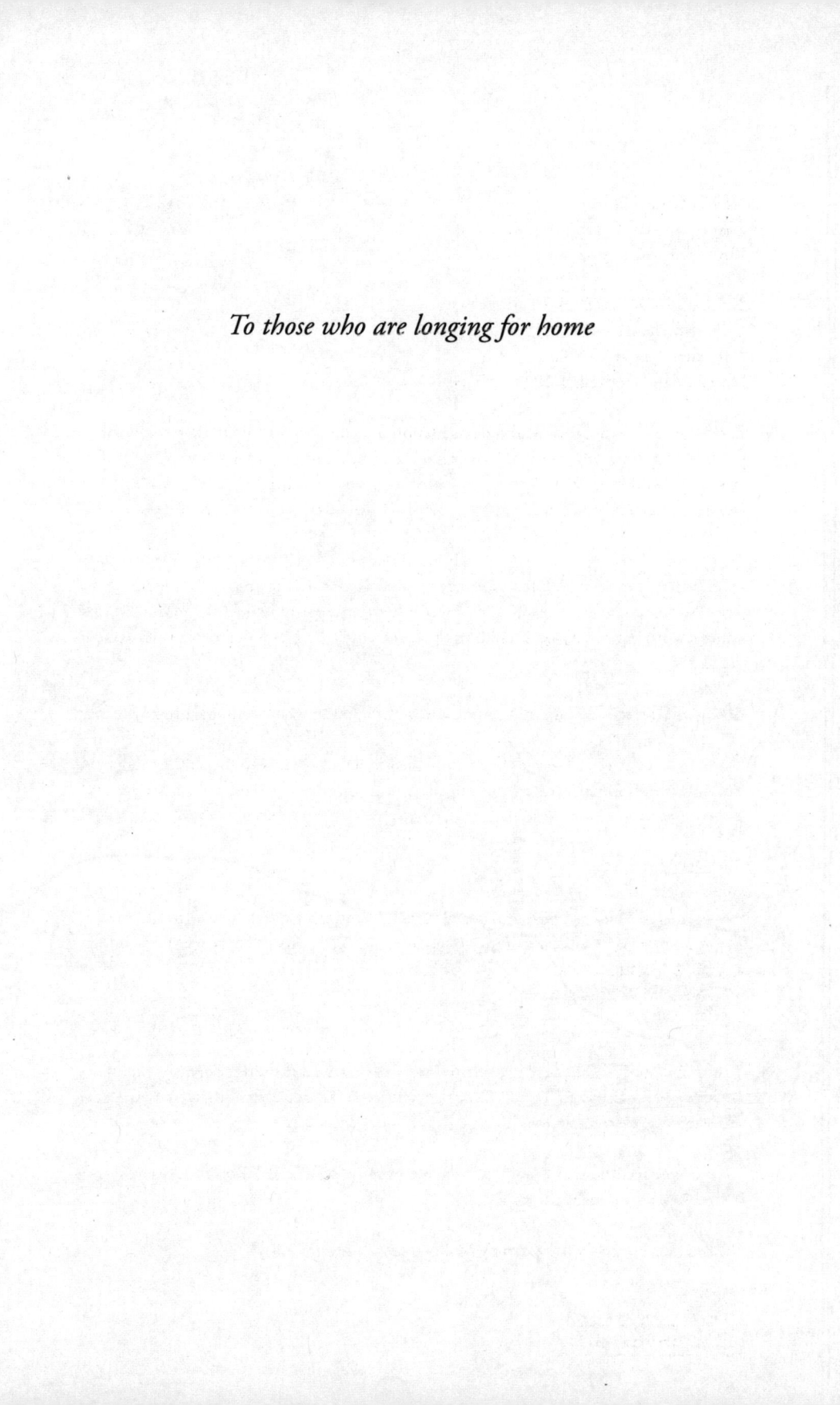

To those who are longing for home

3024 km to go

CHAPTER ONE

Mercy Blain's house was on fire, but that wasn't her biggest problem.

Flames licked orange tongues up the walls; great billows of greasy smoke poured into the night sky. Emergency service vehicles were gathered about the burning house, lights strobing across fences, gardens and the shocked faces of neighbours standing about in slippers, nightgowns clutched at their necks.

An ambulance sat in the middle of the street, back doors flung open. Inside the pool of light spreading from the ambulance doors, Mercy stood with the dog in her arms, ignoring the paramedics. Her body was shaking and tears were coursing down her cheeks. She could hear nothing—not the jets of water shooting into the flames, not the hoses slapping onto the pavement, not the shouted directions of the fire-fighters. Mercy could hear nothing but the high-pitched ringing of her own pure, absolute terror.

It was almost midnight. It was the eve of Mercy's thirty-sixth birthday. None of these things—not the orange flames nor the agog neighbours, not the birthday nor the deafly ringing ears—were Mercy's biggest problem, either.

The dog gave a sudden wriggle and licked Mercy's jaw. Unfamiliar voices swam around her, ebbing vaguely at the edges of her awareness, filtering in through the squeal of horror in her ears.

'Ma'am?

'Can you hear me? Ma'am?'

'Are you her neighbours? What's her name?'

'I don't know,' said a woman's voice. 'We've never met.'

'She keeps to herself,' said a man's voice.

'Ma'am?'

The paramedic was squeezing Mercy's shoulder. The dog began to lick furiously at Mercy's hands. Mercy closed her eyes and the flames were still there, blazing beneath her eyelids. There came a sound like iron cleaving apart, the rush of water battling against flames. Something cracked, groaned, and fell with a crash. Cries rose from the crowd.

'Can she even hear? Maybe that's one of them, you know, hearing dogs?'

'It's a sausage dog.'

It wasn't that Mercy was unconcerned about her house transforming rapidly into the first circle of hell. It wasn't, either, that Mercy was as worried as the paramedic hovering in front of her, calmly desperate for signs of smoke inhalation, or burns, or maybe even concussion from falling debris. No, those things weren't the source of Mercy's current despair.

'Mercy?'

Mercy's eyes flew open. With surprising agility for a Dachshund, Wasabi wriggled free of her arms and thudded to the ground, then took off on his stubby legs towards the figure hurrying up the street.

'Eugene,' Mercy croaked.

Heads swivelled. Onlookers parted. Even the paramedic finally paused in her scrutiny of Mercy as the man strode towards them. He lifted his arms and approached Mercy as if to gather her up in an embrace but, at the last moment, he faltered. His arms lowered awkwardly back to his sides.

'Are you okay?' Eugene said.

Mercy glanced down and saw his feet thrust into sandals. For a long moment she stared, uncomprehending. Since when did Eugene wear *sandals*? The exposed skin on the top of his feet looked pale and obscene. She thought she might be sick.

'Your voicemail didn't make any sense,' Eugene was saying. 'You said you had a small kitchen fire. But oh my god, Merce …' His voice faded as he took in the flames, roaring and crackling into the sky. Glass shattered and the crowd gave a collective gasp.

'We need to take a look at her,' one of the paramedics said, pushing Eugene aside. When Eugene retreated, bending to scoop up the dog, Mercy felt the bones in her legs turn to jelly.

'Don't leave me,' she said.

They took her into the back of the ambulance. Penlights flashed into her eyes. A blood pressure cuff tightened around her arm and the cool disc of a stethoscope slid below her clavicles, across her ribs, beneath her shoulder blades. She inhaled; she exhaled. *Any headaches?* they wanted to know. *Abdominal pain?*

Mercy knew she needed to answer. Dimly conscious as she was, it was enough to know she needed to say *no* to those things, because then they would leave her alone. But her throat was knotted tight and her voice would not come, and without the dog to hold onto her fingers trembled and clutched the pyjama pants at her hips, as if to hold herself together.

Did paramedics carry diazepam? Or maybe, if she asked, they could give her the green Penthrox whistle? Something. Anything.

Eugene and two neighbours stood at the ambulance doors. Eugene was watching her with alarm and something else—anger?—shifting across his features. She noticed he'd cut his hair shorter, and even in the dark she could see the silver that had once feathered his temples had crept upwards and spread, and now covered most of his head. In the flashing lights the silver hair gleamed.

'Lucky I found you, huh?' the male neighbour piped up. It was only now that Mercy noticed the man was shirtless, grey tracksuit pants slung beneath a protruding white belly.

Mercy blinked. Still no words came out.

'Very lucky,' the paramedic said.

'I was just outside, having a bit of a ciggie, when this little dog here—' the shirtless man gestured to Wasabi, who was licking Eugene's face '—appeared out of nowhere, barking its head off. So I look over and at first I thought all the lights were still on, which is a bit weird, because usually it's pretty quiet in that house—'

'Mike,' a woman standing next to him hissed.

'But then I saw smoke and realised it was flames.' The shirtless neighbour shook his head. 'So I ran over. Gave the poor girl a hell of a fright, didn't I, love?' He turned to Mercy. 'Sorry about that. We've never met officially but I just went barrelling into the poor lady's bedroom, found her standing there, smoke everywhere. I grabbed her and took her outside.' He swung his belly towards Eugene and stuck out a hand. 'I'm Mike. And this here's Jenny, the missus,' he finished, stabbing his thumb over his shoulder.

Jenny extended a polite hand towards Eugene, then uttered a shriek as something in the burning house fell with a crash.

The paramedic was taking Mercy's pulse for the third time, frowning. 'Pulse is still fast. You're not coughing though, so that's a good sign. Any nausea? Dizziness?'

Mercy was feeling both of those things, and more, but not for the reasons the paramedic was asking, so she gave a tight shake of her head. The medic's fingertips were cool against Mercy's skin, her thumb pressing gently into the back of Mercy's wrist. The contact was merely professional, and necessary, but to Mercy, the press of the paramedic's fingers was almost unbearably tender. A sob choked out.

The medic smiled at her. 'Bit anxious?'

Mercy's tears flowed faster. She nodded.

'Just keep breathing nice and slow, okay? That's it. In to the count of four, out to the count of … hey, you've got it. Done this deep breathing thing before, huh? Now, here's what I'd like to do.' The paramedic went on to say that Mercy needed to come with them to the Adelaide Northern Hospital, an instruction Mercy vehemently declined. When the medic pressed again, concern and authority sneaking into her voice, Eugene spoke up.

'I'll keep an eye on her.'

The paramedic was unconvinced. She began to say something about smoke inhalation, until Eugene leaned towards her and murmured. The paramedic listened, nodded, looked sidelong at Mercy and smiled.

'Well,' she said, picking up a clipboard, 'if Dr Phelps here is going to take care of you, I feel much better.'

There was more chatter among onlookers and medicos, peppered thick with the sentiments *lucky* and *close call* and *at least it's only things*. Mercy was shepherded out of the ambulance and the doors slammed shut behind her. Once again out in the open, the black night yawning above her and yet more neighbours clustered and gawping, any brief whisper of security Mercy had experienced in the ambulance dropped away. Her heart began to beat so fast and hard that the fat smacking sound of it only amplified her terror. It was like a horse bolting, only to scare itself with the sound of its own hoof-beats and gallop even harder.

Her house. *Her house.* She had lived there for two years.

'Anyway, love,' Mike was saying, 'I didn't catch your name?'

Mercy looked at him. The shirtless man was right. Never, before this night, had they met. For the past two years, all Mercy had known of the people living directly across the street was what she could see from her living-room window. A straggly gum tree was growing beside the footpath, and through its twiggy limbs she could see their carport, where a perpetually half-demolished old car languished beneath an oil-stained sheet. Their front fence was made of green-coloured mesh; their house was of dark red brick. Unlike the people living in the new house on Mercy's left, sometimes the people across the street forgot to put out their bins on a Monday morning and the garbage truck would sail past their house without stopping.

The air was clogged with the stench of smoke and white hot brick, incinerated fabrics and plastics and timber. Voices yelled, water whooshed, truck engines rumbled and dogs all up and down the street were a frenzy of yips and howls. Emergency services personnel in hi-vis scuttled about; Mercy was questioned, her details taken and business cards pressed into her hands. Police sauntered about following directives from the firies. People with FORENSICS written on their backs showed up. Mercy's voice squeaked and shook; she felt as if she were in an alternative reality. As if she were watching all the commotion from a distance, from the surface of another planet. So many people, so much noise. So much attention, all because of *her*. At one point a police officer bent his head to lock into her line of vision and said, 'Can we call anyone for you? Family or friends? Do you have somewhere to go?'

This is not what's wrong, she wanted to tell them all. *This is not my biggest problem.*

Eugene's eyes met Mercy's, then shot away.

Mercy looked towards her house in time to see a huge section of the roof collapse into the flames. Embers shot like fireworks into the dark sky.

And that was when the doom struck. Black and oily as that smoke-filled night, Mercy felt death tap on her shoulder as time ground to a complete halt, the present moment of exquisite pain stretched for an impossible eternity and her lungs filled with a scream of sheer panic.

In desperation, she wheeled to Eugene. 'I don't have—anymore—'

Eugene's face creased. 'She'll stay with me.'

The shirtless neighbour turned to Mercy, surprised. 'Well,' he said, 'I'm glad you've got a friend, love.'

Eugene said, 'I'm her ex-husband.'

'Technically,' Mercy managed to put in, 'we're still married.'

It was the first time Mercy had been outside her house in almost two years.

And *that* was Mercy's biggest problem.

CHAPTER TWO

Compounding Mercy's problem was the fact that she had only set foot in Eugene's new house once.

Eugene bought the house a week after it all happened, and a few days later invited Mercy over for a pizza that, at the time, Mercy could only assume was some perverse attempt at conciliation. They had eaten standing up at the kitchen bench, surrounded by partially unpacked boxes, and she had stayed long enough to eat one slice, then she'd fled. On the drive home, waiting at a red light, she had opened the car door and vomited the pizza right there onto the middle lane. Suffice to say that although he did extend another invitation or two, she never went back.

It was after three am by the time Eugene pulled into his driveway, twenty minutes away from Mercy's house. Every minute of that drive had felt to Mercy like a heavy rope unspooling from her chest, pulling tighter and tighter as the distance from home lengthened. She clung to Wasabi as if the dog was a piece of floating wreckage and she was flailing in a churning sea.

When the car stopped, Eugene turned to her.

'Before we go inside, there's something you should know.' He exhaled, rubbing the back of his head. 'Jose's here.'

Mercy's eyes darted from Eugene's unreadable face to the dark, quiet-looking house. All the windows were black. Above the roof, the sky was murky with Adelaide's ambient light. They were only a few suburbs from the city.

'Jose?'

'Yes.'

'I thought ... I thought you broke up.'

'We did. But now, well, we're not broken up.'

'So ... he's here? Inside?'

'Yes.'

'Eugene. I can't be here!'

'Look,' he hastened to say, 'don't worry about it right now. You've been through a tremendous shock and you just need a shower and some rest. We'll work it all out tomorrow.'

It was then Mercy realised that Eugene was wearing a collared shirt. Despite the urgent midnight awakening, despite the burning-down of his ex-wife's house, Eugene had still managed to put on a collared shirt. Of course he had. And there alongside him was Mercy, wretched with fear, stinking of smoke and melted plastic and blackened brick, in sagging pyjama bottoms and a sweat-stained old T-shirt.

And inside Eugene's dark, quiet house was his off-again, on-again, twenty-three-year-old boyfriend.

The high-pitched whine started up again in Mercy's ears. Everything began to spin, sickening waves pitching her back and forth.

'Eugene?'

'Yes?'

'I'm going to need some Valium.'

'Okay,' he said. 'I've got some in the kitchen.'

Also in Eugene's kitchen was whisky. He offered Mercy a shower but all she could think about was slowing the violent race of her heart. It was basic triage: stop the bleeding before you set the bones. So it was five milligrams of diazepam washed down with three glasses of Glenlivet before a shower, then Mercy climbed into a borrowed pair of jeans and T-shirt, and Eugene steered her into his spare room where she sat on the bed, in the dark, waiting for the sun to come up. Not once did she hear stirring from the master bedroom. Not once did she hear murmured male voices, the reassurances or sweet-nothings her ex-husband might give the young man who had supplanted—several times, it seemed—the woman he had once loved.

Mercy sat on her ex-husband's spare bed, waited for daylight, and tried to breathe.

The next day—Mercy's birthday—the investigator called. Mercy was prostrate on the floor by the window in Eugene's spare room when the phone call came. Being by the window provided the psychological sense that she was closer to her own house, but the curtains were made of a filmy white gauze, useless against the sunny mid-October glare, so she had thrown a blanket over the curtain rail and had just slumped to the carpet when her phone began to buzz.

Wasabi, curled up on the bed, opened one eye. It occurred to Mercy that all she owned in the world now was the dog and her phone. The pyjamas she had been wearing the night before—when her neighbour had dragged her from her smoke-filled bedroom—were now in Eugene's bin. She stared at the phone vibrating in her hand. When her neighbour found her she must have grabbed it from the bedside table, but she couldn't remember.

'It was the toaster,' the investigator told her.

Mercy held the phone tighter to her ear. 'The toaster?'

Eugene's spare room smelled of unfamiliar laundry powder and new carpet. The blanket started to slide from the rail and she squinted at the crack of sunlight blasting around its edge.

'We've established the cause of the fire was the electrical toaster on the kitchen benchtop, on the east wall,' the investigator went on. 'The flames caught what appears to have been a hanging towel, then the overhead cabinets, and then it got into the roof cavity. Once the rafters were alight, it moved very swiftly.'

The blanket slid further. Mercy put a hand up to stop it from falling. 'So when can I go home?'

A beat of silence came down the line. The investigator cleared his throat and said, 'I'm sorry, Ms Blain, I'm afraid you can't.'

Last night, Mercy had pleaded with the fire officers that once the fire was out, couldn't she please just go back inside? She wouldn't mind, she implored, if the carpet was squelchy, or if the walls were a bit sooty. Wasabi wouldn't mind, either. She wouldn't even tell anyone—no one had to know that she was back inside; it could be their little secret. But the wearers of hi-vis had been adamant: under no circumstances was she to go back inside her house. Until they could find the cause of the fire, the house was a crime scene. And besides, they pointed out, half the walls were missing. And the roof was caved in.

'Why not?' she asked now. 'It's not still a crime scene, is it? There's nothing ... suspicious?'

'No, nothing like that. You'll need to speak with your insurer, but at present, the house is unfit for habitation.'

'Unfit?' she echoed.

'I'm very sorry.'

Mercy's throat began to squeeze. She concentrated on drawing air into her lungs, fighting the rising terror. She wasn't safe. She wasn't *safe*. Where could she put herself to be safe? She wanted to climb out of her own skin. She wanted to get out of this terrified body.

The blanket slid from the rail and dropped to the floor. Light flooded in.

Mercy crouched on the floor, her chin on the window sill, blanket hanging behind her head and her breath steaming up the gauze curtains against her face. She closed her eyes and sunlight pressed through her eyelids, casting the world red. If she were in her own home she might have felt cocooned. But she wasn't in her own home. Her home had burned into the night. Her home was *unfit for habitation*. Instead, she was holed up in the spare room of her ex-husband's house, hating its unfamiliar laundry powder and new carpet smells, bristling at the sounds she heard from outside the room: the flush of a toilet; the clink of cutlery;

men's low, muffled voices. They would be talking about her, she knew. When would she come out of this room? When would she leave?

What the hell was she going to do?

Mercy opened her eyes. Another of Eugene's Valium had made her muscles slow, her movements swampy, but the drug had not eased the racing of her mind. It was why she had never really taken to benzos—even right when it all began. Having an out-of-control mind trapped in a limp, gooey body was an unpleasant experience, to say the least.

Mercy's knees ached from crouching. Her ankles were stiff, bent at an angle. Her head throbbed; she hadn't eaten or slept in almost twenty-four hours. From the bed, somewhere behind her, she could hear the dog snoring softly.

She tilted her head, resting her cheek on the window sill. Tears slipped from her eyes, wetting the gauze curtain. She closed her eyes again.

That's when the images came rushing in. Sharp and vibrant, familiar as a movie she had watched a thousand times: naked skin, clammy and pale; a voice, shrill with distress, crying out, *Do something!*

Mercy's eyes bolted open. She stared unseeing into the filmy sunlight until the voices echoed, fading.

When she rubbed her eyes, blinking away the sting of the images, movement caught her attention. Down Eugene's sloped front yard, over the low brick fence and across the street, someone was moving about. Lifting her head from the sill, Mercy squinted through the curtain.

Parked on the far kerb opposite Eugene's house was a very small, square, squashed-looking van. It was mostly beige, although one side panel appeared dark green and there were what looked like red spots in a row under the windows. Something was written in black letters beneath the red spots. Mercy inched the curtain aside, making a gap just large enough to peer through. She pushed her face closer to the glass, but couldn't make out the lettering. Bending down by the van's front wheel was an old man. The man propped a large piece of plywood against the van and on that board were the words: FOR SALE.

Mercy let the curtain drop. Withdrawing from the window, she resumed her prone position on the floor.

A soft knocking on the door. Eugene poked his head into the room.

'How're you feeling?'

Wasabi hopped off the bed and bounced over to Eugene to scramble at his shins. Mercy, lying on the carpet, took her arm from her face. What was the answer to his question? *Lousy? Sick? Homeless?*

She put her arm back over her face. 'I'm so sorry,' she mumbled. She didn't know what else to say.

'I thought you might like some dinner. Jose's made pasta.' He paused, and she heard the door click shut. She waited, thinking he had left, but after a moment he spoke again. 'You should probably eat something. You haven't eaten all day.'

'I didn't realise you've been keeping track.'

'I'm concerned about you. We both are.'

Mercy sighed and lowered her arm. She didn't want dinner. Her stomach was a hard knot rammed against her oesophagus. But after almost twenty-four hours of not leaving Eugene's spare room, she was beginning to despise herself.

Eugene lowered himself to the end of the bed and sat awkwardly. Mercy struggled to sit up. They both looked at the dog, a safe territory, wagging his tail at Eugene's feet, waiting for Eugene to let him out for another lap of the backyard.

'Happy birthday,' Eugene said at last.

'Thank you,' Mercy answered automatically.

'Have you been in touch with your insurer?'

He still didn't look at her. The question was a veiled implication: *When are you leaving?*

Mercy nodded. 'I can get ... they'll give me ... accommodation.'

'That's great news.' Finally his eyes darted to her. 'Not that you're not welcome here, of course. I mean, that must be great news *for you*.'

In spite of herself, Mercy gave a small laugh. Because how could she tell him that she couldn't possibly take herself to a sterile block of furnished apartments? Offices, strangers, bureaucracy, obligation—it was all as incomprehensible a prospect to her, as physically impossible, as growing another limb.

But Eugene was smiling at her, his best calm and reassuring doctor's smile, and the intensity of her wretchedness and self-pity was intolerable to herself so she could only imagine how intolerable she must be to Eugene. So Mercy got to her feet. She said, 'Thank you, dinner would be nice,' and made her way into the bathroom to wash up.

In the shower was where things were unbridled. Lush of belly, bottom, hair. Little firm except her elbows and heels—everything else was pillowy. Thirty-six and already she was a paddock run to seed. Not that she'd minded, really; there was a sublime pleasantness in self-seeding. Nor had there been anyone else close enough to notice. But now, as she stepped out of the shower and tugged Jose's borrowed skinny jeans over the stippled white flesh of her thighs, she remembered Eugene once putting his mouth to that flesh and bit back a yelp of dismay.

She scraped her hands through the limp wet curls tangled over her shoulders and down her back before hauling them into a semblance of a ponytail. She bent to roll up the hems of Jose's jeans.

Finally she straightened up and looked in the mirror. She squared her shoulders. Pinched her cheeks.

You can do this.

In the kitchen she found the table set for three. Music was playing softly, instrumental and tinkling with piano. Wine glasses, bread plates, a bowl of salad. Something with cream and garlic simmered on the stove and Jose was opening a bottle of white wine. It was a lovely, simple scene of suburban after-work domesticity, the sort of thing that friends and family around the world did every day, without even thinking about it. Mercy's heart rocketed up into her mouth.

I can't do this.

But Eugene smiled at her and served pasta and Jose sliced bread, and when Mercy asked what she could do to help, they both made appropriate *tsk, no, you sit down* noises so she sat and said *thank you* when Eugene poured Sauvignon Blanc into her glass. She tried not to recall the last time she and Eugene had actually sat down and eaten a home-cooked meal together, because honestly, did that time even exist?

When they were all seated around the table, Eugene raised his glass and said, 'Happy birthday, Mercy.'

Was that a muscle clenching in Jose's jaw?

'Please,' Mercy said, 'don't worry about it. I'd forgotten. And thank you.'

'We got you something.'

Eugene produced a small, neatly wrapped box with a foil bow on top.

Mercy was aghast. 'You shouldn't have.'

Yes, Jose's jaw was definitely working. He wore huge, round tortoiseshell-framed glasses and a flop of dark hair swept down towards one eye. As the muscles in his jaw clenched, he jerked his head to flick the hair back.

'Should I—would you like me to—now?'

'Yes!' Eugene's voice was over loud. 'Open it.'

Inside the paper was a pink and silver box. Ralph Lauren Romance.

'Perfume,' Mercy said. 'Thank you.' Should she apply some now? It wasn't exactly polite to spritz at the dinner table, but was it a display of ingratitude to set it aside? She settled for dabbing the nozzle on her wrist and making a point of lifting her wrist to her nose.

'Jasmine,' she took a guess.

Forks went to plates. Salad was passed around; bread was buttered. Knives clinked and the piano plunked and it was all Mercy could do to stop the top of her skull from shooting off and affixing itself to the ceiling.

Jose was talking. Specifically, Jose was talking about coffee beans. Oh god, Mercy thought, did he really want to talk about coffee beans? At the dinner table?

Wasabi, sitting hopefully beside her chair and waiting for crumbs, nudged Mercy's leg with a forepaw. It was as if the Dachshund was offering a Zen reminder, a caution not to fall into the trap of following her mind off into the depressing past or an unknown anxious future. Instead, the reminder said, stay right where you are, here, wholly in this present moment. *Be here now.*

Mercy dropped a shred of chicken to the dog and steeled herself.

'Are you …' she began to ask Jose. 'Are you still at the coffee cart, by the hospital entrance?'

A bemused expression crossed Eugene's face. 'Jose has his own cart now.'

'*Mobile refreshment service*,' Jose corrected, giving his head another pert toss. His tone was thick with the kind of loving, resigned exasperation of a long-term spouse. '"Cart" sounds like something you put your groceries in.'

Mercy wanted to put her head on the table. She imagined mashing her face right into the chicken carbonara and just waiting until they had both gone to bed, gone to work the next day, or better yet, maybe moved house altogether.

Clearing his throat, Eugene set down his knife. He glanced at Jose.

'I have to go back to work tomorrow.'

Mercy blinked, looking back and forth between them. 'Okay.'

'I can't take time off.'

'I wouldn't expect you to.'

'I'm about to go back on nights, though, so tomorrow I can run you back, uh, *home*, to pick up your car?'

Mercy felt another paw-nudge on her leg.

'I don't have the car,' she said.

'The Lexus?'

'I sold it.'

'You sold it?'

'Yes. I didn't … need it, anymore.'

'Did you get something smaller?'

'No, I ...' She trailed off. What was the point in telling him? She had sold the car because it was sitting in her garage, largely unused, for almost two years and she was better off with the cash than a whopping great SUV sitting ridiculous and idle. But Eugene wouldn't understand. He would start prescribing, she knew. *You don't face anxiety by hiding from it.*

Mercy felt a shifting, old resentment flaking up like sludge from a stirred pond. The few mouthfuls of pasta she had managed to eat sat like mud in her belly.

The pasta went through Mercy like a hot needle. It was just after midnight when the cramps roused her from a restless half-sleep. Pushing open the bedroom door, she made her way in the dark to the bathroom on her hands and knees, as though taking up less physical space would make her feel less pathetic.

On the way back, she was crawling across the floorboards in a waft of Ralph Lauren Romance (she couldn't find any air freshener) when she heard voices, low and urgent, coming from the end of the hall. Eugene's bedroom door was ajar and light seeped out. The voices began to quicken and rise.

'Seriously?' said Jose.

'It's complicated,' said Eugene.

'It really isn't!' Jose's voice pitched up. 'You bought her *perfume*. It's bloody simple if you ask me.'

Mercy paused, embarrassed, suddenly aware that she had sprayed too much perfume and it was wafting up the hall. She imagined the floral scent of it rolling in a great cloud towards Eugene's bedroom, announcing her presence.

Retreat, she told herself. *Quickly, now, before they find you.* But she didn't move.

'You're not responsible for her, Eugene.'

She couldn't make out Eugene's response.

'—keep her in your life, like this. It's not healthy.'

'—not healthy, Jose. *You're* the one who keeps coming and going—hot and cold—'

Mercy crept further forward.

'She has to go,' Jose said.

'But she has no one else.'

'That's not your responsibility. She's a big girl.'

A hot flash of anger ran over her. For six years she and Eugene had been married. *Six years.* And that marriage had ended as suddenly as a slap. They hadn't drifted apart, her and Eugene, they had severed swiftly, like the chop of an axe. Leaving arteries bleeding all over the place. At least, that's how it had felt to *her*. And Eugene knew that, he had acknowledged that, and *that's* why Mercy was here, now, calling on him when her house had burned to the ground. Not because she wasn't *a big girl*, but because Eugene wasn't an arsehole. Because they had history. Because Eugene, even when he left, had admitted he probably did still love her, and probably always would.

Mercy pressed her face into the floorboards. Her finger-nails scraped as she curled her hands into fists, the square glass bottle of perfume digging into her fingers.

'Jose—'

'She's a thirty-six-year-old woman—a *doctor*, no less—and she can't even get her own shit together?'

'Jose, please—'

'She is not your problem, Eugene. She is her *own* problem.'

The bottle broke when it hit the wall, and the cloying scent of perfume filled the air.

CHAPTER THREE

The next morning Mercy stood inside Eugene's open front door. The day had dawned warm and oppressive. A thin sheet of cloud covered the sky, trapping heat to the earth. It was one of those October mornings in Adelaide where everything felt pensive, paused. The leaves on the jacarandas lining the street hung motionless.

The scent of pine cleaner slunk out from the hallway behind Mercy, but it couldn't quite cover the smell of perfume. Last night she had cried while she mopped, apologising, and although Eugene had sighed sadly and patted her shoulder, saying *Don't worry about it*, she had not seen Jose at all.

Sweat pricked Mercy's temples. She wiped her palms on Jose's skinny jeans, letting out a long, shaky breath. When she had opened the door, Wasabi had uttered an excited, surprised yip then fallen silent, settling his slender bottom on the tiles and looking up at her expectantly. They weren't going for a *walk*, were they?

She bent and picked up the dog. Before she could hesitate, before her mind had a chance to catch up and pounce, burying her beneath reams of terror, she slipped through the open door, hurried across the front yard, and stepped out onto the street.

It was just after eight am; garages rattled open and closed, car doors thudded as people dressed in smart suits and heels hurried brisk and purposeful to work, while Mercy trembled, sweat slicking her skin, thongs on her feet and her arms full of sausage dog.

The badges on the little beige-coloured van read *Daihatsu Hijet*. Now she could see that the red spots beneath the window were hand-painted flowers. In rough brush-strokes below the flowers were the words: *Home is wherever you ARE.*

'She's a good-un, love.'

Mercy shrieked and spun around. Her heart hammered in her ears.

The man at the end of the driveway appeared to be in his seventies. Short and hunched over, a few strands of white hair combed over his scalp. An oil-stained collared shirt was tucked into faded navy work shorts and woollen socks were pulled up to his skinny knees. On his feet were steel-capped boots.

'I'm sorry,' Mercy said. 'I was—I wasn't …'

The man continued forward, coming up to the van and placing a weathered hand on its side. His fingers were as dark with oil as his shirt. Wasabi wriggled in Mercy's arms, straining towards the man.

'Good old bus, this one,' the old man said. 'Doesn't look like much, but the flowers painted on there pretty it up a bit, don't you think?'

'Uh, yes. Lovely.' Mercy focussed on breathing as slowly as she could. In and out. *Just keep breathing.*

The man straightened, looking up and down the road. He frowned at Mercy. 'You don't look familiar. You're not on foot, are you, love?'

Mercy glanced at her feet. Her thongs had cost two dollars; Eugene got them for her from the supermarket yesterday. They were currently the only footwear she owned.

'Well,' she said, searching for something polite to say. 'These—' she gestured to the thongs '—are temporary.'

A confused silence ensued, in which Mercy's pulse continued to race. She realised that he had meant to ask whether she had walked here—*on foot*—and felt heat rise to her cheeks.

'So, the van,' the man said, giving the vehicle a kind of hearty slap. 'You keen? I'll give you a good price. Two thousand.'

Mercy looked towards Eugene's house. Next door a clutch of neatly uniformed children were climbing into a shiny SUV while a woman dressed in active wear with a blonde ponytail and a huge handbag issued chirpy commands. Mercy looked away. Her T-shirt belonged to Eugene (red in colour and printed with, inexplicably, a stylised graphic of a Kombi van), her jeans belonged to Jose, and she had been wearing the same undies for three days now.

She has to go. It's not healthy.

Mercy clutched Wasabi tighter, lifting him to her chin as she considered the little van. *Home is wherever you ARE.*

Well, she thought, presently she was right here on the side of the street in front of her ex-husband's house. She didn't *have* a home, anymore—she had a charred ruin. How could this, where she was right now in this moment, really be *home*? How could it be that simple?

'Eighteen hundred,' the old man said.

'Does it work?' she asked, taking a tentative step towards the van.

'Course it does, love. A little lumpy when she's cold, but aren't we all? Otherwise, she runs just fine.'

'Is it roadworthy?'

The man drew back, looking offended. 'Course it's road-worthy. What do you think?' He stroked the side of the van as though calming a fretting horse. 'She might not look much, but the seatbelts work—coppers really care about that in particular—there's not much rust and all the lights work, and the brakes'll snap your neck, you stomp 'em hard enough. Seventeen hundred, then. Drive a hard bargain, you do.'

Mercy didn't have seventeen hundred dollars on her. In fact she didn't have any dollars on her. All she had was her phone; her purse was melted somewhere into her carpet. The man kept talking and she knew she had only moments left before the fear took her over entirely. She glanced over at Eugene's house, imagining the scent of perfume leaking from the bricks.

She is her own problem.

'There's a gas stove in the back, and a mattress—foam, but good enough—so what else do you need? Tell you what, I'll throw in …'

Mercy didn't hear the rest of that sentence, as the man turned and abruptly toddled off down the driveway. She froze. Was she supposed to follow him? In her head she tried to count the steps back to Eugene's front door. Twenty steps? Thirty? How many seconds would that take, to be back inside? The man disappeared into the garage and Mercy was evaluating how rude it would be to run away now, when the man reappeared with an ancient folding chair tucked under his arm.

'Here,' he said, setting the chair on the ground with a clang. 'I'll throw this in for good measure. *Now* you don't need anything else, love. You've got somewhere to sleep, somewhere to eat, somewhere to sit—' he gave the old folding chair a brief rattle '—and there you have it. Home away from home. So where you headed? North? West? Don't go east—it's all tourists.'

Mercy stared at the van. This was getting out of hand. She should apologise to the man for taking up his time and leave.

Except—where would she go? She heard again the shatter of the perfume bottle breaking, recalled the shock on Eugene's and Jose's faces as they had come into the hall and seen Mercy on her knees. Nausea and panic began to roil in her stomach. She forced herself to breathe slowly.

'You want to take it for a spin?'

'Oh, I'm sorry, I really don't know—'

'Sixteen hundred, then.' The old man laughed and shook his head. 'Talk about wearing a bloke down. Here, I'll show you the trick with the door.' He gave her a conspiratorial smile, as if sharing a secret, and positioned himself at the driver's door. 'You lift the handle—' he did so '—and you gotta get it … right … *here*.' Suddenly he jack-knifed at the waist, slamming his hip into the driver's door in a crunch of metal.

The door popped calmly open.

There seemed to be nothing else for it; events appeared to be unrolling in front of her entirely of their own accord, ever since her neighbour had pulled her from her burning house. Mercy climbed in.

The van had only two seats—driver and passenger, covered in cloth the same beige as the outside, with dark green stripes. The gear shift was a long stick with a ball on top. She turned around, peering into the back. The rear seats had been removed to fit in a tiny, L-shaped unit of chipboard cabinets, one of which had a gas-ring stove on the top. Along one side was a narrow bench topped with foam. A seat? A bed? There was barely room to sneeze, but she could see that it was cosy: the way the walls tucked around; the cheery domesticity of the little cabinets.

'Four-speed manual,' the man was saying. 'Runs like a real little racehorse, though not quite as quick off the mark. But who needs speed? Slow down, take a good gander at life, I say. Everyone's too fast these days. Racing around, putting photos of yourself on the internet all day. Why not just enjoy yourself?'

Mercy felt a squeeze of guilt. She hadn't been online for days. There would be dozens of notifications, all manner of fear and desperation and outrage. As though she'd summoned it, her phone vibrated in her pocket. A message from Eugene:

I want to help you but I'm not sure you can stay. Let's talk tonight. E x.

She could feel herself falling, slipping down a slope that returned her to old habits, old reliances—old hurts. Suddenly, Mercy felt as if a slab of stone had toppled onto her. She was exhausted, crushed; she was defeated, and tired to the marrow of her bones.

Mercy surveyed the inside of the van again. An entire living space, perfectly portable.

'Be home wherever you are,' she murmured.

The man fell silent. He was quiet for so long that Mercy stopped inspecting the Hijet's humble interior and turned to look at him through the open window.

The man was smiling. Tears glimmered in his eyes.

'Fifteen hundred then, love,' he said. 'I think she's saying she's yours.'

When Mercy was fourteen, her classmate Lana Nicholson-Dean had owned a pony. The pony was a brown-spotted, bad-tempered thing, short and round as a barrel. Once, on a rare occasion Mercy's mother had permitted, Mercy had stayed overnight at Lana's house. Early the next morning, Mercy had sat on the fence rail as Lana's pony was having new shoes fitted. The farrier, brow dripping with sweat and blossoms of blood leaking into his shirt from a savage bite on his back, had instructed Lana to rap the pony's forehead with her finger. *Right there between his eyes*, the farrier said. Perplexed by the hollow thudding sound, the pony had stilled its gnashing teeth long enough for the farrier to drive the nails swiftly into the pony's hooves.

This memory came to Mercy now as she pulled out of Eugene's neighbourhood and onto Main North Road. As the traffic closed in around her, the odd sensation of the Hijet's engine buzzing away beneath her seat was a distraction, a physical sensation to focus on, to stop her panic from biting hard enough to draw blood.

'Okay,' she said aloud to herself, 'I'm just driving home. No big deal.'

The van rattled, lurching each time she shifted gears. But Wasabi was unperturbed by the van's clanking and Mercy's clumsy shifting. The dog sat happily alongside her on the passenger seat, tongue hanging out, eyes wide and darting as he took in all the whizzing-by cars and houses.

'It's a good plan, isn't it, boy?' Mercy said. 'It's a little more snug in here than the house, but we'll get used to it. And it won't be for long, just a few weeks, I'm sure. Just until the house is fixed up.' With the campervan parked in her front yard, Mercy had decided, even her view would be the same: she would still see that familiar straggly tree growing beside the footpath; she would still see the neighbour's green mesh fence and their carport with the half-demolished car. She could still watch the garbage truck sailing past when they forgot to put out their bin.

Mercy gripped the old steering wheel and tried to unclench her teeth.

'Just driving home,' she repeated. 'I can do this.'

Mercy pulled onto her street. The taut, heavy rope in her chest began to slacken and her breath came easier. There was the small deli she had once walked to for milk. There was the leaning-over mailbox at number eight, there was the dandelion-strewn nature strip of number twelve. And there, just ahead, was the straggly gum tree growing beside the footpath—

Mercy's body went cold. 'Oh,' she said. 'Oh, *no*.'

The Hijet drifted into the kerb, and stalled.

Skeletal black frames stabbed the sky. There was no roof at all, the walls decapitated and crumbling. The ground was littered with curls of iron, brick rubble and charred detritus. Everything was coal-black, twisted, ruined.

And the *stink*. It was a stink of scorched metal; it was the acrid, toxic reek of melted plastics and cold, sodden charcoal. A breeze came straight from the ruined house, lifted Mercy's hair and etched the stink forever into her pores. Beneath Mercy's feet the earth was muddy and churned. Flakes of soot ticked and sifted.

Mercy stood in front of her house and nothing was the same. Nothing was *safe*. Her ears screamed and her house was the scene from a horror movie. Wasabi sniffed around a pile of bricks, nose searching the ground, and Mercy could not even see where her front door used to be because it was blocked by tangled sheets of roofing iron. Her lounge-room windows were gaping black wounds. As she looked, the charred edge of a curtain fluttered out, and gave the sad, desperate flap of a white flag.

Mercy dropped to her knees. She put her hands over her face. There was a keening sound, and then Wasabi was there, frantically trying to insert his wet warm snout between her hands and her face. His tongue slurped at her nose, her teeth, her eyelids.

Mercy scrambled to her feet. Wasabi yapped and bounced around her ankles.

Mercy fled. Blindly, without thought, without reason— she jumped into the van and drove. She ran as if she could escape her own treacherous, panic-soaked body and into oblivion.

And that is how Mercy Blain's view of the world changed from all she could see through her living-room window, to the world she could see through a windscreen. In a tiny beat-up van that was almost as old as she was, with her Dachshund beside her and the wind in her hair, Mercy's whole world was rattling north along a rural South Australian highway, with only the borrowed clothes on her back, cheap thongs on her feet and adrenaline pulsing through her veins. She had absolutely no idea where she was going, or what she was going to do.

2880 km to go

CHAPTER FOUR

For no other reason than it was the approximate cardinal direction she had been heading since she got out of Eugene's spare bed that morning, Mercy went north.

She drove for three hours, legs quaking on the pedals in a way that could have been caused by the van's engine buzzing beneath her seat or by the fear in her blood. Either way, Mercy drove and drove before she allowed herself any time to think. Adelaide's northern outskirts came and went, buildings and industry giving way to farmhouses, silos and vast slabs of wheat. Beside her on the passenger seat, Wasabi sat, pink tongue lapping the air as he aimed his snout at the wind rushing through the window. His eyes narrowed in pleasure at the new, exciting and very farmyard smells. The paddocks rolling by alternated between cereal crops, cows and sheep. Tufts of scrubby bushes or sprawling, leggy mallee gums lined the road. The sky lightened to a pale gauzy blue.

'Okay,' she said aloud, eventually. 'I guess this is happening.'

The old man had been curious when Mercy drew out her phone and asked for his bank details. 'I don't have any cash on me,' she had apologised. 'But I can transfer it to you right away. Only takes a few minutes.' And sure enough, after the man had insisted she follow him inside for a glass of lemonade and an Iced Vovo, he had checked his internet banking and 'would you look at that, there it is, strike me down with a feather!' Then Mercy had signed a slip of paper and the van was hers.

The Hijet had a top speed of about eighty-five, but according to the old man, you wouldn't want to be in it when it was doing it, so Mercy sat on seventy and watched everyone overtake her: sedans, trucks, caravans. She was the slowest, probably loudest and most hand-painted thing on the road. Google Maps told her she was on the Horrocks Highway, the A32. That meant very little to her other than the fact that she could roughly point out where she was in the event she needed to call roadside assistance. Which she hoped she wouldn't. The old man had been a motor mechanic for sixty-five years, he said, and hand on heart, *if that van wouldn't go until the cows came home he'd go hopping to hell.*

Flat grain fields gave way to rolling hills covered with grapes. Quiet, sleepy towns with slumped old pubs passed in the blink of an eye. After three hours, Mercy felt she had churned through enough adrenaline to stop and take stock of her situation. Up ahead, a sign announced a town called Spalding had restrooms, petrol and food, and Mercy knew that if she didn't want to stove into any innocent oncoming traffic she would have to eat. Low blood sugar and anxiety was an unacceptable combination on the road. Even if she was only puttering along at seventy.

Besides, it wasn't just food Mercy needed. At the very least, she also required soap and a toothbrush. A hairbrush. Something to wear on her feet that wasn't two-dollar thongs. And she would need water, as the few mouthfuls of lemonade she had obligingly choked down at the old man's house now sat uncomfortably in her bladder and her throat was parched.

But the question remained: despite how much she needed all those things—food, water, soap—how was she going to go inside a shop to actually *get* them?

When Mercy thought of her old self, her self from before it had all happened, she wanted to go back in time and shake herself for taking the simplest tasks for granted. The ability to walk into a shop, for instance, and pay no attention to the shop itself whatsoever. To be able to step into a grocery store with a head filled not with bewildering terror but with banal, everyday thoughts: politics at work; the issues of a current client; what she was going to pick up for dinner. Normal thoughts of a normal person. These were the sorts of things that, two years ago, Mercy would have thought about as she mindlessly picked out tomatoes or salted nuts or socks.

But then the shops had become as alien as the rest of the world. Her mind had refused to distract itself with everyday banality and instead became consumed with irrational dread simply for being inside her own skin. The world wasn't safe anymore, it was hostile. And that irrational dread, that sense of hostility, gripped Mercy now as she shut off the Hijet's engine outside the Spalding Welcome Mart.

Wasabi looked at her.

'I don't know, boy,' she said, crouching low in her seat and side-eyeing the Welcome Mart. 'I guess we'll just have to see.'

For a long time she sat in the van, staring into the store windows, hoping to glean a mental picture of the inside—a blueprint or an escape plan—but all she could see was the streetscape reflected back at her, the hand-painted flowers on the side of the Hijet distorted in the glass. The diazepam she had taken yesterday was long gone. She felt tight as a guitar string.

'Here's how I see it,' she said. Wasabi pricked his ears. 'I have two choices. Go into the shop and get what we need. Or,' she exhaled forcefully, 'turn around and go back.'

I want to help you but I'm not sure you can stay.

Without warning, her mind threw her an image of Jose, reclined on a pillow, being stroked by her naked husband, hairy legs entwined. Swiftly that image was followed by the picture of skeletal roof trusses, charred black and reaching towards the sky. When, thirdly, she heard the echoes of a shrill voice crying out, *Do something*, Mercy's shaking hands fumbled for the door.

'Stay,' she said to Wasabi. 'I'll be right back.'

Leaving the windows partially rolled down for fresh air, she left the dog and slid out of the van.

The street was quiet. A magpie warbled from a powerline overhead. From somewhere in the distance came the putter of a lawn mower; the air was warm and still and the sun pressed through a hazy sky. The street was wide, first laid at the time of bullock drays, but there were no cars and Mercy almost expected a tumbleweed to roll past.

Mercy approached the Welcome Mart's front doors. Crates along the window were stacked with nets of oranges, bags of green beans and a pile of cauliflower halves. A sign read ALL LOCAL PRODUCE—SUPPORT YOUR FRIENDS! and Mercy suddenly felt guilty. Food miles were a thing, weren't they? The less miles your food travelled the less you were contributing to global carbon emissions, and she had spent almost two years shopping online, her food trucked for who knows how many miles. Mercy gritted her teeth. There were too many things to feel worried about.

Pushing open the door and setting a bell jangling overhead, Mercy stepped inside.

Bread, Mercy said to herself. *Bread, bread, bread.*

There, on that side wall. She took a loaf of wholemeal. *Okay, what's next?* It was a small store, with two short aisles lined mostly with canned goods. A smaller selection meant easier choices, but less to choose from meant less prompting over what she actually needed, now that she could think of nothing but fleeing the store.

There: cheese? That worked with bread.

Out of the corner of her eye, she saw a woman appear behind the counter, watching her. Mercy felt the weight of the woman's gaze drop over her like a lead blanket. Customers in shops should know what to do; customers in shops should know how to *be* in shops.

Mercy gripped her loaf of bread and small block of cheese and shuffled with deliberate slowness along one aisle. She hoped her slow gait could trick her body into believing there was no threat, no reason to run, but it wasn't working.

How long would it take to pay for these two items and get back to the van? Thirty seconds, if she didn't speak to the woman behind the counter. Could she hold out another thirty seconds? But then she realised that if she only purchased bread and cheese she would have gone through all the stress of coming into the store only to leave again without getting what she needed. That would mean she would, inevitably, have to go back into another store—and it couldn't be this one, the woman would recognise her and that would be embarrassing—and she would have to do it all over again.

Something shifted. The thought of a future fear competed with the current fear and oddly, the future fear started to win. Feeling more afraid of having to do this again at some unknown point made her more convinced to get it out of the way *now*.

At the end of the aisle was a small stack of baskets. Snatching one up, she dropped in the bread and cheese. She added a tin of baked beans and a can of soup. What else?

Stacked in a pyramid shape on the floor by the counter were boxed casks of spring water. The casks held ten litres each; Mercy had no idea how much she would need. She set a cask of water on the counter along with her basket.

'Going away for the weekend?' the woman asked, giving her a big smile and not at all beginning to scan any of Mercy's items.

Mercy shook her head no, then nodded yes. Neither of those answers felt correct. *Please, just start scanning.*

'Good on you for not getting bottled water,' the cashier said, indicating the cask. 'All that plastic, choking all the turtles. Have you seen those photos of the seagulls with their bellies full of plastic?' She clucked her tongue. 'Awful.'

Mercy had seen the photos. Now she added imagery of dead sea life to her distress.

'Of course,' the woman went on, considering it, 'the bladder inside is made of plastic, but it saves a dozen of them bottles, I suppose. In the end it's hard to avoid all that stuff, isn't it?'

Mercy nodded frantically. *Please, for the love of—*

'That your van out front?' The woman leaned to one side, looking out the window. 'Looks cosy. What's it say? "Home is where …"?'

'Home is wherever you are.'

The woman pursed her lips, considering it. 'Well, I suppose that's true enough, isn't it?' Finally she began to scan the items in Mercy's basket. Mercy exhaled silently in relief. She had almost made it.

'The oranges are good,' the woman said, sliding the water cask around in search of the barcode. 'You should get some. Locally grown.'

'Sure,' Mercy said quickly.

The woman beamed, pleased, and punched a few keys on the register.

'That all then?'

Shit. Toothbrush. And soap. Mercy dragged herself up the aisle, grabbed the first ones she could find, and hurried back to the counter.

'Anything else today?'

'No,' Mercy snapped.

The woman's eyebrows jumped in surprise. Mercy swiped her phone to pay and left the store, forgetting entirely to collect her bag of good, locally grown oranges.

Mercy's hands were shaking so hard she couldn't properly grip the steering wheel. Blindly she drove up the street, going only a few blocks before she pulled over, yanked on the park brake and put her hands over her face.

'I can't do this.'

Paws pressed into her leg, then Wasabi climbed into her lap. He snuffled at her hands and she began to cry. The dog licked with more enthusiasm, his little body wriggling, butting into the steering wheel. Warm doggy breath puffed into her face, his damp tongue wormed between her fingers.

'Sit down.' She pushed him away, but he bounced right back, planting a wet slurp right in her eye.

'Hey,' she cried, and she couldn't help but laugh. 'That's gross.'

Her phone buzzed. Mercy took it out, blinking through tears.

You're going CAMPING for a few days? WTF does that mean? Where are you?

Mercy stared at the screen. She started typing replies to Eugene—first indignant, then chirpily reassuring, then meekly asking for help. But in the end she sent nothing. Clicking off the screen, she dropped the phone back on the seat. The tears abated; her chest eased. She waited for her breathing to slow, then she wiped her eyes, clunked the van back in gear, and pulled away from the kerb.

Mercy drove for another hour, following signs to a town named Crystal Brook because it sounded nice: it brought to mind pictures of babbling streams of calming water. There, she managed to fill the Hijet's tank with petrol. When she raced inside to pay she saw cables hanging from hooks behind the counter and bought a car-charger for her phone, which was down to an anxiety-inducing thirteen per cent battery.

It was growing late in the afternoon. In a few hours the October sun would sink towards the western horizon, blazing hot orange through the van's windows, filling it with glare. Mercy rubbed her eyes, already fatigued.

Besides the terror, the sense of doom and the pounding heart, one of the things she found most trying about panic attacks was how *tiring* they were. A flood of adrenaline, blood surging with oxygen, all muscles primed—a panicking body was a body responding to a perceived stressor in a purely reptilian, biological way. See a tiger behind a rock? Flee. Don't think—just get out. A panic attack was her body preparing to run for its life. Digestion halted, all rational cognitive function ceased and she became a helpless passenger in a runaway body.

For hundreds of thousands of years, Mercy knew, that particular survival instinct had not changed in humans, not even a tiny bit. Despite modern progress—despite the decided lack of predatory animals in grocery stores—fleeing from threat was an adaptive evolutionary response. In other words, it was a good idea. You fled, you lived. So it passed down the gene pool. Tiger or no tiger, the ability to panic was hard-wired into Mercy.

And now she was utterly, completely exhausted.

Though she had only been on the road a few hours, Mercy couldn't drive another minute.

CHAPTER FIVE

Up ahead was a sign for the Crystal Brook Caravan Park. Mercy followed the arrows off the main street, through a roundabout and onto a side road. Dipping down through a dry creek bed lined with skinny gums (was this the brook? Mercy wondered), the road finished in a small, sweeping patch of grass and enormous old eucalypts. A stop sign decreed that only caravan park patrons were permitted beyond this point, so Mercy parked next to the sign and sat, staring through the windscreen, engine idling beneath her seat for some time. Wasabi looked at her, ears pricked.

She shut off the engine. Silence descended. Mercy considered the huge old-growth gums. Broad, gnarled trunks the width of three men, limbs soaring overhead; the trees had been there for centuries. Something about that fact was strangely comforting. An unfamiliar calm eased up, sliding over her fear: the thought that these trees, these living beings, pre-dated the stress and the pressure, the arbitrary authority of the current dog-eat-dog world. They represented a time before any of this mattered. They reminded her how short time could actually be.

Scooping Wasabi into her arms, Mercy slid out of the van. The office was a box cabin set under the trees. Three steps up to the veranda, her knees weak, thongs slapping the boards. The door slid open with a whoosh and she stepped inside, clutching Wasabi to her chest. A tiny space, one wall lined with leaflets: Chinese takeaway, a bakery, the local golf course. When a friendly-looking middle-aged man emerged and took a seat behind the counter, smiling pleasantly up at her, Mercy found herself looking down at him and fought an attack of vertigo.

'G'day,' he said.

'Hello,' Mercy managed.

'Where've you come from then?' He was wearing an orange hi-vis shirt; his face was the dark tan of decades working outdoors.

She pointed to the Hijet.

He nodded. 'Not a bad little bus, those. Bit slow, though— you come far?'

Mercy wasn't sure how to answer. She felt as though she had been driving for days. She thought again of the SUV she'd sold; in that, Adelaide was a sleek, comfortable two hours away. In the Daihatsu it was a rattling, teeth-shaking, hair-blowing half-day.

'Just the one night?'

Mercy swallowed dryly. She looked to Wasabi, as if he might have the answer. How long *was* this going to go on? She thought of the old-growth eucalypts outside. To them one night was nothing, not even a heartbeat.

'Okay,' she said. 'One night.'

The site Mercy had been allotted was down the far end of the park. Gravel crunched beneath the tyres as she crept forward, rolling past caravans tethered to power poles like little ships; she waved dutifully at other campers, who stared as she passed as though they had never seen another human before. She found her site and pulled in.

A patch of sunlight fell through the windscreen. Mercy sat in the driver's seat for a long time, tears coursing silently down her face. Eventually, she took a deep breath, wiped her cheeks and stepped out.

The air was dry and warm. Birds screeched. The last of the cloud had burnt off and the sky was a smooth pale blue, the afternoon sunlight coming in bright ribbons through the leaves. Maybe, she thought, in another life— one without existential terror—it could be beautiful.

Popping the back of the van, she clambered inside. Wasabi made a few attempts to jump up behind her, his short legs bouncing, before he sat on his haunches and whined. Mercy climbed out, lifted him inside and climbed back in. The handful of supplies she had purchased at the Spalding Welcome Mart had rolled across the small patch of floor and she gathered up the cans, bread and cheese, and set them on top of the narrow foam mattress. The van wasn't high enough for her to stand; if she sat on the bed her hair brushed the roof. The cabinet with the gas-ring stove butted into her knees.

It was almost four pm and the last thing she had eaten was the Iced VoVo she had dutifully nibbled at the old man's house, and half of that she had shoved in her pocket and afterwards fed to Wasabi. Opening the bread, she laid a slice on her lap then picked up the block of cheese. She ripped it open, held the block in her hand and realised she was out of her depth.

Wasabi stared intensely at the cheese.

'Got a knife?' she asked.

He licked his lips, then sat perfectly still.

Mercy sighed. 'Let's see what we've got here.' Leaning forward, she shifted her knees aside to open one of the cabinet doors. Inside was two shelves, and sitting on one of the shelves was an old plastic ice-cream container, its label faded and peeling. When she picked it up the container was heavy and rattled with something metallic. Peeling off the lid, she found two forks, one spoon, a can opener, a small, fairly rusted pair of scissors and two butter knives.

It wasn't easy slicing the hard cheese with a blunt, rounded butter knife but she hacked off a few pieces, folded the slice of bread around the cheese and bit into it. Wasabi thumped his tail, shuffling forward on his stubby legs. Breaking off a piece of crust, she handed it down; he took the morsel daintily in his front teeth and then it was gone.

Though her stomach growled, her mouth rebelled against the food, refusing to produce enough saliva, so she had to chew for a long time. The bread was fresh and soft and the cheese was creamy and salty but each mouthful tasted like dust. Mercy forced the sandwich in anyway, and when she was done she sat and looked glumly out the open back door of the van, not really noticing the trees, the grass, the birds. If her house hadn't burned down, what would she be doing right now? Sitting on the couch with her laptop on her thighs, web browser open to half-a-dozen groups. Maybe there would be soup simmering on the stove, or chicken portions roasting in the oven, filling the house with their aroma.

After a while Mercy yawned, a yawn so huge her ears rang and her whole body shuddered. A breeze came up and brought with it the smell of barbecuing meat; it was dinner time, and the other campers were firing up their grills. Some-one had turned on a radio and the faint twang of country music filtered through the park. Mercy sat in silence, Wasabi alongside her, curled up and snoring. She remembered a meditation technique she had learned: the intention was to notice the transience of everything—sounds, movements of light, bodily sensations—but also to notice the spaces, the gaps, *between* those events. So Mercy noticed the sound of someone coughing, and then the silence. The thump of a caravan door closing, and then the silence. The indignant shriek of a cockatoo, and then … nothing.

This went on for a while, but Mercy remained uncomfort-able, twitching with unease and exhaustion. She couldn't stop wondering what the hell she was doing here. She really should just turn around and go home.

But she *had* no home.

The sandwich wallowed in her belly and she was thirsty again, so she checked the cupboard but there were no cups to be found. After a brief and decidedly unsuccessful attempt to lift the entire ten litres of water over her head and squirt it into her mouth, she set the cask on the cabinet, cupped her hand beneath the tap, and bent to slurp up palmfuls. It was tedious, and took a long time to drink her fill, but it wasn't as though she had anything else to do.

After giving Wasabi some bread and cheese and a few handfuls of water, she fished her phone from her pocket and created a new note. *Cup*, she typed. She thought for a moment, scratching her chin, then added: *Dog food. Sharp knife.* She racked her brains then added: *Whisky.* Ignoring the glaring red notifications, she shoved the phone back in her pocket.

A cool breeze had come up and Mercy shivered. Rubbing the tops of her arms, she yawned again, then ground her knuckles into her gritty eyes.

She didn't hear the sound of footsteps until it was too late.

CHAPTER SIX

'Knock, knock!'

Mercy froze. Wasabi's head jerked up.

A face peered around the side of the van. A late middle-aged man with silver hair, a generous paunch and a khaki shirt with a vast array of pockets and epaulettes.

'Can—can I help you?' Mercy stuttered, shrinking back on the bed.

'Happy hour!' the man crowed. 'At ours. Site number twelve?' He pointed off to Mercy's right. 'Jayco Starcraft and the silver Cruiser.'

He had just uttered a string of words that meant nothing to Mercy though evidently they should have. He was nodding, eyebrows quirked upwards as though waiting for nothing from her but a confirmation, an agreement.

'I'm sorry,' she said. 'Is there a problem?'

He looked surprised, then laughed. 'Were you planning to have happy hour at yours? Never mind, you can host tomorrow if you like. Unless you're heading off first thing in the morning? Pete and Jules—the Avan, site ten—hosted last night. Oof!' He gave another laugh, shaking his head. 'They can put away the shandies, I tell you! Jan and I couldn't keep up.'

'I see,' Mercy said, though she absolutely did not.

'So,' the man went on, 'you'll be swinging by, yes? Site twelve.' He made to leave, then stopped and turned back. 'I'm Bert. You don't have to bring anything, if you …' He surveyed the inside of the Hijet, as if seeing it for the first time. He took in the tiny cabinet, the narrow bed, the folding chair tucked against the gas bottle. The distinct lack of camping gear or supplies of any kind. 'You just up for the weekend?'

Mercy stared at him, blinking. Eventually, when she didn't answer, Bert rapped smartly on the side of the van.

'Righto,' he said. 'I'll see you at ours, then.' And he left, footsteps crunching away.

Mercy leaned forward, took hold of the door and heaved it closed with a thud. The van shook. She lay down on the stiff, stale-smelling foam, pulled Wasabi to her chest, tucked her arms inside her T-shirt and closed her eyes.

Mercy jerked awake to blackness so complete she could have taken a bite out of it. In the short beat of time it took her to remember where she was—the Hijet, the long drive, the caravan park—she launched into a full-scale panic attack.

Clammy naked skin and a shrill voice: Do something.

Two police officers, expressions calm and loaded.

Oh god, oh Christ, oh god oh Christ oh nononoooo she was so, so, *so* far from home. And there was nothing she could do, no way she could get there, without hours and hours of driving.

Mercy wheezed in a breath, trying with every cell of her body not to scream. Though her fingers scrabbled at the mattress, she tried to keep her body still. If she moved, she might not be able to stop. She might start to run and then where would she be? But then she couldn't breathe, she couldn't get enough air, so she launched herself against the back of the van, flinging the door open. Night air poured in, cold against her burning cheeks.

There was nothing she could do to numb the panic. She had no sedatives, no alcohol, no bed of her own to curl up in. For a frenzied moment she thought of running to one of the other caravans and begging for something—Valium, brandy; hell, even a strong painkiller—but she knew she would only create a scene. Strangers in pyjamas with startled, concerned faces—no.

Mercy was going to have to face the tiger.

She lay down on the mattress. She folded her shaking hands at the base of her ribs, over her diaphragm. Her body screamed and twitched but as she inhaled a long, slow breath, pushing the air into her hands, she said to herself, *Yes.*

Then she concentrated on the sensations: heart pounding hard, fat and juicy with blood. A rushing in her chest like heat. Tears streaming down her cheeks, all her limbs quaking. Her mind kept throwing images at her: the dreadful amount of time it would take to get home; the eternal black night; the horrifying unchangeable *stuckness* of this endless moment. But Mercy tried not to pay attention to those thoughts, tried to let them float past like clouds, tried not to let the images hook her in.

Be here now.

Heart pounding. Tingling limbs. Crying with fear.

Mercy breathed.

This fear was the unadulterated base emotion when all of its defences, its bodyguards—anger, justification, distraction—had been stripped away. Pure. Pristine. This fear was the boiled-down bones, the sheer cliff face, the very bottom of the well. An indescribable terror at the very fact that you exist at all. A headlong plummeting sensation that consciousness is suddenly, exquisitely, unbearable. Cannot be endured for even another instant. But at that same time, an undeniable knowledge that you *do* exist. And therefore, to exist is agony.

Mercy breathed. It hurt. And it took a long time.

Mercy didn't have any siblings. After her, her mother said, there couldn't be any more. When Mercy was younger her mother liked to explain to Mercy that she had taken so much blood to make that there wasn't enough left for anyone else. One time Mercy had skinned her knee on the concrete path between the house and the washing line, and she had looked down at the blood welling in crimson jewels and felt selfish. All that blood she had taken from a potential brother or sister, someone who might have been able to be all the things she tried to be but couldn't. Not on her own. Especially after her father left.

Lying in the thick blackness in the back of the van, Mercy felt the liquid thud of her heart and her own blood. The dog was a warm weight on her lap. Eventually, she began to notice an ambient light filtering through the van's grimy windows. A lone lamp-post over by the amenities block was throwing out a weak yellow pool of light. If she shifted her head a little, she could see out the open back door and up into the night sky. Gum trees made dark cracks like rivers through the landscape of stars. Despite the hour, a magpie sang softly then stopped, and now Mercy could hear another sound: a low, truncated grumbling. What *was* that? She listened harder. Snoring. Someone in one of the caravans was snoring.

She exhaled, feeling her muscles soften, her heart slow. She listened to the snoring from the caravan and felt a bubble of amusement lift into her chest. It sounded like someone starting a chainsaw.

Mercy snorted, then began to laugh. She clapped her hands over her mouth, not wanting to wake anyone, but realised no matter how hard she laughed she couldn't possibly be any louder than that snoring guy, which made her laugh even harder. It was a weak-muscled, delirious kind of laughter. It was laughing-at-a-funeral laughter. Lying on the stiff foam mattress, she wept and giggled and wept again until she was breathless.

And then, with the cold night air pouring in and her dog snuggled into her thighs, Mercy fell asleep.

When Mercy woke again she was freezing. The back door was wide open and the inside of the van was a fridge. The sun was up and the birds were a riot of sound; she could hear the thump of caravan doors, the crunch of leisurely footsteps and murmured voices and above it all, the warble of the magpies. Morning sunlight filtered in through the van's grimy windows and she wriggled herself into a tepid pool of it. All she had on was Eugene's red Kombi T-shirt and Jose's skinny jeans.

Her phone read 7.02am. Although she lay there curled up and shivering, she had done it. She had gotten through the night.

She made a hurried trip to the bathroom, during which the other campers, bundled in puffy vests and socks, called out greetings to her as she passed and she lifted a hand but largely ignored them. As she brushed her teeth, all she could think of was coffee. Hot, strong, creamy coffee.

But of course, Mercy had no coffee. Nor had she a kettle, or milk, or even a cup from which to drink it. Back in the Hijet she considered the loaf of bread, thinking of toast, but had nothing with which to toast it. She also had no butter, jam or Vegemite.

'Christ,' Mercy muttered, the long, panic-filled night coming back to her in flashes. 'Camping is not for the faint-hearted.' Dragging her fingers through her knotted hair, she pulled it up into a big messy bun that scraped along the van's roof as she moved. She caught a whiff of her armpits and grimaced. Picking up her phone, she typed *coffee, deodorant, butter, Vegemite, blanket, jacket.*

'Okay,' she said to Wasabi. 'Not toast. What else?'

She picked up a can of baked beans, frowning at the label.

'In "ham sauce"?' She waggled the tin at the dog, who sat up with sincere interest. 'I must have grabbed the tin without looking. Well, ham sauce it is, I guess. Now then.' She regarded the gas bottle; it was heavy, and the tap made a sharp *pfft* noise as she tried it. Plenty of gas, at least. She turned to the single cooker. 'How do we light this thing, you reckon?' Then she said, 'Oh, shit—what do we heat the beans in?'

Mercy recalled a story she'd heard from the ED, when a young man had been admitted bleeding profusely from a ten-centimetre laceration to the forehead. One of his nostrils had also been ripped open and he had second-degree burns to a fair amount of his upper body. The man had decided to 'go camping' in his backyard. After he had built a roaring fire, he set a can of soup on the coals and a short while later the can had exploded, resulting in his trip to Emergency.

Dropping to her knees on the floor, Mercy checked the cabinet, but other than the plastic ice-cream container of forks, spoon and blunt knives, it was empty. She looked into the second cabinet, beneath the gas-ring, but all that offered up was a curl of gas hose and a box of matches.

Wasabi waited, head cocked. Any sense of accomplishment Mercy had felt upon waking and realising she had made it through the night was leaking away. Who was she kidding? She couldn't do this. She was cold, hungry, sore and still tired. She was desperate for a cup of coffee, a shower and a hot meal.

'All right, Wasabi,' she said, slumping against the bed. 'I think it's time to admit—'

She frowned. Leaning forward, she let herself fall back against the bed again.

Yes, she'd definitely felt it. The bed made a hollow *thunk*.

Turning around, Mercy put her fingers to the edge of the mattress and tugged. The mattress lifted up, revealing another cabinet space.

'Why hadn't I noticed this before?' Filled with a rush of expectation, she propped the mattress against the wall and peered into the cabinet.

It was empty.

Mercy sagged. What did she expect? That someone would sell her a campervan filled with helpful self-sustaining supplies for only fifteen hundred bucks?

She was about to slam the mattress back down when, outside, a vehicle started up and moved, sending a flare of sunlight from its windscreen straight into the back of the Hijet. Briefly lit up, a shape appeared out of the dark. Mercy shuffled along on her knees and found, buried in shadows at the end of the cabinet, a cardboard box.

'What do we have here?'

She lifted it out: plain brown cardboard, a little bigger than a shoebox. The top flaps were folded down into each other. Unlike the ice-cream container, this box didn't rattle when she shook it, but it was too weighted to be empty. Scrawled in blue marker on one side were the words *Jenny Cleggett*. Mercy set the box on the floor and unfolded the flaps. Inside was a thick tuft of scrunched-down clear plastic, held fast with a rubber band. She paused, discomfort creeping over. Wasabi nosed the box.

'No,' she said, gently pushing the dog away.

Carefully, she unrolled the plastic. At the sight of the pale grey grit she wanted to believe it was beach sand. Dry plaster. Anything else. But the larger pieces were unmistakeable. They were chunks of bone.

It was a box of cremated remains. Mercy held in her lap the burned, ground-up skeleton of a human.

CHAPTER SEVEN

When people asked Mercy what drew her to study medicine, or, a little later, why she chose the specialty she did, she usually selected one of two answers to give: firstly, to get away from her mother; or secondly, because of her grandmother.

The first answer she reserved for those she had known long enough and could delve into the whole sludgy mess of it or, conversely, those she had only just met and who could laugh it off—a flippant, throwaway comment. After all, mothers malign easily in this man's world. But the second reason—because of her grandmother—Mercy used far more commonly. Both reasons held some truth, but neither held the whole truth on its own.

The truth was, Mercy never knew exactly why she had chosen to study medicine. Indeed, it was almost a decade of intense study, long years of safely guaranteed reasons to be able to say, *No, I can't*. But that wasn't all of it. Maybe there were lots of reasons: would the prestige of medical school be the thing that finally made her mother proud? Could following in her father's profession help her understand him better? Or perhaps there were no reasons at all besides the fact that her tertiary entrance ranking had been high enough. But one of the easiest answers to reach for was this: Mercy had chosen to learn the intricacies of the human body and its life-giving (or life-taking) forces because, growing up, she had spent countless hours secretly poring over the ashes of her mother's dead mother.

Mercy gaped into the box of cremated remains in her lap now and marvelled at how they looked exactly the same as her grandmother's. Although technically they weren't ashes—they didn't have the silky, powdery appearance of wood ash—they were the carbonised leftovers of the skeleton once all the flesh, muscle, fat and fluids had been vaporised by flames. When the skeleton had cooled, it was swept into a container, put through a pulveriser and poured into a bag. Returned to the family was this coarse, grainy substance scattered through with shards of bone.

And while Mercy held these remains in a plain, slightly battered cardboard box, her grandmother had been housed in a tall brass urn, kept behind a fogged glass door in the cabinet in the living room. Her mother had always kept the cabinet locked, but her mother had also thought Mercy didn't know where the key was (in her mother's sock drawer, buried under all the socks).

Wasabi came forward to sniff the box again and Mercy let him. After all, he too had spent the night with this unknown Jenny Cleggett. It was only fair that he caught some whiff of acquaintance.

Mercy set the box on the floor and rubbed her face. Clearly, she wasn't supposed to do this. She didn't have any supplies, she couldn't easily *get* supplies—let alone know what those supplies should be. And now the crappy van she had unthinkingly purchased from the kerb of Eugene's street had turned out to be a mobile cemetery. She thought of the old man, dropping the price, convincing Mercy this van was *hers*. She could not drive around with a box of unknown remains in the back. Mercy didn't even know where *she* was going, let alone taking along someone else, alive *or* dead.

Home is wherever you ARE.

Mercy stared at the grains of bone. Exactly whose home *was* it?

'Fine,' she cried out, pushing the box away. *'Fine.* I'll go back.'

She had no choice. She would have to return to her ex-husband's house. She would have to face her insurer and their soulless, temporary, unknown apartment. A howl of rage gathered in her chest.

Mercy returned the box to the cabinet under the mattress, climbed out the back of the van and slammed the door.

Then she heard a strange roaring. Looking up, she saw a caravan being towed at speed from the park, rocking as it tore around the corner and up the hill. Close behind it was a second caravan, the engines of both four-wheel drives revving. A third, the last caravan in the park, followed moments later, screaming up the hill and disappearing in a cloud of dust.

Mercy froze, glancing about. The park was empty. Had something happened? Had the owners of those caravans seen her staring into a box of cremated remains and fled in fear? Or was something more sinister afoot? Was there a reason to get the hell out that she wasn't aware of? Marauding bushrangers, a pack of wild dogs, an imminent busload of born-again religious?

She heard chuckling, and turned around to see the man from the office strolling along the grass at the edge of the gravel, a spray pack on his back and nozzle in gloved hands. Periodically he aimed puffs of mist around the base of posts.

'Never mind them,' he said. 'Gotta get there *first.*'

'Where? What's the rush?'

The man shrugged, making the spray pack lift up and down. 'Wherever they're stopping next.'

'Are they in some kind of race?'

'Yep. Hurry up and slow down.' He walked off, still chuckling to himself.

Mercy watched him for a moment, confused, then shook her head. She didn't have time to contemplate the rush of caravanners. She had a box of human remains to return. Hastening to the driver's door, she grabbed the handle and pulled.

Nothing happened.

She wriggled the handle. Fishing the keys from her pocket, she tried the lock but it wouldn't budge. Wasabi was in the van, and he watched her from the other side of the window, head tilted and floppy ears pricked. Feeling a bristle of panic, Mercy rattled the door handle with all her might, until she remembered the old man slamming his hip into the door. She positioned her feet. With one hand she lifted the latch, with the other she steadied herself. Taking a deep breath, she shot sideways, bashing her hip into the centre of the door.

'Ow,' she cried.

The door clicked and swung open.

Mercy climbed in. As if prompted by the fresh throb in her hip, everything the old man had showed her came rushing back. The engine would be cold so she would need to pull the choke. Three pumps on the accelerator. She turned the key, the engine *chug-chug-chugged* for a moment then *brummed* into life. For a minute she let it idle fast, then she pushed in the choke. The engine stalled.

'Crap,' she said. She started again.

Now the engine was flooded, and it turned over uselessly. She had to let it sit for a while. She tried not to think of the box of ashes, or her growling stomach, or the caffeine-withdrawal headache starting to cinch behind her eyes. Finally she got the van running, shoved it into gear and pulled out of the park.

She had almost reached the roundabout onto the main road when her phone began to ring. She glanced at the screen.

Her stomach plummeted. Her vision narrowed and her hands turned to ice on the steering wheel. Blinking to clear up her sight, something appeared in the corner of her eyes. A dark shape on the windscreen.

Mercy looked up and screamed.

Yanking the steering wheel was an instinct, a purely unthinking attempt to fling away the giant huntsman spider. Was it inside or outside the glass? She didn't want to look more closely to see. It was still there, lurking, the size of a bread plate, as she slammed her foot on the accelerator, not necessarily making the van go any faster but sending the engine into a loud whine that at least sounded like it was.

The Hijet leaned perilously as she careened around the roundabout once, twice, three times, trying to fling off the spider until she tugged the wheel again and was on the shoulder, bouncing over rocks and ruts, hitting the kerb and launching finally onto the main road. Pulling back onto the bitumen, she once again stomped the accelerator, hoping that if the spider had managed to cling its long hairy legs to the window as she swerved, sheer speed would blow it away.

That was, if the spider was outside. If it was inside … she didn't want to think about where it could be.

The speedometer needle edged up: sixty, sixty-five, seventy. She kept going. Sweat prickled on her hairline. Seventy-five, seventy-nine. The engine bucked and vibrated beneath her seat. The whole van rattled; Mercy's teeth crashed together and Wasabi's body jiggled.

The engine began to shudder in protest. Mercy eased her foot off the pedal until the van smoothed out. But still she did not look up. Nor did she look down at her phone. Gripping the wheel, she watched the white lines flashing beneath the front of the van and tried not to think.

After half an hour, she finally felt her pulse beginning to slow. Pressing herself as far back in her seat as possible, Mercy allowed herself to glance up at the windscreen.

The spider was gone.

The relief was immediate. She began to laugh weakly, rubbing the tension out of her neck and taking a few more kilometres from her speed. After another half-hour, her breathing was back to normal and she started to pay attention to her surroundings. Surely she should be coming up to Spalding by now? Where were the rolling grape vines from yesterday, the fields of wheat?

And then she saw the large green sign.

'What? No.'

She eased further off the accelerator. A four-wheel drive towing a caravan overtook her like she was going backwards.

'No,' she said again.

Spotting a rest area ahead, she flicked on the indicator and pulled off the road. All around her was flat reddish dirt, low tufty bushes and dry scrub. The sun shone brightly in a clear blue sky. And on Mercy's right was a long, dark green stretch of mountain range.

Bringing the van to a halt, Mercy picked up her phone. *1 missed call; 1 new voicemail.* Ignoring the notifications, she opened Google Maps. Her eyes frantically tracked the screen. Then, setting the phone down, she unclicked her seatbelt and climbed out of the van. She put her hands on her hips and stared at the mountain ranges sitting immovably to the east. The Southern Flinders Ranges. If Mercy was heading back towards Adelaide—if she was heading south—the Flinders Ranges should be *behind* her. Not *next to* her. Because yesterday she was south of them— yesterday, she hadn't even reached them. Now she looked again and they were definitely, undeniably there. A long, rumpled range of mountain, stretching as far north as she could see.

The road sign she had just passed read PORT AUGUSTA 49. Much like the Flinders Ranges, if Mercy was heading south, Port Augusta—the gateway to South Australia's vast northern outback—should be behind her.

Mercy wasn't going back towards Adelaide. She was still headed north.

She had travelled for an hour in the wrong direction.

A string of cars zoomed past on the highway, one after the other. Heat shimmered off the dry earth. Mercy swore under her breath. Then more loudly. Turning towards the mutinous mountain ranges, Mercy opened her mouth and screamed, 'Fuuuuuuck!'

Bending over, she howled into her hands. She couldn't take this anymore. She couldn't take the feeling of her body in a constant state of anxiety, everything tensed like a rabbit awaiting a fox. Unrelenting guilt ate at her, acid sloshing her insides. The waiting, the endless waiting. For what? There was no atonement for her. Nothing could ever fix it, there was no way of going back. Time passed and would always pass and as long as she was so irrevocably *in existence* she would have to face that, the inevitable suffering of her very existence, every single day. Meanwhile people would continue to die—just like whoever was the box of ashes in the back of the Hijet—and she would be alive.

In the shade of the van, the road hidden behind her, Mercy cried until her lungs were raw.

And then a campervan pulled into the rest stop.

CHAPTER EIGHT

The van was a rental camper: tidy and newish, clean and white with a bright orange logo on the side and a sloped pod on the top. It stopped a little way from Mercy and the engine shut off.

Through the windscreen, Mercy could make out only one figure inside. When the driver's door opened and the figure began to climb out, Mercy hurried around the Hijet, readying to climb in.

'They told me to go to Australia in the spring,' said a man's voice. A thick Scottish accent; he sounded amused. 'That's when the weather's the nicest, they said. But if it gets hotter than this—' He paused, and when Mercy looked up he was ducking his head to wipe his face on his sleeve. 'I don't know how you Aussies don't all burst into flames.' He was aged somewhere in his thirties, wearing work boots, cargo shorts and a snug, white T-shirt.

Re-adjusting a navy peaked cap, he gave Mercy a warm smile. 'All right, darlin'?'

'Fine, thank you.' She grabbed the door handle. It wouldn't open.

The man tucked his hands in his pockets, squinting out over the highway towards the Flinders Ranges. A band of sun-pink tinged his right bicep.

Mercy jiggled the latch. Nothing. Wasabi barked from the passenger seat.

'Have a swatch at that,' the man went on, nodding towards the Ranges. 'I mean, they're impressive, right enough, but I must admit for a mountain range I was expecting something a wee bit ... taller? These're really just hills.'

Mercy paused. The ranges weren't magnificent Alps, it was true. But looking at them anew now she thought they were beautiful. Rugged folds of dark jade, rocky outcrops and gentle swells of gold. In a flat, featureless space filled with saltbush and spindly, peeling gums, the Ranges gave the impression of watching over the land, providing relief with their steep damp gullies, shade and sanctuary.

'They probably pre-date the dinosaurs,' she said. 'Maybe give them a break.'

He laughed, toeing the gravel with his boot.

'Nice van you got there,' he said, surveying the Hijet. '"Home is wherever you are" ...' He leaned backwards, looking for the rest of the sentence. 'Och—that's it? Well, I guess that's got some truth in it, eh?'

How easily he stood there, in front of a complete stranger on the side of the road in the middle of nowhere. Feet propped, elbows swinging. Early thirties, then; he certainly couldn't be older than her. And she had to assume he was

a tourist: the accent, the rental van, the *you Aussies*. Mercy
felt a twinge of envy followed by a sharp pang of insecurity
at the sight of him—so easily occupying his freedom. He
appeared as casual and self-possessed as Mercy was iffy and
hysterical.

'Where're you off to then?'

'Oh, just … you know …' Mercy gestured vaguely
towards the highway.

He was smiling at her. There was a dark shadow of stub-
ble across his jaw. 'Is this your van then?'

She looked at it, as if to make sure. 'Yes.'

He nodded appreciatively. 'Bit of a cult vehicle, these.
Japanese.'

Mercy felt a flicker of alarm. She was driving a van from
a Japanese cult?

'If you look after it, you could make yourself a small
fortune. They're only going up in price. Hard to find sometimes. They're a bit of a collector's item.'

Oh, she thought with relief. *That kind of cult. As in
something exclusive.* She considered the Hijet with a new
appreciation. It was battered and grimy and hand-painted.
The bumpers were covered in dents and flecked with rust.
But it was square as a loaf of bread, and with its big rounded
headlights she could see that it was sort of … cute.

If you discounted the box of human remains in the back.

Shit. She really had to get back to Adelaide. Taking a hold
of the door handle, she tried to yank discreetly but the door
stayed closed. Wasabi barked again.

'Well, then,' she said, trying to sound nonchalant. 'Better keep—' more vague gesturing '—rolling, and all that.'
Damn this door. It was going to make a spectacle of her in

front of this man. This Scottish man. This Scottish man whose biceps pressed pleasingly into his T-shirt sleeves.

She was rallying herself, gathering her strength to slam her hip unceremoniously into the door when he said, 'D'you fancy a cuppa?'

A Pavlovian ping of synapses in her brain: *caffeine*. Now she felt the empty growl of her stomach, the dull band of pain tightening around her forehead. Yes, she would love a cup of coffee. Suddenly it was the only thing she wanted. Right now, she wanted more than anything—more than fearing panic, more than her burned-down house, more than cremated remains—to sit, not move, and drink a cup of coffee.

'I'm making one and you're welcome to join me if you like.'

He strode away, disappearing behind his campervan. Mercy heard the side door roll open; the van rocked as he climbed in then she heard rustling, clanging sounds.

Dropping the door handle, Mercy crept sideways. She leaned, peering.

The man appeared to be doing exactly what he'd said he was going to do: make a cup of coffee. He set a small kettle on a cooktop; he took out a jar of instant coffee. His back was turned but she could see the inside of the camper: a small cabinet with a stovetop, just like inside her own van—although his was much larger, and considerably more modern. Off to one side she could see the foot of a mattress, the rumpled end of a blanket.

Mercy stumbled. She had leaned so far she had lost her balance. Her feet scuffed the gravel and the man looked up.

'One for you then?' He held up a plastic cup.

'Yes, please,' she heard herself answer.

'Milk?'

'You have milk?'

'Aye, I do.' He pointed to a small silver box at the base of the cabinet. 'Got myself a fridge here big enough for a carton of milk and not much else.'

Mercy opened the back of the Hijet and lifted Wasabi down. The dog immediately ran to the nearest tree and began to investigate the ground around it.

The man stepped out of his campervan, two steaming cups in hand. He passed one to Mercy. She slurped, burning her mouth.

For a moment they sipped in silence, listening to the cars pass on the road, the birds chirping in the bushes. After a while the Scottish man disappeared back into his camper and reappeared with a folding chair. Setting it down in the shade, he said, 'Take a seat, if you like.'

Mercy retrieved the chair the old man had given her and they sat in the shifting shade of a gum tree, sipping their drinks. Wasabi trotted about on his stumpy legs, belly swinging, sniffing dried leaves and rocks and scraps of bark. Mercy felt the ache in her head slipping away. For a moment she forgot to be anxious until she remembered it again with a jolt.

'So anyway, I'm Andy.' He held out his hand. 'Andrew Macauley.'

Mercy paused before taking his hand briefly in her own. She felt the warmth of his palm beneath her fingers. 'Mercy,' she said.

'Pleased to meet you, Mercy.' He grinned at her from under his cap and heat flushed up her neck. 'So,' he said, sipping his coffee, 'you been on the road long?'

She glanced at the Hijet, as if it could answer for her. 'Not exactly.'

He took another sip from his cup, waiting for more, but she said, 'What about you?'

'Just a couple of days. Picked this thing up from the airport—' he waved in the direction of the camper '—and after a sleep, I took off. Now I'm here.' He settled back in his chair. 'Where're you travelling from?'

Mercy gulped the last of her coffee and stood up. 'Thank you for the drink. But I really have to get going.'

He stretched out his legs; he was in no hurry to move. 'Where're you off to, then?'

'Back to Adelaide, I have to …' She trailed off.

'Have to?'

Rebuild my house. Return a box of ashes. She remembered the missed call, the voicemail on her phone.

I have to face the consequences.

'I have to go. Thank you, again, for the coffee.'

'Cheerio, then.' He smiled and relaxed further in his chair. 'Safe travels.'

Picking up her chair, Mercy closed it with a snap. She flung the chair into the back of the Hijet with such fury it clanged against the cabinet and bounced to the floor. A cry gathered in the back of her throat.

She didn't want to return to Adelaide. She didn't want to go back to it all.

She wanted it to be *over*.

The Flinders Ranges stretched into the distance, disappearing north in a haze of sunshine and cobalt sky. What was at the end of the Ranges? Outback. And what was at the end of that? More outback. And then, eventually, further

north beyond all that outback was the tropics, and then the
sea. Mercy thought of the northern sea, glittering thousands
of miles away. A rippling spread of blue on the other side of
the continent.

She wanted it to be over—she wanted to be *on the other
side* of it all.

On the highway a fuel tanker hauled past, heading north.
One, two, three silver tanks, gleaming in the sunlight, heading goodness knows where. Mercy watched the truck until
it had disappeared. *Hurry up and slow down*, the man at the
caravan park had said. *You'll take her for a good trip, won't
you, love?* the old man who sold her the van had said.

And then Mercy knew. She wanted to be over it.

She would get to the other side of it, literally. She would
take herself to the other side of the country, to the sparkling
blue ocean at the other end. For two years Mercy had not
left her home but now she had a home she could carry with
her. Like a hermit crab. Or more accurately, given her speed
on the road, a snail.

Mercy would drive to Darwin.

CHAPTER NINE

A little under an hour later, Mercy rolled into Port Augusta—grey saltbush, pink earth, sweeping sky—and the first thing she found was a bottle shop. She ran inside and bought a bottle of whisky.

Then she found a supermarket.

Hunched over the wheel, squinting through the windscreen, Mercy drove up and down the rows of parked cars, scoping out the store like a robber at a bank. Would she feel better parking right outside the doors, so she could make a quick getaway? Or should she park on the far side of the carpark, away from everyone else, in that row of empty spaces? In the end she decided on the latter—a quiet place to recuperate, to make a plan. Nosing into a space shaded by a bottlebrush, she saw straight ahead what looked like a river, but when she checked the map she realised it was actually the very tip, the final northward trailing crack, of the

Spencer Gulf. This was where the Southern Ocean ended; from this point on, Mercy would not see the ocean again until she reached the other side of the continent.

The thought was amazing, inexplicable, and terrifying.

But Mercy didn't give herself time to contemplate this ending of the ocean. Instead she unscrewed the lid of the whisky, put the bottle to her lips and took a generous swig. And then another, grimacing as the liquid seared its way down.

Wasabi panted from the passenger seat. Without the wind blowing through, the van had grown stuffy. Mercy rolled both windows all the way down, letting in the cool breeze lifting off the water. Climbing into the back, she tipped the forks, spoon and knives out of the plastic ice-cream container, filled the bottom with two inches of water, and set it on the floor for the dog. Wasabi sniffed, took a few licks, then jumped onto the bed and settled his nose on his paws, tan eyebrows twitching as he watched her.

Pulling her phone from her pocket, Mercy spent the next few minutes making herself a list as detailed and thorough as she possibly could. Mentally she walked through her house, recalling what items she needed in her daily routine: *wake up, make coffee, shower, make breakfast* ... she tried to stay focussed on practicality, concentrating on each step of the task. What would she absolutely need? What could she make do without? What was flexible or versatile enough to serve more than one purpose? She tried not to get lost in the images and thoughts and *what ifs* that swept in, clotting up her mind like storm clouds, taking her away from the *here, now*. Tried not to pay attention to the accusing red circles of notifications, or the voicemail lurking there, unheard.

When the list was done, Mercy took another bracing draught before screwing the lid back on the bottle, then she shoved her phone in her pocket, rolled the windows up high enough so Wasabi couldn't jump out, and hopped out of the van.

Lots of people experiencing a panic attack for the first time, Mercy knew, arrive at Emergency convinced they're having a heart attack. Terrified they are about to die, they front up to the ED and gasp for their life. But when it happened to Mercy for the first time, four days after it all went down, it wasn't her heart she was worried about. It was her mind.

Riding the elevator up to the postnatal ward, checking her watch and running through the countless tasks she'd never be able to complete that shift, what struck her suddenly was a feeling of such intense restlessness she punched the buttons on the elevator to get it to stop. Any floor would do—she just had to stop. Whatever floor it was that the elevator doors had shunted open upon—Mercy still couldn't remember—she had staggered out and fumbled to a bathroom, then locked the door and paced the tiles, tugging at her hair until her scalp burned. All she could think was that she didn't want to be in her body anymore. Didn't know *how* to be in her body anymore. Grabbing hold of the sink, Mercy had stared at her reflection in the mirror and seen the desperation of someone trapped. A prisoner. It was only in hindsight—only when what had happened in the elevator started happening again and again, everywhere—she realised that what she had been experiencing was fear. Pure, unaccountable, insurmountable fear.

But fear of what, Mercy could not say. All she had known was that everything was abruptly and irrevocably wrong.

Mercy thought about that first panic attack now, as she crossed the supermarket carpark feeling for all the world as though she were heading into battle. If two years ago, that day in the elevator, she had been so taken by surprise that she had pulled out her own hair in anguish, then today she had an advantage: at this, at fear, Mercy was now a seasoned pro. There was nothing meek about the way she tackled the whooshing glass entrance doors. Fuelled by willpower and whisky, Mercy fronted up to the tiger that was the Port Augusta Woolworths.

She grabbed a trolley and started at the top of her list: *coffee.*

Her hands shook, and the most difficult points were the ends of the aisles, where her view to the exit was blocked by towering racks of products. The trolley had a shonky wheel and kept humping off to the left; at one point Mercy had to wrestle it away from a precarious display of toilet paper, flooded with a vision of rolls strewn across the floor and a hundred faces turning to stare at her, but she pushed the thought away and concentrated on the next item on her list.

The trolley piled up: canned soup, instant pasta, more baked beans. Apples, tomatoes, a bag of lettuce. Dry food and a lead for Wasabi. More casks of water and, when the display ceased wobbling, a four-pack of toilet paper. There were no blankets as such but there was a display of fuzzy chenille throws with images of cats on them, and Mercy took one, as well as a small blue towel. A man-size puffer jacket, too big but it would be warm. A cheap pair of sunglasses, flimsy as cardboard, but at least she could stop squinting. Several pairs of new underwear, beige coloured and supremely high-waisted but far cleaner than the single pair she had been wearing for longer than she would ever care to admit.

By the time she approached the checkout, Mercy was feeling victorious.

Then she saw the queue.

Why do supermarkets bother installing twelve checkout stations if only two of them are ever open? she wanted to shout. Panic lifted everything in her body upwards, as if she'd been hurled over a speed bump. Blood surged, nerves sang, even her hair stood on end.

How many times in those early days had she run out of the store, a part-filled trolley left to languish halfway up an aisle? Or abandoned a loaded trolley in the checkout queue? *Excuse me*, Mercy had gasped to the other shoppers as she squeezed through, *I just have to check something* ... And she had run through the doors and never gone back.

Trolleys inched forward. Items were scanned through with maddeningly slow, intermittent *beeps*. An older lady was counting out one hundred and eighteen dollars and forty-five cents in coins while she chatted with the checkout operator about someone named Gladys and her broken fridge. Mercy could leave the trolley; there was no obligation for her to buy all this. People would stare but she would be back in the van and driving away in a matter of seconds, never seeing any of them again.

But then she'd have nothing. She would be right back where she started. It was the Spalding Welcome Mart all over again.

If she craned her neck she could just see, through the store windows, the back quarter panel of the Hijet. She pictured Wasabi inside, snoozing peacefully. Silky brown ears puddled on his forepaws, plump belly rising and falling as he waited for her.

Be here now.

The old lady had finished counting out her coins and was shuffling away with her trolley. The checkout operator was turning to Mercy, smiling, asking after her day. Mercy was piling the items on the belt, one after the other, and she too was smiling and saying, *Fine, thanks, how are you?* Damn it, she didn't have any bags, and she was about to say *Yes, please* to the offer of twenty-cent plastic ones when she remembered that plastics were choking the oceans, so she grabbed a couple of hessian bags from the stand and handed those over, five dollars each.

She put the packed bags in the trolley. She asked for some cash out; she paid. She nodded and said *Thank you* again and then—sweet Lord! She'd done it!—Mercy was pushing her trolley through the doors and she was outside, into the fresh air, and she was free.

CHAPTER TEN

Leaving Port Augusta, a large intersection appeared and a road sign loomed, offering Mercy a choice between two monumental destinations, thousands of kilometres away and a continent apart: to the left, Perth, Western Australia; to the right, Darwin, Northern Territory. Flicking on the indicator to turn right felt portentous, loaded. It felt as though she was signalling not just her intention to turn the vehicle, but admitting she was slicing open the future of her whole life. A future she had never considered. The gravel in the median strip was raked into neat broad strokes of dark and light red, like hazard stripes to the beginning of the outback.

Pulling onto the gravel shoulder, Mercy picked up her phone.

'Where the hell are you?' said Eugene. In the background she could hear the sounds of traffic, the blip and burr of a pedestrian crossing. He was on a break. She imagined him standing by the service entrance at the eastern wing of the hospital, where the nursing staff took their smoke breaks beneath a No Smoking sign.

'One thousand, two hundred and twenty-one kilometres south of Alice Springs.'

Silence. Then, '*What?*'

'One thousand, two—'

'I heard you.' He paused and there was a scuffing sound, and then his voice was muffled, as if he'd cupped his hand around the speaker. 'Jesus, Mercy, you must be—'

'Port Augusta.'

'Port *Augusta?*'

'Yes.'

'So—will you be back for dinner?'

'No.'

Another pause. 'Fine. I'll just leave the front door open. You can—'

'Eugene, I won't be ...'

Mercy was twenty-six when she met Eugene Phelps; he thirty-eight. She was into her fourth year of residency, and frustrated, beginning to worry over when she would gain entry into the fellowship. Eugene was bright, serious, older—trailing a kind of effortless Melbourne dapper into the Emergency Department. After four years in the ED at Royal Melbourne, Mercy had wondered if he found Adelaide Northern Hospital to be a little backwater. It was, after all, plonked squarely in a less desirable socioeconomic area, if you considered it from a purely real estate perspective (which of course, Mercy never did, because what kind of an arsehole doctor would that make her?). There'd been a chance bumping-into over the last decent-looking silverside and pickle sandwich at the canteen; quick snuck coffee dates; sex, quite a lot of it somehow, despite their mutually ludicrous work schedules and lack of synchronised time off.

Then, *tra-la-la*, eight years later: all that had happened.

Mercy stared through the windscreen. Up ahead the road disappeared over a low rise; the gravel shoulders were the colour of peaches. The road seemed to aim directly north. To the other side.

'I'm not coming back. Please don't call me. I need to get over it.'

She hung up before he could reply. She set the phone down, pulled onto the Stuart Highway, and drove north.

From here on, as far as routes were concerned, Mercy had very little choice. Australia might be a big country but as far as passable highways went, up the centre it had only one. After Port Augusta, the road north to Darwin was the Stuart Highway. That's it. Unless one had a rugged, kitted-out four-wheel drive and was willing and able to spend weeks traversing sandy desert tracks. Which, it goes without saying, Mercy and her old Hijet were not.

The land rolled by. The highway shimmered a dirty bronze, laying a path through a flat red earth carpeted with low, tussocky shrub. Rutted two-wheel tracks split from the highway to cut through the saltbush. Long stretches passed where Mercy saw no trees at all, only dense thickets of dry bush. Far in the distance, a low string of cloud gathered over gauzy ranges.

The warm wind buffeted Mercy's hair, blowing strands of it in circles around her face. She kept pushing it back behind her ears, only for it to tug loose and fly about again. Wasabi sat squinting on the passenger seat, nose to the wind, ears aflap.

After an hour she passed a rest stop where three caravans were gathered. Someone waved; Mercy hesitated too long and the rest stop was behind her before she had decided whether or not to wave in return.

The scrub bordering the road had grown tuftier, dotted with stunted, straggly trees; the soil popped bright red. Cattle grids sliced through the road, making the van judder. In the rear-vision mirror, Mercy watched four-wheel drives ease up behind her, pause, then overtake, dragging enormous caravans emblazoned with custom decals: *Harry and Bev, channel 18*; *Spending the kids' inheritance!*; *Adventure Before Dementia.* That last one made Mercy laugh, albeit in a thin, slightly crazed sound that was lost in the wind. Salt flats appeared, glinting sheets of pink and silver. Signs warned the road was unfenced and motorists should beware of wandering livestock. Sometimes the road didn't seem to bend or turn at all; it just rolled ever northward, the white lines disappearing under the van with the beat of Mercy's heart.

Eventually, after many hours, all the shrubbery and trees disappeared. The highway unfurled a path over rolling, stony desert; Mercy was left alone with the breeze, the late afternoon light blazing stark over impossibly vast red earth, and the wide flung expanse of flaming sky.

Evening was a blanket of shadow by the time Mercy pulled into Glendambo, a pinprick of an establishment on the elephant hide of the outback. According to a sign on the side of the road, the outpost boasted a population of thirty humans, 22,500 sheep and two million flies. WELCOME TO GLENDAMBO.

More than four hours had passed since Mercy left Port Augusta, which now seemed like a bustling metropolis. She had stopped a few times to drink water and squat self-consciously behind the van, and once for petrol. But now she wanted to eat; she wanted to walk. She wanted to stop driving and sleep. And judging by the caravans she could see clustered about in the square of orange dirt signposted as a 'caravan park', Glendambo, though pinprick it might be, was an oasis off the highway for those much needed things: food, fuel, ceasing of forward movement.

Wasabi sat up and whined as the Hijet's tyres crunched over the gravel. The temperature of the air coming through the windows had dropped sharply; Mercy smelled dry earth, cooking smoke, and diesel fumes from an idling truck.

When she shut off the engine, the silence and lack of vibration seemed absolute. For a moment she sat perfectly still, listening to the silence. Then she climbed out, stretching her legs and lifting her arms above her head.

'Stay,' she said to Wasabi.

The inside of a quiet pub: dark-patterned carpet, the stale stink of beer and the lurid, oversaturated colours of a sports game on a television screen in the corner. Her legs felt weak and cramped stiff.

'Just one night,' Mercy told the older woman behind the counter, who seemed to expect nothing else.

Back in the van, Mercy followed a broad gravel driveway around the back of the pub into a wide paddock also of gravel. Scattered about were spindly, half-dead-looking sticks of trees. Mercy parked on the far side, leaving as much space as she could between herself and the nearest caravan.

She let Wasabi out of the Hijet and he availed himself of the facilities of a nearby fence post then proceeded to trot in zig-zagging circles, nose to the ground. Mercy walked to the toilet block, where crickets sang at the base of tin walls that ended a foot above the ground, then she returned to the van, opened the back and climbed inside, leaving Wasabi out to run around.

Mercy's stomach growled at the scent of grilling sausages floating on the breeze. She felt a pang of envy at the fact of someone's portable fridge. How did it run? Solar panels, gas? The idea of the setup, the complexity of it, boggled her mind. How easy it was to take for granted that which was always readily available, always there. If she was at home, she would be stir-frying chicken tenderloins in soy sauce, or maybe sizzling taco mince in spices. She thought of her couch with its deep, soft cushions, the fluffy green blanket she liked to drape over her knees as she ate, re-watching *The Good Wife* or *Downton Abbey* or *The Crown*. She had taken her comfort and security for granted. Now it was gone.

Mercy selected a single-serve can of baked beans; she studied a tomato, now bruised and dubious-looking after the long drive. The bag of lettuce, once crisp in the store, was now warm and turning to wilt. But she set a bunch of leaves on her brand-new bamboo plate, along with the sliced tomato. While she waited for the beans to heat in her tiny new saucepan, she set out some food and water for Wasabi, whistling him back to the van.

She was scraping the steaming beans onto her plate when she heard a voice.

'Good evening, neighbour!'

Mercy froze, saucepan aloft.

A man appeared: generous belly, buttoned shirt, excessive epaulettes. It was the man from the Crystal Brook caravan park last night. Her mind scrambled for a name but came up blank.

'You made it!' he said, slapping the door pillar of the Hijet.

'Yes,' Mercy said. A single bean oozed from the saucepan and dropped onto her foot.

'Happy hour is at ours again tonight.'

Wasabi pounced and the bean was gone.

'Jayco Starcraft and the silver Cruiser, remember?'

Mercy didn't, because beyond now understanding that 'Jayco' was a brand of caravan (she had been overtaken on the highway by at least a dozen of them) she still didn't quite know what the rest of his statement meant. But she nodded as though she did. She was still holding the saucepan.

'Might be a quieter one this evening,' he went on. 'Pete and Jules haven't shown up yet to get all rowdy! I think they're chuffing off a bit further up the track.'

'I see.'

'Anyway—you don't have to bring anything, just yourself and your … little dog. What kind of dog is he anyway?'

'A Dachshund.'

'One of them sausage dogs!'

'Yes.'

'Yeah, we're from Mannum, Riverland way,' he went on, drawing himself up and stuffing his thumbs into his waistband. He squinted thoughtfully into the distance, as if contemplating something. 'Been on the road about five weeks.'

Mercy set the saucepan back on the stove. Her stomach gave a loud, hollow rumble. Should she start eating? Would he take the hint? Or was that rude—should she perhaps offer the man some beans?

'Jan likes to go places where she can see the horizon, you know? Clear open spaces. Not too many trees, they make her claustrophobic, she says.'

'Then she must love it here.'

He gave a blast of laughter. 'Ahh, but it's magic here, wouldn't you say?' Now he beamed into the distance, flapping his elbows happily. 'Just magic.'

Flies were gathering around her plate; she shooed them away, only for them to lift briefly and land again. Her beans were growing cold.

'So we'll see you at ours then?' He pointed in what Mercy assumed was the direction of his caravan.

Mercy looked helplessly down at her plate, as if it could help her. She thought of the ashes under her seat.

'Thank you, but I really ... um—'

'Bert,' a woman's voice called.

'I've got a nice cask of Shiraz. Not from Mannum, where we're from, but I think it's a South Aussie vineyard. Which reminds me! We were on the Oodnadatta Track once, on another trip, and we saw this rig broken down, and I stopped to help the bloke—'

'*Dinner*, Bert.'

'—he'd let down all his tyres, you see, because he thought that's what you're supposed to do on a corrugated road. But it wasn't like sand, I said, and for rocks you need *more* tyre pressure, not less, right? So he's there with two flat tyres and only one spare, and I said—'

'*Bert!*'

'Oops.' Bert gave Mercy a conspiratorial wink. 'I've over-run my leash. So we'll see you at ours? Happy hour?' And, giving the van another slap, he was gone.

Mercy leaned forward and pulled the door closed. She ate her dinner in silence.

The sun went down and the temperature plummeted. Stars pricked out like chips of ice. Citronella and the scent of mozzie coils hung in the cold air as the park descended into darkness, bracketed by two yellow pools of light from lamps on either side of the gravel lot.

Mercy was tired, but when she lay down on the bed and pulled her new chenille throw with the picture of a cat on it up to her shoulders, she couldn't sleep. Her body felt wired; it was almost too quiet, a suffocating silence so complete it was almost its own noise. Her ponytail was uncomfortable. She sat up, tugging at her hair tie, stuck in a tight clump of knots. Using the torchlight on her phone, she rooted around in the hessian shopping bag she was now using as a handbag and found the new hairbrush, then she sat in the dark and tried to brush out her hair.

She hadn't been to a hairdresser in two years; her hair reached halfway down her back. It was thick, curly and heavy—her mother's hair, but her mother had always worn her curls in a meticulously styled, short, tousled bob. Never a hair out of place on her mother's head. Mercy usually kept her own hair shorter too, but then she had stopped being able to leave the house and that put an end to many ordinary outings, hairdressers included.

The bristles caught in a particularly unruly clump and Mercy gave the brush a vicious tug, stinging her scalp. Driving with the window down all day had turned her hair into a magpie's nest; she imagined it full of twigs, chunks of gravel and the tiny, winged corpses of flying insects.

Her phone vibrated. She glanced at the screen: the red dot on the Facebook icon read *99+*. The last time she had been online her house had been standing, unscathed.

Mercy's finger hovered over the screen. She imagined the chain of tags, mentions, replies. *Em Bee might know; Em Bee can you help? Em Bee was mentioned in …*

For the last two years, this had been Mercy's day: wake up, make a cup of coffee, drink it while checking last night's notifications, then make a second cup and drink that while replying to questions, challenges, sometimes downright vitriol. *How dare you judge me?* She got that one a lot. *You've clearly never experienced …* At first she had been mortified, her face flushing hot as she hurried to type a placating reply. *So sorry. Didn't mean to offend. Just meant to suggest …* But eventually she had come to understand that the outrage of others was always their own pain playing up. Sometimes, no matter what you said, if someone was determined to take offence, they would. Because wasn't she triggered in the same way, by her own pain? When someone held a mirror up to Mercy's face, didn't she want to punch it to shards? Most of the morning would disappear into ploughing through the new posts of more than a dozen groups—*Pregnancy and Birth Chat Adelaide*; *Southern Mamas*; *SA New Mums* and so many more—taking her all the way to lunch time. Then she would set her phone aside and try to do something else for a few hours. Tidy the house, do laundry, order groceries online. Then back to Facebook in the afternoon: cajoling, reassuring, sharing. *Latest evidence shows* and *That's not a peer-reviewed study, sweetheart* and *Check with your doctor, they should know …* After dinner was when things got busy—in the evening, when toddlers had been put to bed and partners attended to and families fed, that's when Mercy's attention was demanded. Through the evenings and into the night, Mercy poured herself out—but not *really* herself, not who she *really* was—trying, somehow, to make amends.

Had it helped? All those hours spent sympathising, advising, sharing the outrage of strangers—had that made up for it?

1 new voicemail. She still hadn't listened to it.

Dropping the hairbrush, Mercy picked up the whisky and swigged it back. She thumbed the Facebook icon, navigated through to *Settings*.

Then she pressed *Delete my account.*

Gasping awake, Mercy lay wide-eyed in the blackness. Sharp hooks remained from the nightmare, squeezing the breath from her lungs. Sweat cooled on her skin. Slowly her surroundings returned: weak light from the lamps outside filtered through the windows; the van's roof was an impenetrable black square. Curled at her hip, Wasabi slept soundly, a small lump of heat. Beneath the cat throw and wearing the man-size puffer jacket, Mercy was warm, but her feet were cold.

Lying motionless, Mercy tried to control her breathing, inhaling to the count of four, exhaling to the same. She softened her fingers, keeping her hands loose and palms open, but her heart raced. The night was so dark, and so incredibly quiet.

When she sat up she knocked the whisky bottle to the floor. Her phone read 12.34am. The inside of her mouth tasted like old carpet. Digging around, she found the toothbrush and tore away its packaging. Tentatively, she pushed open the back door and peered out.

Silence. It was a kind of unimaginable silence—no road noise, no humming radios or electronics, not even a dog barking. Stars stretched an infinite glinting banner. A slight breeze came up but it made no sound; there were no trees to catch it, make it whistle. Wasabi lifted his head and she patted him, whispering, 'Stay.'

Mercy slid out of the van. The gravel was cold and gritty beneath her bare feet. She glanced across the park. The caravans were motionless and quiet. The last thing she wanted was to wake somebody. She imagined Bert tugging on a many-pocketed khaki shirt and accosting her, requiring an explanation for her second absence at happy hour. Would he accept her excuse that she had shared her own version of happy hour with the box of cremated remains under her bed? That she'd lifted out the box marked *Jenny Cleggett*, sat it on the cabinet top next to the gas-ring stove and toasted it with a fair whack of her whisky? An obliging drinking partner Jenny Cleggett had turned out to be—the serene, silent type.

Clutching her toothbrush and tube of paste, Mercy tip-toed across the gravel, towards the bush beyond the fence. The sleeves of the puffer jacket made zipping noises as she moved, so she brushed her teeth with her elbows stuck out, minty foam dripping onto her toes. Opening wide, she scrubbed at her tongue, then the roof of her mouth, brushing harder and harder, scrubbing against the images of blood and naked skin, the faces of the two police officers at her door, the shrill echoed *Do something.* Mercy brushed and scrubbed until she gagged, until tears trickled down her cheeks.

CHAPTER ELEVEN

A snuffling sound, something damp and warm slurping into her ear.

'Wasabi,' Mercy groaned, attempting to push the dog away. But he wouldn't be deterred; the sleepy flail of her hands he chose to interpret as a game, and he began to nip playfully at her wrists before launching a repeated assault on her ears with his tongue.

'No,' she moaned, grabbing hold of his fat, wriggling body. 'Stop it.'

Finally managing to shove the dog away, Mercy sat up. The cat throw slid down and she shivered. Her head swam. The van was filled with light; condensation glistened on the windows and bright, early-morning sunshine reflected off the ridiculously orange dirt, blasted straight through the glass, along her optic nerves and into her brain. How could it be so bright and yet so cold?

The half-empty whisky bottle was on the floor and the box of Jenny Cleggett on the cabinet. Mumbling an apology, Mercy put the ashes away. She gulped a cup of water and opened the back of the van. In a brown blur, Wasabi rocketed out into the crisp morning air, and she wondered how long this burst of puppy energy would last.

Flies came in droves. Choruses of 'Morning!' reached her as she walked to the bathroom. Mercy ducked her face and swatted flies in reply.

Inside the amenities block, the air was already heady with pong. Insects buzzed around the iron walls. At the sink she splashed water on her face and asked herself once again what the hell she was doing. It still wasn't too late to turn back.

But when she lifted her head, she saw the doorway framing a bright slab of sunshine. Birds were singing. A soft breeze skittered across the earth, lifting dusty golden waves, and she recalled the golden flames stretching high into the night sky above her caved-in roof. She sighed, then wrestled her hair into a gnarled ponytail.

Once again outside, Mercy could hear idling diesel engines. Sunlight caught on massive wing mirrors as four-wheel drives were aimed towards awaiting caravans. Awnings clacked as they were rolled snugly away and pop-tops *whoomped* as they collapsed, snapped down tight. Doors thumped; radios crackled.

Mercy tugged her phone from her pocket. 7.12am.

'Yep,' a woman was calling out, waving as if directing an aircraft. 'Straight … straight … left … *left* … I said *LEFT*!'

Mercy needed coffee. And this morning she had plenty. Brightening at the thought of the large jar of Moccona in the van, she hurried back—fielding more waves, more shouted greetings and dutifully conceding that *yes, it's a great day for it.*

As she reached the Hijet the sound of the engines behind her lifted to a roar. Caravans rolled forward, tyres grinding over gravel, gathering speed. Two vehicles swung towards the driveway, creating a brief, tense bottle-neck, before another revved up behind them and the convoy advanced, squeaking, towards the road. The air was filled with the growl of engines as they raced to the highway, square rumps of caravans gleaming in the sun as they disappeared.

Silence descended. A lone magpie carolled; the dry sticks of a tree clicked together.

Mercy stood in the empty lot, staring about. In the space of fifteen minutes the park had emptied, and now her battered Hijet stood alone. Wasabi lifted his nose to sniff at the invisible wake left by the hastily departed. Mercy recalled the park manager from Crystal Brook yesterday morning, chuckling over the vans racing from the park. *Gotta get there first. Hurry up and slow down.*

Almost another twenty minutes passed before Mercy was finally able to drink a cup of coffee. Having forgotten to clean her saucepan the night before, she had to scrub dried baked bean sauce from it at the brackish tap outside the bathroom block, beneath a sign declaring Water NOT For Drinking. The underlined NOT made her so nervous she removed all drips, even from the handle, with her T-shirt before pouring in her cup of spring water. On the small gas-ring the water took almost fifteen minutes to come to the boil. Not having any way of keeping it cold, Mercy had no milk, so the coffee was a swirling tar-black pool in her cup and it burned her tongue, but it was coffee, and as she sat in the back of her van, legs swinging, gazing out into the deserted lot and the blue sheet of sky, she felt, almost, the briefest moment of peace.

Until she wanted a second cup, but realised she would have to wait another quarter hour for the water to boil.

She fed and watered Wasabi, then made herself a tomato and cheese sandwich. After she ate, she slicked on a liberal coating of deodorant, brushed her teeth, fought again with her hair before giving up and piling it into a bun on her crown. Switching on the front camera on her phone, she let out a shriek of laughter.

She looked ridiculous. Puffy purple skin surrounded her red-rimmed eyes. A craggy boulder of frazzled brown hair haloed her head; a handful of inflamed red dots scattered across her forehead. Peering closer, Mercy marvelled at her ability to produce the paradox of both pimples *and* wrinkles.

Her mother had spent hours poring over a mirror, fingertips reading her skin like Braille. As a young child, Mercy had found it fascinating, her mother's ability to spend so much time gazing into her own reflection, and had one day decided to try it herself. Dragging the bath stool alongside the cabinet, Mercy climbed up and sat cross-legged on the cabinet top, then began a protracted study of herself in the mirror. After a few minutes she had grown bored, her attention wandering to the row of baskets filled with glossy metallic tubes, squares of colourful packed powders, pots of exquisitely scented lotions. A while later her mother had appeared in the mirror, face etched with rage, and Mercy had been hoisted from the counter by her arm, smacked on her backside and banished to her bedroom for the rest of the day. Her mother liked to recall the episode to anyone who'd listen, proclaiming it had taken her *hours* to remove all the lipstick and moisturising cream from the mirror. But what Mercy recalled, but never dared mention, was that it wasn't the mess Mercy made that triggered her mother's outrage, but what Mercy had wasted. It was vanity that caused her mother to howl *You little shit, that lipstick was Guerlain!*

Mercy tossed her phone onto the seat.

The sign at the Glendambo petrol station read LAST FUEL FOR 253KM.

Holding the nozzle in the Hijet's tank, Mercy was considering the sign's implications when she heard the sound of a vehicle pulling into the bowser behind her.

'Mercy, hiya!'

At the Scottish accent, Mercy's grip on the nozzle faltered. The pump chugged to a halt.

'How's it gaun?'

The rental camper was parked so close to the back of her van their bumpers were almost touching. Andrew Macauley stood with hands on hips, smiling widely.

Mercy was suddenly aware that she hadn't showered in three days.

'Hello,' she said, fumbling with the nozzle and restarting the petrol flow.

'Did you stop here overnight?' He pushed his sunglasses up onto his head.

'I did,' Mercy answered, thinking of the half-empty whisky bottle.

'Maybe I misheard, but I thought you'd said you were headed back to Adelaide?'

'I changed my mind.'

He waited for her to say more, but she stared hard at her petrol cap.

'Fair enough, then,' Andy said cheerfully. He cranked up his own flow of fuel, and gazed about Glendambo's bleak surroundings with an amused expression. 'Minimalist,' he said.

'Except for the flies.'

Last fuel for 253km. Travelling at seventy, that was over three and a half hours. How long could the Hijet go without filling up? She thought again of her SUV, purring along at one hundred and fifteen—that distance would barely skim the top off a tank of premium unleaded. But this thing?

Home is wherever you ARE. Flakes of paint were peeling from one of the flowers, stone chips marked the green panel. She noticed that the back bumper seemed to be sagging and touched it with her toes; it wiggled. Wasabi was in the driver's seat, front paws propped on the window frame, tail wagging.

'I had a bit of a fright yesterday, by the way,' the Scottish tourist was saying. 'Have you seen those signs on the road saying "watch out for livestock"?' He lifted his eyebrows. 'Sound advice, eh?'

Mercy glanced at the front of his camper, but it appeared free of dents or smears of cow hide.

'Near miss,' he explained. 'Good brakes on this thing, thank Christ. Although I gave the auld yins in the caravan behind me a right scare.' He laughed. 'Reaction times all round were impressive, I must say.'

'What about the poor cow?'

'I don't think it minded at all, to tell you the truth. It just glared at me and wandered off. I got the impression that *I* was in *her* way.'

Petrol gurgled up into the filler and the pump clicked off. She set the nozzle back in the bowser with a clunk and turned again to consider the sign. Once she left Glendambo it would be just her, the rattling Daihatsu and the road (and the threat of wandering livestock) for almost half a day.

'So how far are you going today?' Andy asked, replacing his petrol cap.

Mercy touched the mess piled on top of her head, attempting to smooth it somehow. When she lifted her arm she realised her deodorant was not working. No wonder she had her own cloud of flies. She wiped her palms on her jeans, hoping the petrol fumes would drown out any other smells and thinking, right now, she could really use that bottle of Ralph Lauren Romance she had smashed against Eugene's wall.

'Hopefully further than 253 kilometres.'

'Coober Pedy?' He stepped closer, looking in the direction of the highway. A roadtrain thundered past, clattering and roaring. 'Opal mining town, so they say.'

Well, *he* had showered, that much was clear. Soap, toothpaste and a hint of something else, alpine and decidedly masculine. Mercy clamped her elbows at her sides.

And that's when she felt the first kick of discomfort. Perhaps it was the baked beans; perhaps it was the whisky. Or maybe it was six hundred kilometres of anxiety. Whatever it was, Mercy felt a low growl of gaseous pressure rumble through her insides. Andy leaned himself comfortably on the side of her van, his right arm now looking more tanned than yesterday, and she thought, *Oh, god.*

Andy was looking at her, waiting, and Mercy realised as her guts gurgled unmistakably that he had asked her a question.

'Sorry?' she said, voice strained.

'D'you think we'll find any opals on the side of the road?'

'Opals?' The hair on Mercy's arms was standing up.

'Yeah, you know, 253 kilometres that way.' He pointed. 'Opal mining town?'

'Oh,' Mercy said. She was clenching so hard her voice had risen to a squeak. But there was no more petrol to pump, and they were both just standing there, and there was nothing for it but to start walking towards the store to pay for their petrol. Could she move without anything slipping out?

Mercy tried to walk normally as they made their way to the shopfront, and she didn't realise until she had stepped inside that she really should have stayed outside. She had only seconds left. Heat bloomed in her chest as a chill ran down her spine. On the far wall she spotted a self-service coffee station. It was abandoned. Muttering about caffeine, she made a beeline for it. She punched buttons and waited. She turned her back to the machine and affected a casual pose and when the coffee machine let out an eruption of steam, so did Mercy.

Then she took her coffee, paid, and hurried back outside. *Last fuel for 253km.*

The Hijet looked so *small*. While she had been inside, a semi-trailer had pulled up and her tiny van sat beside it like a fly spot on a watermelon. It was even dwarfed in comparison to the Scottish man's rental camper parked right behind.

In the middle of the concrete forecourt, Mercy spun around.

'Woah!' Andy jumped sideways as Mercy's coffee sloshed over the rim of her cup. 'You all right—?'

But Mercy couldn't stop; she had to keep going, she couldn't give her mind time to catch up with her. Back inside the shop, she marched to the rear wall. Batteries, ropes, torches … there. Plastic fuel containers. Mercy picked one up, went outside to the bowser, filled the container, returned inside and paid.

Then she was back in the van, heading towards the highway. For a few minutes Andy drove a polite distance behind her, but when it became clear that the Hijet was maxed out, its juddering top speed reached, Andy tooted the horn and waved as he pulled out and overtook, before he accelerated ahead and, eventually, disappeared into the distance.

At least with both windows down and the wind buffeting through the van, the petrol vapours oozing from the spare fuel container in the back were blown away. So were any other smells.

As Mercy drove on, the sun climbed higher over the arid landscape, a fierce, white-hot ball glaring through the windscreen. Wasabi panted, leaning against the seat, and after a while he jumped through into the back, escaping into the shade.

'You really should have a seatbelt on,' she scolded the dog, glancing into the rear-vision mirror.

And then she saw the truck.

Not so much a truck as it was a colossal steel bull-bar filling her entire back window, the word MACK stretched in thick chrome across the grille.

Involuntarily Mercy's foot pressed on the accelerator, speeding up as if to outrun a pursuer, but within a few moments it became clear that going faster was not a good idea. The engine whined; the van began to vibrate like a speedboat smacking over choppy water. Mercy eased off, but the bull-bar remained, bearing down mercilessly through her rear window.

'Go around me,' she pleaded.

Although they were rounding a long curved stretch in the road, the white lines were broken; it was safe to pass. Mercy couldn't see any oncoming traffic. Why wouldn't the truck overtake?

The immense grille inched closer. Every instinct was to flee, to go faster, but Mercy lifted her foot further off the pedal; the speedometer needle began to ease down. Seventy, sixty-five, sixty. They were now travelling at the speed limit of the middle of a town, but the truck stayed glued up her arse.

'Why won't you just bloody *pass*?'

Then, she said, 'Oh.'

In her mirror the bull-bar migrated to the right, and as it did, she saw what stretched behind it. A long—impossibly long—row of gleaming fuel tanks.

Mercy's whole body began to shake. She gripped the wheel but it suddenly felt flimsy in her hands, as though she might swerve without even trying. On her right a shadow loomed, blocking out the sun as the roadtrain's prime mover inched past her open window. If she reached out, she could almost touch it.

The first tank crawled past. Then came a second.

A huge stretch of roadtrain now loomed in front of her, on the wrong side of the road, and yet more truck lagged far behind. To her left the gravel shoulder flew past, murderously slippery and dry. All she could hear was the roar of wind and the howl of dozens of huge wheels churning the bitumen an arm's width from her head.

'Aaargh!' Mercy cried.

A third tank eased past. A fourth. The little van rocked and jumped.

'Shiiiiit!'

After a long time, daylight appeared. Far ahead the truck began to list to the left, a slow, languid movement like a blue whale lazing in the ocean, and Mercy's speed had dropped to fifty, and kept dropping even as the roadtrain finally pulled ahead. When she looked up, she saw the truck's indicators flash: left, right, left.

What did that mean? A threat? A chastisement? A warning that if he ever saw her and her piece of shit van on the highway again he would crush her into the heat-hazed asphalt—and her little dog, too?

A rest stop appeared. Mercy slowed, pulled into the rest area and clambered out of the van on shaking legs. At first she thought she needed to pee but when she squatted over the grey desert vegetation it was clear a different kind of voiding was in order.

'Crap,' Mercy said helplessly.

She didn't have a shovel, so she scrabbled at the hard dirt with her fingers, which achieved nothing except to graze her fingertips and cement red crescents under her nails. Sweat beading her brow, she picked up a rock and scraped at the dirt, which was exactly like trying to dig through shower tiles with a shampoo bottle. She flung the rock down in despair.

She would sacrifice a pair of underwear, she thought, pressing her quivering body against the side of the van. But then she remembered that she had only one pair of pants, and oh god it was about to come out, there was no denying it anymore, and Mercy swiped away a patch of pebbles and that's where she went, right there on the red dirt.

That was also when a truck drove past, horn blaring in approval or disapproval, Mercy wouldn't ever know. But even though her pale naked arse was aimed at the highway, she waved, because that felt like the polite thing to do, and when she was done she tried to wash the ground with cask water until she realised that dying of thirst was probably worse than leaving a little bit of excrement on the dirt, so she heaped up a pile of stones, like a cat in a litter tray, and then she climbed back into the van, crawled into the driver's seat and once again headed north.

CHAPTER TWELVE

As Mercy approached Coober Pedy, strange pale cones began to appear on the treeless landscape. Triangular mounds of white earth were scattered randomly about; some of the mounds were huge, grouped together in quarry-like excavations, others were singular and small, barely bigger than anthills, huddled close to the highway.

Signs began to appear, propped upon the barren ground: UNDERGROUND HOTEL; UNDERGROUND B&B; UNDERGROUND CHURCH. A bold warning popped in bright red: DANGER. UNMARKED HOLES. That one was complete with a series of line drawings of deep shafts and stick figures falling perilously.

And then, on the horizon, Mercy saw something she hadn't seen in almost four hours.

'Look, Wasabi,' she said. 'Trees!'

Mercy slowed, indicated right and took the turn-off.

At first she didn't have a plan. The trees she had spotted from the highway were limited to a handful of wiry gums clinging to dry soil. Not a blade of grass appeared in the desiccated ground—everywhere was brittle yellow and grey. Rolling through the dusty town, she passed petrol stations, opal shops, chain-link fences around bare gravel yards, more opal shops. Flat roofs, sun-baked lots, and rattling, big-wheeled utes. Many buildings were only visible by their entrances peeking aboveground, the rest of the structure burrowed into the earth to escape the blinding heat: underground restaurant, underground bookstore, underground gallery.

Just driving through town was making her thirsty and hot. The sun was belting directly through the windscreen onto Jose's black skinny jeans.

And here, Mercy realised her supply shopping was not complete. At Port Augusta all she had purchased to wear were spare undies and a puffer jacket. The only shirt she had was Eugene's red Kombi T-shirt and her only pants were Jose's jeans—and they almost hadn't made it, she thought, recalling her helpless gut-clenching stop on the roadside earlier. Going north, it was only going to get hotter. Her single T-shirt was only going to get filthier and the jeans only more unsuitable. Two-dollar thongs weren't exactly outback-savvy footwear, either.

A familiar sign caught Mercy's eye: VINNIES—an op shop. She followed an arrow up a side street, where a break in a corrugated iron fence pointed her up a sloping driveway.

Mercy found herself in a sudden oasis. Under a cluster of gum trees stood a little mud cottage, walls the colour of caramel. A shrubby garden nestled against the cottage, bordered by a ramble of stones and spattered with shade.

Parking under a tree, Mercy shut off the engine and stepped out of the van. She stretched her arms above her head, the muscles along her spine shuddering. She lifted Wasabi out and set him on the ground, where he trotted to relieve himself beneath a bush. When he was done she tied his new lead to a veranda post in the shade by a plastic container filled with clean water.

A dry breeze clacked through the trees, cooling the sweat on Mercy's skin. The back of her T-shirt felt damp from pressing against the seat for so many hours. Tucked away up here, in a shaded patch on a hill away from the road, Mercy felt a peculiar sensation. It took her a long minute to realise what it was: simply, an absence of nerves. She was waiting for anxiety to sweep in, clouding her mind, bringing its urgency and dogged single-mindedness. But, as she warily made a scan of her body, she noticed it wasn't there. Not yet, anyway. Instead she felt something like a careful, quiet waiting. A pause—but there was nothing in it. No expectation.

'Weird,' she muttered under her breath.

Wasabi twitched an ear, then settled his belly onto the cool concrete.

Mercy went inside.

Though an air-conditioning unit blasted valiantly from the wall, the inside of the tiny store was only a couple of degrees cooler than outside. The air was thick with the scent of musty fabric, laundry powder and old carpet. Crammed racks of clothing clogged the floor and the walls were covered with framed paintings, cross-stitches of country houses, mirrors, clocks.

Mercy stepped into the sea of clothes, hangers catching her shoulders and screeching on the racks.

'G'day, love. Where you from then?'

Mercy glanced around. The voice had come from somewhere on the other side of the room.

'Looking for anything in particular?'

Tentatively, Mercy rose onto tiptoes but saw only swathes of fabric: colours, patterns, greys that probably used to be white. She said, 'Shorts?'

'This way.'

'Sorry, which way?'

'Take a left, dear, at that big stuffed bear.'

Mercy reached the end of a rack and propped against it was a gigantic teddy bear. Matted yellow fur, glassy brown eyes; its forepaws were stitched to a basket in its lap. The basket was empty, and Mercy was briefly filled with an inordinate sadness at the idea of this bear condemned to forever hold an empty vessel. Casting about, she spotted a bunch of faded silk flowers in a vase.

Mercy glanced from side to side. She still couldn't see the owner of the voice. Lifting the flowers from the vase, she slipped them into the bear's basket.

'He'll like that.'

Mercy jumped. Right behind her, a saleswoman, ostensibly. A kind of ample floral sacking draped over one shoulder and knotted beneath the other. Greying, stout, and smiling as if Mercy was a friend she hadn't seen for twenty years.

The woman grasped the fur on the bear's crown and tugged him upright. The bear obliged, sitting up straighter.

'Oh yes, that's much better.'

'Sorry,' Mercy said. 'I just thought …'

'Where've you come from, then?'

'The van?' Mercy pointed, but any view outside was obscured by mountains of clothing.

The woman gave a generous laugh. 'Good one, love. You're up from Adelaide, then?'

Mercy nodded. The woman was watching her with such frank, non-judgemental warmth that Mercy almost confessed it all, there and then in the Cooper Pedy op shop: the fire; the not-technically-ex-husband; the lurking voice-mail that she still hadn't listened to and all the awful shit it would dredge up. The not having been able to leave her house for two years.

'Shorts,' Mercy blurted again.

'Right you are.' The saleswoman beckoned Mercy to a nearby rack. 'Take your pick, love. You'd be—what, size twelve, fourteen?—here we go. Now, they're all clean, of course, and in good condition. Some people, bless their hearts, just leave *rubbish* in the donation bin, torn and stained. It breaks my heart but all I can do is throw them out. I can't have anything not up to scratch for sale; that wouldn't be right, would it?'

'No, I suppose it wouldn't.'

'Oh, would you look at these?' She lifted a hanger from the rack with a hoot. 'Have you ever seen so many sparkles?' She laughed, then looked abruptly mystified. 'Goodness knows where these would've come from—no one round here in their right mind would wear something like this. Must've been a tourist up from the city dumped 'em.' She shoved the pair of glittering silver hot pants back onto the rack. 'Now, *here's* something you'll like.'

She held up a pair of cut-off jeans. The denim worn pale blue, the hem a fringe of fraying threads. They were so short the inside of the pockets protruded out the legs but the fabric was soft and stretchy, and Mercy imagined the air swirling through the van as she drove, cooling her bare skin.

'I'll take them.'

The woman rifled through the rack, handing Mercy several more pairs: a multi-pocketed khaki number, reminding Mercy of an archaeologist kneeling in pits of dinosaur bones; a simple pair of grey running shorts; and a pair made of dark brown linen with a wide bow at the front. Shooing Mercy towards a curtain in the back corner, the saleswoman insisted Mercy 'try before you buy'.

'And if you like 'em, love,' the woman went on, head buried among the hangers, 'I'll give you two for the price of one.'

Mercy looked at the price tag on the pair of denim cut-offs, a torn scrap of card affixed with a safety-pin: $2.

The change room was a broom handle with a sheet draped over. A shard of mirror leaned against the wall. Nerves flickered in Mercy's belly as she drew the sheet, but she imagined Wasabi just outside, sitting patiently, waiting for her. She pictured the dappled shade and the pretty garden tucked against the walls. And when she pulled off her hot jeans, she sighed with relief.

'You staying in town?' the woman called out.

'Just passing through,' Mercy answered, hopping on one leg.

'That's a shame. There's a film at the drive-in tonight.'

'Sorry.'

'Never mind. It's just all local miners going anyway, probably not your type.'

Mercy didn't know if she had a type anymore.

'You gonna try some noodling before you go?'

Pulling on the pair of brown linen shorts, Mercy banged her knee into the wall. 'Some what?'

'Noodling, love. You can fossick through the mullock heaps anytime you like. Plenty of folks find opals in the miners' leftovers. Just watch out for open shafts. Whatever you do, don't walk backwards if you're taking photos.'

'Is that what all those piles of white sand are? Mullock heaps?'

'Yes, love. That's what comes out when the shafts are dug. Plenty of good opal chips in there—some townsfolk make a good enough living just picking the scraps up off the ground.'

'Wow,' Mercy said. The brown linen shorts were giving her a ferocious wedgie. She yanked them off.

'Of course, it's not just opals in the shafts, unfortunately.'

'Oh?'

'Plenty of bodies, too, I'm afraid.'

Mercy froze, one foot in the air. 'Bodies?'

'Sad, isn't it?'

'Do people fall down often?'

'Yes and no. Some fall; others get pushed.'

The hair on the back of Mercy's neck stood up. 'Pushed?'

'Sorry, dear, I shouldn't be saying morbid things. Don't let an old bird like me scare you. We're a lovely bunch here, truly. It's just some unsavoury types think the outback is a good place to dispose of their … rubbish.' She sniffed, and Mercy could hear what sounded like real tears in the woman's voice.

Mercy saw herself in the shard of mirror. Red-eyed, wild-haired: she had the look of a caged thing. 'I guess everyone's got their secrets.'

The woman sighed. 'Too right, love.'

Mercy hurried out from behind the sheet. She had decided on two pairs of shorts: the denim cut-offs, which she left on, bundling Jose's black skinny jeans into a ball, and the grey running shorts.

A large bin was filled with shoes held together in pairs by rubber bands. Mercy rooted around in the bin, fishing out squashed strappy sandals, sad old pumps (who wore pumps in an opal mining town?) and more thongs until she found a pair of floppy leather lace-up boots, tongues lolling like a dog in the sun. The boots were half a size too big, but far better protection against snake bites or bindi-eyes than her supermarket thongs. She also grabbed another T-shirt, pale pink marle with I ♥ SYDNEY above a screen print of the Sydney Harbour Bridge.

'Good one,' the saleswoman said, motioning to the T-shirt and tapping the side of her nose. 'Act like a tourist, people might give you a bit of space.' She chuckled, counting out Mercy's change.

Mercy stared at her. How did she know? Could the woman tell, just by looking at her, that Mercy was crowded by everything? That everything—the whole world—had piled on top of her and she couldn't breathe anymore? She pictured bodies crumpled at the bottom of mine shafts; judging by the amount of mullock heaps she had seen, there were thousands of open shafts out there. Hundreds of kilometres from anywhere, at the bottom of a vast, ancient inland sea.

Each human life was so tiny, so ephemeral, compared to the inescapable march of time, the earth, infinite space.

'There you go, dear.'

The saleswoman held out a weathered hand, change for a twenty sitting in her palm.

'Keep it,' Mercy said. 'A donation.'

The woman blinked, cleared her throat. 'Well, good on you, love.' She closed her hand. 'It's all for the hospital.'

A beat passed. Fighting the urge to hug the saleswoman tightly, Mercy turned and left.

CHAPTER THIRTEEN

The treeless landscape went on and on.

Mercy drove, stopping to drink water, eat an apple or nervously splash petrol into the tank. In every direction as far as she could see the earth stretched out, rocky and bare beneath the never-ending sky. Which meant, of course, that whenever she needed to pee, there was no privacy. No trees to hide behind, no bushes or thickets of shrubbery in which to tuck herself away from the eyes of the highway. Just spiky grasses and creeping saltbush all the way to the horizon. When she pulled off the highway, all she could do was take a long look in both directions, listening hard for any traffic, and then, crouching next to the van, go as quickly as possible.

The earth slide-showed a glorious palette of changing colour. Sometimes the soil was bright orange, sometimes a rich blood-like scarlet, sometimes a pale sandy yellow. But always: flat, wide open. A moonscape. When Mercy stopped she heard the breeze whispering across the open land and imagined it unimpeded for hundreds of kilometres, finally reaching her to wrap around her legs and lift the sweat from her brow.

About two hours on from Coober Pedy, the landscape changed again and wiry shrubs began to spring up. The soil deepened to the colour of rust. Overhead a low blanket of silver clouds drifted in.

Mercy drove on. The Stuart Highway might have been crossing some of Australia's most remote outback country but it was never quiet. She was passed in both directions by a steady stream of caravans and trucks, campervans and sedans that sped by in an instant and were gone, almost as quickly as they had appeared.

The sun wore a track through the sky, until it began to sink in the west, flaring hot through the passenger-side window. After a very long, straight stretch, the highway began a gentle curve to the west. A sign appeared, displaying icons for bed, fuel, food—even a police station. MARLA, THE TRAVELLERS REST. POPULATION: 72.

'Whatcha think, boy?' she said to Wasabi.

The dog sat up, lifting his snout to inspect the air.

'A rest sound good?'

Wasabi blinked at her, then yawned.

Mercy looked in the rear-vision mirror.

'What do you think, Jenny Cleggett?'

Mercy intuited the silence as satisfied.

She eased off the accelerator, flicked the indicator and followed the signs into town.

Town was probably a generous moniker, Mercy thought as she rattled into the fifty zone. She was following a caravan with *Grey nomads: age is an attitude not a condition* across the back.

She rolled through a roadhouse forecourt giant enough for roadtrains, past a bar with a row of saddle-bagged motorbikes parked out the front. Faded red Coca-Cola signs, a strip of pay-phone boxes. And everywhere— caravans. Big caravans, small caravans. Long vans with jacked-up suspension and checkerboard plating, low vans with gauzy curtains and swirly decal. Squat four-wheel drives, dusty four-wheel drives, shining expensive beasts of four-wheel drives.

A strip of tree-studded lawn edged the forecourt, and Mercy nosed into the shade by a picnic table. The Hijet puttered to a stop. Heads turned. She tried not to notice.

It was almost five thirty; she had been on the road more than eight hours. She thought of that morning in Glendambo, making coffee in her saucepan, and it felt like a month ago.

When she opened the door to climb out, the mess of her hair scraped along the roof lining. It moved like a solid entity. She touched it; it felt like a pile of carpet. She scratched at the grit in her hairline and her fingernails came away crusted with red dirt.

For a few minutes Mercy stood out the front of the roadhouse, partly watching Wasabi trotting about, partly watching the shopfront and its lazy bustle of travellers. It appeared that the roadhouse was in fact a grocery store, petrol station, café, bar, motel and caravan park all rolled into one. Several more caravans pulled in, stayed a few minutes and drove off again, disappearing into the park around the back.

'Rush hour,' Mercy muttered.

There was no avoiding it; she had to go in. Bracing herself with a few deep breaths, she hurried across the asphalt, op-shop hiking boots flapping at her ankles, tied Wasabi by the door and stepped inside.

Mercy selected supplies: a fresh loaf of bread, a packet of chicken flavoured freeze-dried rice, crackers. In the van she still had a few apples and one lone tomato that she could slice the bruised patches off, but she would have to throw away the lettuce. Though she longed for fresh food, the selection was limited to a few browning bananas, hard, pale tomatoes and bags of potatoes she had no way of cooking if she didn't want to spend hours boiling them in her tiny saucepan. Which she didn't. So, at the fridge, Mercy selected a decadence she would eat straight away: a tub of strawberry yoghurt.

Approaching the counter, Mercy picked up a brochure from the stand. According to the stylised map she was east of the Anangu Pitjantjatjara Yankunytjatjara Lands, over 1000 kilometres north of Adelaide, and less than 160 kilometres south of the Northern Territory border.

She was almost in the centre of the continent. She felt a little sick.

A tremor shook her hands as she paid for her groceries and a campsite for the night.

It was as Mercy had feared: the caravan park was filling up. Unlike Glendambo's dusty gravel lot, the park here was a square of lawn dotted with shade trees, surrounded by a picket fence, backing onto the endless bush. Prime vanning real estate.

When she reached twenty-one caravans, Mercy stopped counting. She parked in her allotted site, trying not to think of the gathering horde of grey nomads with which she would be spending a long, dark night deep in the outback. Instead, she focussed on the hungry growl of her stomach.

She opened the back door, letting in the warm late-afternoon air. Though she could hear doors thumping, footsteps crunching and voices murmuring, she couldn't see any other caravans. From the back of the van, her view was a strip of lawn, the back fence, and the desert scrub beyond it. The setting sun burnished the red soil and leeched the scrub silver.

Kicking off her floppy old boots, Mercy sat on the floor of the van and let her legs dangle out the back, flicking her toes against the grass. She slid forward until the earth felt solid and sure beneath her feet. At the edge of the park, a group of local Aboriginal kids were playing in a swimming pool. Slim bodies jumped and splashed, shrieks echoing up into the sky. She waited for her pulse to settle.

'You made it!'

Pocketed shirt, beer belly: Bert. He appeared without warning around the side of the van, clutching a pewter mug in one hand, the other tucked into his waistband.

'The bus running well?' he asked, lifting one foot to prop it on the Hijet's rear tyre.

'Very well, thank you,' Mercy said. Orange dust coated the wheels and clung in a fine film over the side panels.

The green panel now looked more of a dark brown, but she could still read the hand-painted *Home is wherever you ARE*.

She said, 'How is your … um …'

'Cruiser? Ahhh.'

If she wasn't mistaken, Mercy thought he grew a little misty eyed.

'She's a magic bus. Just magic.'

'That's …' Mercy didn't know what it was. She assumed he used *magic* as a metaphor for something wondrous—the vehicle was phenomenal, perhaps. Out of this world. It seemed a rather hyperbolic way to describe a tow vehicle, but Mercy did have to concede towing and caravanning in general was an area about which she had proved to be fairly uninformed. After all, she was driving a near-forty-year-old van with a top speed of eighty-five from one side of the continent to the other.

Wasabi jumped from the van to sniff Bert's shoes, then proceeded to dance around him excitedly, long body curled into a tight semi-circle.

'Good company on a trip like this, dogs,' Bert said, leaning down to give Wasabi a series of pats that were more like resounding thumps. Wasabi snuffled happily. 'Although you can't take them into the national parks.' Bert said it sternly, and Mercy felt told off. 'That's why Jan and I haven't had a dog for, oh …' he considered it, scratching his gut, 'twenty-five years or so now. We used to have a big dog, a black Labrador. Named Charlie. What a scoundrel he was! Broke into the neighbour's yard and killed all his chooks. I came home from work one day and there was feathers everywhere …'

Mercy glanced longingly into the the van. Her yoghurt would be getting warm. Could she just climb in and start eating it? What was the etiquette around showing up uninvited in someone's campsite? Was it like when someone knocks on your door when you're about to start dinner at home, and you can simply … not answer?

'… show-quality hens, he reckoned …'

The scent of grilling onions wafted on the breeze and Mercy's stomach gave a loud growl. Sweat clung to the backs of her knees. She imagined the smooth, cool cream of the yoghurt.

'… five bucks each! A bloody rip-off …'

Mercy stood rooted to her patch of lawn, vacillating between waiting until Bert had naturally concluded his story and walked away or simply retrieving her strawberry yoghurt and eating it, regardless of how long he continued talking. Eventually even Wasabi grew bored, abandoning her to utilise the facilities of a nearby fence post.

'… and then I said, "You can stuff your own goddamn pillow, mate," and he—well, g'day!'

Mercy startled, then flushed hot.

'Hiya.'

A freshly showered Andrew Macauley appeared. Wet hair, thongs on his feet.

And, yes, Mercy was into her third unwashed day. She could almost *see* the waves of stench lifting from her body. Flies darted about her eyes but lifting her arms to shoo them might expose them all to a dangerous biohazard. She recalled the shag carpet of hair on her head with horror.

'How's your bus going?' Bert asked. 'You're the rental camper, the Toyota, right?'

'Aye, that's me. And you're the silver LandCruiser?'

Bert beamed and inflated.

Andy turned to Mercy and grinned. 'How's it that you managed to beat me here?'

'Magic,' Mercy said.

Bert roared with laughter. Red wine sloshed from his pewter mug.

'So happy hour's at Pete and Jules's tonight—the Avan—' Bert pointed towards a caravan in the next row, where Mercy could see a gathering of silver-haired folk on folding chairs around a card table holding three, no, *four* casks of wine '—so it should be an absolute *pearler.* Those two know how to throw happy hour, let me tell you! We'll see you kids there?'

'Sounds like fun,' Andy said.

Mercy panicked.

'But I was about to invite Mercy here for a walk, if that's all right?'

'Sure, sure.' Bert held up his hand, backing away. 'Far be it for us oldies to get in the way of you young whippersnappers.' He laughed again, turning to walk away, then called over his shoulder, 'No need to bring anything—I've got a great box of Shiraz.'

'Excellent,' Andy said.

'A walk?' Mercy said.

'If you'd like? Thought we might explore the town. It's Friday night, after all.'

Mercy swallowed. Wasabi had returned and was rolling onto his back to show the Scottish man his undercarriage, paws flopping. Andy obliged, scratching the dog's belly. Wasabi squinted in ecstasy.

Mercy's mind raced, but three things shouted the loudest: firstly, her unwashed state. Secondly, the strawberry yoghurt she desperately wanted to savour while it was still cold, and thirdly, the disgusting state of her hair.

The shower won, closely followed by the yoghurt.

Mercy's heart was thumping but the words came out as if on their own.

'A walk sounds great. How about you come back in twenty minutes? I just have to, uh …' She flapped her T-shirt to demonstrate, immediately regretting it.

'Sure,' Andy said. 'Looks like it's going to be a spectacular sunset.' He smiled and all the saliva disappeared from Mercy's mouth.

Mercy walked with Wasabi across the park to the amenities block. She raised her hand to called-out greetings, agreeing that *yes, it is a perfect evening for it*, and even conceding at one point that *yes, this is the good life*. Criss-crossing the grassy space were lines of electrical cords, rolled-out green matting, chairs and tables. Awnings unfurled and pop-tops unpopped; everywhere were relaxed limbs, drinks in hand, laughter.

The median age was somewhere close to seventy.

The shower block was a timber frame with tin walls and a tin roof. Mercy set her bag on a slatted bench. She picked up her hairbrush and looked in the mirror. What she saw would have been hilarious if it wasn't so mortifying. She had been speaking to people looking like *this*? Actual human people, with *eyes*?

The top of her hair wasn't visible in the mirror—it lofted up, beyond the mirror's boundary. But what she could see was a sweat-matted lump, coated in a layer of red dust. The same red dust that covered her van, and the same red dust that covered her face, except for the sunglasses-shaped pale patch around her eyes. There was even dust across her collar bones and caked in the hollow of her throat.

Locating her hair tie, she tugged, but it held fast.

'Good god,' she cried as her scalp burned. Strands pinged and snapped. Eventually, with a tearing sound, the tie wrenched loose, trailing long strings of hair. But, even with the hair tie gone, the bun stayed largely in place. She tried untangling it with her fingers, but that succeeded only in turning her hair from a loose knotted bun into a voluminous greasy halo. After attempting to run the brush through it, she gave up. She had a big enough bottle of conditioner.

Red dust rained down as she stripped out of her clothes. Chunks of it ticked onto the tiles. She dropped her dirty clothes into the bottom of the shower stall, turned on the water and stepped in. The water was blissfully warm; needles of water pelted her dusty, wind-battered skin and aching muscles. Rivulets of brown ran down her legs and whirled into the drain. Wasabi pressed himself into the corner of the stall, face turned away from the water.

'Soap!' she said into the spray, closing her eyes as the water sluiced over her face. 'How good is soap?'

Shampoo foamed up and plopped onto the wet tiles; handfuls of conditioner disappeared but still her hair stayed somewhere aloft, defying gravity. She stomped soap into her clothes, bending down to scrub them clean with her hands. She rinsed dust from Wasabi's fur, making him sleek as an otter.

The water began to feel too hot, so she adjusted the taps. After a moment, she turned the hot down again, adding more cold. But still an uncomfortable burning sensation crept over. Rinsing as much of the conditioner as she could, she shut off the water and stepped out.

Touching the towel to her legs, she let out a gasp of pain. Her thighs were a strident, hot red. Sitting all day with the sun glaring through the windscreen in her tiny new (used) shorts, the sun had baked her bare skin to a crisp.

She touched the tops of her thighs, wincing as if her fingertips were razors. Carefully she dried herself and stepped gingerly into her change of clothes: the pink I ♥ SYDNEY T-shirt and grey running shorts. Never in her life had she worn a more comfortable outfit.

Hurrying back across the park in a cloud of shampoo scent, damp clothes clutched in a ball and thighs pulsing with heat, she waved and greeted and agreed once again, before arriving back at the blessed quiet of her van.

After laying out her wet clothes to dry on the grass, Mercy gave Wasabi a handful of kibble, then opened the cabinet and lifted out the strawberry yoghurt. The plastic sides of the tub retained a cool hint of the fridge, but it was fading fast. She peeled off the lid, put it to her mouth and licked it clean. Velvety sweet cream melted on her tongue. She dipped in her spoon and brought up a piece of soft strawberry flesh. Her skin tingled. Never in her life had she tasted anything more delicious.

She was sitting on the bed savouring the last sugary spoonful when she heard Andy's voice.

'Anyone home?' Knuckles rapped lightly on the door pillar and his head appeared. 'Got all the dust off then, I see.'

Mercy flushed beyond her sunburned thighs. 'I think I was wearing half the outback,' she said, wiping her spoon with her towel. 'The other half is inside the van.'

When she climbed out, Andy noticed her legs.

'Ouch.'

'It's not too bad,' she lied, clipping Wasabi to his lead. He spun in excited circles. 'But I might just stop at the store and see if they have aloe vera ointment. Or some new skin.'

She could feel her pulse ticking as they walked through the park. Each step that took her further away from the safety and privacy of her van felt like leaving home. She knew a rattly old camper wasn't *really* safe, nor was it private, but so far it had kept her cocooned. She thought of the roadtrain belting past her on the highway, the little Daihatsu valiantly shepherding her and Wasabi—and the cremated remains of Jenny Cleggett—to safety.

Andy offered to watch the dog while Mercy entered the store, but the idea of it made her fingers tighten on the lead.

'It's okay, I'll just … take him inside.'

'You sure? I don't mind.' He reached down to scratch under Wasabi's collar.

'He's … an assistance dog.'

'That's cool.' Andy slung his hands in his pockets.

'Emotional assistance. I have … emotions.'

'That's fine. I'll just wait here.' He smiled and Mercy's thighs sang with heat.

Inside the store, Wasabi's claws ticked on the lino. She swallowed nervously but told herself that surely a roadhouse/store/bar in the middle of the outback had seen far more threatening things than a sausage dog on a lead.

Mercy made a hurried scan of the shelves. There was sunscreen (she already had a tube that she'd forgotten to apply but she grabbed another, anyway), toothpaste, deodorant, generic brand moisturiser, but no aloe vera ointment. She found a bottle of 'after-sun gel', a gelatinous, vivid blue mixture in a clear tube. The ingredients were a list of multi-syllable chemical equations with a ten-year shelf life. It probably shouldn't be applied to healthy parts of her body, let alone skin so severely burned little blisters were beginning to appear. But she had no other choice. The label on the front promised a 'cooling effect' and she couldn't deny that cooling was precisely what her poor legs needed.

Glancing out the window, she saw Andy sitting on a picnic bench, leaning back on his elbows, legs stretched out. The tube of after-sun lotion squelched. She hurried to the counter.

'He's an assistance dog,' Mercy said hastily, when she had to tug Wasabi away from the display of potato crisps.

But the cashier just shrugged and said, 'Twenty-nine fifty,' which was at least a two hundred per cent increase on what the gel would retail for a thousand kilometres ago.

Once again outside the store, Mercy squirted a handful of gel into her palm.

'It looks like the stuff an ice pack is made of,' Andy observed. 'You know, the packs you put on your ankle when you sprain it. The stuff that says "Poison, do not eat".'

Carefully, barely making contact with her skin, Mercy slicked the gel onto her burned thighs. It felt gooey and icy cold, and the effect was immediate.

She let out a relieved laugh. 'That's better than the shower.'

Thighs glistening, Scottish tourist laughing alongside her, Mercy set off on her walk around Marla.

CHAPTER FOURTEEN

Six minutes later, Mercy said, 'I think this is it.' The narrow strip of bitumen crumbled to a halt. Red dirt stretched to the horizon.

Town, it turned out, was a narrow grid of four streets surrounding weatherboard cabins, dusty lots and barking dogs. A runty police station, a parched oval. Mercy imagined how it would look from high above, this tiny town dropped onto the outback: a sandy patch on a blanket of red.

'It's pretty incredible,' Andy said, gazing out over the bush. The setting sun made long shadows and stars were beginning to show in a pink sky. 'I'd no idea it was going to look like this. It's the middle of nowhere but it's that ... *nowhere-ness* itself that feels huge. Like, huger than if you were in the middle of the city.'

For a moment Mercy couldn't speak. She knew exactly what he meant. As they stood at the road's end, the rocky scarlet earth stretching flat as a board, as far as they could see, it was as though they stood in the centre of a vast, breathing space. A heart in the stillness between beats. A lung between breaths. Out here, in the absence of *stuff*, there was an immense, deeply silent, very real *presence*.

Sweat trickled down Mercy's spine, snapping her out of her reverie.

'We should probably get back,' she said, tugging Wasabi to heel.

They turned to walk back, and now that each step took her closer to the van, Mercy began to relax. Their footfalls crunched and Wasabi panted, collar jingling.

'So you're from Adelaide?' Andy asked.

Mercy hesitated. 'I wasn't born there, but yes. That's where I ... live.' *Lived*, she thought. Her house was a charred ruin. She glanced at him. 'You?'

'Glasgow.' He stooped to pick up a pebble. 'Or just outside it, a wee farming village.' He threw the pebble in a straight line, down the centre of the deserted street. 'So where were you born then, if not Adelaide?'

He was looking at her openly, kindly. It was nothing more than the polite getting-to-know-you small talk people engaged in every day; she didn't have to answer the question if she didn't want to.

But something in her wanted to.

She cleared her throat. 'South of Adelaide. A town on the river called Murray Bridge.'

He picked up another pebble. This one he handed to her, then he selected another for himself.

'I moved to Adelaide to go to uni,' she found herself saying. 'Straight out of high school. I wasn't even nineteen.'

'What'd you study?'

Mercy turned the warm stone over in her hand. Even before it had all come undone, his was a question she rarely answered—outside of work, to strangers—with honesty. It was too much of a conversation stopper; it inevitably introduced a divide between her and the other person. Telling people she'd studied medicine meant she became an authority figure, an immediate confidante. She would be treated to questions about ingrown toenails, or this itchy patch on their left butt cheek, or their cousin's prostate cancer treatment—whether or not she was practised in those things. The moment someone knew what Mercy did she became not a normal flawed person but someone infallible. Someone more than. Someone with the answers to life's grievances. When the truth was she was just as messy and breakable as everyone else.

'Medicine.'

'You're a doctor?'

'Yes.'

'Then you should know better than to go without sunscreen.'

She laughed and tried to throw the stone the way Andy had, straight down the road. It slanted to the left, plummeting immediately into the dust.

'What d'you call that shite?' He handed her another stone.

'Should we really be roaming the streets at twilight throwing rocks?'

He took her hand, looking down at the stone in her palm. 'I don't know about you Aussies, but back home we wouldn't call that a rock. It's barely a wee pebble.'

His fingers left a lingering warmth on hers. Mercy tried again; the rock sailed a few metres and fell.

'So what's a doctor doing driving an old Japanese import across the country?'

'What's a Glaswegian doing driving a rental whatever-yours-is across a foreign country?'

'All right.' He whipped the pebble, low and quick, and it skittered over the asphalt. 'Shall we count to three and answer at the same time?'

Andy counted to three, but when neither of them answered, each just looking expectantly at the other, they laughed again.

As the sun slipped below the horizon the air temperature dropped, but heat continued to radiate from the baked earth. Wasabi's panting and the sound of their footsteps carried into the night air. They arrived back at the caravan park to the sizzle of grilling meats, the smoke of mosquito coils, chimes of laughter. Wine glasses and coiffed silver hair.

'Is this what they call "glamping"?' Mercy wondered.

'I think this is what they call "spending the kids' inheritance",' Andy said. 'Listen.' He turned to her. 'I've a can of beef stew I'm willing to share. How'd you fancy joining me?'

Mercy paused. She thought of her freeze-dried rice, tucked alongside the box of Jenny Cleggett. She formed the words to turn him down. But when she opened her mouth to decline, she realised that beef stew sounded good. And in spite of her anxious pulse and scorched thighs, she had enjoyed her walk with the Scottish man. Something about his company felt easy, unpressured. How long had it been since she had laughed with another person?

'Yours or mine?'

'You choose,' he said. 'Although if it helps, my gaff has more room for your head. And two burners on the stove.'

'Okay,' she heard herself agree. 'I'll bring the rice.'

'"Chunky Beef and Meat stew"?' Mercy asked. 'What kind of meat if it isn't beef, exactly?'

'I'm not sure,' Andy said, studying the can of stew. It was twice the size of a normal can, the label a riot of aggressive colours and slabbed print: *chunky* and *meaty* and *man-sized*.

He was right; there was room enough to stand upright inside his campervan. The kitchenette had a sink, a two-burner stove, a fridge, and cabinets filled with helpful utensils and cookware. There was a tidy double-bed at the back and, up front, the seats were plush as armchairs.

Andy's van also had air conditioning; the inside was free of dust, insect carcases and other detritus. And according to Andy, the van was perfectly comfortable cruising the highway at a hundred and ten. When Mercy had asked how, in that case, she *had* managed to beat him to Marla, he had picked up a small vial of stone chips.

'I went noodling in Coober Pedy,' he said, tipping the vial so its contents caught the light: chips of creamy rock glinting gold, blue and green. Thinking of all the missing bodies, Mercy told him she hoped he'd kept a close watch on the open shafts.

'Oh wait,' Andy said now, 'apparently it "may also contain chicken, pork or ham".' He lowered the can. 'D'you reckon the makers of—' he tilted the can to read the front label '—"Blokes R Tuff N Stuff Stew" know that pork and ham are from the same animal?'

'Well,' Mercy said, taking the can from him to study it herself, 'they seem to think that beef and meat are different things.'

Andy heated the stew while Mercy stirred boiled water into the rice. When the food was ready they sat outside, steaming bowls in hand, and looked over the evening-shrouded desert.

'Whatever this actually is,' Mercy said, her mouth full, 'I don't care. It's delicious.'

'It's the meat that makes it so good,' Andy agreed.

Mercy spooned up another mouthful. Salty, rich with gravy—she could almost feel her hungry, wind-pummelled muscles plumping in pleasure. They ate in companionable silence, listening to the birds going quiet, hearing the gentle chatter and hum of the other campers. The kids in the swimming pool had gone; lit from above by a moth-flecked lamp, the water was rippling blue.

Andy wolfed his meal then produced a bottle of red wine and, after digging around in the camper, reappeared with two plastic flutes.

'It's right classy this van, so it is.'

Mercy didn't tell him that her camper might not have plastic glasses, but it did contain a box of cremated remains.

'Will you tell me a wee bit about yourself, Doctor Mercy?' Andy asked, glugging wine into the flutes. 'At home is there a husband or kids?'

Mercy worried a grain of rice with her spoon. 'No,' she said eventually. 'Neither.' She took a flute from him and sipped. 'You?'

'If you're asking if I've a husband the answer's no,' he said with a grin. 'But I did once have a wife.'

'Oh,' Mercy said.

'I don't anymore.'

'Oh?'

'And I've two weans, a boy and a girl. Eleven and five.' Pulling his phone from his pocket, he scrolled for a moment before leaning forward to show her the screen. A boy and a young girl crouched in bright white snow, red-cheeked and beaming with fluffy scarfs around their necks and jackets so puffy the little girl's arms were stuck straight out. They both had honey brown eyes, lighter than their father's, but there Andy was in the smiles lifted higher at one corner of their mouths.

'Beautiful,' Mercy murmured. 'You must miss them.'

'I do.' After smiling again at the photo, he tucked his phone back in his pocket.

'So.' Mercy studied her last grains of rice. 'What happened to the wife?'

He gazed into his glass and Mercy thought suddenly, *Oh god*. He wasn't widowed, was he?

'We married too young. Ended up just …' He spread his hands. 'Going in different directions. Maybe I changed, or maybe she changed, but in the end it doesn't matter, does it?'

'Probably not.' Mercy exhaled silently.

'One day we realised that, besides the kids, we didn't have anything in common anymore. We could be eating dinner or driving somewhere and neither of us would talk the entire time. Not because we were raging with each other, or anything like that, but just because we had nothing to say.' He sounded rueful. 'When she said she was moving out I think I was relieved, more than anything else.' He paused to take a swig of wine. 'What's that word they always use when you're just lucky enough that your divorce isn't completely

god awful? Amicable, aye, that's it. But it's just that she's ...'
He paused, looking out over the bush.

Mercy waited.

'She's getting married again.'

'I see.'

'I'm happy for her. I know it's a cliché and it probably
doesn't seem like it—what with me flying to the other side
of the world to drive across the outback—but I really am
happy for her, because I've not seen her this happy in ...
well, years. You know? And when she's smiling, the little'uns
are smiling. But it's just ... ach.' He cut himself short. 'It's a
bit shite, is all.'

'I understand,' Mercy said, because she really did. 'Were
you together long?'

'Since we were kids.'

'That's tough.'

Another silence settled. Mercy set down her empty bowl
and rested her head against the musty canvas chair.

Andy was sprawled with his arms and legs out, head
tipped back and gazing up at the stars. At length he asked,
'Is it your turn now?'

Mercy breathed in the sharp night air. She swallowed her
wine. After a while she said, 'My house burned down.'

Andy said nothing, and she wondered if he was struck dumb.

'It was the first time I'd left it in two years.'

He lifted his head. 'Wait—at all?'

'Pretty much.'

'That's a long time not to leave your house.'

Mercy squeezed the plastic wine flute in her fingers, making the stem creak. 'It wasn't like in the movies. I wasn't
newspapering up the windows or fumbling to the letterbox

with my eyes shut. I'd go out into the yard, and sometimes I'd walk up the street, but …' She went quiet.

Andy's body was relaxed, splayed out on his chair, but his face was alert, his expression one of restrained shock. 'D'you want to talk about why?'

Mercy knocked back the last of her drink. 'Panic attacks,' she said, and left it at that.

'Have you …' he began. 'Had you always been …?'

'House-bound?'

'Yeah.' He gave her a little smile.

She shook her head. 'No. Just these past two years.' Then she heard herself say, 'Something happened. At work. There was—' Her throat tightened, choking off the words, refusing to make them real. 'A lot of things happened all at once. And at the time, my husband had just left me. He met someone else.' She twirled her empty wine flute, adding, 'He fell in love with a man. Now *there's* your cliché.'

Andy picked up the bottle and held it forward, and she let him fill her glass to the brim.

'Wow,' he said. 'I don't really know what to say.'

She shrugged.

'I mean, to not be able to leave your house must be hard enough, but then it burned down?'

'Yes.'

'That sucks. Christ …' He puffed out his cheeks. 'I'm really sorry, Mercy.'

'Thanks.'

A long silence fell.

And then Andy said, 'What happened at work?'

She clamped her lips, shook her head.

'So now you're seeing the country.'

'I was getting nowhere. I was so tired of being stagnant. I wanted to be on the other side of it all. So that's what I've decided to do.'

'I have to say, that's a hell of a way to end two years of not leaving your house.'

'By watching it burn down then buying a crappy old van and driving through the desert?'

'Aye.'

Stars wheeled. Crickets chirped. The waxing moon poked its pale face over the saltbush. Around them the park slipped into nightfall; plates clinked as they were packed away, caravan doors snicked open and closed, water pumps groaned.

'That sounds heavy, Doctor Mercy. And I guess that explains the assistance dog.'

For a long time Mercy didn't reply, slugging back wine like it was water, sunburn throbbing on her legs.

That's not all, she wanted to say. But she didn't. Instead they sat together in the quiet, looking out into the velvet black of the outback night.

CHAPTER FIFTEEN

Dawn was a pale pink smudge on the horizon and the inside of the van was cold when Mercy was awakened by a rising chorus of engines.

Yawning, she lifted her head and made to shuffle up the mattress until the movement of her burned skin on the velour made her yelp in pain. Wincing, keeping the throw rug tucked around her neck, she craned up on her elbows to peer outside, watching as men in puffy vests and shorts climbed into driver's seats and women checked indicators and brake lights before climbing into passenger seats. It was never the other way around, Mercy had noticed.

Engines roared and caravans rocked and squeaked out of the park, one after the other, chasing each other towards the highway.

Mercy groaned, shivered, and pulled her warm cat blanket back over her head.

It was just after nine am when she awoke again. Her phone was vibrating on the cabinet.

She ignored it, and it went quiet. Almost immediately it started up again. Then again.

Eugene.

It was as if the world came flooding in. As though a flock of news cameras suddenly appeared inside the Hijet, the seeking black eyes of lenses pointed straight at her. Clickbait headlines blared, commentators frothed outraged op-eds, Facebook groups imploded. The quiet thrum of the desert, the red dust, the crackling silver bush—it all disappeared. The world and its screaming opinions pressed down on her chest, flattening the air from her lungs.

'Mercy, where are you?'

She had to take a deep breath. 'Marla.'

'Where?'

'Not far south of the border.'

'Border? What border?'

'For god's sake, Eugene,' she said. 'The fucking Arctic Circle.'

He was quiet. No chatter of background noise; he must be at home, Mercy realised. He was calling on his day off. She pictured him sitting alone in his silent kitchen, in his T-shirt and track pants, coffee steaming beside him as he made a phone call through obligation. She imagined him pinching the bridge of his nose.

Mercy sighed. 'The Northern Territory border. According to the map, I've got just over two hours left in SA.' She gave a wry laugh. 'Or ninety minutes in a normal car.'

Eugene exhaled against the speaker. 'I've had a phone call from Legal.'

A bolt of nerves shot up her spine. 'Why are they calling you?'

'Because they can't get hold of you. I'm your ...' He paused again. 'I'm still your next of kin. There's been some movement on her case.'

Mercy hesitated. 'I know,' she admitted. 'They got in touch again, last week. Just before ...'

Before the fire.

Images snapped into her mind unbidden: Standing in her bedroom, watching smoke curl in wisps under the door. Stark silence from the fire alarm. The shirtless neighbour, Mike, suddenly appearing wide-eyed in her bedroom.

Naked, pale skin. *Do something.*

'Merce, you there?'

Be here now. Mercy heard the warble of a magpie. Out the window she saw the bird perched on the fence, right behind the van. If she opened the back door, she could reach out and touch it. Jet black and snowy white, the bird lifted its vicious-looking beak, opened its throat to the sky and sang a beautiful, lilting song.

Mercy looked over at the cabinet where she'd set the box of ashes. She didn't like to keep them under the bed over-night; she didn't like the idea of sleeping over whoever it was.

Mercy said, 'I'm still travelling right now.'

'I know that. But you'll need to keep an eye on your email—can you do that?' He paused, and the silence stretched heavy. 'And you have to take their calls. It's ... it's the law, Merce. You don't have a choice.'

Mercy hung up. The magpie opened its wings and was gone.

Mercy continued north. As she drove out of the park, she saw Andy's campsite was empty. She wondered if he had left in the mass exodus at the crack of dawn, embracing the race to hurry up and slow down.

See? Andy was running from something too, she reminded herself as she pulled onto the highway. The happiness of his ex-wife had sent him across the planet to try and reconcile or escape it.

Maybe they were all running from something. Grey nomads with their caravan slogans: *Living the dream* or *Not dead yet*—who were they trying to prove it to? Themselves? Everyone else? Aren't we all, Mercy thought, seeking to validate ourselves? To know we're *okay*—no matter what we've done?

The red dirt and low scrub continued. In the distance flat-topped peaks appeared, eased closer, then disappeared behind her. Trucks and vans overtook, belching hot, dusty air. A stretch of half an hour passed without a single bend in the road, the ribbon of asphalt stretching endlessly in front and behind.

After a while, Mercy noticed the vegetation began to change. From the sparse silver it had been yesterday it was now tinged with green, growing thicker. The soil lightened to apricot. The trees remained stunted and stick-like but foliage turned lime green.

A bridge approached and Mercy perked up, hoping to see water, but Tarcoonyinna Creek turned out to be a wide, flat expanse of tyre-tracked sand and sprawling low mallees.

Mercy drove on.

It was too hot to wear Jose's jeans, especially on her sunburned thighs, but Mercy had draped her towel over her lap to shield herself from the sun. Still, the heat of the sun's rays baked through the fabric, setting her burned skin howling. More bridges appeared; more broad dry creek beds. Though the land was parched, the presence of these water courses buoyed Mercy, as she pictured them as run-offs from the monsoonal tropics far ahead. She imagined them swollen with leftover floodwater, wide and shallow and teeming with life. Arteries of nutrients and oxygen and moisture for the thirsty outback.

Mercy passed a single tall tree and cried, 'Look, Wasabi!' That single tree became another, then another.

As she was driving along a flat field of pale green, her stomach rumbled and her bladder squeezed uncomfortably. She was considering stopping when a sign appeared: STATE BORDER, 1 KM.

Mercy's heart leapt. One kilometre to go.

She gripped the wheel. A minute passed.

The road widened as a slip lane appeared. There, up ahead. A turn-off to a parking bay, a low, studded-post fence surrounding a broad patch of sand. And alongside the road, a huge slab of orange concrete with an enormous triangular brown wedge soaring up:

WELCOME TO THE NORTHERN TERRITORY.

1791 km to go

CHAPTER SIXTEEN

Mercy stood in front of the state border marker and stared at her phone. It occurred to her that she had no one to send the selfie to. No friends to share it with, no family eager to hear about her progress, not even a bunch of acquaintances on social media anymore for whom to confect airs of *living the road-trip life* and being *so blessed*.

Running across the ground below her was a straight concrete path denoting the divide between the two states and Mercy was standing with her feet on it, imagining she had one foot in the south, the other in the north. Was she balanced on the tipping point, leaving the *before* and ready to fall into the *after*? On the highway a car drove past without bothering to stop for the border's concrete ceremony; one moment south, the next, north. The sun was too bright for Mercy to see the screen of her phone with any clarity, but she could make out the outline of her head, the ludicrous bouff of her hair and Wasabi's snout mid-lick on her chin, and behind them the hulking shadow of the concrete slab that read Welcome to the Northern Territory.

Two other vehicles were parked in the rest area: a car towing a caravan, and a tremendous, slick-looking RV, which had pulled in a few minutes after Mercy and from which a pair of teenage girls had slunk, followed by a man, a woman and a toddler—floppy hatted, hiking booted, fly swatting.

As Mercy's thumb hovered over her phone, wondering if she could send the photo to Eugene as a kind of olive branch for hanging up on him, the woman from the RV approached, toddler clinging to her hip.

'Excuse me,' the woman said. 'Could you take our photo?'

The woman's floppy straw hat drooped down over her face. Though she backhanded the hat up with her wrist, the child kept grabbing at it and the woman was fighting a losing battle. All Mercy could see of the woman's face were spots of sunlight coming through the weave onto her cheeks and chin.

'Sure,' Mercy said, shoving her phone away, selfie sent to no one. She glanced around for Wasabi; he had wandered a short way to inspect a patch of shade and she felt the invisible string in her chest pull tight.

The woman handed Mercy a brand new iPhone, twisting it away from the plump little hand reaching for it. 'Sorry,' she said, 'but there's three of them altogether—' tucking her free hand into her pocket she dug out another two phones '—if you wouldn't mind? The older girls, you know. For their Snapchats.' In the woman's voice Mercy heard the roll of her eyes. 'Or whatever.'

'Right.' Mercy juggled the phones, hoping she wouldn't drop one onto the sun-baked ground and break a teenage girl's heart. Possibly ruin her life forever.

Wasabi had found a scent and was zigzagging further away, nose pressed to the ground. Mercy wanted to call him back but Floppy-hat, the man and two teenage girls were standing in the shade of the border sign, waiting for their photo. One girl was chewing a nail, the other had her arms crossed and was glaring in the direction of the highway as if she had a personal grudge with it.

'Do you want us to say "cheese"?' the woman called out.

Wasabi's brown body disappeared into a thicket of bush.

'Uh … sure.' Mercy aimed the first phone in their direction.

Wasabi reappeared. Out the corner of her lips, Mercy tried to whistle him back, but all that achieved was a fly lifting from her cheek and re-settling on her ear.

The adults called, 'Cheese!' One girl spat out a sliver of fingernail and the other continued to hate the highway. Once the toddler started exclaiming, 'Sees! Sees!' she didn't stop, and Mercy juggled phones and snapped as many group photos as she could until the scene organically dissolved all on its own. When the father said something about sausages and Coke, the teenagers showed mild interest and they all sloped off back to their RV.

Now Mercy whistled to Wasabi, calling him sternly as he made to dash off after the man who'd promised sausages. The dog came trotting back, sheepish, and Mercy bent down to run her hand over his fur.

The mother, hauling the toddler, jogged back to Mercy.

'Thanks!' She retrieved the phones, stuffing her pockets while Mercy apologised for anything blurry or for chopping anyone's head off.

'I'm sure they'll be fine,' the woman said, waving a hand. 'It's rare these days to get the girls out of their rooms long enough to get all of us in one shot.'

Mercy laughed obligingly. The toddler glared at her. A breeze came up then, a sudden swirly gust, and blew the woman's hat right off her head. She tried to lunge after it but the toddler slowed her down. For a beat, Mercy watched the hat bounce and roll across the gravel, before she hurried after it and scooped it up. Dust littered the brim and she brushed it off, handing it back to the woman.

'Thanks.'

'No problem,' Mercy said.

'I'm Ann, by the way.' Early forties, short blonde curls, eyes a remarkable greyish colour over sharp cheekbones. She held out her hand to Mercy and Mercy shook it, feeling an uneasy flicker.

'Mer—' Mercy began. Those eyes, those cheekbones. Had she seen them before? The woman had three children, one of whom wasn't even two years old. Had Mercy seen her at the hospital? What if she participated in one of those online groups? After all, it's not as though *Mercy* was a particularly common name.

'—becca,' Mercy finished.

'Merbecca?'

'Yes. That's me.'

Ann seemed to be waiting for something, so Mercy added, 'My mother was unusual.'

Ann gave a short laugh. 'Aren't they all?'

Mercy didn't know how to answer.

'Thanks for playing photographer. I hope we haven't held you up too much.'

'Not at all.' Mercy pointed to the Hijet. 'I couldn't be in a hurry if I tried.' Immediately she regretted identifying her vehicle.

'Wow, what a fantastic little van!' Ann said. Mercy realised they were strolling back towards the carpark together. 'We've got plenty of sausages, and cold drinks,' Ann was saying. 'Would you and your little dog like something to eat?'

Mercy felt the familiar squeezing inside, the sense of internal shrinking away. The rising desperation to be alone, inside, safe.

'Uh, thanks,' she said. 'But I couldn't. I've got to …' She flapped a hand towards the van.

'No worries,' Ann said with a shrug and a smile. Giving a final wave, she trotted back to her family, the sound of sausages sizzling and the *pop-fizz* of soft drink cans rising up into the sunshine, and then it dawned on Mercy.

Those grey eyes. Sharp cheekbones. Blonde curls. That was Ann Barker.

Ann fucking Barker.

CHAPTER SEVENTEEN

Eugene had told Mercy that the problem with her reading the articles was that it made things feel a lot worse than they were. Which was true—among other things, reading the headlines and blog posts had made Mercy feel invaded, personally violated. Like the opinion writers and commenters had shoved a scope up Mercy's nostril and into her brain. Really jerked the camera around in there. *Just forget it,* Eugene had tried to tell her. *It's all rubbish, it will blow over.* If they hadn't been dividing up their stuff and selling their house at the time—boxes of clothes, a walnut tall boy and the faux-suede two-seater couch sitting in the middle of the driveway—Mercy might have been better able to swallow such blithe reassurances.

Besides, Mercy had tried to point out to Eugene, *Oh, Annie!* had more than a million followers. Roughly equivalent to the entire population of Adelaide. Try blowing over that.

Four long hours passed between leaving the border and reaching Alice Springs. And in those long hours of thrumming bitumen and slow-flashing white lines, Mercy could not be distracted by the red dirt and big sky, the stiff-bloated roadkill kangaroos and hopping crows, nor even the maddening crawl of burned skin on her thighs. No, for those four hours, all Mercy could think about was population statistics again. All she could think about was how in a country of twenty-five million—the majority of whom lived thousands of kilometres away from where she currently was (the middle of the outback, for crying out loud!)—Mercy could run into *her*.

'Haven't seen a set of traffic lights for two days,' Mercy shouted into the wind, 'but I have seen *her*. Of all people. Her!'

What were the chances? Mercy wasn't a mathematician but the odds, surely, had to be stacked in Mercy's favour. One in a million? One in *twenty-five* million?

But, as slim as chances could be, awful things happened. Mercy knew that. Statistics could be used to argue against all kinds of unlikelihoods but still, no matter how impossible the odds seemed, tragedy struck. Being struck by lightning, or hit by a falling coconut, or squashed by a meteorite might make you a minuscule percentage of the population but it doesn't make the fact of it happening any less real. Any less painful.

Mercy slowed for the outskirts of Alice Springs. Traffic thickened, more traffic than she had seen since Port Augusta. The ridge of the MacDonnell Ranges rose up like a wall, running as far east–west as she could see. The highway aimed towards a narrow gap in the range and Mercy felt herself squeezed towards a certain doom. On the other side of that ridge was Alice Springs township: the only large metropolitan centre for another fifteen hundred kilometres. What if Ann Barker was in town, on the other side of that looming ridge? An hour after leaving the border, Ann's RV had appeared in Mercy's rear-vision mirror. When the RV pulled out to overtake the Hijet there had been convivial waves exchanged and tooted horns and Mercy had tried to tell herself that, back at the border, the journalist had not recognised her. If she had, surely she would have said something?

Trepidation rose as the Hijet rattled along the highway, cars slipping in close on all sides, until they were squeezed through the gap in the ranges and disgorged into the sedate streets of Alice Springs on the other side. Mercy felt chewed up and spat out. All at once that familiar, tremendous exhaustion dumped itself over her.

Whether or not the opinion writer who had called her a *murderer* was in town, Mercy had to stop.

The first caravan park she came to appeared to be full. The square white rear ends of caravans were packed to the fence lines, but when Mercy cruised a slow lap around the block, peering into the park, she couldn't see anything that looked like Ann Barker's RV and the sign out the front of the park said VACANCY and KIOSK so all in all, those things appealed to her. It was just after five pm; gum trees threw long shadows across the road and the afternoon light was bright yellow. She was hungry, tired and anxious.

Mercy parked the van in front of the office and stepped out. Her legs felt doughy, not quite connected to her body. Inside, an air conditioner pumped frigid air into a small space. Leaflets rustled on a squeaky stand; a potted plant trailed waxy green leaves down the side of a desk, and when Mercy asked the lady behind the counter for a campsite for the night, the woman asked, 'Just yourself?' and Mercy replied, 'Me and my dog,' and the woman looked outraged.

'No pets,' she said, in the same tone as if Mercy had asked if she could dismember a corpse on the shared barbecue tables.

Cheeks flaming, Mercy left the office.

Following signs down a side street to another caravan park, she found a notice that said Pets welcome and her heart lifted but then she saw the small no taped in front of Vacancy. This park was complete with a boom gate and high corrugated iron fences, so Mercy couldn't see inside, and she figured the welcoming of pets, the security and the signposted 1 hour free wi-fi must be a favourite with the grey nomads. As she drove away she was beginning to understand why they all left their camps in the morning in such a rush.

The third and final caravan park, tucked down the end of a dead-end street behind a pub, had no boom gate, mesh fences and a faded three-and-a-half star rating sign swinging by one corner, and when she went inside she was told they accepted neither pets nor mobile payments and anyway, they were fully booked. Biting back a retort about putting those things on their sign instead of coin-operated laundry, Mercy slunk out.

Shadows inched longer; the sun sank towards the Ranges. The thud of bass and the smell of cigarette smoke emanated from the pub up the road. Sitting in the van, Mercy wrung her hands. Wasabi looked up at her from the passenger seat.

'What are we going to do?'

There were always rest stops on the side of the road—could she drive out of town a little way and camp at one of those? After all, she had a bed, a gas burner and a can of soup—she didn't really *need* a caravan park. But then more headlines began to flash into her mind: backpackers stabbed to death; tourists kidnapped at gun point; travellers vanishing into the outback, never to be seen again. She thought of bodies dumped down mine shafts and saw what they would write about her now: *Women should know better than to camp alone. Women should stay in well-lit areas at all times. A sausage dog is no protection.*

Or, Mercy thought with a jolt, maybe they wouldn't. Maybe they'd write *Doctor gets what she deserved.* Maybe that random anonymous AngelJax2917 would crow that their email to Mercy suggesting she *die bitch die* had come true.

It was almost six pm; less than an hour of daylight remained. And Mercy might have a can of soup but she had no other food and she was almost out of water. Scrubbing her hands over her face, she felt the road grit and dust sliding under her nails. She stank, she was afraid and god only knew what could be going on with her hair.

Pulling back onto the road, she drove to the Coles she had passed at least eight times while searching for a caravan park. Leaving the windows cracked for Wasabi, she hurried into the store and began piling boxes, cans and packets into the trolley. Fear tasted like metal on her tongue but at least the anxiety over where she was going to sleep tonight and not get murdered topped the anxiety over being in the supermarket.

As she loaded casks of spring water onto the checkout belt, the operator, a pimply youth surely no older than twelve, asked, 'Passing through or staying?'

'Staying,' Mercy said. 'Well, I'm supposed to be. If I can find somewhere.'

'You looking for a place to stay?'

Mercy glanced up from a pack of two-minute noodles in alarm. The boy wasn't offering, was he?

'It's just I know they're still taking campers at the show-grounds.' The cashier glanced from side to side, then leaned towards Mercy and stage whispered, 'Only they don't want people to know about it.'

'Who doesn't?'

'The local caravan park owners.'

'I see.' She didn't. After a confused beat she asked, 'So … can I camp there, or not?'

'Oh, yeah,' the cashier said confidently, waving her question away. 'You totally can. Anyone can. You just rock up. First in, first served. They're only supposed to take thirty campers, and it's supposed to be *only* the overflow from the caravan parks. But …' He hesitated over a can of spring vegetable soup with real croutons. 'I don't think anyone's policing it, you know? Like—' he snorted a laugh, '—no one's fangin' around taking a rollcall.'

'I see,' Mercy repeated, but at least now she was beginning to. 'So … just go to the showgrounds?'

'Yep.'

'And I can camp there overnight?'

'Yep.'

'With my dog?'

'Absolutely.'

'And if it's already full is there anywhere else?'

He hesitated before shooting another furtive look around. 'It won't be full,' he said. 'It never is, get me?' Knowingly, he tapped the side of his nose and went back to scanning.

Mercy thought of women after sixteen hours of labour, how they looked at the anaesthetist after the first squirt of epidural into their spine. Relief and gratitude crossed with a profound amazement, as though they'd just experienced something inexplicable, something holy.

Stuffing loaded bags into the trolley, Mercy looked at the checkout boy and knew her expression would be the same.

CHAPTER EIGHTEEN

The showgrounds were on the southern fringe of town, back the way she had come, through the gap in the Ranges. Mercy drove onto the grounds slowly, gripping the wheel and waiting for an enraged local caravan park owner to leap out from behind a bush and yell *Gotcha!* She was comforted to see that in the row of caravans and motorhomes parked beneath the trees, none of them looked to be Ann Barker's. And at least, she thought, if she was to be caught red-handed somewhere she wasn't supposed to be, she wouldn't be alone.

It struck her, that feeling of solidarity with the other campers, because she realised she hadn't felt solidarity with anyone—least of all strangers—for a long time.

Driving along the row of campers, she spotted a familiar setup and recognised it belonged to Bert, of the multi-pocketed shirt. There was no one outside the caravan, so she didn't wave, but the realisation that she would have came as a shock. Once again there were neat chairs and tables set out on mats, tidy silver-haired folk in clean pressed linen, everyone appearing organised and fresh while Mercy rocked up late, covered in dust, sweat-rumpled and wind-blown. She felt like the drunk uncle at a Sunday morning christening.

And there, at the end of the row, was the rental van of Andrew Macauley.

He was sitting in a folding chair, a beer cradled in his lap, and when he saw Mercy drive in his face lit up in a way that made her entire body feel sunburned. Parking a polite distance away from his camper, she shut off the engine and climbed out.

'Hiya,' Andy said, waving. 'Following me, eh?'

'I think we're all following each other.' She pointed to the other caravans. It occurred to her that Ann Barker could still arrive at any moment. Nervously she scanned the highway, a murmur of traffic at the far edge of the park.

'So now I'm supposed to ask you how your vehicle is going,' Andy said, getting to his feet and coming over. 'And then I'm supposed to stand with one foot up on your back wheel and talk about where I've been while you try and set up.'

'I don't have much to set up, I'm afraid.' Lifting Wasabi out, she set him on the grass. 'There,' she said. 'Done.' The dog rocketed towards Andy, his back end curling towards his front in happiness. Andy reached down to pat him and the dog rolled onto his back, tongue lolling. 'But be my guest,' Mercy added, gesturing to the Hijet's wheels, caked with orange dust. 'And the vehicle is going fine, thank you. If a little slow.'

'How'd you go with the roadtrains?'

'Windy.'

Andy laughed.

'And on that note,' Mercy said, looking around, 'I've really got to find a bathroom ...' She wanted to reach up and try to smooth her hair, but that would only draw attention to it—if it wasn't already up there whistling and swinging its hips like a showgirl.

Andy pointed, and Mercy picked up her hessian shopping bag and hurried across the grass towards a small stone building. No showers—what could one expect when camping on the sly?—only a toilet block with a black water dump point out the back. But there was a sink with clean running water. Above the sink serving as a mirror was a sheet of hammered steel. Her reflection was only a vague blur, but that was enough to see that her hair had reached the proportion of something extra-planetary.

Peeling off her T-shirt, she washed up as best she could, plastering on deodorant and brushing her teeth, and then she set about trying to do something with her hair. Rooting about up there, she found the hair tie snagged in tight as fencing wire. There was no retrieving it, no matter how hard and painfully she tried. Eventually, using her hands like bulldozer blades, she coaxed it all back into some kind of bun and then looped a new hair tie over the top to hold it all in place. Then she leaned over the sink, splashed water onto her face and up into her scalp. When she was done she rinsed a slick of blood-coloured mud from the bowl.

'Can I have a wee bit of your piece?' Andy was looking down at Mercy's lap.

Mercy dropped her fork. 'My what?'

He gestured towards her lap. 'I've never tried it.' At the expression on her face, he laughed. 'Sorry. A piece. You know—a sandwich.'

Mercy looked at her plate: pasta salad from a packet and a brown bread sandwich cut into quarters. 'Sure,' she said, holding it out. 'But you've never tried a sandwich?'

'I've never tried Vegemite.' He took a triangle and gave the bread a sniff. 'I'm told it's salty.' He took a tentative bite and chewed, his face expressionless. After a moment, his cheeks sucked in and his eyes screwed up. 'Christ!' he said, coughing and swallowing with difficulty. 'That's dead nasty, that is.'

'It also doubles as a good engine degreaser, I've heard,' Mercy said mildly, taking a large bite.

'Aye, noted,' he said, wiping his eyes.

Mercy and Andy were sitting on the grass between their vans. The sun was setting and the sky was spectacular. The face of the Ranges rolled like a movie screen of colour and shadow. With the liberal application of more after-sun gel, the sting in Mercy's thighs had eased and they were now giving off more of a dull burr than a smarting heat. Laughing at Andy, with Wasabi stretched out peacefully between them and the grass turning gold in the setting sun, Mercy felt a slow, spreading warmth sink over her shoulders and down her spine.

It didn't last. As if registering the moment of peace, her mind knee-jerked with a swift reminder of Ann Barker lurking out there somewhere and that voicemail lurking on her phone. She stabbed her fork into her pasta salad. She should just listen to the message. A heads-up from a legal assistant, a formality or paperwork—it wouldn't be anything she needed to panic over. Surely.

But as long as she didn't listen to it, as long as whatever information that message contained went unacknowledged, Mercy could continue to remain *here now*: where there was no obligation, where there was only a Scottish man laughing about Vegemite and the sunset gilding the Ranges and the warm, cottony evening air. To hear what Legal had to say would not only be admitting to the future, but confronting the past all over again.

Mercy set her plate on the grass. Wasabi took the rest of her sandwich.

'So listen,' Andy said at length. 'There's a waterhole not far from here, and I was thinking of going swimming tomorrow. Would you be up for it?'

Mercy looked down at the smears of mayonnaise on her plate. Overhead in the trees, cockatoos squabbled over evening roosts.

'Unless you're taking off in a hurry.' Andy inclined his head, indicating the row of caravans. 'Like this lot.'

Mercy's mind raced. She tried to recall the last time she had been invited swimming by a friend. She tried to recall the last time she had done *anything* with a friend. Once, there had been colleagues—drinks after work at the pub, synchronised days off where they might have met for lunch. At one point she had joined a book club started by one of the nurses, but after six books in a row that she didn't get to read she had stopped going. Between work, and Eugene, and her mother, Mercy simply hadn't done a lot of swimming with friends. And then, two years ago, those last few people she could have called friends had slipped away. Or been pushed: when she started giving excuses, stopped returning calls and, eventually, changed her number.

Could she? The thought made her stomach squeeze. Strapped into the passenger seat, someone else in control. What if she drove herself, offering to meet him there? But that would be a waste of petrol (and here she thought of the sea life again, suffering with carbon emissions and global warming), and she considered suggesting they take her Hijet, until she recalled how the inside of it must smell: road dust, sweat, petrol and a hint of cremated remains.

She couldn't. Besides, what would she do with Wasabi?

'I don't know—'

'It's not at a national park, so this wee fellow can come for a dip, too.' Andy reached forward to pat the dog. 'We can't leave an assistance dog behind.'

Could she?

Mercy thought of a day of not driving, a day of open sky and sunshine and cool water; the crunch of dry gum leaves beneath her feet, the trickle of a creek. She thought of talking and laughing. She thought of Andrew Macauley's dark eyes and warm smile and deep voice.

'Okay,' she said, finally meeting his eyes.

'Yes?' he said.

'Yes.'

CHAPTER NINETEEN

The thud of the van door closing echoed across the red cliffs.

'Are you *sure* it's not part of the national park?' Mercy asked again, nervous, as she lifted Wasabi from the van.

'I'm ninety-nine per cent certain,' Andy said, waving the map. 'That track we just drove down is definitely not in the green section. The guy at the tourist information centre yesterday swore to me the land is privately owned—said it was a sheep station once upon a time—but the owner is old, no longer has sheep, and lives about a hundred kilometres further in that direction.' He pointed vaguely west.

Mercy remained holding the dog, reluctant to step away from the van.

In the end, they'd taken the Hijet. When she had awoken that morning, Mercy knew she could not sit in a strange vehicle and drive to an unknown destination with a man she hardly knew. She simply could not. Even if that man was charming, inexplicably trustable and had lovely brown eyes. Fortifying herself with a few deep breaths, she had shown up at Andy's camper that morning as he'd been munching buttered toast and said, 'Okay if we take my van?' Then she'd clamped her hands together to stop them from shaking. 'For sure,' Andy had replied without hesitation. 'I'd love a lift in that beast.'

And so after more than an hour of juddering and teeth-clattering down a two-wheel track, bushes screeching like fingernails along the sides of the van, they had arrived at the waterhole. Dusty, sweaty and out of breath, but here they were. After finally coming to a halt, Mercy had clung to the safety of the steering wheel for a full four minutes before finding the courage to open the door and slide out.

She gazed now around the tree-lined hollow. Rocky bluffs rose up, a split of daylight blasting through the centre where a shallow creek trickled between the cliffs and ended in a deep pool. A sandy beach curled around one side of the waterhole. Insects buzzed and clicked; a bird gave a long, whip-like call that echoed around the rocks before fading into the heat.

'Okay,' Mercy conceded. 'It's nice.'

As Andy took out the esky, Mercy set Wasabi down and made her way to the water. Dry leaves crunched underfoot; sweat beaded her lip and she wiped it with the back of her hand. Wasabi trotted off into the bushes, nose to the ground, and Mercy hoped he hadn't scented some endangered native marsupial and was about to dig it out of its hole and devour it.

At the water's edge she stepped out of her boots. The sand was hot and gritty beneath her feet. Algae slicked the shallows. Dipping her toes in the tea-coloured water, she let out an involuntary shriek. The sound ricocheted across the cliff faces.

'All right over there?' Andy called.

'It's freezing!'

He came down the sand and crouched, putting his hand in the water. 'Ah, what're you on about? It's lovely.'

'After you, then,' she said, opening her arm towards the pool.

'All right.' Lifting his T-shirt over his head, he stepped out of his boots and peeled off his socks. He dropped his clothing on the sand, grinned at her, then plunged into the water. Icy cold droplets showered Mercy's legs and arms and she gasped and stepped back. There was a second, smaller splash as Wasabi rocketed after Andy.

Mercy watched Andy's arms lifting and slicing through the water, Wasabi trailing behind like a seal. Ripples spread out in their wake, bobbing twigs and pieces of leaf litter. Below the surface Andy's torso and shoulders looked green-brown.

A memory began to stir, dredged up from the bottom of the pond of her mind. Mercy fought it, trying to press it down but it floated up, lifting higher and higher until, like it or not, there it was, grabbing at her insides.

Two police officers came to her door, and told her they had found her mother in the bath. Two days she had been there, they said. It looked as though her mother may have tried to climb out, but never made it over the rim, falling back into the water. Mercy often thought that if her mother's heart had kept beating just a few moments more, the neighbour who met her mother for coffee every Thursday morning might not have found her in the bath, but on the bathroom floor, and Mercy wasn't sure if that would have been any better, to be honest. Loretta Blain's body was still in rigor mortis when they found her; there was no water in the lungs. She had died of a massive heart attack. This information they had delivered to Mercy gently but assertively, leaving no room for misunderstanding, and Mercy knew this tone so very well because how many times had she delivered that same irreversible, life-altering news?

There is no heartbeat and your baby has died.

Watching TV, Mercy always scoffed at the way doctors or police officers delivered the news of death to loved ones. Lots of *We did all we could,* or *I'm afraid I have bad news,* or sometimes nothing more than a sad shake of the head while holding tragic, beseeching eye contact. No, that's not how it was done, not in real life. Breaking the news of death takes exquisitely firm clarity and the use of correct, unmistakeable words.

Dead. Died. Dead.

Andy was saying something, his voice skipping across the water and echoing around the rocks. He was laughing at Wasabi.

When Mercy had broken the news to the woman's husband, he had looked around the room as though he suddenly didn't know where his wife had gone. As though he was waiting for her to appear. When Mercy said, *Your wife has died,* it was as though he heard: *Your wife has just popped out to the shops, she'll be back in a jiffy.* Even though his wife had been lying right there on the bed in the ICU, still attached to all the tubes and hoses that hadn't saved her.

'You coming in?'

Mercy blinked. Sunlight flared off the water. The scent of sunscreen rose from her warm skin. *Be here now.*

And now she was crying, tears sliding down her hot cheeks, the silent kind of crying that happens all on its own, without any shuddering or sobbing or honking, just tears leaking like pus from an abscess that has gotten so swollen the fluid and mess can no longer be contained.

'Hey—are you okay?'

Mercy looked up. Andy was swimming towards her. His hair was slicked back, water gleaming on his shoulders, a concerned expression on his face.

Mercy hauled herself up straight. Her whole body felt too hot, like she was burning up from the inside. Pain flared like a blowtorch in her chest.

She didn't think about it. She yanked her I ♥ SYDNEY T-shirt over her head. She wriggled out of her shorts, kicked them across the sand, and in her bra and undies she ran forward, cold water churning up her legs, until the silty floor of the waterhole fell away from under her feet and she flung herself in.

Cold slapped her skin. Bubbles roared against her ears. The water tasted of earth and metal. She may have laughed, or screamed, and when she surfaced, she was breathless and shrieking.

'Oh god!' she cried, unsure if she was exclaiming over the cold, or the pain, or the fact that she had just leapt into the water in her only bra.

Andy was treading water a few metres away from her, Wasabi paddling in circles around him, wet nose pointed into the air.

'Better?' Andy said after a few minutes.

Mercy's legs pedalled. Below the surface the water was even colder. She imagined the water seeping up from deep fissures in the earth. Hair plastered to her cheeks and scalp, the sun heated the top of her head. Above and below. Heat and cold. Light and dark. Life had both extremes—all human experience existed on the one spectrum. Sometimes you felt one side, sometimes the other. It was a physical fact, as real and immutable as the necessity for air.

Life and death.

Mercy was here now, in this moment. That was all she had, or could ever know, really.

Mercy exhaled. She said, 'Better.'

Mercy had seen a lot of men in their virile prime. Large men, small men, men built like broom handles and men who could lift a bus with a single bicep. She had seen gym-pumped men with shaved heads, sensitive-looking graphic designer types with coifs, shopping centre security guards smelling of cigarettes and big city bankers reeking of cologne and sexual infidelity. But Mercy had never seen a man pull off a man-bun. Until now.

After a swim, Mercy and Andy had climbed out of the waterhole and staggered, shivering, across the sand. Before collapsing onto towels in the shade, Andy had lifted his arms, loosely raked his fingers through his hair, and snagged it up into a top knot with an elastic tie he'd taken from his wrist. And he'd left his shirt lying on the sand.

So there he was, lounging back, eyes closed and face tilted to the sun and gloriously man-bunned, and Mercy, tugging her T-shirt back over her damp body, was trying to look anywhere but directly at him. Because where did all that definition in his shoulders and chest come from? Was it there before? When he lifted his arm again to scratch between his shoulder blades, was that … was she *salivating*?

Mercy dropped her gaze to her toes. It was amazing how something she'd assumed was long dead could actually snap awake and announce itself with an unmistakeable pang. Yes, it had been a long time. A very long time. To many it would be painfully long, but to Mercy it had simply never come into her mind because for two years (and not to mention the long marriage to a man who had quietly harboured a hankering for the pleasures of his own sex) her mind had been too busy freaking out about how she was going to pick up that parcel the courier had taken to the post office instead of dropping on her doorstep, or what might happen if a Solar Roof salesman came to her door and refused to be rebuffed with any haste. Life had been reduced to moments of fear strung together like beads on a wire of anticipation.

Until finally that string had frayed, unravelled, snapped—beads falling to the floor and scattering everywhere. Flames licking the night sky.

Andy leaned over to drag the esky closer, the muscles along his spine doing all kinds of wonderful things.

'D'you want a piece?'

Mercy unstuck her lips. Her stomach growled. Yes, she wanted a piece. They'd bought the pre-packaged sandwiches that morning from a deli—ham, cheese, tomato and white pepper on multigrain bread. Biting into the soft bread, she ate hungrily. Pepper pleasantly opened her sinuses, eucalyptus-fresh air filled her lungs and Andy appeared in no hurry to reapply his shirt.

She didn't even mind the flies.

They chatted about pleasant things, personal things: Andy had two younger sisters and had always felt the protector, even though one of his sisters was a pro wrestler and the other was a diesel mechanic. 'And they're both six foot two,' he added, holding his hand flat a few inches above his crown. 'Like, they don't need me.'

They chatted about normal things, everyday things: Mercy preferred *Armageddon* when it first came out—'I was fifteen,' she declared—but now she had to concede that *Deep Impact* was, well, deeper.

They chatted about family things, let-go-of things: Andy's ex-wife's wedding was yesterday, Saturday, and Mercy's father, even though he had cut ties almost entirely when he left, still sent Mercy a card every year for her birthday.

'I got the most recent one the day before my house burned down.'

'Are you angry at him?' Andy asked. '*Were* you ever angry?'

'Maybe,' Mercy said. 'Yes. Of course. But I think, in a way, I sort of got it. I understood.' She fed Wasabi the last crust of her sandwich and brushed crumbs from her fingers.

'How old were you when he left?'

'Eight, I think. Nine.'

'That's fairly young to understand something like that.'

Mercy shrugged. 'Everything seems to make more sense in hindsight though, doesn't it? It ends up that we view our childhood memories through an adult lens. That changes things. Even if it didn't make sense to me at the time, it makes sense to me now. At home, when I was a kid, things were … intolerable.' She left the rest unsaid.

'So you're not angry—at either of them?'

She looked at him. 'Are you worried your kids will be angry at you?'

He picked up a twig and began to snap it into small pieces. 'I don't know,' he said. 'Maybe. Yes. Of course.'

'You know,' she said, 'I don't think it's possible *not* to have hang-ups about your parents. I think even the happiest, most loved children in the world grow up wishing something could have been different.' She offered him a smile. 'Just be there for them when they need you to be, and let them be whoever they are. Do that and you'll be a better parent than the shittiest ones, I guarantee it.'

'What a bar to aim for, eh? One up from the shittiest.'

'Everyone's got standards.'

A warm breeze eddied across the water, shifted over the sand and lifted hair from the nape of Mercy's neck. Her skin was dry but her bra was still damp, pressing dark circles into her T-shirt.

Andy turned to her, and she held his gaze.

'So what now?' she said.

A beat of silence passed. Eucalypts tipped their limbs and rustled their leaves. Then, carried on the breeze, they both heard it at the same time: an engine. A car was coming down the track. A minute later a dusty troop carrier arrived in the clearing, voices whooping from open windows, and Mercy and Andy were alone no longer.

It was about halfway along the rutted, rocky track back to the highway when the loud clang sounded under the van.

'Shit,' Mercy said, wincing. 'What was—'

She was drowned out by a tremendous, deafening roar. It sounded like a herd of Harleys had just opened the rear door and begun driving through the Hijet.

If Mercy could have heard Andy, she would have heard him mutter, 'Damn.' But she couldn't, so she didn't; instead she applied the brakes and the van jerked to a stop. The thundering continued. As the engine idled, Mercy realised the racket was the sound of the Hijet itself. It had gone from making its usual happy little burble to an ear-splitting crashing sound.

Andy was speaking, but Mercy couldn't hear him. He mimed turning a key.

She shut off the engine. Silence fell.

'What the hell was that?' she said.

'Sounds like the muffler.'

'The what?'

'I'll take a look.' Andy opened the door.

'Do you know about … mufflers?'

'Enough to know if they've fallen off.'

As Mercy went to open the door, Wasabi jumped onto her lap. Ears flattened, he was quivering and showing the whites of his eyes.

'That was loud and scary, huh?' she said, stroking his fur. 'Sorry, boy. It's okay.' Running her palms over his body, she waited until the dog settled before climbing out. He whined and put his paws up on the window.

'Stay,' she told him. She was still nervous about the national park's boundaries.

Squinting against the blaring afternoon sun, she hurried around the side of the van in time to see Andy's head and shoulders disappear under it.

'Okay,' he said from under the vehicle. 'The muffler's fallen off, all right.' He reappeared with a grunt. Red dirt smeared his shoulder and one side of his head. 'And great Christ, is this sand hot.'

'Is it serious?' Mercy said. 'Can it drive?'

He got to his feet, brushing his hands on his shorts. 'It can drive, but we'll both be deaf as a post by the time we're back in town.'

'Oh.'

'That is, if we're not dead from carbon monoxide poisoning.'

'Oh,' Mercy repeated. Frowning, she squatted and peered under the van, but on first glance all she could see was sand, rocks and shadows, with bright daylight out the other side. Looking more closely, she identified a piece of pipe hanging down.

'Is that it?' she asked, pointing. 'The muffler?'

'Yes.'

'It shouldn't be hanging down in the dirt like that?'

'Nope.'

'So how do we—can we get it back ... up?'

Andy was walking a lap of the Hijet; he appeared to be looking for something. He put his hand on the back door. 'Mind if I take a look, see what we've got to work with?'

'Sure.'

The rear door lifted open with a squeak. Wasabi barked again, bounding from the front into the back to lick Andy's face as he climbed in.

'What are you looking for?' Mercy asked.

'Something I can tie it back up with.'

That sounded simple enough, Mercy thought, brightening, as she examined the fallen piece of pipe again. Of course. It just needed to be tied back up.

'Is that why it got so loud, all of a sudden?' Mercy said. 'Because it wasn't *muffling* anymore?'

'That's right,' came the sound of Andy's voice. 'Hey, d'you mind if I take look in this cabinet? The one under the bed?'

'Sure, go ahe— Wait!'

Andy's head appeared.

'Sorry,' she hastened to say. 'There's just, under the bed, there's, um …' *Jenny Cleggett.* Cremated remains. A box containing the ground-up skeleton of an unknown human. None of those statements were utterable, probably not even in ordinary circumstances, let alone while they were stranded on a two-wheel track in the outback with a muffler dragging in the dirt, an hour from the main road.

'That's, uh … my underwear.' Her face was already hot from the sun, but heat flooded it anyway. 'Maybe I should just take a look myself.'

Mercy climbed into the van, and Andy shifted aside to make room. He smiled at her. She smiled back.

'I'll leave you to it,' he said, and hopped out.

'So would anything do in particular, to tie the pipe back up?' she asked, lifting the mattress and checking the box of ashes. The rough track had loosened the flaps and she re-tucked them firmly, apologising to Jenny in her head. *But he did say to take you for a good trip.*

'We need a length of wire,' Andy said, his voice coming from somewhere outside. 'Or maybe some nylon rope, although that wouldn't last as long.'

Mercy was considering whether an emptied out can of condensed tomato soup could be fashioned into some kind of muffler-holding device when Andy reappeared.

'How attached are you to listening to the radio?'

'I didn't even know there was one,' she replied honestly.

'Good.' He lifted his hand, and in it was a bent-up coat hanger. 'Because now you don't have an aerial. Sorry.'

After convincing her she wouldn't asphyxiate running the engine for a few more seconds, Andy directed Mercy to position the van at an angle over the track, straddling one of the wheel ruts to allow more space underneath. The un-muffled engine roared like an angry god. When it was silent again, she climbed out and walked to where Andy lay in the sand.

'How's it going?'

A string of expletives issued from under the van, punctuated with words Mercy didn't recognise—she caught what sounded like *bawbag* and *bampot* and something about being *fucking scunnered*.

'Need some help?'

'It's all right,' he said, strained. 'Pipe's just a bit fuckin' hot.'

'Please don't burn yourself. We can't fix that with a coat hanger.'

Mercy lowered herself to the ground next to his legs. For about ten minutes she sat quietly, listening to the *tink* and *thunk* of whatever Andy was doing to tie the pipe back up. Occasionally, when she heard his breath labour or a few more heavily accented curses roll out, she'd say, 'All right?' and he'd reply, 'All right.' Beneath her the sand was warm and the afternoon sun was turning sharp and yellow. Andy had one leg stretched out, the other bent at the knee and his heel on the ground. Red dirt streaked his bare skin and caked into the tops of his boots.

She did it without thinking. With the flat of her fingers, she swept her hand over Andy's thigh, brushing the dirt off.

Andy jumped. Something went *thud*.

'Sorry,' she said, laughing. 'Didn't mean to startle—'

Wriggling backwards, he emerged from beneath the van. Red dirt coated his whole body, dark oil smudged his arms, and trickling from his forehead and dripping from the end of his nose was a bright trail of blood.

And then Mercy realised Wasabi was missing.

CHAPTER TWENTY

All Mercy could find to treat Andy's scalp wound were tissues, and as she was digging through her supplies hoping she might have, at some point, bought hand sanitiser, she realised Wasabi wasn't yapping at her, waggling his fat body or licking her face.

'Wasabi?' Craning to look over the seat, she checked in the back but it was empty. Wasabi wasn't in the van at all.

Slamming the door, Mercy jogged a lap of the van. She whistled, calling out, 'Here, boy!'

Nothing. Just the track disappearing around a bend, the breeze *shush*ing in the bushes, sunlight and shadow.

Andy was crouched in the shade of the van, palm to his forehead. Flies buzzed at the blood seeping down his forearm and dripping from his elbow, plopping into the dust.

'I can't find Wasabi,' Mercy said, alarmed.

'What?' Andy looked up. His face was pale.

Pushing him gently off his haunches, she sat him on the sand and lifted his palm away from his forehead. Fresh blood welled up. Matted hair clumped over the laceration in his hairline but Mercy couldn't see bone so, reassured, she wadded a large handful of tissues and pressed them onto the wound.

'Ow!' Andy cried.

'Sorry. Here, hold this.' She took his hand and pressed it back over the tissues. 'Keep some pressure on it. You'll live.'

After giving Andy a cup of water, Mercy jogged up the track, calling out to the dog. Putting her fingers between her teeth, she gave a long, sharp whistle, a shrill burst that echoed through the scrub and sent birds aloft and screeching.

'Wasabi!'

Spinning on her heel, she saw Andy staggering towards her, hand on his head.

'What's going on?'

'I can't find the dog. He's run off. And you should be sitting down.'

'Ah, shit. Are you sure?'

'Wasabi!' she bellowed.

Andy winced. 'I'll check the van again. Maybe he's tucked himself away somewhere.'

'The noise of the engine frightened him. I shouldn't have left him.'

'Was the door open?'

'The windows are down. He must have jumped out. Oh god,' Mercy said, putting her hands to her own forehead. 'It's such a long jump for his little legs. What if he's hurt? *Wasabi!*'

They checked under the seats, inside the cabinets, and Mercy even checked under the mattress but there was nothing but tinned beans, cask water and human remains. Andy needed to sit down again, so he leaned against the van and checked underneath, looking behind all the wheels while Mercy wove in and out of the bush along the edge of the track, calling out, her voice growing increasingly panicked.

'Wasabi, come here!'

But Wasabi did not come.

Digging out a can of beans, she whacked it with a spoon, yelling out, 'Din din dinner!'

Nothing.

'Shit!'

Stepping off the track, Mercy pushed further into the bush but thick melaleuca clawed at her and when she turned in a circle, she momentarily lost sight of the van and then she couldn't breathe.

A typical puppy, Wasabi had been. Chewed what he wasn't supposed to: books on the bottom shelves of the bookcase; the vacuum cleaner cord; shoes (he particularly loved Mercy's work sneakers, redolent of blood and piss and vomit). He shat where he wasn't supposed to (for weeks Mercy had picked tiny curls of turd off the living-room floor mat) and he yowled plaintively at three am. A typical puppy behaving the way a puppy was expected to, and doubly so because Mercy was never home. Could she scold a three-month-old puppy for upending the kitchen rubbish bin and spreading smelly litter all over the house when he had been left alone for twelve hours? Could she expect a six-month-old puppy *not* to jump all over the couch and rip the cushions to shreds when he hadn't been taken for a walk for three days?

She'd bought him just before she started her internship, naively thinking that the end of med school signalled the beginning of control over her own life. Maybe a cat would have been a better choice, Mercy had thought to herself in the early days, coming home in the bleary dawn after night shift to an avalanche of exploded toilet paper up and down the hallway. Or even a goldfish, she had thought, walking an excitable, yapping, twisting Dachshund in the dark streets at two am before work.

But Mercy had gotten Wasabi for the same reason anyone gets a puppy: because they embody happiness. Their fuzzy little faces are gorgeous and irresistible. Their love is unconditional. And no matter how long Mercy was gone, no matter how wrecked she was when she came home, no matter whether she had snapped at him or even ignored him, Wasabi was always there. He never blamed her, never criticised her, never expected *her* to actualise *him*. Always wagging his tail. Always happy to curl up on her lap and be petted, for as long as Mercy needed.

Simple. Everything.

Mercy scrambled her way out of the bush and back to the track. Colour had not returned to Andy's face, but the blood was no longer dripping.

'I can't find him,' Mercy said. She could feel herself slipping, losing her grip on the ground as if she was floating up into the air. 'He's gone.'

'Don't worry,' Andy said. He tried to get to his feet but his face turned a nauseated green and he slumped back down. He took his hand away from his head and the wound began to ooze again. In the dim recesses of her mind Mercy had the vague thought that she should be concerned about Andy's wound, but panic was flashing through her like fireworks. She shoved more tissues at him and muttered to keep the pressure on.

'What am I going to do?' she said, scanning the bush. 'He could be anywhere.'

'He can't have gone far.'

'Wasabi!'

'Wait,' Andy said, grabbing her arm with his free hand. 'Hear that?'

'What?' Mercy held her breath, but all she could hear was the thump of her own heart.

'It's an engine. Someone's coming.'

No sooner had he said it than the vehicle burst into view. Roaring up the track was a troop carrier, covered in dust and packed with bodies. It was the carload of people that had arrived at the waterhole earlier.

The vehicle pulled up behind the Hijet, engine idling. Three faces crammed through the window.

'You all right?'

Mercy hurried over. 'Have you seen a dog at all? A little brown sausage dog? He might have been running along the track.'

There was a brief conference inside the troop carrier, then: 'Haven't seen a dog. Are you missing one?'

Mercy wrung her hands and glanced at Andy. He was trying to stand again; blood crusted his eyebrows.

'Yes,' she said. It came out in a sob.

The engine shut off. A crowd of Aboriginal youths poured from the vehicle. Ten people altogether, aged between what looked to be fourteen and early twenties.

An older girl in a bright yellow T-shirt asked, 'What's he look like?'

'He's dark brown,' Mercy said around the lump in her throat. 'With light brown paws and eyebrows. And he's got two tan patches on his chest, here,' she added, pointing to her own breasts. 'Like he's wearing a bikini. He's small. Are you sure you didn't see him?'

The driver was a tall, lithe guy in his early twenties, and before Mercy realised what was happening the man had issued instructions, dividing the group in two, then each smaller team was disappearing into the bush.

'Wait,' Mercy said. 'I don't want anyone getting lost.'

'It's okay,' the driver said. 'We'll find him.'

'I can't—' Mercy tried to keep sight of each body as they took off into the scrub. She threw another glance at Andy; he was leaning heavily against the Hijet, clump of bloodied tissues pressed to his head, blinking as if he had water in his eyes.

Mercy's voice was thin. 'I really don't feel comfortable—'

'No worries,' the driver said with a big smile. 'This is our backyard. We know every rock and tree in this place.'

'Wasabi!'

'Wasabi!'

'Wasabi!'

The scrub echoed with whistles and calls. Mercy was too panicked about teenagers disappearing into the bush, and losing Wasabi, to worry about the colour leaching from Andy's face and the blood that began to trickle again when he insisted on standing up to help search.

Mercy walked a long way up and down the track, calling until her voice was hoarse. Standing on tiptoes to scan the bush, she tried to listen for all ten voices but it was impossible. Petrified of not only losing Wasabi but ten other people as well, after thirty agonising minutes she was seriously considering driving—muffler or no muffler—to the highway to call for help when she heard a far-off shout, replies lifting up into the late-afternoon air, and a few minutes later, all twelve of them—a relieved Mercy, a sore Andy, and ten perfectly happy youth—were back at the vehicles.

Thirteen if you counted the sausage dog in the arms of the girl with the yellow T-shirt, tail wagging, pink tongue delightedly licking the girl's face.

CHAPTER TWENTY-ONE

Bert's first aid kit was better described as a surgical theatre in a box, Mercy thought. The thing had an actual suture kit. Not that Andy would need stitches, much to Bert's disappointment. (Nor would Andy need an IV for that matter, as Bert had suggested to Mercy, producing a 20 gauge cannula needle, to Andy's alarm.)

They had made it back to the showgrounds by late afternoon, the van popping and farting more than usual but otherwise back to its regular volume. After Andy's colour had returned and his wound had stopped bleeding, Mercy had made Andy drive while she clutched Wasabi in her lap. Though the dog was untroubled by his brief yet profound junket alone in the bush, Mercy was too afraid to let him go. Even now, as she leaned over Andy, swabbing away his blood with his breath on her throat, Wasabi was tied to the leg of Andy's chair.

Mercy rinsed away dried blood and shreds of tissue from the wound in Andy's hairline in a state of hyper-awareness of her surroundings. The crackle of swab wrapping prickled her scalp. Wasabi flopped on the grass, panting, and Mercy imagined she could feel the blades of grass tickling her own belly. One of Andy's knees was between hers, nudging the inside of her thigh.

When she asked if Andy learned how to tie up mufflers from one of his sisters, he laughed and admitted he wasn't entirely unskilled in that area himself.

'What do you do, then?' she asked, squirting disinfectant and realising she still didn't know.

'Aircraft mechanic.'

'You work on planes? Plane engines?'

'Aye, so I do. Ouch. That stings.'

'I pulled your hair, sorry.'

'Some bedside manner you have.'

'Wrong end,' she said, without thinking. 'I'm not usually at people's heads.'

His eyes flew open. 'What end are you usually at?'

She applied a Steri-Strip with more vigour than necessary and he winced. 'You'd think someone who works under vehicles all day would know not to hit their head on it,' Mercy pointed out.

'You would think that,' Andy said, meeting her eyes. 'Just like a doctor knows not to get sunburnt.' For the briefest moment, his fingers brushed the skin above her knees. Mercy felt it through her whole body.

Moonlight sifted in through the windows. A low growl of thunder rattled the van. The air was dead calm, sticky and warm, the eerie quiet that precedes a storm.

Mercy lay on her back, cat throw puddled around her legs. She rolled her head to the side; the box of ashes sat on the cabinet. The time on her phone read 1.30am. The park had gone quiet hours ago; from up the row of caravans she could hear someone snoring. But Mercy could not sleep. Every time she closed her eyes she felt the plummeting sensation she had felt hours earlier when she realised Wasabi was gone. What if they hadn't found him? What if those kids hadn't been there? Worse still, what if one or all of them had gotten lost, or been hurt? Racking through those *what ifs*, of course, opened the floodgate on all the other *what ifs* and into her mind they poured, gushing and churning, irrational and pointless but oh-so-seductive to chafe over, until sweat sprang out on her skin and she sat up, thinking she was about to be sick.

When the nausea passed, Mercy looked at the cardboard box resting quietly on the cabinet. *Jenny Cleggett.*

'What should I do?' she whispered.

The box was silent.

Thunder cracked, closer now, and she heard a low shushing noise as a breeze began to stir the treetops. Bright blue light flashed as a bolt of lightning split the sky, followed by a loud crack of thunder. Wasabi whimpered and tried to burrow under her legs.

Mercy grabbed the dog's collar, panic spiking. She swung her legs off the bed and the throw slipped to the floor.

It was as though the inside of her body was trying to push out in all directions. She should go back home, but she had no home. She should be responsible but to whom? A good person ('a good girl', said her mother) doesn't take off across the country in a crappy old van, ignoring voicemails, hiding from journalists, bumming mechanical repairs from Scottish men, animal rescue from local teenagers and medical supplies from better prepared, responsibly-stocked retirees.

Be a good girl. Make Mummy proud.

Mercy stared at the box of ashes. 'If you happen to know my mother, wherever you are,' she said, her voice strained, 'can you kindly ask her to shut up?'

Thunder boomed, rattling the van. Wasabi yelped.

'Oh, so you're still blaming me?' Mercy tipped her face to the roof of the van. 'I'm so tired of never being good enough for you!'

It was the ultimate one-upping, really, to go ahead and die. When Mercy had finally, bravely—painfully—cut off contact with Loretta Blain, by the time she opened Facebook the next morning her mother had already de-friended and blocked her—and so had five other people. Mercy had messages from those few who hadn't taken her mother's side: *Are you okay? / Your mum said she's had to cut off all contact with you / She actually used the word 'toxic'.* An ego that large simply cannot fathom being the one who does things *second.* So if all else fails—lie. To everyone else, Loretta Blain had always been the gener-ous, bubbly, life of the party. It was only Mercy who saw the shadows. Copped the storms. Shouldered the blame and guilt.

'Well, you died, Mum,' Mercy said. 'You win. I will for-ever be the bitch.'

The wind began to pick up, lashing at the trees. A few spots of rain ticked onto the windscreen.

Mercy couldn't take the buzzing in her veins any longer.

With shaking hands she picked up her phone, thumbing through to the voicemail. The idea of putting the phone to her ear, as if the words would be injected right into the centre of her brain, was unbearable, so she put it on speaker. But as soon as that tinny electronic voice announcing her voicemails crackled through the van, projecting out into the world, she fumbled to shut the speaker off and lifted the phone to her ear.

'Mercy, this is Alison Webber from Legal Governance and Insurance Services Unit in regards to the matter of the inquest into the death of Tamara Lee Spencer. We have received the summation from the solicitor, and you will be emailed confirmation of the inquest date in due course. If you could please return my call, I just need to confirm …'

Alison Webber's sleek and professional voice faded away as Mercy took the phone from her ear and dropped it onto the bed. Clambering through into the driver's seat, she fumbled the keys into the ignition. She pulled the choke and tapped the accelerator. Lightning split the sky and thunder crashed as the engine thrummed into life.

Putting the Hijet into reverse, she swung away from the row of campers. Headlights flashed across Andy's van and she thought of the muffler tied on by a coat hanger. A surge of irrational anger swept through her at the sense that her liberty was conditional. So the muffler might need welding— so what? So Legal were leaving sleek-voiced voicemails—so what? Why should that stop her? Right here, right now, she was *fine*. And besides, she was a surgeon. Surely if it came to it she could re-twist a piece of wire around a pipe.

'*I'm* leaving first this time!' she cried, zooming past the sleeping caravans.

As the thunderstorm surged over the Ranges, Mercy gunned it out of the showgrounds and turned left onto the highway, out through Alice Springs, heading north into the wind-whipped night.

Rain sheeted in the headlights. White lines on the bitumen flashed and disappeared; the road whooshed and rumbled under the wheels.

Hunched white-knuckled over the steering wheel, Mercy peered through the windscreen. Visibility was down to a few metres. After the streetlights of Alice Springs had faded behind her, the night was black as the belly of a beast, lit up for split-seconds as lightning flashed the desert blue-white.

When the van rattled over the first cattle grid, Mercy held her breath. The engine burped and puttered but remained quiet and she exhaled, silently thanking Andy's skills in wire tying. When she bumped over a second cattle grid unscathed, she allowed herself to relax even further.

Almost as suddenly as it had started, the rain stopped. Stars reappeared in the sky; the road dried and the head-lights scooped out the night. As the moon-shadowed desert materialised around her, dark and still and endless, Mercy began to question her ill-considered decision to flee Alice Springs, to leave the showgrounds and her band of fellow travellers. Somehow, the storm had provided a cocoon, blanketing the world's *bigness*, reducing it to a cosy centre. The urge to move that had taken over her body had quieted.

Two and a half hours after leaving Alice Springs, it was a third cattle grid that finally did it: the muffler fell off, and the Hijet howled like a jet engine.

🐾

Mechanically, it was perfectly possible to drive a vehicle without part of its exhaust system, Andy had explained to her earlier. Provided the windows stayed open to let all the carbon monoxide out, it was just going to be loud as hell. Maybe out here on the deserted outback highway no one would mind, but in town, people would. So would any cops. And so would her ear drums, eventually.

'And if I were you, I probably wouldn't want to draw too much police attention to that thing,' Andy had said, pointing his sausage in bread towards the Hijet.

'Why not?' Mercy had replied, indignant. 'The lovely old man I bought it from swore it was roadworthy. The brakes are excellent. So are the seatbelts.'

'I'm sure the guy who sold you the car was convinced of it.'

Mercy had felt a rush of defensiveness for the little van, the camper that had shepherded her and Wasabi so far, safely. It had become her home. She had bonded with the Hijet, imprinted on it like a newborn deer.

Now, as the engine thundered like two ships banging together beneath her seat, Mercy realised she may have become overly, and problematically, sentimental. Taking a firm hold of Wasabi's collar, she steered the van one-handed onto a gravel siding, applied the park brake and turned off the engine. The silence blared.

'Bloody hell,' she said, ears ringing. 'Now what?'

Cold, dew-damp gravel scraped against Mercy's ear and shoulder. The smell of hot metal and road dust filled her nose. From inside the van, Wasabi whined—he was tied to the gear shift. Holding up her phone as a torch, lying on her side, Mercy wriggled her head and shoulders under the Hijet.

'Okay,' she said to herself as she shunted her hips forward. 'This should be simple enough. One pipe has come out of another pipe. All I need to do, once they've cooled down, is slide them back together. All I need to do is …'

Mercy looked. Halfway along the underside of the van, the broken-open exhaust pipe hung by a tidy twist of coat-hanger wire. The second piece of pipe should be right there beside it.

She turned her head. There was no second piece of pipe. The remainder of the undercarriage was bare.

The muffler was missing altogether.

CHAPTER TWENTY·TWO

'Shit,' Mercy said. 'Shit and bugger.'

Wasabi whined again.

In the light of her phone she checked the underside of the Hijet thoroughly but the muffler was nowhere to be found.

Wriggling out from under the vehicle, she stood up and shone washy light over the ground around her. All she saw were rocks and more rocks. Tentatively she walked towards the highway and cast her eyes up and down the dark stretch of bitumen. The muffler could be anywhere. It could have bounced off the road into the mulga. It could be bent, battered, smashed into pieces.

The highway disappeared like a throat into the blackness. Cold air lifted from the asphalt. Mercy shivered and hurried back to the van. Leaning against its side, she slid slowly down until she was crouched on the gravel. Wasabi yowled and scrabbled at the closed window.

It was just after four thirty am. Dawn was over an hour away. The cold was breathtaking, and the silence was incredible, absolute, its own shouting force. No cars passed on the highway; not a single insect clicked or buzzed in the rocks; not a breath whispered over the saltbush. The Milky Way rolled overhead, the moon cast a dim light from the far horizon, and Mercy's heels ground through the gravel as she stretched her legs out in front of her, propped against the van in the dark, alone in god knows where.

Google Maps was unresponsive. There was no service. Her phone was nothing but a clock and a torch.

Should she just keep driving? Mercy racked her brains for the last time she'd looked at the map. About two hundred kilometres north of Alice Springs, she recalled, there was a small town, a dot on the map. How far away was it? She'd been driving for almost three hours: the town must be close, within fifty kilometres. But what if it wasn't? What if she was remembering incorrectly? On the road she had seen no signs for an upcoming town. Besides, even if there *was* a tiny town up ahead, would it have a mechanic with a spare muffler? A twenty-four-hour mechanic, who'd be happy to weld someone's busted old Daihatsu Hijet back together at five am?

Mercy put her hands over her face. Inside the van, Wasabi howled with injustice.

In the end, the weariness that slunk over her like a drug made the decision for her. Starting the van for another few seconds, she tucked it a little further off the highway, behind a row of low scrubby bush. Quivering all the way to her toes, she locked the doors, crawled into the back, and pulled Wasabi to her beneath the blanket. She tried not to think of dingoes and horror movies and murderers.

Sleep came in pieces. The sky turned grey. As the birds began to twitter in the saltbush, she finally dropped off.

Sunlight shone straight onto her eyelids. Everything was red. For a brief moment, Mercy's mind was completely, peacefully blank. And then it came flooding back to her: the highway, no phone service, the van—its un-muffled engine thundering into the night.

Groaning, Mercy uncurled herself slowly; she'd awoken folded into a tight ball against the cold.

Pouring the dog some kibble and water, Mercy considered her options. She could hear the occasional vehicle passing on the highway now—could she hitch a ride back to Alice Springs? But there was little for her to do there besides fly back to Adelaide. Admit defeat, crawl back to Eugene, live in a strange, soulless apartment until her house was rebuilt.

'No,' she said. Wasabi paused over his food, looking at her. 'Sorry,' she added. 'Not you. As you were.'

In Alice Springs she could rent a car—something with air conditioning, something with speed and a firmly attached muffler—and keep going north. Get to the other side. Could she just leave the Hijet here, on the side of the Stuart Highway? What would happen to it?

Smashed windows. Spray painted with graffiti and its wheels stolen, axles in the dirt. Ruin, just like her house.

'I know,' Mercy said to the box of cremated remains sitting on the cabinet. 'That's abhorrent. Next option.'

She could hitch a ride to the nearest town north, wherever that was. From there, if it wasn't too far, maybe she could arrange for the van to be towed?

She climbed out of the van and stood on the gravel, looking towards the highway. The morning sun was warm on her bare legs. Her sunburned thighs itched with dry skin. It took twenty minutes before she heard the sound of an engine, a dull rumble in the distance. The sound came closer, and a truck appeared. Mercy watched it approach, gleaming chrome and jerking trailers, until it roared past, wheels churning, spitting grit and hot air. A glimpse of the driver revealed a bull-like shape filling the cab, dark glasses and hi-vis.

Mercy said, 'No way in hell.'

A headache was starting to tap behind her eyes. Andy was heading north, and so was Bert, too. If she waited long enough, maybe one of them would come past. So far neither of them had proven to be a kidnapper or axe murderer. Nor had they been overly judgemental, Mercy thought, recalling Bert watching her clean Andy's wound and nodding approvingly; remembering that even though it was Mercy's hand touching Andy's leg that had startled him into head-butting the underside of the van, he had only smiled and laughed about it after.

And it was with that thought that Mercy bore herself up. The past two years might have passed largely inside the four walls of her own house, but in doing so she had successfully avoided the anxiety and obligation that comes from contact with other people. She had learned a kind of dignity in aloneness. An independence. So, no: this, Mercy decided with a flare of indignation, she would return to doing *herself.* She ate a floury apple and drank a cup of water. Puffing out her cheeks, she stood back from the van, put her hands on her hips. She jogged on the spot, executed some arm stretches: first one side, then the other.

'Okay,' she said, her voice carrying into the bright desert morning. 'Let's do this.'

After checking everything was packed away, she rolled both windows all the way down, tied Wasabi securely in the back, and tucked Jenny Cleggett into the passenger side footwell. 'For moral support,' she told the box.

Then, twisting two tissues into wads, she stuffed them into her ears.

Her heart leapt into her throat as the van boomed into life. Birds shot into the sky. Wasabi burrowed beneath the cat blanket on the floor.

Mercy put the van in gear and pressed the accelerator. Engine screaming, she drove back onto the highway.

Praying that there was a town, and that it wasn't too far away, Mercy headed north.

Forty-five minutes later, the speed limit dropped and a sign appeared. Mercy could have wept with relief. Ti TREE, said the sign. POPULATION 70.

CHAPTER TWENTY·THREE

Mercy pulled the roaring Hijet off the highway into the Ti Tree service station, a wide flat concrete lot open to the huge burned-out sky. Even though the forecourt was empty, Mercy was too afraid to take the thundering van near any people, so she drove to the far side of the asphalt and parked alongside a corrugated iron fence, then turned off the engine.

Her ears rang. Her pulse pounded. As she untied Wasabi, the headache that had been hinting earlier now felt like it was cleaving apart her skull. Pushing open the door, she lost her footing and fell onto the pavement. For a moment everything swam: the blaring sun, the fence, the bitumen. Putting a hand on the ground to steady herself, she tried to suck in a few slow, deep breaths. Wasabi had clambered out of the van and started to lick her face.

'Jeez, love, that's quite an entrance.' A man's voice, rough and weathered.

Shakily, Mercy got to her feet, grimacing against the sun and the pain in her head.

'Where'd you lose it?'

'Sorry?' she croaked.

'Lost the muffler, did ya? Whereabouts?' Tall and broad-shouldered, the Aboriginal man approaching her had clumps of curly silvering hair and wore a pale blue polo shirt with *Ti Tree Roadhouse* embroidered on the pocket. He squatted and peered under the van.

'I'm not sure where it is,' Mercy said, trying to unglue her mouth. 'Somewhere south of here.'

'Hmm.' The man studied the van's underside, then straightened up. 'It's Tate you'll need.'

'Tate?'

'Round the back.' He jerked his thumb over his shoulder. 'Me nephew. He'll fix you right up.' He wiped a sheen of sweat from his forehead, glanced at the van, down to Wasabi and finally back to her. 'You by yourself?'

Mercy couldn't answer. Everything was swimming again.

'Headed north?'

She tried to nod.

His voice took on a gentler tone. 'Come inside, out of the sun. You don't look so well.'

Wordlessly, Mercy followed the man across the empty forecourt towards the roadhouse—a long, low-slung building with a sloped veranda and a cluster of fuel bowsers out the front. A row of air-conditioning units hummed; a huge sign reading FOOD • FUEL • SUPPLIES soared from the roof. The sky was impossibly huge.

A buzzer sounded as they passed through the door. Inside was cool and quiet. Wasabi followed her in; she didn't bother making an excuse to bring the dog inside, but the man didn't seem to care, either. Nausea rolled on Mercy's tongue and she paused, putting fingertips to her mouth as saliva gathered in her cheeks.

'There, now,' the man said quietly. 'You're all right.'

Tears pricked into her eyes. He led her to a group of plastic tables by the front window.

'Have a seat. How do you like your tea? White? Lots of sugar? Never mind, I'll just bring it over.' He disappeared, and returned a few minutes later with a large mug.

'I made it not too hot, so you can drink it right away. You want some chips? Wendy's just put 'em in the fryer. Won't be long. I'll bring you some.'

Mercy looked into the mug. The tea was the colour of a paper bag. She took a sip. Sugared and warm. She took another sip, feeling it moisten her throat, then a big gulp.

The man had disappeared again. Mercy looked out the window. Apart from the Hijet sulking by the fence, the forecourt was empty. A lone four-wheel drive passed on the highway. Over the road, spread across a flat expanse of red earth and pale green grass, a scatter of buildings shimmered in the heat, white iron roofs reflecting the sun.

The door buzzer sounded, and a wiry young man approached Mercy.

'Uncle Kev says you've got a broken muffler?' He wore long, shiny black shorts and a red Sydney Swans jersey, baring lean, muscular shoulders. 'Reckon I've got something that'll fit that.' He nodded towards the window, looking out at the van. 'That's deadly, that one. You had it long?'

Mercy took in the Hijet, parked sheepishly in the sun. Flat-nosed, it looked like it had been pinched by a giant hand. *Home is wherever you ARE*. It had only been five days since she had compelled herself across Eugene's street to the van on the side of the road, FOR SALE sign propped against the tyre, but it felt like months. Years.

'A little while,' she said. The sweet milky tea was starting to make her feel better; sitting in the cool quiet of the roadhouse was easing the sickening pulse in her head. 'You must be Tate.'

'If you want to bring it around the back—' the young man made a sweeping motion with his arm '—I'll take a look at that muffler.' His face broke into a grin. 'Or lack of.' His eyes caught on something behind her. 'Or if you want to eat your brekkie, I can move it for you.'

Mercy turned to see Tate's uncle Kev bearing a tray with a large steaming bowl of chips, a plate with two pieces of toast, two fried eggs and a fat sausage, sliced up the centre.

'Oh,' Mercy said. 'Did I order—?'

'Took the liberty,' Kev said, setting the tray in front of her. Scents of sausage grease and toast wafted up. 'Figured you'll be waiting a bit, and you can sit and relax here before the lunch rush.'

Mercy glanced at her phone; it was just before ten am. Outside a plastic bag tumbled across the empty forecourt. Heat haze shimmered off the blacktop.

'Gets pretty busy around here, weekday lunch,' Kev added, as if he'd heard her thoughts. 'We're the only major stop between Alice and Tennant Creek. Coupla hundred clicks each way. Anyway, eat up. Let bub here see to that vehicle.'

In a daze of nausea mixed with hunger, Mercy handed over her keys. When the Hijet started up the windows rattled in their panes. Mercy watched the little van rolling across the bitumen roaring like a 747; Tate stuck his arm out the window and waved before he disappeared from sight, but she could still hear the engine blaring behind the building, before it finally shut off.

Sitting on the floor at her feet, Wasabi shuffled closer, eyes fixed on her plate. His brown eyebrows twitched.

Mercy was alone again. The sheer volume of food in front of her made her feel slightly panicked. Cutting off a piece of sausage, she glanced from side to side before dropping it surreptitiously to the floor. Wasabi swooped and it was gone. She dropped another, bigger piece. Picking up a chip, she nibbled one end. Salt dissolved on her tongue. She dipped the chip in the bowl of tomato sauce and took another bite. When her stomach began to growl, she took progressively bigger bites, slicing a knife into the egg yolk and watching it melt like butter into the toast. Slowly, the meal grew smaller and smaller on the plate, disappearing between mouthfuls of warm tea. Eating a fresh hot meal with a knife and fork, at a proper table and chairs, in the air conditioning: she felt like she was at the Shangri-La.

With her belly full, the ringing in her ears dulled and her headache fading, Mercy became aware of a stink. Something acrid and petrochemical, like burned fuel. When she realised the stink was coming from her, the Hijet's exhaust fumes ingrained in her clothing, she groaned. She didn't have a clean change of clothes—her other set was still dirty from yesterday's trip to the waterhole with Andy.

She was staring out the window, stomach starting to churn with too much food, when she saw the giant RV pulling off the highway. Cruising up to a fuel bowser, it came to a halt in a squeal of brakes, and out piled two adults, two surly teenage girls and one toddler.

Mercy's heart stopped. Ann fucking Barker.

CHAPTER TWENTY·FOUR

Mercy watched Ann cross the forecourt, teen girls scuffing their feet, toddler trailing after her mother like a duckling. As Ann approached the door, Mercy could feel her muscles tensing up, excuses flitting into her mind as she prepared to flee. But flee to where? And in what? The Hijet was somewhere around the back, likely on a jack with its wheels off the ground.

Before Ann entered the store she turned suddenly; her husband at the bowser had called something out to her, and she flung her head back and laughed. One brief moment surging with confidence and nonchalance.

Mercy cast about the store. Could she hide over there, behind the biscuit aisle? Scanning the table top, her eyes lit briefly on the butter knife. Now *there's* a headline, she thought: *Doctor shivs journalist in outback servo.*

The door opened and Ann's laughter floated inside. Wasabi's tail began to beat rapidly against the lino.

For a moment, Mercy felt her body curling down in her seat, her face inclined towards the window. She saw herself as if from above, cowering towards the egg smears on her plate. If it was possible to be ashamed of one's own shame, Mercy was. And certainly, if anyone had the look of a person with something to hide, at that moment, Mercy was sure she did. What a way to advertise that you're hiding from something, she thought. So, turning in her seat, Mercy looked straight at Ann and heaved up a smile. 'Hi.'

Ann Barker took her in for a moment before recognition crossed her face. 'Oh hi!' she said. 'From the border crossing. It's …' She snapped her fingers, searching for the name Mercy had given her. Mercy went cold as she realised she had forgotten the lie, too. What made-up name had she given the journalist?

'Merbecca,' Ann said.

'Right,' Mercy said.

'You had a funky little van, didn't you?' Ann Barker glanced out the windows. The toddler began to tug on her shirt. 'I didn't see you parked out front.'

Figuring honesty was the best way to continue not to appear suspicious, Mercy said, 'It's round the back. It needed … repairs.'

Ann's eyes widened. The toddler tugged harder. 'Nothing serious, I hope?'

In lieu of answering, Mercy gave a small laugh and flapped a hand.

'Wouldn't have thought they could fix anything here.' The journalist looked dubiously around the store. 'But I guess that's lucky.' Without breaking eye contact with Mercy, Ann hiked the toddler up onto her hip. 'Thank goodness for outback mechanics then, huh?'

Mercy thought of Andy, smeared with red dirt, man-bun dishevelled.

'Yes,' she said.

Without warning, Ann plopped into the chair opposite, huffing hair out of her eyes. Mercy's heart ratcheted up into her mouth. Wasabi wriggled forward to lick the woman's ankles and Mercy shot a foot out to stop him.

'Food here any good?' Ann glanced down at Mercy's empty plate. 'They ate breakfast two hours ago but, you know,' she leaned forward, 'that's about a thousand years in a teenager's life.' The girls scuffed into the store, thongs slapping feet and low voices murmuring to each other. The fridge doors *whomped* open and closed.

'Hey,' Ann said sharply. Mercy flinched, then realised Ann was talking to her children. 'In or out—not both. Cara, can you tell your sister—' she half-stood to project her voice across the store, '—tell your sister to put that energy drink back? We don't need her trippin' halfway across the Northern Territory.

'Anyway,' Ann went on, plopping back down. 'When will you be back on the road?' She made a steering-wheel motion with her hands. The toddler copied, lifting her little hands as if gripping a wheel.

'I'm not sure—'

At that moment Tate appeared, sloping through a door on the other side of the room.

'I've found something that should fit,' he announced. 'Might take a bit, though. I've gotta make some alterations to the pipe. But job's right, you can be on your way soon.'

Relief flooded over Mercy. 'That's great,' she said, stopping short of kissing the mechanic's hands. 'Thank you so much.'

'That's lucky,' said Ann when he'd left. 'You know,' she leaned back in her chair and her eyes crinkled, 'when I met you at the border I could have sworn you had longer hair.'

Automatically Mercy's hand went to her head. Her hair seemed to be shrinking up into knots.

The journalist gave Mercy a long look, and appeared about to say something when one of the girls appeared, scowling.

'Gretta's hogging the iPad.'

'So do something else.'

'There isn't anything else to *do*.'

'Read a book. Go for a walk. Here—take the baby.'

'Go for a *walk*?' the girl said, aghast. 'You mean we're *staying* here?'

'Long enough to get something to eat, sure.'

'That *sucks*, Mum,' the girl said, loading so much exasperation into the statement that Mercy almost said in solidarity, *Yeah, MUM. Fuck OFF.*

The girl stared at her mother. Ann stared back. This went on for what felt to Mercy like a solid ten minutes before, jaw clenched, the girl slunk off, muttering.

Mercy checked the time. It was almost midday. Tate had said *soon*. How soon was soon? Ann Barker took her phone out of her pocket, set it on the table top, and then fluffed up her short curls and settled back in her chair to read the menu on the wall.

Beneath the table, Mercy's heels began to jog up and down. 'You're staying here the night?'

Ann assured Mercy that she was not. 'I have a deadline for work and I need to get somewhere with internet service.'

The polite thing to do here, Mercy knew, would be to ask after the other person's work. But Mercy already knew what Ann Barker did. And there was no way she would be revealing that.

But Ann said it anyway. 'I'm a writer. I have my own website.' Then she laughed. 'Which will fall apart if I'm out of service for more than a few hours.'

Mercy said, 'I see.'

Finished with the menu, Ann turned back to Mercy. She seemed to be waiting for Mercy to say something—perhaps to acknowledge the enormity of what Ann had just disclosed, entire websites crashing without her—but Mercy's voice wouldn't come.

Finally she said, 'It must be ... flexible, writing. That's ... handy.'

'Oh, it is,' Ann said with enthusiasm. 'Although—' she gave a self-effacing laugh '—it's not so easy, sometimes, because there's no such thing as anonymity anymore. Not on the internet.'

Mercy swallowed dryly. 'Right,' she said.

Ann laughed again. 'And there's certainly no anonymity when you have opinions like mine.'

There was nothing for it. The conversation was a railroad the journalist had laid to go only in one direction.

'You write opinions,' Mercy echoed.

'I *like* to write about all sorts of things—travel, for instance, and I *love* to cook—but my advertisers always say, "Annie, nothing drives traffic like abortion, vaccination and childbirth. So put us on *those* articles."'

Mercy couldn't respond.

'Anyway.' Ann shook her head. 'What do you do, Merbecca?'

'I, uh—' Mercy blanked. Ann was regarding her pleasantly, waiting for her to respond. *Lie*, Mercy instructed herself. *Just make something up. Anything!* 'Well, I—'

She saw it come over Ann's face. Slowly at first, a glimmer. A frown, then the slow widening of her eyes.

'I *knew* you looked familiar.'

Mercy's stomach bottomed out.

'Yes!' Ann clicked her fingers, looking down at the table, and Mercy could almost see the writer's mind ratcheting furiously to find it. Then, *ping!*, there it was: 'You're that doctor.'

Mercy said, 'Well—'

'From Adelaide Northern Hospital.'

'I think you've gotten me confused—'

Ann Barker's eyebrows rocketed up as recognition flared. 'You're Mercy Blain.'

How many headlines does it take to reduce a person's world to the four walls of their house? For some thick-skinned, shameless individuals who are happy to wear public commentary like a coat, it may be none. Shock jocks and politicians, for instance, seemed to Mercy not only indifferent to howls of criticism but completely incapable of considering that life could be—or should be—anything else. Then there were those sudden media sensations, flaring into newsfeeds and fizzling out just as quickly: a minor sports star in a doping scandal; an illegal au pair pregnant by the married Minister for Foreign Affairs; a reality TV star's drunk fat-shaming tweet.

But for Mercy, it had taken only a single headline: *Obstetrician should never have let dead woman go into labour, husband says.* That single piece, tagged to Mercy by a sticky-beaked distant colleague one mid-morning in the weeks after, had been the final stressor, the final assault of adrenaline on her already over-taxed system. It was nothing more than pixels, words on a screen, but it had sucked her up like a tornado. Mercy couldn't stop following it. The way the comments had run into the hundreds. After everything else that had happened, that single article had made Mercy's last panic attack so painful, so unbearable, that the outside world became impossible, utterly and exquisitely hopeless.

For a while after that, there had been more than one headline, Mercy knew, and even though she had stopped reading, the messages and emails and tags had found her, anyway.

That single article, written by Ann fucking Barker.

The high ringing sound returned in Mercy's ears.

'Oh, no,' Mercy said with a nervous laugh. 'I just have one of those faces—'

'You've been MIA for a couple of years,' Ann said. 'Where have you been?'

'I'm really not—'

'Doctor Blain,' Ann said, frankly. 'Come on.'

Mercy felt like she'd walked into a furnace.

Ann snatched up her phone and her thumbs typed in a brief flurry, but then the writer cursed and leaned back to stuff the phone in her pocket. 'No bloody service. I can't look up the particulars but from memory you retired. Is that true?'

The line from PR came back to Mercy easily. 'I'm not in a position to comment.'

Ann smiled. 'Sure you can. It's been years. We're out here together in the middle of the Territory.' She made a show of looking around the room, opening her palm to the sun-baked forecourt. 'It's just you, me and the outback.'

Mercy said nothing.

'Didn't it get the coroner's attention? That must be pretty stressful.'

There was something odd in the way Ann was leaning to one side. She seemed to be affecting a casual pose, looking for all the world like she was lounging nonchalantly in her chair, but Mercy could see that what Ann was in fact doing was straightening her hip pocket so as not to muffle the mic on her phone.

'Or maybe you don't remember the delivery? I mean, you would have been attending, what—hundreds of deliveries a year? They probably all start to blend in together.'

Now Ann had presented Mercy with a choice, giving her the option to either admit that she didn't recall the event, which made Mercy a terrible person, or confirm that of course she remembered Tamara, she would never, ever forget Tamara, in which case Mercy's decision not to speak to Ann about it made Mercy not only terrible but guilty to boot.

'But I suppose,' Ann went on, tapping her lip thought-fully, 'women don't die in childbirth very often. Not in a privileged first world country like ours. That's got to stick with you. Right?'

The sense that Ann had stopped seeing Mercy—let alone Tamara—as a human being and instead as a source of click-bait was instantly infuriating. The fury came surfing in on top of an undercurrent of fear, but at least the anger was something to cling to. Grabbing onto the floating slab of rage gave Mercy much more oxygen than sinking into the depths of terror.

Mercy's voice was cold. 'Of course it sticks with me.'

Ann said nothing, shifting her hip ever so slightly forward. But when Mercy remained silent, Ann went on: 'You know, generally, medicine is off limits. It's protected, a no-go zone. Doctors don't usually find themselves in head-lines like that. Not unless they turn out to be, you know, a closet paedophile or something.'

Mercy blinked in horror.

'But *you* ended up in the media.' Ann said it lightly, curiously, like she was still contemplating what to order for lunch. 'Why is that, you think?'

'Will you excuse me?'

Without waiting for an answer, Mercy got to her feet, sweeping up the dog and tucking him under her arm. She crossed the store and pushed through the door Tate had earlier appeared through, and found herself in a small vestibule. In front of her was a door to the outside, framed with bright light, but to her dismay it was locked. She rattled the handle and cursed. To her left was a unisex bathroom, and because her only other choice was to return to the store, she went into the bathroom, locking the door behind her.

Blue-tiled walls, a water-stained sink, the overpowering scent of commercial-strength cleaner. Mercy could feel her throat closing, her lungs heaving for air. Her mind threw at her all the terrifying facts: she was trapped in the bathroom, she didn't know where her van was, and even if she could get on the road, Ann could easily follow her. It was a bloody big country but there was only one damn highway, and they were both on it.

Home was a very, very long way away.

Time unspooled and stopped. Mercy's heart pummelled at her ribs like a fist. A silent scream bubbled up because she couldn't get any air into her body. Clambering onto the toilet lid, she groped at the small awning window, pushed it open and shoved her face towards the fresh air.

Mercy leaned her weight against the wall and tried to breathe. The air coming through the window was hot and smelled of oil and fuel. Off to the side, Mercy could see a large shed, sliding doors pushed open and there, propped up on jacks, was her Hijet. A radio was playing and she could see the bright sparks of an arc welder spitting out from under the van.

On the bathroom floor, Wasabi began to whine. He jumped up to scrabble his paws at Mercy's feet, balanced on the lid of the toilet. She felt his wet tongue at her ankles.

Mercy fixed her eyes on the Hijet, as if she could suck herself into it with willpower alone. She pushed again at the window, and it opened an inch wider then stopped, held fast by a small chain.

Mercy looked down at Wasabi. He stopped whining and cocked his head.

The chain broke easily enough when Mercy hit the frame with her shoulder. The pane of glass swung wide on its hinges. Dropping to the floor, Mercy picked up Wasabi, lifted him to the window, said, 'Sorry, boy,' and shoved him through. Then she climbed back onto the toilet lid and tried to hoist herself up, but her arms weren't strong enough to lift her entire body. Dropping down again, she shoved the sanitary bin under the window and used it to lever herself up higher. Just as she hauled her belly onto the window sill, the sanitary bin crashed sideways. Mercy kicked her feet against the wall. The window frame dug into her belly and then, as she lifted one knee, very painfully into her crotch. Rolling to the side, she fell through the window.

CHAPTER TWENTY-FIVE

One leg took the brunt of her fall, then her knee and wrist.

For a long minute, Mercy lay gasping on the ground, pain jarring through her bones. Wasabi came over to lick her face. She sat up; her right palm was grazed and her knee was scraped open and oozing blood. She winced as she brushed grit from the wound. Her wrist throbbed. Then, remembering the journalist waiting for her inside, Mercy got up.

She limped across the gravel lot. Overhead the sun beat down and the gravel radiated heat. Cars were strewn about in varying stages of dismemberment: some missing doors, others without wheels—one small car was missing its entire front end. Columns of tyres lined a chain-link fence matted with dried spear grass.

Inside the shed, the Hijet was propped up on an angle, two wheels in the air and, from underneath, Tate's legs protruded. Mercy flashed back to yesterday, when she had

brushed Andy's leg with her hand; she recalled his bleeding
head and the voices rising out of the bush calling for Wasabi.
Mercy picked up the dog, clutching him to her chest.

Tate was lying on a wheeled mechanic's creeper. Over the
fizz and crackle of the welder and the radio blaring on the
back wall, Mercy could hear him whistling. She said, 'Hello?'
but was too afraid to make any noise that Ann might hear,
which meant it was too soft for Tate to hear, either.

'Hello?' she tried again, louder. She was standing next to
Tate's legs now. Remembering the dull smack Andy's head
had made on the underside of the van, she didn't know how
to get Tate's attention. She was clearing her throat to try a
loud hiss when Tate shifted, spotted her and scooted out.

'Hi,' he said, sitting up on the creeper. 'You finish your
lunch already?'

Mercy glanced back at the roadhouse.

'I've got a bit of a problem,' she said.

Tate paused, a look flickering across his face. Steeling
himself for the complaints of a white city woman.

'There's someone inside that I need to get away from,'
Mercy told him. And then she found herself telling him the
rest. Not all of it—she didn't want to assail the guy with her
whole sorry tale of incinerated houses, gay ex-husbands, death
and despair—just enough of her brush with the media and
subsequent need to avoid it that his face changed from appre-
hension, to understanding, to something close to amusement.

'So,' Mercy said when she was finished, 'I don't suppose I
can hide out here until you're done?'

'Well, it's done.' Tate stood up and wiped his hands on a
rag. 'So as much as you'd be welcome to stick around,' his
face broke into a smile, 'you can take off if you want.'

Mercy staggered with relief, until she remembered that the highway was right out front of the roadhouse, and there was only one highway, and she could outrun no one in this thing, not even a heavy luxury RV.

Tate seemed to know what she was thinking. 'But listen,' he said, tucking the fifties she handed him into his pocket, 'if you're looking to keep your head down, don't take the highway.'

And then Tate told Mercy where she should go.

The track was hard-packed, carved into orange dirt and stones, with deep drifts of sand piled along its shoulders. As Mercy juddered along, glimpses of the highway flashed between gaps in the scrub, before the track wended its way east and it was just her, the bush track and the enormous sky.

Mercy was too rattled to be terrified. Her knuckles were white on the wheel and she leaned forward, every muscle tensed, because if she eased back in her seat the bumps mashed her vertebrae together like an accordion. Tate had shown her the welds in the new muffler—thick bands of cooled molten steel—but Mercy held her breath against each rock that pinged against the undercarriage, each deep rut that swallowed the wheels.

Running mostly parallel to the highway, Tate had told her this track went north for over a hundred kilometres. If she wanted to she could take it all the way to Karlu Karlu, the Devil's Marbles.

Which was precisely what Mercy did, for more than two hours. For two dusty, fly-strewn, bone-jarring hours, she clattered along a dirt track, hidden from the flowing artery and prying eyes of the highway.

CHAPTER TWENTY·SIX

People smuggle worse things every day, Mercy told herself. Weapons over borders. Human beings in shipping containers. Balloons of heroin up rectums into prisons. As far as smuggling outrages go, a sausage dog into an outback hotel room was a minor offence. But as she stuffed Wasabi into her hessian shopping bag and unlocked the door to the room out the back of The Devil's Marbles Hotel, Mercy felt like she was sweating through Customs with a suitcase of marijuana.

It had been a long drive from Ti Tree. By mid-afternoon Mercy had re-joined the highway, which, after two hours thumping along a dirt track, felt as if she were sliding onto butter. It had been another hour on the highway, nervously checking her mirrors for rogue journalists, before she reached the southern outskirts of Karlu Karlu Conservation Reserve, and there, off the highway beneath a fringe of tropical palms, sat an outback pub. Steep pitched-iron roof, shadowed veranda, campsites and cold beer. It wasn't until Mercy was in the air-conditioned front bar and asking after a campsite that she realised how desperately she wanted to get out from under the sky. She wanted four walls, a door that locked: she wanted the outside to stay out, if just for a night. With the freakish, one-in-however-many-million chance meeting with a single opinion writer had come the weight of an entire aggrieved, hurting planet, and Mercy felt pinned like an insect to a board, run through the thorax by sharp wire for all to see. So she heard herself asking for a room, and told herself that she had done far worse things in her life than take a small dog inside a small room into which dogs (or any animals, for that matter) of any size were not supposed to go.

Glancing both ways, she stepped through the door and closed it quickly behind her. The lock gave a satisfying click.

The room was simple, with bare white walls, a rickety bedside table and a lino floor, but to Mercy it felt like a palace. It was clean and smelled of fresh laundry. The inside of her van, along with sweaty human and dog, still gave off the faint pong of exhaust and was covered with a layer of red dust so thick even the box of Jenny Cleggett, tucked inside the bed cabinet, was starting to turn orange.

Mercy lay back on the fluffy quilt and let out a soft moan. Spreading her arms and legs, she wriggled deeper into the mattress with pleasure. She had just decided there was never a more wonderful invention than the inner spring mattress when she heard the water start in the shower next door and a man's voice break into song.

Mercy sprang up, face flaming. Wasabi was sitting obediently on her towel on the floor, looking at her.

'Lie down,' she hissed, as if someone might see him through the window. After a long moment the dog obliged, resting his chin on his forepaws. The man was still singing; Mercy couldn't make out the words but the tune was vaguely familiar. She was desperate for a shower herself, but the idea that she and this unknown singing man would be naked at the same time, mere feet away from each other, made her insides squirm. So she sat on the end of the bed. She picked grit from the still-smarting graze in her knee. She scratched her thighs: the sunburn was beginning to heal and it itched like ants were nibbling her skin.

A laminated note in the bathroom reminded patrons to *Please be mindful of our precious water*, and Mercy imagined banging on the wall and pointing it out to the singing man, until she remembered the illicit sausage dog on the floor and bit her lip.

Finally the water next door shut off, and the man went quiet. Mercy dragged a reluctant Wasabi into the shower with her, and although she could have soaped and scrubbed for a week she kept it to two minutes. To counteract the smuggled Dachshund she would otherwise be a model guest, so she pulled the plug of hair out of the drain that was both hers and Wasabi's, and plenty that wasn't, then wiped the cubicle clean and dry.

Finally Mercy squared herself in front of the mirror—the first proper mirror she had looked in since Marla, three days ago.

Her curls came from her mother: loose springs that Loretta Blain had always worn in soft honey-coloured waves about her face. But she had never let Mercy wear her own curls the same way. Every morning of Mercy's primary school years, her mother had scraped Mercy's hair into a tight braid, gelling back each loose wisp. For years Mercy's nickname had been 'Ten Pin' because her head resembled the smoothness and shine of a bowling ball. When she had come home crying one day because Stuart Hoggarty had slapped her head and yelled out, 'Gutter ball!' her mother had laughed until her face turned pink, then told Mercy she had no sense of humour. When Mercy reached her teenage years and her mother could no longer exercise the same amount of control over Mercy's appearance, Loretta Blain instead resorted to taunts and sneers. *Trying to impress someone, are we?* or *The eighties called and wants its hair back.* They were never overt insults, nothing her mother could be condemned for. If Mercy became upset, that wasn't because of the *joke* her mother made, it was because Mercy was *too sensitive.*

Mercy ran her fingertips along her jaw, stippled with tiny bumps: she might have her mother's hair but she had her father's chin, square and pronounced, where her mother's was pointed like a fox. Her arms and neck were a patchwork of sunburned pink and T-shirt white; purple crescents sat beneath her eyes but her eyes were bright with fresh air.

Mercy turned away from the mirror.

Only eight kilometres north of the hotel was the sacred site of Karlu Karlu.

'You've gotta see the Marbles at sunset,' the barman had told Mercy when she paid for her room. 'You can't come all this way so close to sunset and not see it. It's spectacular.'

Mercy was reluctant to leave her room, but the barman had a point. Two days ago, three hours south of Alice Springs, Mercy's heart had squeezed as she passed the turn-off to Uluru, a further three hours' travel to the west. Australia might have some ancient, world-famous attractions but they sure were a bloody long way away from each other, Mercy thought. If only the same could be said for its journalists.

So Mercy once again shoved Wasabi into her bag. Cracking open the door, she squeezed her head out, checked both ways, then hurried to her van. Overhead the sky was already turning pink. A handful of caravans were parked in the campground out back and Mercy could hear murmured voices and the snick of van doors, but otherwise the outback was huge and still.

Mercy drove with both windows rolled down, letting in the warm evening air, scented with far-off smoke. For ten minutes the highway rolled up and down, left and right through rocky ridges, before the land opened out in a wide, shallow valley. Thin columns of smoke rose lazily in the distance. And there, just off the edge of the highway, were the first glimpses of the giant granite boulders.

Mercy slowed, turning onto the access road, and as she rolled along more boulders revealed themselves, turning gold in the late afternoon light. Huge round stones, smooth as eggs; some sat alone on the grass, taller than two men; some were the size of a child, tumbled against one another, and others towered in enormous piles, storeys high, one on top of the other in a mammoth ancient jumble. Shadows plunged in cracks and crevices.

The access road ended in a dirt carpark dotted with picnic tables. A few vehicles were scattered about. Mercy pulled up a short distance from another van just as it was reversing out, revealing beside it Andrew Macauley's rental camper.

'It's a small world, eh?' Andy said, strolling over.

'I'm beginning to understand that,' Mercy replied.

Mercy and Andy sat on top of a picnic table and watched the sun go down over the valley. In the sacred site pets were permitted only in the carpark and Wasabi was tied to the table leg; Andy had offered to stay with the dog while Mercy walked around the trails, but Mercy had said no. She couldn't leave him again.

Mercy watched the setting sun paint the boulders all shades of fire and felt both awed and very small. Here she was, breathing in land old as creation, traditional and important country for its Aboriginal custodians for all time. Geology explained the impossibly balanced piles of granite as the remnants of once-molten bedrock rising up, cooling, then eroding away and Mercy felt keenly how very short a human life is in comparison to the earth. But rather than being terrifying, something about that thought was deeply comforting. No matter what happened, you were always going to be cradled by the earth. It wasn't possible for it to be any other way.

When the sun had slipped below the horizon and the marbles were the colour of cocoa, Mercy said to Andy, 'I'm sorry for taking off so suddenly, back in Alice.'

He turned to her, surprised. 'That's nothing to apologise for. You're free to go where you like.'

'I know. But still …' She shrugged.

'D'you often apologise when you haven't done anything wrong?'

'Yes,' she answered with a rueful laugh.

'Why?'

Mercy twisted her fingers, eyes on the glowing horizon. All that remained of the sun was a gold band. 'Probably my mother.'

They were quiet for a time. The gold band thinned, then was gone.

Mercy took a deep breath and held it in. Then, slowly, she let it out. 'On the Tuesday, Eugene left. Then on Thursday, I found out my mother had died. And then on Sunday, a pregnant woman died in the delivery suite.' Mercy paused. Her heart was beating very fast. 'I was the obstetrician on call. She was under my care. This all happened two years ago. Within the same week.'

Andy was quiet.

'Six days, that's all it took. Everything was normal and then, a few days later …' Mercy spread her hands and left the sentence unfinished. 'I'd never had a panic attack before. I didn't recognise what it was. It wasn't like what I'd always heard.'

'What was it like?'

Mercy frowned, trying to find the right words. 'It's hard to explain. Everything just felt suddenly … wrong. Like, really, catastrophically *wrong*. Because fear usually comes *from* something, right? Like, standing on top of a tall building, or seeing a snake, or whatever. But I was at work, the same place I'd been every day for years. Nothing scary. But they kept happening.' She paused again, watching a small lizard dart over a rock. 'And then when I knew what they were, I started to become afraid of the attacks themselves. Terrified, actually. Because things like deep breathing, identifying the thought pattern and changing it—all that stuff we're taught? It didn't work. It's like my brain leaked out my ears and I was nothing more than a skin full of existential horror.' She looked down at her hands. 'You can't be a doctor without a brain.'

Andy remained quiet.

'I told myself the same thing I'd tell a patient: "Of course you're anxious." A marriage break-up, the death of a parent, and the death of a patient under my hands, all in the same week? That's enough to send anyone's adrenaline and cortisol levels into orbit.'

'I'm sure it is.'

She looked down at her hands. 'I tried different therapists, counselling and CBT. But nothing seemed to work. I couldn't find a solution. They kept telling me to give it time, that I had to be willing to *do the work*, but I just couldn't … It's like I didn't know how to *exist* anymore. I thought I was losing my mind. The world wasn't safe. *Nothing* was safe; no*where* was safe. I couldn't even human.' She smiled sadly. 'And I couldn't take tranqs at work.'

Andy touched the cut in his hairline. 'Maybe not.'

Mercy recalled the sound of the thud from under the van. 'Does it hurt?' she asked sheepishly.

'Nah, it's all right. Go on.'

Mercy watched a star blink into the sky, then another. 'Everyone kept telling me it was just trauma. Lots of people experience trauma. And then there was the media ...' She shook her head, refusing to give that part any more of her attention. 'It only took a few months but it got to the point where staying in was easier than going out, because staying in was the only break I got. The only break from the fear. I felt like such a hypocrite, because I can't tell you how many times I told anxious pregnant women, or even their partners, "anxiety is made worse when you give in to it". God,' she said with a bitter laugh, 'only someone who's never actually experienced ongoing panic could say that. When you're in it, the only thing you want is relief.'

'That's all anyone wants, isn't it?' Andy said. 'To live with ease.'

Mercy looked out over the boulder-strewn valley. 'Her name was Tamara,' she said quietly. 'She was so close to having her baby, and then she said she couldn't breathe, and she was saying she was going to die. It all happened so quickly. I tried ... but I couldn't—' Mercy stopped, swallowing. She stared into the stars until her vision blurred them all together. 'I had four minutes to get her baby out. It wasn't enough. They both died.'

She heard Andy's breath falter. A mosquito landed on her hand and she didn't brush it away; she felt the tiny sting as it drew up her blood.

'Her partner kept saying, "Do something." I can't stop hearing it. And I keep seeing the police officers at my door, before they told me my mum was dead.'

Then the mosquito lifted as Andy took Mercy's hand in both of his. His warm fingers laced into hers, sending sparks of electricity up her arm and across her scalp. He ran a hand over her wrist, up her forearm and squeezed gently. Mercy's heartbeat went into her hands. Minutes passed where they sat, watching the stars come out one by one. Andy's thumb traced a soft line back and forth on her own.

'Fucking hell,' he said in a thick voice. 'That's all just so— fuck me, I'm really sorry. That's just utter shite. And then your house burned down? I mean … Christ, Mercy.'

'Yeah.'

'Can I ask though …' He paused, studying her face in the last of the light. 'You said you feel the need to apologise because of your mum. Is that because she died? Were you close?'

Mercy shook her head.

Andy waited.

'I loved her. Most people only get one mother in their life and she was mine.' In spite of it all, Mercy felt herself smile. 'Even when she woke up in the morning she smelled like perfume. Physically, she was perfect. Stunning. And it was effortless, too, you know? It's just who she was, like it was her identity. I'm a doctor and you're an aircraft mechanic and my mother was beautiful. She loved mandarins, and anything with raisins in it, and at Easter she'd make a huge slab of chocolate cake because she said there's nothing like too much chocolate. And we lived in a small town; everyone knew who she was. Loretta Blain, wife of beloved local GP Harold Blain. Mother of one dutiful daughter, president of the Parents' Committee, the Country Women's Association, and maker of the best lemonade scones this side of the equator.'

Andy was quiet.

'But it was all on the outside. Inside, she was a mess. Fucked up by a dad who fixed things with his fists, she used to say in her rare honest moments. And she took that out on me. Her need to be beautiful and validated and adored—I had to provide that for her, every day. Sometimes I could, and that's when she was good to me, and I would move heaven and earth to try and keep it that way. But most of the time I couldn't, or worse, sometimes I did something or achieved something that might take the focus away from her …'

For a long time Mercy was quiet. The sky went dark. The marbles slid into the night. Andy's hands were warm on hers; she could feel his breath.

'When I got into a medical degree at Flinders, do you know what she said?'

She felt him look at her.

'She said, "Yes, everyone knows their standards are slipping."'

A long silence passed. The grass whispered. A cricket chirped.

Mercy said, 'In the end I wasn't in contact with her at all. It took me a few tries, but I'd finally done it. I hadn't spoken to her for seven months before she died.'

Andy didn't say anything. The air was motionless and warm. More mosquitoes came out and Mercy felt stings on her ankles, elbows, the backs of her knees.

Eventually, Andy said, 'Shall we have some tea, then?'

CHAPTER TWENTY·SEVEN

Dinner was steak sandwiches big as pallets and slabs of chips that they ate outside in the beer garden, sitting at a table made from old railway sleepers. Planter boxes around the tables had little white flowers that spilled out towards the ground, glowing in the evening light and looking to Mercy like fallen stars. From a jug they poured cold beer with heads so creamy Mercy could almost chew them, and the more creamy beer she drank, the brighter the flowers glowed. For the first time since leaving Adelaide, nightfall didn't come with a drop in temperature; the evening air that circled Mercy's bare arms and legs was warm as bathwater.

Andy was nursing his beer and considering her, empty plates between them. At length he said, 'Tennis.'

'What?'

'Or hockey, maybe. Horse-riding lessons?'

'What is this?'

'There had to be something in your childhood that you did, that was yours and that wasn't … you know.'

'My parents'?'

'Right.'

Mercy thought about it. It had been too easy to forget that before everything, in spite of everything, she was perhaps still a person. What were the niceties, the pleasantries, the normal and simple things that spaced out all the darker chunks?

'Well,' she said. 'When I was thirteen I went to the roller-skating rink every Thursday night. Does that count?'

'Oh, aye,' Andy said. 'That counts. So you roller skated. You zoomed around the rink, maybe to Kylie Minogue or Hanson and a disco ball. And did you get to be yourself then?'

Mercy gave a small laugh. 'I don't know. Maybe.' As if joining in their conversation, from a table nearby came a burst of laughter. Country music twanged from speakers hanging from the rafters. Mercy tipped the last of the jug into her glass; it wasn't quite half full. 'You know, I don't miss being stuck inside my house.'

'That's understandable,' Andy said.

'But I think you might be onto something. I do miss dancing.'

'Dancing?'

'Yeah. When it started I couldn't exercise, and I got to the point where I was going stir-crazy. One day I just started dancing, right there in my living room. And then it was something I did every day. After dinner or whatever, I'd put on some music, put in my earphones and dance. Or in the afternoon. Or in the morning. Or sometimes in the middle of the night when I couldn't sleep. It made me feel like I wasn't completely dead.'

'What kind of dancing?'

'The probably very bad kind.' She emptied her glass in a few mouthfuls.

'I've never heard of this probably-very-bad kind of dance. Is it modern? Classical? Do you need wee steel tips on the toes of your shoes for it?'

Mercy stacked their empty plates and beer jug, and stood to take them to the bar. 'Definitely no steel toes. Nothing that draws attention.'

When she returned from the bar with another full jug, Andy wanted to know if she'd ever done any dance as a kid. Ballet maybe?

Mercy poured. 'Nope.'

'So I'm wondering where the—' he grooved in his seat, wiggling his shoulders, clicking his fingers '—comes from.'

'You're overestimating the dancing. There's nothing deeper about it.'

'Is that so?'

What followed was inevitable. The steak sandwiches, the beer, the warm outback night: it was just that kind of evening. It couldn't have gone any differently. Glass in hand, Andy sprang up and went to the jukebox in the corner. A country song halted mid-warble and someone from the table nearby called out, 'Hey—' but then the first strains of 'Copperhead Road' came on and everyone cheered.

'Let's do this,' Andy said, holding out his hand.

Mercy got up. And she danced.

If Mercy had to guess what songs would be played in the beer garden of an outback pub she would have picked the exact same songs that played that night at The Devil's Marbles Hotel: 'I'm Gonna Be (500 Miles)'. 'Brown Eyed Girl'. 'Run To Paradise'. But when 'Mr Brightside' came on, Mercy just about lost her own marbles.

'Oh my god!' she exclaimed to Andy, beer slopping over her fingers. 'In my last year of med school I was *obsessed* with this song. I swear to god this got me through all-nighters poring over pharmacology text books.' And then Mercy had an epiphany and she realised *that's* exactly who Andy looked like, the lead singer from The Killers. And not only that, but that Mercy's hair looked *exactly* as big as the woman from the 'Mr Brightside' video clip's hair did. 'Only she was blonde,' Mercy finished.

'Your hair's not that big,' Andy said, doubtfully. His eyes roamed up over the top of her head. 'I don't think.'

'It is,' Mercy said vehemently. Then she had another epiphany. She was positively popping with light bulbs. 'I'm too recognisable like this,' she said. 'I can't hide from Ann fucking Barker when my head looks like an alien space craft.'

Andy threw his head back and laughed so hard he had to momentarily stop dancing.

Mercy had a plan.

'I have a plan!' she announced. 'Hold my beer.'

The barman's name was Steve—returning four times for a jug of beer will get a person fairly familiar with a barman—and while Mercy, Andy and the locals were cutting a rug in the star-flowered beer garden, Steve was looking on, smiling like a fond parent while he sliced up lemons.

'Okay, here's what's gonna happen,' Mercy explained to Andy, pressed right up against him to speak in his ear, because someone had turned the music up yet again and the Screaming Jets really were. 'You're going to distract Steve, and I'm going to get it. Got it?'

'Yes,' Andy said emphatically, although Mercy knew he had absolutely no idea what she was talking about. But right at that moment, as sweat sheened Mercy's forehead and skin peeled from her thighs and they were running to paradise, she knew that Andy would agree to hide a dead body with her if that's what she wanted to do.

'Go now,' Mercy said.

'Okay,' Andy said.

Andy sauntered over to the bar. 'Hiya, Steve,' Mercy heard him say as she danced casually past. 'Listen, I think there's been an unfortunate situation over there by the flowers. Looks like someone couldn't keep their tea down, which is a right shame really, because those piece and chips were pure dead brilliant. Have ye got a mop?'

Steve sighed and plunked the knife onto the chopping board. 'If that's Larry who's chundered again, I'm not letting him back in for a week ...' And Steve was gone, leaving the bar unattended.

Mercy sidled up. Leaning forward, she stretched but couldn't quite reach. She wriggled, heaving her belly up onto the bar, and leaned again. Her toes left the ground; her lungs squashed but her fingertips caught the knife and she grabbed it and kicked her legs back towards the ground but for a brief moment she was suspended, see-sawing over the bar on her guts, and she laughed until Andy grabbed her legs and tilted her back down.

'Thanks,' Mercy said. 'Close one.' Pushing the knife into her back pocket, she hurried out of the beer garden and back to her room.

The knife was sticky with lemon juice. The light above the bathroom mirror was bright, and Mercy had to squint until her eyes adjusted. Wasabi sat at her ankles and looked up at her.

The paring knife was small but ruthlessly sharp: the blade had sunk through the back pocket of her op-shop shorts right to the hilt, and now when she put her hand in her pocket she could stick her index finger through the seam and waggle it in the fresh air.

She tried to comb up a neat section of hair, like hairdressers did, but her fingers were tacky with beer and lemon juice. Her grazed palm stung like buggery. In the end her fist was easier. Beginning at the top, Mercy took up a chunk of hair and lifted the knife.

Clumps of matted hair fell into the sink. Mercy chopped and chopped and it worked: the face staring back at her became completely unrecognisable.

'Hello, Eugene.'

'Mercy?'

'Yes, it's me, Mercy Blain. You might not recognise me because I'm incognito.'

She heard the shuffle and scrape of a man waking from sleep. 'It's two am. Are you all right?'

'I'm fine.' Mercy smiled. A slow, genuine smile that stretched her cheeks. 'You know? I really am fine.'

'What's going on? Where are you?'

Mercy was sitting cross-legged on the bed in her room. A shaft of light from a lamp outside came in through the window. Wasabi was curled on a towel on the floor; she was not an inconsiderate smuggler, she would not let the dog on the bed. She had thoughtfully cleaned all the hair out of the sink—once again some of it didn't even appear to be hers. In the corner, the lid of the bin bulged up and coils of hair snaked out.

'I wanted to say that I'm sorry.'

'For what?' Eugene sounded clearer now; she heard the click of a bedroom door closing. 'Where are you?' he repeated.

'Karlu Karlu.'

'Where?'

'The Devil's Marbles.'

'Really? That's ... wow.'

'It *is* wow. But anyway, I am very sorry.'

He sighed. 'You're drunk, aren't you?'

Mercy considered it. 'Look, I might be,' she admitted.

'I'm on an early shift in the morning; can this wait?'

'Probably, but I'll be quick. I'm sorry.'

'You've said that already. What you've not said is why. Have you done something ...?'

'You know what, Eugene? I actually haven't. That's partly what I'm sorry for. I'm sorry that, for the past two years, I have done absolutely nothing. I have stuck my head in the sand like an emu, and refused to face what was going on.'

'I don't think it's emus that stick their heads in—'

'I've done nothing for two whole years, Eugene. I shut myself in the house and hoped it could all just go away. I mean, isn't that the cardinal sin of anxiety treatment—to give in to it?' Her voice had pitched up, and she was waving her free hand. 'The clinically effective treatment for panic and generalised anxiety disorder is medication and cognitive behaviour therapy,' she recited, 'not online shopping, denial and Facebook forums.'

'Merce—'

'Eugene,' she said, stern now. 'I'm terrified it's my fault.'

She heard the soft squeak of his office chair.

'It wasn't your fault, Mercy,' he said quietly.

'But what if—'

'You can't keep blaming yourself. You did everything you could. Everyone did.'

'No.' Mercy shook her head. 'I should have done more.'

'There was nothing else to do.'

'I could have sectioned her earlier.'

'Stop,' he said, not unkindly. 'You can't go back in time. What happened, happened the way it did. Tamara didn't *want* a C-section earlier, and you can't give women surgery against their will.'

'She didn't want the induction either, but I still gave it to her.'

'She was overdue, Merce. It's hospital policy.'

'Bollocks to policy. When did we stop seeing women as people?'

They were quiet for a time.

'It's always been my fault,' Mercy said softly, running her fingernail back and forth across the bedspread. 'My whole life I've been blamed and scapegoated. It was my fault that Mum couldn't have any more kids after I was born. Did you know that even when my dad left, Mum blamed me? I was only a kid.'

'Your mother was a narcissist. The coroner won't—'

Mercy wasn't listening. 'I tried my best and she died, that woman *died*—' Her throat jammed with a sob.

'Mercy? Please listen to me. You're drunk. I want you to have a glass of water and go to sleep. I know it feels very real and very scary right now, but this isn't real, and it will pass, okay? Just know that these feelings will pass.'

His voice was calm and contained, the authoritative doctor soothing an irrational, panicking patient. But rather than surge with irritation, Mercy watched with mild surprise as her body simply accepted it. Heard his words and shrugged. Something deep inside her, some sober part, was already there—the place he was trying to show her. Already centred and calm, and didn't need his coaxing. Peace was already a seed lodged within her.

Suddenly, Mercy felt very tired.

'Okay, Eugene,' she said, patting the bedspread as if it was the top of his head. 'I'll go to sleep. But I *do* want to apologise. My house burned down and you were a very kind ex-husband, taking me in to bunk alongside your barista boyfriend, and I repaid you by throwing perfume against the wall and buying a Daihatsu Hijet and running away up the track—that's what they call the Stuart Highway here in the Territory, "the track"—and I hung up on you and made you talk to Legal. I shouldn't have treated you that way and I'm sorry.'

'Okay, Mercy,' Eugene said patiently. 'I accept your apology. Now get some sleep.'

'One more thing?'

'Yes?'

'Tell Jose I'm sorry about his jeans.'

'His what?'

'His skinny jeans. I left them in a truck stop bin an hour north of Ti Tree. They smelled like arse.'

There was a long pause, and then Eugene said, 'Goodnight, Mercy.'

Mercy pressed the phone to her cheek. 'Nighty night, Eugene.' Dropping the phone to the bed, she stood and crossed the room, then pressed her palm against the door and whispered, 'Goodnight, Andy.'

CHAPTER TWENTY·EIGHT

Road travel, Mercy had learned, came with certain unwritten rules and conventions, social niceties that formed on the road to ensure everyone's comfort, safety and forward momentum. For instance, that roadtrain that had first overtaken her, south of Coober Pedy? The left-right indicator blinks the trucker had flashed weren't a caged threat, as she had initially feared—it was a *thank you*, because Mercy had slowed her own speed and gotten the hell out of the truck's way. Some drivers didn't do this. Some drivers, Mercy had seen, actually sped up or cruised closer to the centre line when they were being overtaken, in some kind of egotistical testosteroney knee-jerk, a need to *win*, so Mercy figured that *thank you* was probably closer to code for a relieved *cheers for not being an inconsiderate prick*.

And so as Mercy tumbled out of bed the next morning, dull-headed and with her mouth tasting like cardboard, and found the note slid under the door, she realised another road-travel convention was not to assume that any folk you met along the way by coincidence of timing and location—even if you'd shared your life story over sunset the night before—would make the assumption that you wanted to drive along together from now on, continuing to hold hands. Road-trip etiquette dictated that travellers value their solitude and autonomy and will, pretty much, *catch you later.*

That's what Andy's note read: *Hey Mercy, great hanging out last night. Didn't want to wake you—hope you enjoyed your sleep in the luxury of a bed and your head's not too sore this morning. Catch you later up the track. Andy. x*

It was nine thirty am. In a soft bed, with curtains over the windows and the white-noise hum of the air conditioner, Mercy had slept like a corpse. She tucked Andy's note into her pocket and, in spite of her hangover, smiled. Then she remembered her conversation with Eugene and waited to cringe, but didn't. Instead, she felt even lighter.

This sense of lightness was made manifest when she went to scratch the back of her neck, found it bare, and remembered the sound of the paring knife sawing through her tangled locks. She ran her fingers through the shorn curls: ragged and uneven, and very short. This morning, Mercy had awoken with a lot less baggage—both on the inside *and* out.

The room belonged to Mercy for only thirty more minutes. It was time for one last shower and to remove any and all traces of her hair or her contraband sausage dog before she was back on the road.

DARWIN 1094.

'Look at that, Wasabi,' Mercy said, shifting into top gear. 'If we were driving a normal car, that's only about ten hours. We're almost down to three figures! But we're not in a normal car, are we, boy?' She ruffled the fur on his head and Wasabi thudded his tail on the seat. 'We're in no hurry.'

With the smoky-sweet breeze caressing the bare nape of her neck, the scent of soap and sunscreen rising from her skin and her belly full of The Devil's Marbles Hotel's eggs-and-bacon breakfast, she could almost believe it. *No hurry.* Free of time limits.

No looming date.

Termite mounds cropped up, rising between the grass and scrub like brown-robed old women. Some were only feet from the blacktop, and as she drove on, Mercy felt a strange admiration for those brave ants imperious to the churn and bluster of the highway. They were *here now*, without time, and fearless.

Heading north, the highway passed right through Karlu Karlu. The morning daylight painted the marbles a different shade to the brilliant golds of the evening before; now they were paler, colours of sand and rust. Mercy drove through the valley remembering the fiery sunset, pools of warm shadow and the feel of Andy's hand in her own.

An hour and a half later, Mercy found herself slowing for the first fifty zone she'd driven through since Alice Springs; five hundred kilometres later and she was once again capable of breaking the speed limit. And of driving at a speed that let in clouds of flies through the window.

Tennant Creek—named for yet another European explorer's exultation over a water source—was a flat, spread-out town, split up the centre by the highway. Mercy stopped for groceries (water, canned beans, rice crackers, oranges) then pulled into a service station to top up the fuel tank.

She was paying for her petrol when her phone buzzed.

If you get this, please call?

Eugene had never been known for the verbosity of his text messages, but this one was particularly skimpy. Mercy's thumb hovered over the call button. The night before, Mercy had said everything she wanted to say. She had hung up feeling eased, washed clean like linen. Maybe *he* had things to say now, she thought. Maybe it was Eugene's turn to get things off his chest, to take responsibility and apologise. Or maybe he was angry at Mercy for opening up a dialogue he didn't want, especially at two am.

Her screen displayed only one bar of service. A voice call would be irritating for them both, patchy and dropping in and out. Besides, Eugene had used the fairly non-urgent *if* and a question mark—desultory enough for Mercy to click the screen off and shove the phone back in her pocket.

If only he hadn't used that question mark.

CHAPTER TWENTY·NINE

Driving out of Tennant Creek, Mercy passed a woman walking along the side of the road. Barefoot, in a colourful flowing skirt, the woman carried a young boy up on her shoulders, her hands clasped around the child's feet.

Leaning her elbow on the window frame, Mercy drove one handed, watching the woman and child disappear in the rear-view mirror.

Once, Mercy had lifted a newborn baby to its mother's chest and the mother had uttered in a terrified voice, 'I don't know how to hold it.' The mother's hands had fumbled to clasp the tiny slippery body and the infant's head had flopped and thumped over the woman's swollen breasts. It was true: the woman had not known how to hold her baby. Unpractised and clumsy, her elbows had stuck out as she stared wide-eyed down her nose, her face etched with fear as if on her chest was not her own new baby but a gigantic tarantula.

Mercy had seen all kinds of mothers: competent, confident mothers eating a sandwich with one hand while breastfeeding with the other; teenage mothers whose babies shot out like slippery fish while a clutch of girlfriends slurped Frozen Coke in the corner; women having their first baby in their forties: studious, well-read, questioning everything. Into the hospital women came in droves, waddling, panting, moaning or nervous and eager-eyed, waiting to be told what to do or growling not to be told what to do. But if there was one consistency among all these women—happy, scared, confident or even ambivalent—it was that they all wore their pregnant bellies with a look of ease. Even those huge women whose spines crunched and ankles ballooned tight, they all looked as though they *should* be pregnant. Like they couldn't *not* be pregnant at that exact point in their life, no matter how willingly or with what fore-planning they had gotten there. It seemed to Mercy as if everything in the universe had conspired to end up at that moment, where Mercy was catching a baby, blood-slicked and blue, from their body.

Mercy squinted into the mirror, but the barefoot woman and child were gone. A four-wheel drive and caravan overtook her; *Born with nothing*, it read. *Still got most of it.*

No matter how Mercy had tried to explain it to Eugene—this sense that when women were supposed to bear fruit it happened naturally—it was something he had never been able to understand. 'IVF is hardly natural,' he'd argue, 'plenty of women go through that,' to which Mercy would reply, 'Yes, but it *happened*. You see my point?' To Eugene, married couples had kids. It was simply what they did, like mowing the nature strip and paying the bills in a timely manner. And to Mercy, women who were meant to had kids, like they were meant to breathe and blink and grow hair. Even if they were scared.

Mercy wasn't meant to have a baby. Two miscarriages wasn't a lot of miscarriages compared to some women, but for Mercy those two early losses had been enough to tell her she just wasn't meant to have a child. Medicine had trained her as a scientist—rational, logical—but her mother had trained her to know that maternal love could be heart-breakingly conditional, and for Mercy, two miscarriages was enough to put a firm stop to the idea of ever passing that conditional love on. Nature had warned Mercy, and so Mercy wouldn't ever be pregnant again. Eugene had been crushed. And the irony of her husband then choosing a life partner who happened not to have a uterus would not have been lost on Mercy had life not then thrown her that entire life-shattering week, and by then irony was something Mercy couldn't care less about.

It didn't mean, however, that Mercy couldn't look at a mother–child pair—a barefoot woman carrying a child along the road, hands clasping little feet to her breast—and feel that deep heart swoop, that tug, that reminded her that maternal love was inexplicable, and fleshy, and as pure and simple as it could be sickeningly complicated.

Mercy sighed, and her breath tugged away in the breeze.

'Wasabi, stop that,' she said, as the dog began to lick his crotch, as if he could hear her musings on reproduction and decided to check if his testicles had miraculously grown back. He desisted with regret.

Mercy realised she hadn't steered for a very long time. Lost in thought, she had travelled for an hour in a straight line, and for as far as she could see ahead the highway continued to roll dead straight, disappearing into the shimmering horizon.

DARWIN 780.

Late in the afternoon, the speed limit reduced and a tiny town approached. Mercy noticed the afternoon sunlight looked different. The landscape had changed: colours were sharper, the vegetation more lush. Through patches of bright green grass the soil was the colour of dark blood. The heated air felt thicker; low banks of cloud smothered the sky.

Elliot was another blip on the highway: fuel, a pub, a tired-looking caravan park tucked off the highway. And it was as Mercy turned off the highway and onto the service road that she saw, through the trees, Ann Barker's RV.

'Bloody *hell*.'

She kept rolling along the service road, too afraid to put her foot on the brake in case Ann happened to glance up and see her: the doctor she had slandered, the doctor she had impossibly run into in the middle of nowhere, the doctor who had climbed out a service-station window and travelled for two hours along a dirt track to escape her.

Scattered weatherboard buildings trundled past the windows and the end of the Elliot service road approached, curving back towards the highway. It was late in the afternoon; Mercy was tired and hungry. She needed a place to stop for the night—but Ann Barker had already laid claim to it, this particular place of possible rest. There was an irony in that, too, Mercy thought—that the unforgiving opinions of the world could not be avoided, no matter how literally you isolated yourself.

The highway approached. The service road rose up to rejoin it, and Mercy found herself once again staring down the endless stretch of bitumen. The next town was one hundred kilometres away.

CHAPTER THIRTY

Clouds continued to thicken across the sky, closing over the sinking sun and casting an eerie green pall over the earth. The road turned the colour of slate. Mercy switched on the headlights, but they provided little illumination of her next options. On the passenger seat, Wasabi sat up and whined, giving her a meaningful look; he needed to stop.

Grabbing her phone off the dash, she glanced at the screen: no service. She cursed and tossed the phone down. About thirty minutes had passed since she'd left Elliot; could she just turn around and go back?

But. Ann fucking Barker.

A few drops of water ticked onto the windscreen. The clouds had turned bruised-looking and angry. Wasabi whimpered again.

'Darn it,' she muttered.

Her foot eased off the accelerator. She would have to turn around. The next town was still over an hour away, and even then, what if there was nowhere she could camp? She recalled driving nervously around Alice Springs, finding everything booked out or pet prohibitive. Journalist or not, Mercy needed to stop.

Easing onto the brake, she was looking for a smooth patch of shoulder where she could turn the van around when the headlights lit up a sign.

REST STOP 2KM.

Mercy looked at the dog. 'Two more minutes, boy. Let's hold on.'

The rain held long enough for Mercy to pull into the rest area, and then it poured. She could see it coming from the west, a dense grey sheet of water sweeping towards them across the scrub, then meeting the windscreen and the roof of the van with a patter then a roar. She hastened to roll up the windows and the insides of the glass quickly began to fog. Startled by the downpour, Wasabi flattened his ears and she petted his head but after a few minutes he returned to his original complaint and began to whine with urgency.

Clambering into the back, Mercy found the puffer jacket she hadn't needed since leaving Alice Springs, threw it over her head, and climbed out into the rain.

The heady scent of wet earth rose to greet her. Water pattered into the red sand, warm drops dripped off the jacket and onto her elbows. Wasabi trotted off into the downpour and she hurried after him.

A small tin shed housed a composting toilet, and after Wasabi had relieved himself by a post, Mercy went inside, taking the dog with her.

The rest area was deserted. Three poles held up a triangle of iron sheeting and Mercy took shelter beneath it, hugging her elbows to her sides in spite of the warmth of the air.

It rained for a long time. The setting sun was hidden by the dark bank of raincloud and the light gradually faded. Muffled roars came as trucks passed on the highway, wheels hissing through water, but by the time the rain eventually eased the highway had turned quiet. Insects came out in the grass and bushes, clicking and shrieking. Water dripped and a dull humidity clogged the air. Ravens cawed in the trees; a pair of them, huge and blue-black, hopped across the rest area, their cries moaning out into the evening.

Mercy brought the Hijet close alongside the desultory triangular shelter and sat inside the van, chewing her lip. As the light disappeared, her belly churned with hunger and a growing unease.

Recently, Mercy had seen headlines that one of Australia's most notorious serial killers had died in jail. The victims, all hitchhikers, had been found buried in shallow graves, their bodies filled with bullet and stab wounds.

Mercy thought now of how many times the outback had thrown up murderous mystery, how many times she had sat safe and quiet in her city home and read the terrible, scandalous stories with the comforting security of distance. Sometimes, those people who had been claimed by the outback were never even found, their deaths only implied through their disappearance, any searches or investigation futile against the vastness, the isolation, the impossible remoteness of the space.

Sitting in the back of the van, Mercy opened a can of baked beans in ham sauce and as she emptied the tin into the saucepan, the red drip of sauce reminded her of blood. She gave Wasabi a handful of kibble and waited for the beans to heat, but her hunger had leached away with the last of the sunlight.

'You're being silly,' she scolded herself, and opened the back door to let in the fresh, damp air. 'You are perfectly safe.'

But of course, that wasn't precisely true. She *wasn't* perfectly safe. This was not some irrational, supermarket-based anxiety playing tricks on her mind in the toilet paper aisle: this was real. She *was* alone. She *was* a very long way from home.

People *did* meet their death out here—stabbed, shot, stolen. From the time Europeans had first trawled along this route more than a century ago, searching for water and naming things after themselves, brutal massacres had followed in their wake.

'Oh, for heaven's sake,' Mercy shouted, dropping her spoon. Ham sauce splattered her T-shirt and Wasabi looked up from his kibble. 'This is *not* helping.' At that moment, a roadtrain began its long haul past on the highway and Mercy took the growl of its engine and the churn of its ninety-six wheels as a reminder that she was not *that* removed from civilisation.

And then she remembered that the serial killer who had recently died in jail had snatched all of his victims from the side of a major highway. She slammed the back door closed, locked all the doors, and when she ate, beans quivered on the spoon with the shake of her hand.

Mercy awoke in a murky dark. Disoriented, and with her lower back aching, it took her a moment to remember where she was—the rest area; fleeing from Ann Barker back at Elliot. Somehow she had fallen asleep sitting up on the bed, leaning against the wall. After eating she had not intended to fall asleep right away; Jenny Cleggett was still in the cabinet beneath her. Wasabi was curled up asleep at the foot of the bed.

In the dark, music was playing. Loud, plaintive vocals and the whine of electric guitar echoed out in the blackness.

Mercy froze. Where was the music coming from?

The volume was suddenly turned up even further as cymbals began to crash and a drum beat thudded. The vocals began to shriek.

Mercy peered out the back window but all she could see were stars. Heart rising into her mouth, she crawled along the mattress towards the driver's seat and slowly lifted her head.

On the far side of the rest area, a row of spotlights blared from the roof of a vehicle, illuminating the scrub in stark pools. Mercy could only make out the shape of the vehicle but its large wheels, blinding spotlights and the chunky squares of rear cages were enough to strike metallic fear into her mouth: it was a pig-dog ute. A hunting vehicle.

Silhouetted in the spotlights was the tall, dark figure of a man. His arms were raised, his feet planted wide, and he was howling along with the guitars of Led Zeppelin's 'Stairway To Heaven'.

The highway was silent. All the grey nomads would be tucked safely away in their parks for the night; now, the road belonged only to long-haul truckies on amphetamines.

Certainly, for Mercy, fear had been a daily companion. For the past two years, fear had draped itself like a scarf around her neck and stayed put, no matter how much she tried to take it off. But this? This was something other than fear. At the sight of that male figure silhouetted in the spotlights, the sound of the electric guitar yowling out into the night, at the understanding that the highway was silent and unfriendly, Mercy felt not a rush of irrational, consuming terror, but a very calmly voiced, clear and simple threat: *If you don't leave now, you will die.*

It wasn't an anxious *what if*, it was a certainty. It was knowledge. For once, Mercy's fear did not seem like something to try and overcome, but something to listen to. Respond to. Something she should obey.

A cold sweat broke out on her temples as she tried to climb into the driver's seat, keeping her body as low as possible in the windscreen. Because what if the man looked over to the Hijet and saw movement? He must have seen her van when he drove in, surely, and it occurred to her that maybe he had stood and watched her sleep, waiting for her to awake before he made his approach.

Her movements woke Wasabi, and he bounded up the mattress and clambered over the seats, trying to lick her face.

'Not now, Wasabi,' she whispered. 'Down.'

But the dog wouldn't be dissuaded. He darted and panted, he bounced back and forth as Mercy tipped her upper body forward over the seat and tried to bring her legs over. His paws landed on her face; his tongue slurped at her ears.

'Wasabi, no!' she hissed. He ignored her. The music continued to blare, drums rumbling and guitar screeching.

Somehow, she had contorted herself into the driver's seat upside down. Her legs were up where her spine should be, and her spine was down where her bum should be. Drawing her knees to her chest, she tried to roll undetectably sideways but her shoulders jammed under the steering wheel.

Wasabi let out a string of loud, playful yaps.

The music went silent.

'Shit.'

Wrestling herself out from under the steering column, Mercy sat up and fumbled for the keys. She looked up and saw the figure standing there in the spotlights, unmoving. She couldn't see his face. Was he looking at her? She thumbed the ignition but the engine didn't start: it was cold. Tugging open the choke, she tried again and the engine *chug-chug-chugged* but didn't catch. She looked up and saw the figure start to move. He was walking towards her.

'Shit!' Mercy repeated. Pumping the accelerator, she pleaded with the van, 'Come on, *start*.'

Now she'd flooded the engine. It coughed and stopped, filling the air with the fumes of unburned fuel.

The figure continued, his stride slow but purposeful.

Mercy's fear turned to a cold rage. 'I will not go down like this,' she cried. 'After everything, I will not see it end this way! Start, now!'

The engine turned over, spluttered, and came to life. She shoved at the gear stick, hauled on the steering wheel and roared back onto the highway, gravel skittering and the man standing silently in her wake.

CHAPTER THIRTY·ONE

With the dawn of the following morning came, of course, feelings of doubt. Even a sense of silliness. Shaken, Mercy had fled back to Elliot, each kilometre feeling like a hundred, each minute stretching like an hour, her eyes glued to the rear-vision mirror as she waited for a row of bright spotlights to bear down on her little van and shotgun pellets to shatter the back window.

None of that happened. The only thing that had happened after Mercy fled the rest area and peeled into the Elliot caravan park was she had pulled into a campsite—a scrappy patch of grass under a tree, as far away as possible from the dark, hulking shape of Ann Barker's RV—and then she'd tucked the cat throw over her head and quivered until the sun came up.

So, as Mercy lay now in the balmy sub-tropical morning, listening to the trumpeting of peacocks strutting around outside the van, the threat of the previous night felt surreal, something she had entirely imagined. The man was probably only walking towards the Hijet to offer assistance in getting it to start. That is, if he was even walking towards her at all. Maybe he was just walking to the toilet?

Naturally, she was also kicking herself for choosing the very real threat of facing the opinion writer who had called her a *murderer* over the imagined threat of a single man at a rest stop.

But when she considered it that way, even Ann fucking Barker won out. Because if Mercy *had* died last night, as she had at the time been entirely convinced she was going to, people like Barker would have positively *crowed* all over the internet about how much of an idiot Mercy was for putting herself into that situation in the first place. A deserted rest area, at night, in the far reaches of the Territory outback? It was the road-trip equivalent of walking home alone in the dark with her earphones in—they would have said Mercy was *asking for it*.

'But this is what we do, isn't it?' she said to herself, pushing down the cat blanket and letting Wasabi lick her hand. She couldn't escape the collective female conditioning that ensured she be fearful of everything—her environment, her male counterparts, her body hair—but then, on top of that, to feel ashamed and silly for being afraid of everything.

Groaning, Mercy rolled onto her front, stuffing her face into the mattress. She had already decided she'd simply wait in the van until Ann Barker's RV left. After all, a few weatherboard shacks and herds of peacocks surrounded by rusted car bodies and shoulder-high spear grass would hold very little appeal for two teenage girls—especially without any internet or phone service. They would be gone very soon.

Along with Mercy's Hijet and Ann's RV, there were only two other campers in the park: a pair of grey nomads in caravans, both of whom roared out predictably not long after the crack of dawn. Inside her van, Mercy stayed low, lifting her eyes above the window frame, watching the luxury RV on the far side of the park and waiting for it to leave, but by the time nine am rolled past, Mercy was busting for the facilities and there was no sign of the RV going anywhere. In fact, there was no sign of life from Ann Barker's RV at all. No chairs or tables unfolded for breakfast outside, no movement through the windows, all the curtains were drawn.

As the sun rose higher, the inside of the van began to swelter. Reluctantly, Mercy rolled down the windows, eyeing the lurking RV, but without any breeze there was little relief. Last night's downpour was swiftly turning into this morning's sauna.

After making coffee and eating an apple and a few slices of cheese, Mercy couldn't hold out any longer. Neither could Wasabi: his whines had grown squeakier and more urgent. For a long minute she studied the silent RV, and after convincing herself that Ann and her family were either still sound asleep or had gone for some kind of inexplicably lengthy morning walk around the unglamorous facilities of Elliot, Mercy cracked open the back door and slipped out.

Eyes low, she hurried across the grass. Bull-ants swarmed over patches of damp sand, causing her to take large, jolting steps that strained her full bladder. Wasabi trotted in circles, sneezing at the ants, panting after the peacocks and availing himself of more than one tree. When he wandered in the direction of the monstrous RV, she hissed at him, glancing anxiously at the windows, but the vehicle remained quiet.

The amenities block was a small brick building painted bright blue. Inside, Mercy locked herself and the dog in a shower stall and stood under an invigorating stream of cool water. As soon as she finished her shower, she would leave. All she had to do was dress herself, return to the van and drive away. Even if she ran into Ann, she told herself as she scrubbed her face, Mercy was under no obligation to speak to her. Who did the woman think she was? Mercy thought now, soaping under her arms. The writer was just a mouth-piece for clicks. Mercy owed her nothing.

Emboldened, she shut off the water. She towelled her newly cropped hair. She stepped into her shorts, pulled on her T-shirt and opened the stall door as Ann Barker turned from the sink and gave her a smile.

'Doctor Blain,' the opinion writer said around the tooth-brush in her mouth. 'Good morning.' Ann spat toothpaste into the sink. 'I thought that was your funny little van outside. Obviously you had no trouble after it was fixed? I didn't even see you leave, back at Ti Tree.'

Mercy was clean, dry and dressed. All she had to do was say, *Excuse me*, and slip past Ann, get into her van and drive away. She owed Ann nothing, right? But as the writer stood there with a smile, those piercing grey eyes bright, head tilted, wiping toothpaste from her chin and smelling of shampoo and bold self-entitlement, all the resolve Mercy had found in the shower only moments ago vanished. Before Mercy's eyes all the comments came racking up, unfiltered and into the hundreds, bursting with high drama. One comment had even read, *Fuck that! Fuck her! BURN THEM ALL.*

And how Mercy had burned indeed.

'How are you enjoying your trip?' Ann asked, picking up a tube of sunscreen. 'It's starting to feel a little tropical, wouldn't you say?' She tilted her head, narrowing her eyes. 'I'd *swear* your hair looks shorter. Anyway, we're going to make straight for Darwin today, I don't care if we have to drive into the night. Without phone service, we're all going a bit mad.'

'Yes,' Mercy heard herself say. 'God forbid you're not stoking public outrage about something.'

Ann paused, a dob of sunscreen in her palm. 'What?'

And then it was coming out of Mercy's mouth. It was coming out all by itself, as if it had two thousand kilometres of velocity behind it, a continent of flames, and it seemed all Mercy could do was bear witness to it. 'You called me a murderer, if I recall. Admittedly I only read the article once, but I don't think being called *that* is something I could have misread.'

Slowly, Ann set the tube of sunscreen down. 'Really?'

'Yes.' Mercy's mouth was dry. 'You did.'

'Look,' Ann said, rubbing cream into her upper arm, 'since I ran into you a couple of days ago, I've been trying to remember the case. But I know people were up in arms about it, that much I do recall, and I remember thinking that was remarkable in itself, because, by and large, doctors are immune from public criticism.' She squeezed more sunscreen into her palm. The beachy scent of it filled the steamy brick building. 'I mean, why wouldn't you guys be? You save lives. You're miracle workers.' She bent forward to wipe sunscreen on her thighs, looking up at Mercy from under loose, swinging curls. 'So what was different, this time? And then.' She straightened up. 'Then I remembered who she was. That influencer. How many Instagram followers did she have? A million?'

A beat of silence passed, the sound of Wasabi's panting echoing around the brick building.

'One-point-three million,' Mercy said at length. 'And her husband had about half that.'

Another silence ensued. The tap dripped in the sink.

Then Ann slapped her palms together. 'Well,' she said briskly. 'There you go.' She shrugged. 'People knew who they were. Her followers had shared every moment of that pregnancy—photos of her stretch marks, her maternity knickers, the beautiful nursery. And then she died and, as usual, there had to be a scapegoat.'

Was it because Ann used that word, *scapegoat*? When Mercy was growing up, she had often felt as though her mother had created her just so she would have someone to *blame*. Mercy never had any choice in the fact that she existed, that she was Loretta Blain's child, living in her mother's house by her mother's say-so. Mercy's mother made her, so when she had insisted Mercy be the person *she* wanted her to be—which Mercy never could be, of course—it felt devastating and hypocritical. Why did her mother resent Mercy's existence when she had chosen to make her exist in the first place? How come, no matter how much you tried your best, some people would choose your very existence to tear down in order to make themselves feel bigger?

The back of Mercy's throat began to ache; hot tears swam into her eyes.

'You had no right to put her family through that.'

Ann looked surprised. 'Me? All I did was report the facts. A bit of a flurry online? That's nothing compared to the grief of losing a loved one.'

'You're right,' Mercy said, anger flaring. 'Nothing compares to losing a loved one. *Nothing*. And that "bit of a flurry online"—which you instigated, by the way—was the soundtrack for me at a time when I'd lost not one but *two* loved ones. Not in the same circumstances as Tamara's family, but to me, they were still gone. Grief is grief. It's complicated and awful and hard and it can only be weathered with time. But I couldn't weather it. I could not. Because I was too busy hiding, keeping my head down, barricading myself against all this confected rage when all I had done was *my job*. To you, words are nothing but lures for traffic, fodder for advertising revenue. But your words have real-life consequences, Ann, they have a human face. Without any actual understanding of what happened—without a single scrap of empathy or nuance or *humanity*—you turned that family's grief, the most awful thing in their life, into nothing but clickbait. To make yourself feel bigger.'

Mercy's breath was coming fast and shallow.

Ann stared at her. She opened her mouth to speak, and then they both turned at the sound of a toilet flushing. The end stall opened and Ann's teenage daughter stepped out.

'Yeah, *Mum*,' the girl muttered. 'And you lecture *me* about the consequences of posting online. *Jeez*.'

Shaking her head, Ann's daughter washed her hands and left. Wordlessly, Mercy watched her go. Then she said, 'Excuse me,' stepped around Ann Barker and walked outside into the sunshine.

Maybe, Mercy thought, she had come so far that she had left fear behind and entered apathy. Or even oblivion. Whatever the case, as she filled the Hijet with petrol at the Elliot service station, she could feel her mind reaching out, searching for the reliable old hit of fear like an addict for the pipe, only to find a sense of ... nothing. What actually was this? Who was plumbing the depths of her mind, looking for anxiety, or regret, or angst, and coming up empty-handed? And what was it that she had instead? Without fear, what did Mercy feel?

After paying for the petrol, Mercy poured herself a cup of water and stood in the shade at the back of the van to drink it. An ingrained sense of habit wanted to replay those moments with Ann Barker in the amenities block, but bizarrely, she also found that, right now, she genuinely did not care. Ann Barker's RV had gone and the opinion writer was in the past, and Mercy was here, now, drinking cool water and listening to the insects shriek in the warm red dirt, looking at the blue sky stretching forever.

Lifting her foot, she rested it on the rear bumper. There was a metallic clunk and her foot skidded onto the gravel. Startled, Mercy turned and saw the bumper hanging at an angle.

Carefully, she gave the bumper an experimental jiggle. When it didn't fall off she jiggled harder, but rather than being loose, it now seemed to be wedged in position, sloping like a frown towards the shiny new tailpipe Tate had installed back in Ti Tree.

In truth, the Hijet was starting to make more noises than it used to. Sometimes it skipped a beat, gave an unusual little burp, barely perceptible but there nonetheless. New rattles had evolved, different squeaks. The rear-vision mirror had begun to sag and the driver's side window no longer rolled all the way up.

But, like the old mechanic had assured her, the steering was tight and the van still stopped on a dime. Just yesterday afternoon, Mercy had slammed on the brakes for an echidna waddling across the highway and the Hijet had stopped so swiftly and completely that the tyres had chirped. And the temperature gauge never rose above cool, even in the heat of the mid-afternoon sun. Mercy kept its liquids topped up: petrol and water. The bumper didn't matter, it was only aesthetic.

Giving the drooping bumper a final shove, Mercy nodded, satisfied, then drained her cup and got back into the van.

Only three hundred kilometres up the road, Mercy had been told by the petrol station attendant, was a place she absolutely had to visit. She simply could not miss it.

After she had laughed about how it was only in the outback of Australia that a distance of three hundred kilometres could carry the sentiment 'only'—and then fell about over how, for most drivers, three hundred kays was almost a single stretch of driving but for Mercy it was more than half a day, even without stops—the attendant had produced a map and pointed to the Mataranka Thermal Pools.

'Is it a dirt road?' she'd asked.

'Sealed all the way,' he'd assured her.

So, with her ears peeled for the sound of the rear bumper hitting the bitumen, Mercy pulled onto the highway and continued north.

Gradually, she felt a change in the atmosphere. The air grew stickier, heavier; the heat became more consuming. Three hours north of Elliot, she rolled into the tiny establishment of Larrimah with her T-shirt clinging damply to her sides and her stomach growling. Strung up on a fence was a chalkboard sign reading THE BEST PIES IN TOWN! and although she wanted to get to Mataranka, to immerse her sweating, dusty body in clear thermal waters, Mercy's hunger pulled her off the highway, only to discover another sign promising THE BEST HOME MADE PIES IN TOWN and now she was stuck for too many choices of pie. But then she saw yet another sign that said YOUR DOG IS WELCOME HERE! and her decision was made.

The café was a weatherboard-and-shadecloth shack covered by a sprawling pink bougainvillea. Inside, a large-bladed fan squeaked in lazy circles from the ceiling, stirring the warm air like soup. Declining offers of camel or buffalo pies, Mercy chose two beef pies and took them outside, where she sat in the shade of a violently blossoming flame tree and ate, giving the second pie to Wasabi.

The highway was quiet; the few dirt tracks that comprised the township's streets were empty, baking red beneath a hard sky. From somewhere nearby came a lonesome, metallic whine, like a windmill shifting in an errant breeze; a skinny dog trotted in the distance and Mercy put her hand on Wasabi's collar but he was too busy studying his pie, pawing away green-ants and waiting for it to cool.

Despite the heat, as Mercy ate she felt the hairs on her arms standing on end. Tied to fences, tacked onto power poles and plastered across the facade of the pub across the road were blue-and-white chequered posters. MISSING read the slab headline. When Mercy went back into the café for a lemonade and asked after the missing man, she was met with pursed lips, a shaken head and a dark look. Mercy thought of the man in the pig-dog ute from the previous night, the strident guitar twangs of 'Stairway To Heaven' echoing into the outback, the impossible vastness of the space. How small the human body was, she thought. How small and vulnerable. She looked down at the remains of her pie and felt a wave of loneliness come over her. Abruptly her appetite was gone, along with whatever quietness she had felt earlier at Elliot, replaced by crawling skin and fear skittering up her spine. She picked up the dog, climbed into the van and hurried back onto the highway.

As the hours passed, the vegetation continued to evolve. Undergrowth thickened, greens intensified. The red of the dirt began to fade, losing the shades of blood it had carried for more than two thousand kilometres. Termite mounds grew taller, as if to keep up with the grass. Open glades of dry gum trees were replaced with forests of whip-thin, fire-charred sticks. The highway crossed over a wide monsoonal floodplain and Mercy's pulse quickened.

She had entered the tropical north.

DARWIN 450.

It was about three pm when Mercy rolled into Mataranka, a clutch of stores tucked against one side of the highway. Palms waved, bougainvillea frothed purple and an enormous woody frangipani dropped blossoms onto the road and perfumed the sticky air.

Mercy selected a camping ground based on a sign that said PETS VERY WELCOME! and when she drove in, she found a tree-studded grassy space dotted with picnic tables, wallabies and more peacocks.

And there, parked under the trees, was Bert's silver Land-Cruiser and caravan, and a polite distance away from it, Andy's rental camper.

CHAPTER THIRTY-TWO

'The whole gang's here!' Bert said happily, propping his foot up on the Hijet's back wheel. 'Although you just missed Pete and Jules. They chuffed off this morning. We decided to stay an extra night, because look at this place.' He swept out his arm. 'It's just magic.

'So listen,' Bert went on without stopping. 'Happy hour's at four, at ours. Silver Cruiser and Jayco Starcraft.' He pointed, then beamed. 'But you know that by now! Bring whatever you've got, and if you've got nothing, bring that. This bumper's looking a bit average, did you know that?' Bert frowned at the van's rear bumper, clinging at an angle over the tailpipe. He bent down and gave it a test wiggle. 'Anyway,' he said, straightening up. 'I'll take a look at it later. I've got a wrench that'd fit those bolts.' He patted several of his shirt pockets, as if checking for spare wrenches.

Mercy had only just shut off the engine and stepped out. The driver's door swung on its hinges; she still had the keys in her hand. Wasabi shot over to a nearby tree, squatted and pooped.

'Thank you,' was all Mercy could think to say.

'No problem. So, happy hour—we'll see you there? Your mate's bringing a bottle of whisky, apparently.' Bert laughed. 'Like a true Scotsman. So I'm sure it'll be a great night, even without Pete and Jules.' He looked so pleased Mercy had to give him a smile. She looked over at Andy's camper. The canvas awning was pulled out and a small table and chair were set in its shade, but she couldn't see the whisky-bringing Scotsman.

Finally, Bert frowned at her. 'Something's different about you.'

Mercy put a hand to her chopped curls. 'Just gave it a trim.'

'Huh? Oh, no, I don't mean your hair. Can't put my finger on it, but you seem, I dunno—'

'Bert!'

'Oops, that's me,' Bert said, and left.

Mercy hurried to clean up after Wasabi before his little turd attracted half the flies in the Northern Territory.

After showering off her coating of red dust and sweat, Mercy clipped on Wasabi's lead and walked back into town. On one side of the highway was a grocer, petrol station, police station, another petrol station and a shop selling stockwhips, hat bands and leather belts. The other side of the highway was a large grassy park: white-trunked gums, shade trees with thick, sprawling roots like rainforests. Trucks rattled along the highway, pushing hot air, and Mercy felt glad to be resting, relieved to be off the road.

And: it was hot. The heat seemed to come not just from the sun overhead, but from the ground. Heat seemed to radiate from the grass, the trees, the flowers. From the moist, motionless air itself.

Mercy stepped into the air-conditioned grocer with relief.

Standing in front of the fridge, studying its contents and wearing thongs on his feet, a towel around his waist and seemingly nothing else, was Andrew Macauley.

Mercy sidled up. 'You know, we have standards in this country.'

'Doctor Mercy! How's it gaun? Wow,' he said, taking in her short hair. 'So that's what Steve's knife was for.' He gave her a smile that she felt all the way to her toes. 'Now, what're these standards you're on about, eh?'

'These things called "shirts",' Mercy pointed out. 'Miraculous inventions that don't give poor old ladies coronaries.'

'Ah, come on now. You're not old, not yet. This heat is taps aff, so it is.'

It took her a moment. *Tops off.*

'I've been swimming,' he clarified, bumping his bare shoulder gently into hers. 'Are you camping at the thermal springs?'

Mercy nodded, trying to ignore the sudden hyperawareness of the skin on her shoulder. 'Bert's already invited me to happy hour.'

'Aye, me too.'

'I don't think I can get out of this one. He's been asking me since Crystal Brook. I've been antisocial for almost two and a half thousand kilometres.'

'Don't worry, Doctor Mercy. I'll be there. And you can bring your assistance dog.' He looked around. 'Speaking of, where's your assistance dog?'

'Outside.'

'Look at you!'

'I know, right?' Mercy selected a packet of sausages, placing it ceremoniously into her basket. 'Like an ordinary shopper. Talking to another shopper, in a very ordinary fashion. That is, you know, if most ordinary shoppers browsed for French onion dip half-naked.'

'It's the only way to shop, I find. You should try it.' He grinned. 'It's the liberation you're searching for, darlin'.'

The Roper Creek wound through thick cabbage palms. Blue as lapis, clear as cut glass, warm artesian water rose from deep underground and poured into creeks and springs. Lily-pads hugged the hot water like a lover.

For a long, hushed moment, Mercy stood on the cobblestone steps and watched the jewelled, steaming water. Any anxiety she'd felt a few minutes ago over leaving Wasabi with Andy was forgotten. Then she couldn't get her boots off fast enough. She slid into the water like it was her sole purpose in life.

Mercy had the sensation of everything heavy lifting away. As if she was entirely weightless. Aching muscles unwound.

Wind-chafed skin softened. The pleasure was so intense she saw stars.

The water tugged her gently downstream. Floating on her back, Mercy watched palm fronds slip by. In the trees overhead bats chattered in clumps. And in the sky, thunderheads were forming the size of skyscrapers. Held by the warm water, cushioned by palms, Mercy watched the palms and bats and thunderheads and felt safe, removed. Gliding in this ancient earth-heated water, there was nothing she needed to do but watch. All she had to do was *be.*

The spring narrowed, turning a corner. Mercy ducked beneath the surface, and when she came up, the spring had opened out into another pool. A sign at the water's edge warned swimmers to be aware of freshwater crocodiles. Although not the same level of threat as their man-eating saltwater cousins, freshwater crocs *can become aggressive if disturbed.*

Then it came to her, without warning, as it always did.

A bath: one of the midwives had offered Tamara a bath, to take the edge off the pain. Dutifully Mercy had been informed of this development, and how had Mercy responded? Treading water, she tried to remember. All of these details would be recorded in the notes, both her own notes and those of the midwives, but right now, Mercy's mind was blank. Mercy had delivered two to three hundred babies a year and Ann Barker, Mercy realised, was right—each labouring woman, each infant, was blended in together, wadded into a series of bradycardias and tachycardias, primips or multiparas, obstructed labours or failures to progress.

Lying on her back, water lapping her skin, Mercy watched a purple-black thunderhead sprawl across the sky, blocking out the sun, casting an unearthly twilight. Thunder growled. Mercy felt the slow *ba-boom* of her heart. She was alive. She was here, now. But Tamara Lee Spencer and millions of women just like her over the course of human history, was not. And men, too. All kinds of people, all ages. In the past, and now, and into the future. No matter what Mercy or the best, most qualified, most senior of her colleagues did. No matter how people fought it, or denied it, or outraged about it. Death happened. Birth happened. *Life* happened.

It was as devastating, as transformative, and as simple as that.

If it could have been possible to have more than a quintuple bypass, Mercy was sure Bert's brother would have had one. Or at least, Bert would *claim* his brother had had one. Sextuple bypass? Octuple? That's nothing—Bert's brother can top that, he's got failing coronary arteries in abundance.

They were sitting around a crackling campfire: a group of chattering grey nomads, Andy with his man-bun and single malt, and Mercy, Shiraz and sausage dog on her lap. Happy hour had been delayed due to the tremendous, crashing tropical thunderstorm that had poured buckets and raged for half an hour, then ended as abruptly as it had begun. Everything was wet, dripping and steamy. Puddles gleamed with the last reflections of the pink-orange sunset.

The man who had recently come through a triple bypass was a robust, chrome-haired fellow named Graham, and his wife, a thin woman draped in floral scarves despite the humidity, Eileen. Both in their seventies, they'd had to put the van 'up on blocks' for six months while Graham recovered from his surgery last year, Graham was explaining.

'Oh yeah,' another man piped up. 'I had a quadruple bypass two years ago. Sure takes it outta you. You know they have to saw open your ribs?'

'My brother had a quintuple bypass,' Bert said. 'Doctors did it in one surgery. Rare as hen's teeth, that kind of operation. Took all day. They had to bring in another team of surgeons from Melbourne. Practically closed down the operating theatre for a week.'

No one could one-up Bert's brother for that, so there was a moment of obligatory silence, before they moved on to cancer: who'd had a scare, who'd had something removed and from what part of their body. (Graham: cousin with first stage lung; Quadruple Bypass: prostate; Bert's brother: had a lump removed from his groin that doctors had been very worried about, only it turned out to be a cyst. Had the pathologists and oncologists completely bamboozled, though, and they're thinking of naming it after him.)

Listening to their tall and competitive tales of medical woe, Mercy couldn't help but feel entertained. She sipped her glass of wine, offering requisite gasps, murmurs and sympathetic winces. This was the sharing of battle stories, retiree style. This was how they proved to themselves that they were indeed *living the dream*. Because why else would you buy yourself a big-arse caravan and drag it around the country, racing a troupe of other big-arse caravans for the best campsite? To prove how damn blissful life is, that's why. And to acknowledge how bloody short it is, too.

And to prove to Millennials the value of superannuation.

Leaning over, Mercy asked Andy under her breath, 'What's the collective noun for a group of caravans?'

Andy pondered it. 'A swagger.'

'A gloat?'

'A boast.'

'A grandstand.'

Andy asked, 'What's the opposite of an apology? A confession?'

'A flagrant?'

'An entitlement?'

This went on for a while, back and forth, until Andy finally suggested, 'An ostentation. An ostentation of caravans,' at which Shiraz came out of Mercy's nose and the subject was settled.

'What about you, Mercy?' Bert said, as Mercy wiped red wine from Wasabi's fur. 'What do you do?'

Mercy said, 'I work for the tax department.'

'Don't we all?' Quadruple Bypass declared, and everyone rolled about laughing.

Eileen passed around a platter of devilled eggs and Mercy asked if she'd bought them here in Mataranka.

'No, dear,' Eileen said pleasantly, 'I made them.'

Mercy looked down at the tray and imagined hard boiling all those eggs in the poky back of her van. She took one, thanked Eileen, and bit into it. It was delicious, creamy and spicy.

'Wow,' she murmured. 'Amazing. You must have more than one saucepan.'

Eileen gave a happy titter. 'I have a full kitchen in that ridiculous thing over there. Here, have another.' And she placed two more eggs into Mercy's hand. Wasabi sat up, sniffing, and Mercy pushed him to the ground, whereby he immediately began to follow the tray of devilled eggs around the circle.

Flames crackled; a log fell and sparks shot into the fading light. Laughter spilled out. Andy leaned over to whisper jokes to Mercy and she smelled his soap, his breath tickling the soft, short hairs behind her ear. Wasabi trotted up to each person, accepting pats and scruffs and titbits of egg, sausage, crackers and cheese.

It took her a while to name the sensation in her body. A softening, languid and non-urgent. Like she had noticed at Elliot that morning, if she paid careful attention, she could almost *feel* her mind hustling for something to *think* about, something to fret over, something to dread. But instead, Mercy felt something else, something other than nerves and disquiet.

It was calm—that's who Mercy was. That's how Mercy felt, here and now.

Mercy was calm.

In the end, happy hour went far longer than one hour.

422 km to go

CHAPTER THIRTY-THREE

7.40 am read Mercy's phone. *No service.*

Yawning, Mercy rolled onto her back and stretched. The van felt like a sweat lodge. From outside she could hear the sounds of the other caravanners packing up, readying to race each other for the next camp.

This was the seventh morning Mercy had woken up on this narrow, velour-covered foam mattress, box of ashes watching over her as she slept. How many more would there be? She was only four hundred and twenty kilometres from Darwin. So far, the biggest stretch she had driven in one day had been just over five hundred kilometres, from Glendambo to Marla on the third day. If she got up and started driving soon, it was entirely possible to be in Darwin by dinner time. Provided nothing important fell off the van, Mercy thought, remembering the sagging bumper.

Wasabi snuffled, stretching out along her leg. Mercy had slept without the cat throw. Mosquito bites itched around her ankles and knees. Absent-mindedly she dug one heel into the other ankle, scratching. Her sunburned thighs were peeling and the scab on her knee was starting to itch, too.

What was between here and Darwin? Nitmiluk, she knew. Spectacular, picturesque gorges carved through sandstone cliffs by the Katherine River. Another iconic, world-famous piece of Australia. She couldn't take Wasabi into the national park but there would be places she could go, lookouts and swimming holes. There would be roads that took her to the feet of the dramatic sandstone escarpments. What else? She decided she would pick up a tourist brochure in town.

Humming to herself, she climbed out of the van and visited the amenities block to wash up. When she returned, Andy was standing in the shade by her van. Her heart tripped against her ribs.

'So listen,' Andy said, 'I don't know about you, but I could do with a breakfast that wasn't campervan toast.'

'I *miss* toast,' Mercy told him. 'I only have a saucepan. It's a bit hard to cook toast in that.'

'All right then. I need something other than toast, you need toast. It's only an hour to Katherine. Would you be up for a wee convoy?'

'A breakfast convoy?'

'Aye. The best kind.'

Mercy reminded him that an hour for him was an hour and a half for her.

'I've factored that in.' He patted his flat belly. 'Already had a bowl of cereal for the road.'

Mercy smiled. 'Okay. It's a date.'

'A breakfast date?'

'The best kind.'

Mercy pulled onto the highway at eight thirty am. *No service.* She tossed her phone into the door pocket.

The heat was stupendous. The sun was a white hot ball in a flawless sky, roasting the bitumen a molten silver. Mercy rolled the windows up, trying to keep out some of the heat, only to roll them down again a few minutes later, desperate for a breeze. Sweat slicked her spine and the backs of her thighs, turning the seat cloth into a swamp. Eventually she settled for the windows halfway.

The dog sat up on the seat, tongue hanging out in a long pink ribbon. After a while he retired to the deeper shade in the back. Mercy thought of the box of ashes under the bed; poor Jenny Cleggett, flaming hot once again.

Andy was driving ahead; she could just see his van further up on the highway, a white speck in the heat haze. She thought of him sitting comfortably in the air conditioning, man-bun dust free, snug white T-shirt.

Ninety minutes later, the highway split into a dual lane. More traffic appeared. Warning signs bristled up on the roadside: alcohol prohibitions, quarantine restrictions, flood threat levels.

WELCOME TO KATHERINE.

DARWIN 320

Mercy's phone began to ping.

❧

A truck passed on Mercy's right and slipped in front of her, obscuring Andy's camper.

She glanced down at her phone, buzzing like an angry insect. She looked up but she still couldn't see Andy. It had not occurred to them to pre-arrange a meeting location; they had both just assumed 'Katherine' was accurate enough. But Katherine turned out to be a small metropolis, with branching-off streets, clusters of industrial stores and cars everywhere. Vehicles boxed Mercy in on all sides; the traffic slowed. Her phone was almost vibrating itself right out of the door pocket.

Mercy could feel her pulse ticking. In front of her, brake lights glowed as traffic came to a halt. At a standstill, with hot exhaust-filled air coming in through the window, Mercy picked up her phone.

Twelve voicemails.

Nine unread emails.

Thirty-six messages from Eugene.

Frowning, Mercy opened her voicemails. Setting the phone on her lap, she switched it to speaker as the traffic moved off and she craned forward, looking for Andy.

'Mercy, it's Eugene. Please call me right now, it's urgent.'

'Mercy, I'm getting worried. Legal said they can't get hold of you either.'

'Mercy, you need to call me immediately. They've moved up the date of the inquest. It's Monday. As in, *this coming Monday.*'

Mercy slammed on the brakes. The phone shot from her lap and clattered into the footwell. Behind her a horn blared angrily.

'Oh god,' Mercy said.

Yanking the wheel, she lurched into a parking space. The engine stalled as she lifted her feet from the pedals, scrambling for her phone, knocking her forehead against the steering column.

She listened to the rest of the voicemails, all from Legal. She clicked through to her emails, eyes scanning frantically. She read Eugene's increasingly hysterical text messages, ending with:

MERCY. INQUEST MONDAY 28 OCT. CALL ME NOW.

Mercy glared at the date on her phone but it didn't change. Yes, today was Thursday 24th October. The coronial inquest into the death of Tamara Lee Spencer wasn't in two weeks, like she had thought all along.

It was in three days.

CHAPTER THIRTY-FOUR

Traffic trundled past. Mercy's hands shook as she swiped through to Eugene's number.

He answered on the second ring. He was mad as hell. 'Where the fuck are you?'

'Katherine,' she answered.

'I'm looking at a map.' She heard the swish of paper that confirmed he was indeed looking at an actual physical map, like the old man he was. 'Okay, that's at the top, right? Near Darwin? Can you get to Darwin?'

'Have they really moved up the inquest?' She knew the answer; she'd seen the emailed confirmation from the solicitor.

'Yes. To Monday.'

'Can they even *do* that? That date's been fixed for months—'

'Looks like it. Something about a surgery the coroner needs to have. Doesn't matter. All the submissions were already prepared weeks ago, everyone's briefed and evidently no one batted an eyelid that the key fucking witness had gone AWOL in the fucking outback, Mercy.'

Mercy had never heard Eugene—kindly, docile, unflappable, ED senior consultant Eugene—say *fuck* so many times in one sentence. What could she do? Legal bureaucracy was a machine that churned as unstoppably as a steam engine. Despite anyone's agoraphobic tendencies, it would roll inexorably forward.

The inquest into the death of Tamara Lee Spencer was not in two more weeks. Mercy did not have two weeks to collect herself, to recover from the burning down of her house, to atone.

She had three days.

And she was nearly three thousand kilometres away.

Cold panic rushed in. Her throat tightened and she couldn't breathe. Heaving down the window, she gasped the hot air.

Eugene was still talking; she could hear the hurried clicks of a keyboard. 'There's a flight leaving Darwin at five this afternoon. What's the time now …? Ten … okay, that's seven hours away. How soon can you get to Darwin? It doesn't look that far on the map. You can get there in time, right? I'll book you this flight now. The dog can go on it, too. Mercy?'

Mercy gazed into the traffic. She'd lost Andy entirely. They had not exchanged numbers—why would they? Things were entirely too casual, too road-tripping, too *catch you later up the track* for that. Her only option might be to cruise around the muggy streets of Katherine until she found him.

'Mercy?'

Maybe three days was plenty of time. She could fly out tomorrow, or even the next day. She could find Andy and have breakfast, and then drive to Darwin in an orderly fashion, calmly, feeling collected, grounded, and with time to spare.

Except she couldn't. Mercy knew that. Three days was nothing when two of them were a weekend, devoid of office hours. She needed to meet with the solicitors. She needed to prepare. Her house had burned down and so had everything in it: she needed to buy court shoes, make up and clean clothes—she couldn't show up to coroner's court and say, *I did everything I could to save this woman's life* in too-large boots, a sweat-stained I ♥ SYDNEY T-shirt and cut-off denim shorts from the Coober Pedy op shop. And, it went without saying, she required the skills of a qualified hairdresser.

Mercy had to get to Darwin today, and she had to get on that plane. And to make it in time for a five pm flight, she had to leave now.

'Book the flight,' she said to Eugene. 'I'll make it.'

She didn't wait to hear Eugene's response. Dropping the phone on the seat, she started the van, knocked it into reverse and pulled back onto the street.

When she caught her breath, she whispered, 'Bye, Andy.'

Then she drove through Katherine and out the other side. As she raced over the bridge, the deep bed of the Katherine River was far below; for Mercy now there would be no sandstone escarpments, no beautiful waterholes and hidden rock pools. Her trip was over. Pedal pressed to the floor, she headed north because she had no other choice.

CHAPTER THIRTY-FIVE

Mercy drove for twenty minutes before she realised she could not keep driving like this.

Trembling, bowels in a knot, she crouched over the wheel as if clinging to the handlebars of a motorbike. The van rattled and skipped, burped and wobbled. She needed to stop and fortify herself. Having missed breakfast—not even a cup of coffee—she needed to eat something, drink something.

You have time, she told herself. *It's going to be okay.* Legal obviously weren't falling over themselves with angst—they'd moved up the inquest without her—so she shouldn't be worried either, right? She still had six and a half hours until her flight, and only about four hours of driving. Better to take a few minutes and be calmer, thinking more clearly, than frazzled and heat-stroked and upside-down in a ditch.

So Mercy pulled over. On a nondescript piece of highway she found a narrow track leading off into the bush and pulled in a short way. Surrounded by a copse of small, toothpick-like gums and watched over by the burning sun, she parked in the dappled shade and took deep breaths. She checked her phone but she'd lost service again. Eugene would have booked the flight for her; the thought of him dropping hundreds of dollars on her and being unable to pay him back right away set her teeth on edge. Eugene to the rescue. Eugene, the sensible one, the sane one, the rational one whose father hadn't left when he was eight and whose mother hadn't treated him like a mirror to reflect only her own grandeur and then gone ahead and died when that mirror had the audacity to finally turn away. Eugene, who even managed to make leaving his wife of six years for a hipster male barista seem like a sensible thing to do.

It was too hot for a hot drink but Mercy needed to be alert. Properly alert, not anxiety alert, so she heated a cup of water, scooped in a half-teaspoon of coffee, then set it aside to cool while she chewed a muesli bar. She ate standing outside the van in the spotted shade. Insects whirred in the bush around her, singing with heat. Every now and then a vehicle sped past on the highway. Wasabi sniffed about, perfectly unhurried, while Mercy's jaw worked fiercely as she chewed. She swallowed her lukewarm drink in three gulps.

Ten minutes passed. Fifteen. She gave a sharp whistle and the dog came running and, in a slam of doors and belch of exhaust smoke, they were back on the road.

As Mercy rushed up the highway, an old sense of powerlessness came over her. It was the irrefutable knowledge of fact: that no matter what she did, certain things could never be changed. Time, for instance—it moved the way it did regardless of what Mercy wanted to savour, or flee. No matter how much she coaxed the accelerator now, pushing the Hijet up the Stuart Highway, the clock ticked as it always had. It did not care about her plight, her need for time to *please slow down.*

And genetics—that she was born the sole child of Loretta Blain was a biological fact she could never escape.

Grief had come to Mercy in an erratic way when her mother died. It came late, of course—between the confusing, heart-breaking logistics of Eugene leaving and the bureaucratic and public shock of Tamara's death, Mercy had had to close the door to grief over her mother and wait for it to pound the door down when it could no longer be denied. Because it would, that much she had known—and it did. In life, Loretta Blain would not endure long any wane in Mercy's attention, and nor would she in death.

Beneath her seat the engine was starting to whine. Mercy flexed her ankle, easing up on the accelerator. She glanced at the temperature gauge but the needle still hovered over *cool.*

The grief had come between panic attacks. Sickening, angry, ugly grief. Grief that caused Mercy to throw coffee mugs against her kitchen wall and leave the shards on the floor for days. Grief that caused her to sit on the couch and stare at the wall, dry-eyed and parch-mouthed, unable to move. Grief that had slithered into her chest cavity like a slug, trails of slime up and down her limbs, and gorged itself on her heart until Mercy was nothing but flat, grey nothingness.

The van shook with a sudden convulsion. Wasabi lifted his head and Mercy sat back in her seat, briefly lifting her hands from the juddering steering wheel. The van smoothed out, returning to its normal hum.

Mercy drove on.

'Mercy?——you hear me?'

'I can hear you, Eugene. But I've only got—' she took the phone away from her ear and checked the screen, setting the van into a swerve '—one bar of service.' She grabbed the wheel more tightly.

'——much longer?'

'What was that?'

'Are you——sport——junction?'

'Sport *what*? Eugene, sorry, I can't hear you.'

The phone beeped. Eugene disappeared.

An hour and a half after leaving Katherine, the highway was rolling up and down slow, sweeping hills, curving back and forth around long bends. Fuzzy clouds sat low in the sky; the humidity continued to soar.

The van was halfway up a long incline when it started to shake. Mercy backed off the accelerator again, but the engine coughed and rattled.

Mercy frowned, and said, 'Oh—?' before the Hijet wheezed like a choking animal, the wheel shook in her hands with the violence of an earthquake, and there was a tremendous, bone-shattering *BANG*.

And then silence. The van slowed, moving without sound. All she could hear was the breeze against her ears and the tyres rolling over the bitumen. Terrified, Mercy tugged on the wheel, crunching off the road and coming to a halt on the shoulder.

She was two hundred kilometres from Darwin. Dead silence filled the van. Smoke lifted, drifting lazily in the hot, breezeless air.

CHAPTER THIRTY-SIX

Stunned, Mercy sat in the driver's seat of her silent van, watching curls of blue smoke drift past the windscreen.

Then she jumped. Kicking open the door, she grabbed Wasabi and was running away from the van, sprinting into the vegetation. After crashing through the treeline, she spun on her heel, leaves crackling underfoot, looked back at the van and waited for it to burst into flames.

A last puff of smoke dissolved, and then there was nothing. The van sat on the edge of the road. Not on fire. Not even a spark. It just sat there quietly in the baking heat, red dust covering its hand-painted flowers and obscuring *Home is wherever you ARE*.

Mercy was having an out-of-body experience. Perhaps she was dreaming. Her consciousness was floating up, up, high up above her head and then it drifted around in a circle up there above the van, above the highway, above the sparse, endless scrub going *Ha ha ha, would you look at this mess?!*

And then—THUMP—Mercy was back to earth. Back in her body, Mercy bent down, placed Wasabi on the ground, brought her hands to her face and, slowly, her eyes and mouth opened. Wider and wider, inch by inch, until her jaw hurt and her eyeballs stung in the swampy heat.

She gaped down at Wasabi. He looked up at her, panting. She gaped at the van. It ticked quietly. Insects in the bush around her shrieked.

'Oh,' Mercy said. 'God.'

Gingerly, tentatively, she inched towards the van. She tiptoed, as if the stalled Hijet was a sleeping dragon. She sniffed the air for petrol fumes. She waited long agonising minutes, but the van just sat there on the side of the highway, not catching on fire.

The driver's door wouldn't open, but Mercy wasn't willing to thump her hip into it in case the whole thing exploded, so she crept to the passenger side, opened the door and clambered across the seats. Her hands shook dreadfully as she gripped the key in the ignition. Closing her eyes and holding her breath, she turned the key.

A single click, then nothing.

She tried again. Click. Silence.

And again.

It wasn't out of petrol; she had filled the tank from the jerry can when she had stopped just out of Katherine. But mechanically, it could be anything else and she wouldn't know how to fix it. It didn't matter whether it was a simple, easily remedied technical fault or something catastrophic—there was nothing she could do. Nothing she knew *how* to do.

'Oh *shit*,' she yelped. 'Oh Christ, no!'

It was almost noon. She had just over five hours left.

Now Mercy panicked.

Never leave your vehicle.

Wasn't that one of the fundamental rules of being stranded in the outback? Mercy wondered as her anxious footsteps crunched along the highway shoulder. *Always stay with your vehicle.* Like in a horror movie—never say, 'I'll be right back.' The viewer just knows that the character who says 'I'll be right back' is about to meet the wrong end of a long knife. Repeatedly.

Wasabi trotted along beside her, zigzagging about on the end of his lead, sniffing the ground, lifting his short leg over tufts of weed. Having a grand old time, blissfully oblivious to their predicament. Mercy tried to draw some strength and calm from his oblivion, but she was failing. Her entire body was quivering, as if it was held together not by bones and sinew but by cotton and string.

She turned around to look back at the van, stalled halfway down the hill. The highway was a silver cut in a shroud of green; the van was a sad dot of dusty metal. She hadn't walked far, only a hundred metres or so; she was heading towards the top of this long rise, hoping that when she reached the crest she would see a town on the other side. Or a petrol station. Or even just a bar of phone service.

Besides, she tried to tell herself, she wasn't *stranded* in the outback. Not technically. Stranded in the outback would be one's vehicle shitting itself in the middle of a desert. Here she was, at the side of one of the country's major highways. She wasn't going to perish alone, slowly dehydrating, eroding into a skeleton and getting covered by the dusts of time.

No. On this highway, vehicles zoomed past every few minutes. There was plenty of civilisation here. Mercy was going to be *fine*.

The problem was, none of those vehicles were stopping. And compounding that, Mercy didn't *want* any of them to stop. Because that was another fundamental lesson from a horror movie, wasn't it? Just when you think the character, filled with relief and gratitude, is about to be rescued by a kind stranger, the kind stranger turns out to have a shotgun under their seat and a penchant for making handbags out of human skin.

Which, she reminded herself, was the exact reason she had fled the rest area outside Elliot. Strident bars from 'Stairway To Heaven' wailed into her mind.

Down the bottom of the hill, a fuel tanker glimmered into view, the long white barrels of its trailers gleaming in the sun. A truck driver whose salary was paid by a major fuel franchise would surely be trustworthy, wouldn't they? Mercy watched the truck approach, and felt her hand lift meekly. She thought of her five pm flight and lifted her hand higher. The truck barrelled closer and closer, hauling up the hill, engine roaring. Mercy waved her arm.

The truck roared past in a shower of grit and diesel fumes. Hot air blasted her body. The driver gave her a friendly wave.

'Thanks, jerk,' Mercy cried at the truck's retreating trailer.

She checked her phone again. Still no service. It was just on noon. She had five hours before she had to be on that plane.

So, trucks were a lost cause. The only trucks Mercy would have been comfortable flagging down were the big, shiny corporate ones—yet those were clearly the trucks that would not pick her up. The absurdly rich multinationals probably had a whole procedural manual's worth of policy about not picking up hitchhikers, broken-down travellers or stranded women and sausage dogs, no matter how sweaty and frantic they appeared.

No trucks then. No sedans, because they slipped past without even looking at her, giving off an *in your dreams* vibe. Grey nomads in their four-wheel drives and caravans slowed enough to stare, and sometimes the wives gave a sympathetic little smile, but none of them stopped. And definitely no battered utes with huge wheels and pig-dog cages on the back—those, Mercy hid from by dashing into the bush.

Another half-hour passed. Forty-five minutes. The sun was an inferno and the air pulsed with heat. Mercy crouched in the shade of the Hijet and tried to conserve water by not crying.

Just before one pm, Mercy heard an engine approach, the sound of it slowing down. Peering around the side of the van, readying herself to hide or signal for help or curse at the vehicle's retreating form, she instead jumped to her feet and waved.

The silver LandCruiser and Jayco Starcraft pulled off the road and came to a stop, idling behind the Hijet. The driver's door opened and Bert called out, 'Got yourself in a bit of a jam, did you, love?'

Mercy had never been so happy to see a shirt with so many pockets.

CHAPTER THIRTY-SEVEN

Bert stepped out of his four-wheel drive and strode over. 'Want me to take a look?'

'Could you?' Mercy said gratefully. 'I've got to be at the airport at five to catch a flight.'

Bert glanced at his watch. 'Crikey, love, you're cutting it a bit fine.'

'Well, earlier I wasn't … but, yes, now I am.'

'Did it overheat?' Bert ran a hand over the front of the van, squatted down to peer underneath.

'I don't know.' Mercy chewed her lip as Bert moved to inspect the inside of the van, studying the dashboard. 'The temperature gauge didn't seem to think so.'

'That's because the gauge is cactus.'

'It's a what?'

'The temperature gauge.' Bert tapped the dial. 'It's stuffed. The needle's stuck on cold, see?'

Mercy moved closer and looked. She said, 'Oh.' She put her head in her hands and tugged on the remaining tufts of her hair.

'Never mind, dear.' Bert's wife, Jan, came alongside Mercy and patted her back.

Deftly, Bert flipped up the seats and the top of the engine appeared. Swells of metal, tangles of wire and hose. Mercy peered around Bert's crouching form, hoping she might be able to identify something and say, *There! Look, that's come off and simply needs to be reattached!*

After a few minutes of poking, prodding and wriggling, Bert made a noise and retreated from the van, shaking his head. Mercy was almost waiting for him to produce an oily rag from his belt and start wiping his hands.

'You've got a split radiator hose,' he said. 'Real nasty—the hose is busted right open. What happened before it stopped?'

'Well,' Mercy said, 'it shook a bit, and made a funny noise, and then it just—' she swallowed a tightening in her throat '—stopped.'

'Did it go bang?'

'Bang?'

'Yeah. Boom. Like a gunshot.'

Mercy nodded. 'Yes. Now that you mention it. It did go bang.'

Bert's face fell.

'What is it, dear?' Jan said. 'Can we call someone to fix it?'

'I'm afraid not.' Bert turned to Mercy and said gravely, 'I think it's cooked.'

'Cooked?' Mercy repeated, uncomprehending. 'Can it be … uncooked? Because it's one twenty, and I have to be at the airport by five.'

Bert and Jan exchanged a look.

'I'm sorry,' Mercy was rambling now. 'I lied, the other night at happy hour. I don't work for the tax department. I'm a doctor—an obstetrician, to be precise—and I've got to be in Adelaide on Monday. I have … well, I have to attend an inquest.' Tears welled in her eyes. 'I thought I had two more weeks but I don't, and …' She put her head in her hands. 'I really, really have to get *home*.' The last word came out a sob.

'Oh, you poor dear.' Jan continued to rub her back. Wasabi licked her ankle.

Mercy looked up at Bert, the man with all the pockets. She remembered his brimming first aid kit; she remembered applying butterfly strips to Andy's bloodied face. *Andy.* Her heart gave a kick. Would he be back in Katherine, thinking she had stood him up? Would he be worried? Beginning with dashing across the street from Eugene's house that morning eight days ago, it seemed she was making a habit of running off on men who were being helpful to her. Or at least trying to.

Mercy took a deep breath. 'You said it has a split radiator hose?'

'Yes.'

'Okay. I can get another one from a service station, right?'

Bert shook his head. 'It's not just the radiator hose. Your oil looks like iced coffee—there's water in it. The head's cracked.'

'Oh dear,' Jan said.

Mercy looked between then. 'So it needs new oil? And a new head?'

'I'm real sorry, love,' Bert said gently. 'The engine's dead. As in locked up. As in pistons jammed into the block never to come out again. As in,' he looked at her sadly and gestured to the van, 'what you've got here is nothing but a boat anchor.'

Mercy wanted Bert to tell it to her straight. She needed to hear the correct, unmistakeable words.

'Bert, is the van dead?'

'Yes, love. The van is dead.'

Jan continued to pat Mercy's back. Pat, pat, pat.

The sun beat down. It was one thirty.

'You got your ears on there, Pete?'

Bert toggled the radio in a squelch of static. The Land-Cruiser was an air-conditioned oasis. Jan had produced two ice-cold apple juice boxes from a refrigerator and Mercy sat in the back seat, sipping from her straw, trying to ignore how much of a child she felt. Wasabi was sitting at her feet, panting, filling the car with his doggy breath.

'Pete, comeback, Pete,' Bert tried again.

Another burst of empty static.

'He wouldn't have left the vehicle, would he?' Jan murmured to her husband. Bert shook his head.

And then a man's voice crackled over the radio: 'Loud and clear, Bert. Go ahead.'

Bert's whole body beamed with happiness, but his voice was perfunctory as an airline pilot. 'We got a situation here, Pete. Got a lady stranded on the side of the highway. Vehicle situation dire. Repeat, dire. Are you still at Emerald Springs? Over.'

There was a pause, then, 'Affirmative. Current location Emerald Springs. Over.'

'Roger that. Are you still heading up to Darwin today?'

'That's an affirmative.'

'Request you have seat for one extra soul?'

A long pause ensued. Mercy held her breath. The whole LandCruiser held its breath.

'Affirmative.'

Jan exhaled and turned to Mercy with a smile. 'There, now. See? We'll have you there in no time.'

Mercy looked at her phone. One forty.

Bert put his hand on the gear shift.

Mercy said, 'Wait!'

Startled, Bert turned to her. The engine idled.

'There's something I need from the van.'

Without waiting for a reply, Mercy slid out of the car. She walked to the poor dead Hijet, a corpse on the gravel. She opened the back and smelled the musty, dusty inside. The scent of the last seven days. Clambering in, she lifted the mattress and drew out the box of ashes. *Jenny Cleggett.* Mercy ran her hand over the box. Looking up, out through the windscreen, she remembered the huntsman spider that had appeared on the glass as she left Crystal Brook. The spider had never reappeared—it must have been outside the glass after all. Although she was thankful not to have seen it again, that spider had determined that Mercy had headed north, instead of returning to Adelaide. For almost three thousand kilometres, this little van had carried her across the country, trying its best to get her to *the other side.*

Running her fingertips over the creased, dusty cardboard, she smiled.

For the last time, she climbed out of the Daihatsu Hijet. She closed the door, her hand lingering on the warm metal.

Home is wherever you ARE.

Mercy said, 'Thank you.'

Tucking the box of ashes under her arm, she turned and walked away.

CHAPTER THIRTY-EIGHT

Bert and Jan weren't going as far as Darwin today. Instead, Bert had plans to disappear 'off the beaten track' for a week or four, maybe head out to Kakadu or Arnhem Land. Maybe over the border into Queensland.

'Otherwise we'd be happy to take you to the airport,' Bert said. 'But lucky for you, Pete and Jules are headed that way! Ho ho,' he said, laughing, 'you're in for a real treat with those two!'

'Oh, Bert, stop it,' Jan said, playfully swatting her husband's arm. 'You'll scare the poor girl.'

Mercy attempted to make reassuring noises. She would have liked to set Wasabi in her lap, but she didn't want to put the dog on Bert and Jan's pristine seats. Instead she clutched her hessian shopping bag, the dank scent of her own clothes rising from within it. Surreptitiously she dug out her deodorant and tried to roll some on without lifting her arms.

The LandCruiser sped along, air-conditioner purring, nobody having to shout to be heard over the wind. Even travelling at a hundred and ten, dragging a caravan, the engine did not die in a smoking ruin. When they arrived at the roadhouse, Mercy's face was cool, dry and dust free. If the Hijet had held out for another ten kilometres, Mercy would have at least made it to Emerald Springs: a roadhouse, truck stop and leafy camping area on the side of the highway.

Bert parked in a truck bay. Leaving the engine idling, he turned in his seat.

'Well, love, this is where we leave you.' He pointed to the roadhouse. 'That's Pete and Jules waiting up there. See?' He waved at someone.

Mercy's chest began to tighten. She was about to get into a car with a pair of complete strangers, a mythical couple who existed only in tales of outrageous happy hours. Bert had shown no hesitation in suggesting Mercy catch a lift with the pair of grey nomads to Darwin. The question wasn't so much could she trust this Pete and Jules, but did she trust Bert?

He was turned towards her, one elbow propped on the centre console, other hand resting on the steering wheel. The epaulette on his shoulder bent up in a loop. He was smiling. She had known him since that first night in Crystal Brook. He was *livin' the dream*.

'Thank you both so much,' Mercy said.

Jan reached back and took Mercy's hand, giving it a tender squeeze. 'You take care, dear. Good luck with whatever it is you need to do.'

Mercy squeezed Jan's hand, picked up her bag, her dog and her box of cremated remains, and hopped out of the car.

Wasabi trotted along beside her. Her footsteps crunched across the gravel. She heard the sound of Bert and Jan pulling onto the highway; a horn tooted. She turned and watched them go, waving.

Parked up ahead, alongside the roadhouse, was an enormous Dodge Ram. Jet black paint, gleaming chrome and Mafia-tinted windows. Radio aerials bristling like a police car. Attached at its rear was a caravan made of checker-plate steel. Standing out the front of the vehicle was a smallish, grey-haired man and a tall, willowy woman. Mercy looked from side to side, expecting the real Pete and Jules to show up any minute, decked out head to toe in camo print.

Nervously, Mercy approached.

'Are you …' She cast about again. 'Are you Pete and Jules? I'm Mercy Blain. Bert called you just now on the radio, about Darwin …'

Stepping forward, the man extended his hand. 'Peter Boothey. A pleasure to meet you. Bert indicated you had some trouble with your vehicle. I'm sorry to hear it. How stressful, when you have a deadline to meet at the airport.'

Mercy blinked, shaking his tiny, cool hand. The man was a few inches shorter than her and his hair was combed neatly from one side of his head to the other. His short-sleeved, button-down shirt was tucked into belted plaid shorts. Mercy wasn't sure what she was expecting Pete to look like, but, coupled with the giant Dodge Ram, it wasn't … *this*. Courtly and unassuming, he almost needed a British accent and a monocle.

'Allow me to introduce my wife, Julie. Goodness, it's almost two o'clock, we must be pressing on. Your flight is at five, yes? Okay. Well, let's be timely. Here, let me pack that in the back for you.'

He made to take the box from Mercy but she tightened her grip on the cardboard. 'Thank you, but there's no need. I'll keep it with me.'

'Nonsense,' he said. 'I'll stow it safely with our canned goods.'

'I'll just nurse it.'

A brief yet exceedingly polite tug-of-war ensued, Mercy smiling, Pete smiling, box of cremated remains shuttling between them, until Pete stepped back. 'As you wish,' he conceded with a nod of his head.

Mercy was about to shake Jules's hand when the woman leaned towards Mercy in a waft of frankincense, touched her cheek to Mercy's and squeezed her shoulders. She said nothing, just smiled, took Mercy's hessian bag and turned towards the vehicle, long purple skirt billowing out behind her.

Mercy's insides felt sloppy as she climbed into the Dodge. The dark window tint gave the interior of the vehicle a greenish hue. Mercy's sweaty thighs squeaked across black leather seats. Wasabi put his paws up but she pushed him down into the footwell, thinking of dog hairs and red dirt across the leather. She clutched Jenny Cleggett in her lap.

On the dashboard, all manner of handsets hung from loops of curled cord, digital displays cycled radio frequencies, touchscreens glowed with maps. Mercy wanted to ask how it was possible to operate so many radios at once, but then she realised one of those radios had saved her stranded arse.

So she said, 'I like all your radios.'

Jules waved a hand at the dashboard but said nothing.

'And your car is lovely.'

'It gets us from A to B,' said Pete, pressing the start button. Mercy couldn't hear the engine, but she could feel the sudden subtle vibration; the dash lit up like a cockpit.

'Did you know there used to be an open speed limit in the Northern Territory?' asked Pete as he navigated the Dodge onto the highway, his seat racked in close to the wheel so he could peer through the windscreen.

'Anything would have been faster than my poor van,' Mercy said.

'Pity,' Pete said. 'We could have had you at the airport in less than ninety minutes.' He was turning the wheel by shuffling it carefully through his hands. Mercy opened her mouth to laugh at his joke.

And then the Dodge rocketed forwards. Mercy fell back in her seat, spine flattening against the leather. Jenny Cleggett shunted into her guts.

In the front, Jules calmly popped the top on a tube of hand cream. Squeezing a dob into her palm, the car filled with the scent of roses.

No service.

Scenery blurred past silently, like a fast-forwarded movie screen on mute.

No service.

Although they were speeding along at an effortless 130— nearly double Mercy's top speed of the last seven days—the minutes crawled by, drawn out like taffy.

No service.

'Come on,' Mercy muttered at her phone.

In the twenty minutes they had been speeding up the highway, Mercy had learned Pete and Jules had two sons and three grandchildren. Both sons worked in finance; both were happily married. Pete was retired now, but he, too, had worked in finance. Mercy waited for the punchline, the upsurge of laughter to reveal their true party-animal selves, but nothing came. After asking Mercy a few polite questions, for which she breathed deeply and answered with the truth (separated; no kids; an obstetrician, not presently practising), they seemed perfectly satisfied to let her be. Jules produced a set of knitting needles and quietly clacked; Pete drove, hands at ten-and-two, occasionally touching a screen, tapping a button or silencing a radio.

And Mercy stared down at her phone, willing it into service.

Eighty kilometres out of Darwin, it happened. Her phone lit up, pinging and buzzing. One bar of service: in came text messages from Eugene. Two bars: voicemail.

Three bars: Mercy opened a web browser.

CHAPTER THIRTY-NINE

White Pages displayed twenty-eight listings in South Australia for *Cleggett*. Closing her eyes, Mercy recalled the moment she had dashed from Eugene's house and across the street, the heady scent of perfume trailing after her, Jose's words ringing in her ears: *she is her own problem.* She remembered the nauseating, blinding soup of confusion and panic as she had tried to listen to the old man's sales spiel about the van; she remembered charred roof frames stabbing the sky. Opening her eyes, she typed the name of Eugene's street into the search bar, but there were zero results. No listings for a Cleggett on Eugene's street. She tried Eugene's suburb but that also yielded nothing. Eventually, she opened the White Pages search to Cleggetts in the greater Adelaide region (nine) and started dialling.

'Hello,' Mercy said, when the first call was answered. 'This might seem strange, but I'm looking for an older gentleman who lives in North Adelaide, a retired mechanic, who recently sold me a Daihatsu Hijet … No? Don't know anyone by that description? What about the name Jenny Cleggett, do you know anyone by that name—' Glancing at the front seats, Mercy lowered her voice, turning her face towards the window '—possibly deceased? Oh. Okay, well, sorry to bother you. Thank you for your ti—'

They hung up.

'Everything okay?' Pete asked. 'Can we get you anything? Might you need to stop and use the facilities at all?'

Now that he mentioned it, Mercy did, but she steeled herself and declined. It was just before three pm. At this rate, Mercy was going to make it to the airport on time. There was no way she would ask them to stop.

The next two calls went to voicemail. The fourth and fifth went unanswered, ringing for an eternity before finally going dead. The next two calls were answered, and Mercy repeated her request to the same end. No old mechanic named Cleggett, no dead Jenny.

She dialled the last number. It rang and rang.

'Shit,' she muttered. She was about to hang up and google *Can I take human cremains on a plane*, when the line clicked.

A shuffling noise, and then, quietly, 'Hello?'

'Hello?' said Mercy.

'Hello?' The man cleared his throat, then demanded, 'Who is it?'

Mercy's free hand tightened around the cardboard box. 'I'm looking for a man named Cleggett.' Repeating her spiel about the Hijet, she finished, 'Does that sound like anyone you know?'

'Of course it does,' said the man.

'It does?'

'Yes. It's me, you goose. Harry Cleggett. How'd you find me?'

Exhaling with relief, Mercy explained dialling all the Cleggetts in Adelaide.

'Oh, sorry,' Harry Cleggett said with a laugh. 'Forgot to tell the phone company I moved. Sadly, it's one of the reasons I had to sell her—this new place has a shed the size of a matchbox.' He muttered inaudibly and sighed. Then, more brightly, 'So—how's the old girl doing?'

Mercy wanted to laugh. She wanted to weep. What she ended up doing was somewhere in between, chuckling and wiping her leaking eyes, her breath coming in halting puffs that were neither happy nor sad. Jules's knitting needles paused, then resumed their tidy clicking.

'Mr Cleggett,' she managed to say. 'Is Jenny … your wife?'

'I don't mean Jenny. I mean the van. How's she doing?'

Mercy's last glimpse of the Hijet had been through the window of Bert's LandCruiser, her view swallowed up by the white box of his caravan as they had pulled onto the highway. The faithful old van, filled with her own sweat and tears, stalled on the side of the Stuart Highway, three thousand kilometres of dust caked to its flanks, bleeding out its milky oil into the gravel.

'I'm sorry,' Mercy said. 'It—*she* didn't quite make it.'

Another sigh. 'Ahh, well. How far'd you get? Please, I'd like to hear about it.'

So Mercy told him. Starting at Crystal Brook, she told him about the huntsman spider, the decision to keep going north. She detailed the trip across the desert, the roadtrains blasting past. When she described the muffler falling off on the way back from the waterhole, the old man hooted with laughter. She told him about driving into the tropics, the way the humidity crept in first as a hint, and then all at once, like opening an oven door.

'Sounds like you did all right,' Harry said when she was done. He sniffed, and the catch in his throat was back. 'I asked you to take her for a good trip, and you did.'

'I'm sorry to leave her on the side of the road,' Mercy said. 'I'll arrange for a tow truck or a car carrier. Or something.' She glanced at the time. Three ten pm.

'No.'

'No?'

'I want you to leave her there. What you've described sounds like an adventure. A fitting end for her. Don't worry, the cops will pick her up eventually, and she'll be taken to the impound, and one day, who knows? Maybe she'll be recycled into something brand new. She might end up in a Mercedes Benz, or a refrigerator, or a fancy new television. Anything.' Quiet came over the line for a few moments. 'That sounds like a fine end for a fine girl.'

Mercy looked out the window in time to catch a glimpse of a sign: Darwin 45. Her pulse fluttered.

'If you're sure …?'

'I'm sure.'

'Mr Cleggett?'

'Yes?'

'Who is this box of ashes?'

'Why, that's Jenny. Doesn't it say so on the box?'

'It does, sir, but what I mean is … who is she? And what shall I do with her? I mean, should I post her to you?' Mercy dug through her bag, looking for a pen. 'If you remind me what street number your house is, I can—'

'No.'

'No?'

'Don't put her in the mail. I don't want her back.'

Mercy's eyes slid to the box in her lap. With a whole new feeling of wariness, she considered the box of remains.

'Can I ask … why not?'

Now Harry Cleggett laughed. 'Do you think she'd want to be stuck in the post and end up back here, with this pissant shed, right back where she started? No!' He cackled so hard he stopped to cough. When he recovered, he went on. 'She's had the time of her life with you. She always wanted to go up the centre, but she never got to. She didn't travel so well, you see, when she was alive. Got terribly car sick. She was never able to stay in a vehicle too long. Even driving to the shops would upset her.' He sounded sad. 'But now? Well, she's got what she always wanted. A journey through the entire country.'

Mercy didn't know what to say.

'You're in Darwin?'

'Almost,' Mercy said. Paddocks had begun to appear, the wild scrubby green giving way to cleared blocks. The speed limit dropped to 110, and Pete veered left as the highway split, opening out into dual lanes. Water pipes and power lines flanked the highway. Civilisation was nigh. Leaning towards the front, Mercy asked, 'How far?'

'Thirty-five kays,' Pete answered. 'Half an hour, traffic willing.'

Jules smiled and kept knitting.

'Mercy,' Harry Cleggett said, suddenly serious, 'can you do me a favour?'

'Anything,' Mercy said. 'Except I can't take any more of your relatives on road trips, at least not in the next couple of weeks.'

Harry laughed again. 'Can you leave her there?'

'Where?' Mercy looked around the polished Dodge.

'In Darwin. Leave her there, somewhere nice. Like a park, or the beach. Oh, she did love the ocean. I bet the ocean up there is real nice and warm. Can you do that for an old man, Mercy? Can you ...' He stopped again.

Mercy waited.

'Can you please take my mother's ashes to the ocean?'

CHAPTER FORTY

Mother. *My mother's ashes.*

Mercy had been travelling across the country with someone's mother. All along she had assumed *Jenny Cleggett* must have been the man's wife. Other relatives or friends had come to mind: a sister, or maybe a lonesome cousin; at one stage Mercy had considered it could perhaps even be a beloved pet horse. But, driving along and pondering, always Mercy had returned to wife. It was the safest, most likely assumption. And given how easily the old mechanic had parted with the van and its cargo of cremains, Mercy had, deep down, assumed that, between the man and this Jenny Cleggett, no love had been lost.

But Jenny Cleggett was his mother. A woman who had wanted, and hoped, and despaired, and battled her own frustrations in this world in order to provide life for someone else. Did Harry love his mother? Was she kind to him, patient with him? Or did she yell at him, call him names? Did Harry Cleggett grieve the death of his mother in a raw, plain way? Or in the elaborate, tangled way Mercy did? After all, he *had* left her ashes inside the cabinet of a van he'd sold on the side of the road for fifteen hundred bucks.

Mercy looked at the clock. It was three forty. Her flight was at five thirty. The Dodge was hurtling along the highway, shuttling around the thickening traffic with ease. If they got to the airport in half an hour, that would give her almost ninety minutes to spare before her flight.

So she could detour to the beach first, couldn't she?

Until she checked her ticket and discovered that the dog had to be checked in at the freight terminal no less than ninety minutes before the flight.

Shit.

She thought she had uttered the curse in her head, but then Pete spoke up. 'Something the matter?'

Anxiety competed with embarrassment, and both competed with the terrible gnawing sensation of relying on someone else—strangers, no less—to provide everything she needed right now. It made her feel both small and weak, and bloated and burdensome, all at once. Biting the inside of her cheek, she was trying to decide where to begin when Pete went on.

'Forgive my overhearing, but it sounds like you've had somewhat the unwitting adventure.' He smiled over his shoulder. 'We grey nomads have been known to pack quite a lot, but I don't believe I've met anyone who has packed, how should I say ...'

'A dead relative?'

'Yes.' Pete gave a small laugh.

Mercy looked at the box in her lap, so much more banged-up and dusty than when she'd first found it. 'I'm sorry to have brought it in your car without telling you what it was.'

Between the front seats, Jules's slender hand appeared, gave a dismissive wave and disappeared again. Outside, a truck-sized depot of fast-food restaurants rolled by. Pete manoeuvred the Dodge around traffic, nipping in and out, and Mercy had forgotten they were actually towing a caravan.

'My mother died when I was just a boy,' Pete said, startling Mercy out of her mental counting of minutes.

'I'm sorry,' she said.

'My father married again, very quickly, because a man in the early sixties with three children and no wife is a man quite out of his depth indeed.' He flicked on the indicator to zip into a gap in the next lane. 'Our stepmother was a tremendous woman. Selfless, patient, kind-hearted—to be honest, I've never known how my father managed to make her agree to marry him, to take on his motherless children and raise them as her own. But she did. And do you know what my brothers and I did in return?'

Jules's hand reached out and squeezed Pete's forearm.

'We made her life quite unpleasant. We put mulberries in the washing machine, so all the laundry stained purple. We threw mud on the clean washing. We took her best church dresses and hid them under the chooks' nesting straw, down the bottom of the yard. We swapped the sugar for the salt, so one day she put salt in all the CWA ladies' tea. None of our pranks were terribly original, I'm afraid, but they were awful all the same. And this went on for *years*. But our stepmother never complained, never even mentioned it to our

father. Kept it all to herself. And we didn't even have the
decency to feel bad about it until we'd grown up and had
children of our own.'

Mercy imagined Peter Boothey as a child, muddied hands
throwing dirty globs on pristine white sheets. She saw the
pain and anger in his face. Then she saw her own coffee
mugs smashed against the wall, she saw herself sitting on
her couch for weeks, months—years. The unreturned calls;
the abandoned world. Flames licking the dark sky.

'Somehow,' Peter went on, 'Stepmother knew that we were
acting out our pain, so she simply endured it.' He paused for
a long moment. 'We've all done things we regret.'

Mercy saw Jules nod her head in silent agreement.

'Because, do you know what I think?' Now Pete sounded
quite chipper. 'Sometimes, pain is simply pain. It hurts, and
when it is felt in the moment, there's nothing can be done
but endurance.'

Mercy looked out the window. 'Be here now,' she said.
Wherever you *ARE*.

A red light approached and the vehicle rolled to a stop.
Traffic congested. Palm trees fanned a blue sky. It was
three fifty-five pm; she needed to check Wasabi in for the
flight *now*.

The airport was fifteen minutes away.

And she still had the box of a mother's remains on her lap.

CHAPTER FORTY-ONE

The heat was stupefying. Mercy crossed the blistering carpark and headed towards the freight terminal, clutching Wasabi and gasping like a fish. She couldn't get enough air. She felt like she was trying to breathe in an armpit. The thick smell of jet fuel; cicadas screaming, frogs shouting. Sunlight pelted onto water from a recent downpour lying everywhere and she was sweating from every single part of her body. Even her eyelids.

'It's going to be okay, Wasabi,' she said, voice shaking. The dog licked her chin.

There would be no convincing the airline that Wasabi needed to stay with her. She was trying desperately not to picture herself sitting alone, strapped into her seat awaiting take-off, while her little sausage dog was in a crate below, in the dark guts of the plane. Other than his brief jaunt into the bush at Alice Springs, it would be the furthest she had been from her dog for two years.

She stepped into the terminal and her sweat-slick skin
turned immediately frigid. Outside, her shorts and T-shirt
had seemed too much clothing; inside she felt naked. The
hot-cold flash felt exactly like the first sensations of panic.

Digging her fingertips into Wasabi's fur, Mercy
approached the counter. Pete and Jules were waiting for her
in the carpark. They would accept nothing less than taking
her and Jenny Cleggett to the beach. 'It's not far,' Pete had
promised, checking the map. 'Only a few minutes. And better you dipping your toes in the water than waiting at the
airport for an hour, isn't that right? Besides,' he added, 'you
wanted to get to the other side. You're not quite there, yet.'

'You're late,' the woman behind the counter said now,
tapping at a keyboard. The attendant was a smallish,
pinched-looking woman in her thirties, with hair gelled
into a bun so tight the skin around her eyes was strained.

'I know,' Mercy said. 'My car broke down. I had to—'

'Check-in for accompanied animals closes ninety minutes before a flight.' She pointed to the clock. 'That was
seven minutes ago.' There was not a single hair loose on the
woman's head at all, and Mercy self-consciously patted her
chopped curls. The humidity had sent what was left of them
into wild puffs.

'I'm sorry. Can you please …?' Mercy lifted her arms,
holding Wasabi forward like an offering.

The expression on the attendant's face was both conde-
scending and long-suffering. If Mercy had to guess, she
would say this woman adored how much power she had.
Mercy imagined her going home at night, perhaps to a
thin, nervous-looking boyfriend, and gloating over who
she had turned down, chastened or reduced to tears that

day. Airports were emotional places at the best of times, what with all those grief-filled farewells, separations or joyous reunions. Mercy could almost feel the bitterness seeping from this woman, resentment that she was stuck handling dogs and cats and oversized packages instead of being up there, at the main terminal, where all the real heart-rending happened.

Though Mercy wanted to snap or beg, she felt an old, practised calm come over her. When confronted with a desperate need, most people reached for anger, threats or emotional blackmail. But now Mercy felt her old tools dredging up, rusty and unused, and turned to the best one in her arsenal: empathy.

'I'm so sorry,' Mercy said. 'It sucks that I'm late. That must be really hard for you.'

The woman looked at Mercy warily.

Shuffling Wasabi onto her hip, Mercy leaned forward, putting one hand on the counter and stage-whispering, 'And you must deal with this *all day.*'

The woman waited.

'I bet you get all kinds of people. And you have to be nice to them. Even the cranky ones. And that must be very frustrating.'

The attendant continued to stare, although Mercy detected the smallest upwards shift in her brows.

'And besides, you're probably not paid enough, right?'

There was a beat, and then the woman said, 'Who is?'

'Lawyers. And politicians.'

That got a small laugh.

'I'm *really* sorry to be a pain. You must work very hard to stay so nice to people.'

The attendant gave a short sigh, glancing at her watch. 'Look, I can't—'

'Please.' At that moment, Mercy knew she wouldn't be above begging. If she had to get on her knees, she was quite certain she would. Maybe from there she could crawl onto the conveyer belt, disappear into the building and put Wasabi onto the plane herself.

'A random act of kindness,' Mercy said. 'That always gets likes.'

The woman glanced from side to side. She sighed again. She deliberated so hard Mercy restrained herself from grabbing the counter and wailing. Then, after a long, long time, her hands pecked at the keyboard. Labels shot out of a machine.

'All done,' she said. 'I'll take him through.'

Mercy lowered her face to Wasabi's silky fur, then handed him over.

By the time Mercy returned to the Dodge, tears were rolling down her cheeks. Her legs were quivering so much she thought she might pee right through her shorts.

'I don't think I can do this,' she said to Jules. 'I don't think I can leave him. I think I'll have to go get him.'

Jules gave her another frankincense-scented hug.

Mercy couldn't tear her eyes away from the freight terminal. Wasabi was in there, somewhere, his plump little body being packed into a crate. Would he be frightened? Would he be wondering where Mercy was? Would he think, after all he had done for his mistress, that she had abandoned him?

Mercy put her hands over her face. She was falling to pieces, and she couldn't believe it. She had come so far and now she was going to fall apart entirely.

But before she knew it, the Dodge was away and they were slipping down palm-lined streets. Pete kept up a steady stream of chatter about the dog, asking her when she had first got him, and what he liked to eat, and where he slept, and what tricks he knew. It wasn't to distract her, Mercy realised, it was to keep her connected to the dog. To help her understand that her companion hadn't disappeared, that her comfort—her ability to be comforted—had not left her forever.

'Imagine how happy he's going to be when you hop off the plane,' Pete said. 'That little tail will be waggling like a propeller!'

And that made Mercy think of landing in Adelaide, of getting off the plane, and it halted the narrow, throat-closing myopia of anxiety. It made her remember that *this too shall pass*.

Be here now, and know that whatever *now* is, is transient.

It took ten minutes to get from the airport to Nightcliff Beach. Skirting a peninsula was a winding drive lined with palms and frangipannis. Houses on stilts hid in shady frond canopies. Through mangroves lining one side of the road, Mercy spotted glimpses of blue, until the mangroves and palms opened up and fell away revealing a wide, flat, sparkling sea.

Once, several years ago, Mercy went to have her teeth cleaned and her regular dentist had been away. Mercy reclined on the chair under the hands of a small, ferocious woman, who had handled the sharp steel instruments with the ease and grace of a baton twirler. After she had ground away inside Mercy's mouth for forty-five minutes, Mercy had come away feeling nothing short of excavated. Her tongue couldn't stop probing the back of her lower incisors, feeling the deep, rough chasms that had never been there before. It had been unsettling, imagining the chunks of calculus that might have been sitting there all along, unbeknown to her, so smooth and familiar but underneath quietly rotting.

At the sight of the ocean, Mercy felt that sensation now—excavation. As though something long calcified inside her had just cleaved up and lifted away. The Arafura Sea stretched to the horizon in a flawless sheet of blue. No surf, rips or rocks marred the glittering sheet, no bruises of seaweed or deep holes. For as far as she could see, there was just calm, supreme, breath-taking blue.

Mercy had made it. She was here.

Mercy had made it to the other side.

Atop a low cliff was a small carpark, and Pete pulled the vehicle off the road.

'We'll wait here for you.'

Mercy shook her head. 'You've been so kind. I don't want to keep you any longer. I'd like to do this alone, if that's okay.'

'If you're sure?'

'I'm sure.'

Pete inclined his head.

Mercy double-checked nothing important had fallen from her bag; Pete took her phone off the charger. Then she tucked Harry Cleggett's mother under her arm, opened the door and slid out into the heat.

She was preparing to wave the couple off when Jules suddenly opened her door and stepped out.

In Jules's hand was an amber-coloured glass dropper bottle. She tucked it into Mercy's palm, closed her fingers around Mercy's hand, and squeezed.

'What is it?'

Jules gave a beatific smile.

The label was a sticker that read *Skullcap*. Nothing else. Mercy held the bottle up but the liquid inside was obscured by the dark glass.

And then Jules spoke the first words Mercy had heard from her for the entire two-hour journey.

'There's a difference between pain, you know, and suffering. The former is a fact to surrender to, the latter is a choice.' Jules gestured to the bottle. 'One dropperful, under the tongue. Sometimes we all need a little help for calm.' She winked.

Purple skirt fanning out behind her, Jules climbed back into the Dodge.

'Wait!' Mercy cried, stepping forward.

Jules rolled down her window. Cool air billowed out.

'There's something I have to ask.' Mercy hesitated. It seemed a ridiculous question, but the idea of letting them go without knowing felt impossible. 'For the last week, every time I've seen Bert he's mentioned you two, and I have to say, the picture he painted was ... well, to be honest, it was very different.'

Pete and Jules exchanged an amused look.

'Nothing impolite, mind you,' Mercy hastened to clarify. 'He just implied that the two of you were, well ...'

'Wild?' Pete said.

'Right.' Mercy laughed.

Jules's eyebrows quirked.

Pete seemed to consider it for a long time. Then he said, 'It's not just herbs for calm that Jules works with.'

Jules gave Mercy a wink.

And then the window rolled up. They waved, pulled out onto the street and were gone.

CHAPTER FORTY-TWO

Descending a concrete ramp, Mercy stepped onto the sand.

Other than a lone walker and a dog far ahead, the beach was deserted. Heat shimmered up. Mercy could feel her exposed skin roasting and sweating at the same time. Leaving her hessian bag on the dry sand, she walked towards the water's edge.

The sea was like a lake. Flat and unhurried. Ripples lapped against the damp sand. Mercy shuffled towards the water, letting it touch her toes. She gasped, but not from cold. The water was balmy and perfect. How was it that Bondi, the Gold Coast or Cottesloe claimed all of Australia's waterside glory? This beach was everything: creamy sand, clear waters, placid and warm.

Except for the occasional saltwater crocodile they coaxed out of the harbour, she thought, and the warning she'd passed on the foreshore for box jellyfish, which can kill within minutes. BETWEEN OCTOBER AND MAY, DO NOT ENTER THE WATER, the sign read. As the warm water washed up over Mercy's feet, she was very aware that it was late October. She examined the sea, looking for floating transparent blobs, dangerous wispy tentacles, but she could see only sand and ripples. She waded in a little further, letting the water wash up over her ankles. Invisible threats were all around her, she realised. She was surrounded by them in countless numbers; at any moment she could be brutally stung, her body lashed with welts.

But—she also might not. She also might feel nothing but the pleasure of warm saltwater and the sun on her bare neck. It's true that she could be reckless, thoughtless, and dive headlong into the water and all of its unseen harms— or she could be the opposite: timid, withdrawing and staying on the sand.

Or she could find somewhere in that great in-between, that place of nuance and clarity and balance. That place where she could do her best, do what she needed to do, and not let the fear of pain and hurt, all the infinite *what ifs*, crowd her mind until she could do nothing but stare longingly from the shore. Hidden away, watching the outside world from inside the walls.

The sky that had only twenty minutes ago been an unblemished sapphire was now knotting with swollen, greenish clouds. An onshore breeze had come up. If Mercy opened the ashes here, they would blow back onto the sand.

Scanning the water, she waded out further. Further still. The shallow sea bed barely sloped at all: no matter how far Mercy waded, the water stayed just above her ankles.

She glanced back at the shore. Where was Wasabi now? Was he crossing the hot tarmac in his dark crate? Was he waiting somewhere in a shed? Was he parked beneath the gaping belly of an aircraft?

With a final nervous scan of the water, Mercy opened the box. Lifting out the plastic bag, she dropped the box to the water, where it floated, butting against her shins. Stepping first one foot then the other into it, she pushed the box down onto the sandy floor. The bottom half of the cardboard darkened as saltwater seeped in, but she felt at least temporarily protected from the water's deadly flotsam.

Her hands were sticky on the plastic. As she unrolled the bag, a small puff of grey ash lifted up and disappeared. Mercy hesitated. It didn't feel right for her to put her hand inside; it was too intimate a thing, to touch the ground-up bones of Harry Cleggett's mother. But somehow, it didn't feel right to just *upend* the bag, either.

A strong breeze skittered across the water. In the space of minutes, clouds had boiled up in the sky. Mercy saw a flicker of lightning; a few beats later, thunder rolled. She thought back to that stormy night in Alice Springs, when she had fled the showgrounds at midnight, muffler hanging by a thread. As the thunder had cracked overhead, rattling the van, Mercy had cried out to her dead mother, *I'm so tired of never being good enough for you.*

Be a good girl. Make Mummy proud.

Turning away from the breeze, Mercy slowly tipped the bag. It would have to be good enough, she thought, that she had loved her mother. Because she was the only mother Mercy had, and Mercy was the only daughter Loretta Blain had. That was what Mercy had to give: eternal love. Forever now, there could be nothing else.

The ashes began to shift. Straightening the top of the bag into a chute, Mercy shook the bag, gently, and a grey stream began to sift into the water. It made the sound of rain. A silver cloud fanned across the surface, rippling and bobbing, and Mercy kept shaking the bag until it was clear the final clumps weren't going to shift without help.

'Okay, Jenny,' Mercy said, 'after all we've been through together, I can do this for you.'

Mercy dipped her hand into the bag: coarse grit, sharp pieces of bone. Scooping up the last handfuls, she flung the remains downwind. Bigger pieces hit the water in soft plops. Another clap of thunder boomed and, despite the heat, goose bumps lifted on Mercy's skin. When the bag was finally empty, Mercy's hand was covered in grey powder. Bending down, she dipped her hand into the warm saltwater, rinsing away a mother's ashes.

'Bye, Jenny,' she said, as the last of the powder drifted away. 'Thanks for coming with me to the other side.'

Thunder cracked. The sun disappeared. The box in which Mercy stood was full of water and the cardboard was falling apart. Wind whipped up a low chop of waves.

Mercy tried to think of something profound to say, some final words to mark the end of Jenny Cleggett's journey, but nothing came to her. Nothing but silence, and the sound of the wind eddying the water, and the thunder rolling across the sky.

Then Mercy heard it, her own voice in her head but spoken as clear as if it had been uttered aloud: *Run.*

Run!

It wasn't a voice of fear. It was a voice of pure delight.

Taking a deep breath, Mercy stepped out of her box. She scooped it, dripping, out of the water and began to run back to the shore. Saltwater foamed her legs and sprayed up her back, wetting her through to the skin as she picked her feet up as high as she could, running as fast as she could, as if she could skip across the surface and avoid all the stinging jellyfish, as if she could float across all the pain that wraps its tentacles and burns into flesh.

As she ran, the wind caught Mercy's laughter and took it high up into the air.

Here, now

CHAPTER FORTY-THREE

It took longer to wait for a taxi than Mercy expected, which meant that by the time she arrived at the airport, she was running again.

Inside the passenger terminal the air conditioning was frigid, and Mercy made it to the check-in counter shivering and breathless. There was no time to change out of her damp, sand-gritty clothes—and besides, all she had to change into was another T-shirt and pair of shorts. The puffer jacket and cat throw were all the way back in her dead Hijet. So Mercy stood in line for security, trembling and hugging herself, and when she was taken out of line to be scanned with a wand and patted down she wasn't at all surprised—she looked as pale and quavering as someone with a pistol strapped into their underpants might.

'Have pets been loaded on board, yet? Is my dog on the plane?' Mercy had asked the young man behind the check-in

desk, and he had smiled and assured her that the airline
loved pets as much as their owners did and her beloved animal would be very comfortable, *don't you worry at all*, which
was a reassuring change from the woman at the freight terminal earlier. But as Mercy stood with her arms out to the
sides and the wand hovering over her body for anything
malevolent, she could feel all that worry leaking back in,
seeping like fresh blood through the soft plasters of any tentative, new-found calm.

When it was ascertained that there was nothing suspicious on her person, Mercy was finally allowed to move on.
Over the loudspeaker, Mercy heard her flight called. She ran
to the gate, one arm pumping, the other gripping her hessian shopping bag as it flapped against her hip. The crowd
parted as she barrelled through. If there was anywhere on
the planet where you could run as a woman—even a woman
as wind-swept, sunburned, damp and salty as Mercy was
right now—and not cause even a raised eyebrow, it was at
the airport.

So as Mercy ran, floppy boots clumping across the floor,
an insane, drunken sensation bubbled up out of her chest.
Her breath wheezed and salt tightened on her cheeks and up
ahead she saw the queue forming at her gate.

Oh my god, I made it!

Joining the end of the line, Mercy bent over, shoulders
heaving. A suited man in front of her turned, performed a
quick assessment, and stepped forward, giving her a little
more space, then faced the front again.

Mercy was grinning at her feet, heart stammering, trying
to catch her breath, when another pair of feet appeared next
to hers. A man's feet, in work boots. Pale shins, muscular

calves. Cargo shorts, a clean white T-shirt, biceps swelling pleasingly into sleeves. A warm, broad smile. Dark-stubbled jaw and a man-bun.

'Well, hiya, Doctor Mercy,' said Andrew Macauley. 'How's it gaun?'

And then they cancelled Mercy's flight.

CHAPTER FORTY-FOUR

Murmurs of consternation fluttered along the queue. Voices raised in question as the announcement came over the loud-speaker, and a red box flashed onto the departures screen: *Cancelled*.

'What the hell?' Mercy said.

'I'm not sure,' Andy replied, frowning towards the jetway. Outside the floor-to-ceiling windows, the sky was black and great sheets of rain hurled against the glass. 'Don't reckon a thunderstorm would cancel the flight entirely. If they can't fly around it, they'll just wait it out.'

'No,' Mercy said. 'I meant—'

But what *did* Mercy mean? She was as equally *What the hell* about her cancelled flight as she was about Andy's sudden appearance. She didn't know where to look first: at the strained-smiling aircrew who were listening into phones and talking into radios and being swamped by confused passengers, or at the lovely Scottish man who had miraculously arrived at her boarding gate.

'What are you doing—hang on, I've gotta find out about—'

Andy shoved his hands into his pockets and smiled. 'Probably a mechanical fault. Jet engines don't have mufflers, though, so don't worry about that.'

It took a while, but Mercy learned eventually that, yes, there was a technical fault and that, yes, her flight was absolutely cancelled. Waiting in more queues, surrounded by irate, flustered or frustrated passengers, Mercy stood, breathing against her fluttering pulse, because she could only *be here now* and this too would pass. The next available flight from Darwin to Adelaide was at 12.50am.

Seven hours away.

Wasabi's tail wagged so happily that his entire body spasmed in her arms. The sausage dog licked her face, butting his snout into her teeth.

'Okay, okay,' she said. 'Stop it, Wasabi. Calm down.'

By the time they had stepped out of the terminal, the storm had eased. The sky was washed pale green and everything was soaked and steaming, but the fierce heat was gone.

Andy's camper was in the middle of the carpark. Seeing the rental van, rinsed of all its red dust by the rain, Mercy felt a pang of longing for yesterday, or the day before: when she had no phone service and there was no panicked rush and the Hijet was still running like a slow little train. She recalled the sharp, clear scent of the outback, the lazy caw of crows and the morning warble of magpies. How quickly memories take on a rose-coloured tint, she thought ruefully, as she recalled her cold fear at the rest stop outside Elliot, the stomach-dropping sight of Ann Barker standing at the sink, the ear-splitting *BANG* of the van's death throes and the terror of being stranded on the highway as the agonising minutes ticked by. But those things, so scary at the time, now had gone. As she stood here in the rain-soaked car-park with Andy and seven more hours stretching ahead of her, she knew that being *here now* meant the past itself had vanished. It existed only in her mind, which meant it didn't exist at all.

Crossing the water-strewn bitumen, they made their way to Andy's van.

'It's too convenient,' Mercy said, 'that you're here right when my flight is cancelled.'

'Convenient or lucky?' he replied, jangling the keys.

'Convenient.' She narrowed her eyes. 'You didn't do anything to that plane, did you?'

He halted mid-stride. 'Who's flattering themselves, eh? Sabotage, wilfully disabling an aircraft—I'd be arrested on terrorism laws. They'd probably string me up by my thumbs, attach electrodes to my nipples.'

Mercy held his gaze. 'How did you know I was here?'

He held her eyes in return. 'I caught up with Bert on the highway. When you didn't show in Katherine, I kept going. I …' He lowered his eyes to the ground. 'I don't know why, but I just knew you'd kept on heading north. I thought it'd be *you* I'd catch up with, given how slow you were. I just wanted—' He reached out with a finger and poked her hip. 'I wanted to make sure you were all right.'

For a moment, all of Mercy's blood rushed to that point in her hip.

'But how did you catch Bert?' she said at length. 'He went on ahead of me.'

'Ah, you know them grey nomads,' Andy said. 'One minute here, the next minute there. He changed his mind and decided to go over east, or something, and so he was heading south again for a bit. That's when I passed him, coming towards me. It was not far from—' He stopped.

'Far from what?'

He looked discomfited. 'Not far from your van. I saw it, not long after I saw Bert. He flagged me down. He looked a bit desperate, poor guy. He was worried about you, I think. Actually,' he said with a soft laugh, 'I think your van breaking down took the stuffing right out of our friend Bert. I know he thinks he's some kind of king of the outback, but in reality he's got so much luxury in his setup he's a mobile Hilton. He talks big, but I think the most outback he deals with is the dust in his wheel rims.'

Mercy smiled with a sudden fondness, thinking of Bert with all his pockets and his pewter mug, and Pete and Jules in their Dodge Ram, smelling of rose-scented hand cream. Ultimately, isn't that what everyone wanted? To be comfortable. To live with ease. Some people found that ease in spaceship-like four-wheel drives and caravans with porcelain toilets, some people found ease in prayer, some people found it at the bottom of a bottle. Some people scrambled for it by hiding themselves in a house for two years. And then turning away from the flames.

As Mercy had said to countless frazzled new mothers over the years, all anyone can do is the best they can with what they have, at any one time.

And right now, Mercy had her happy little sausage dog, a Scottish man with a top-knot whose muscled arms she wanted to lick, and seven hours to spare.

'I wanted to see you again, before you left,' Andy said. 'I hope that's all right.'

Mercy reached out a fingertip and poked his hip. 'That's all right,' she said.

And so, in spite of Mercy's nerves, she made the best of it.

It was the last sunset beachfront market before the wet season, and it was packed. Traffic crawled, clogging the streets; families strolled along the median strip carrying picnic rugs, eskies and folding chairs. The scent of grilling meat, spices and smoke filled the air, and the thrum of music, laughter and voices beat in Mercy's chest.

They bought spicy curries in paper boats and drank iced mint tea that was so good Mercy went back for more. They wandered among the crowd, Wasabi weaving at her ankles, inspecting local artworks and wooden knick-knacks and hippie clothing. Mercy bought Andy a small stuffed kangaroo wearing a tiny Akubra hat, and then two more for his children. Andy bought Mercy a pair of ballooning crepe pants with elasticised ankles in patches of green, purple and fuchsia pink, so she wouldn't get cold on the plane.

'And if the plane crashes, I can use them as a parachute,' Mercy said.

'Both practical and optimistic,' Andy observed.

When the sky started to glow, the market began to clear. Everyone wandered out of the palm trees, across the grass and over the dunes. Drifting down onto the beach, they stood about hushed and worshipful like devotees at a temple. For half an hour or more they watched in silence as the sky flamed and blazed and carried on like a show pony before the sun finally disappeared, exiting the stage and leaving a dazzling lightning display far out to sea.

It was so beautiful Mercy didn't even realise how desperately she needed to pee until it was over and she had to excuse herself.

'Three iced teas,' she explained to Andy as she stood, brushing sand from the backs of her legs. She left Wasabi on the beach with Andy and hurried back over the dunes, through the crowd to the bathroom. A familiar song was playing and she sang along under her breath. She smiled at people whose shoulders she bumped into. Someone else was drinking iced mint tea and she stopped briefly to congratulate them on their choice of beverage.

It was only when she was returning to Andy with two cups of pistachio gelato that she realised what the sensation gently ebbing through her was. It was something she hadn't felt for a very long time.

Normal. Mercy felt, somehow, the glimmer of a normal person.

Mercy felt like a teenager.

Three hours remained until she had to be back at the airport, and her phone was running low on battery so they were driving around the city in Andy's rental van while it charged up.

Windows rolled down, balmy night air filling the van, they cruised in a loop up and down the main street of Darwin, past bright heaving pubs and bass-throbbing bars. The median age in the city seemed to be about nineteen, and the kerbs were crammed with tottering heels, short skirts and military crew cuts. Mercy had her feet up on the dash and she was laughing so hard she honestly had to pee again. Andy had shifted his seat right back, reclined it so low he could barely see over the steering wheel, and turned up Roxette's 'Sleeping In My Car' on the crackling, tinny radio so loud the speakers were threatening to burst. Mercy sang at the top of her lungs, Andy held one fist to his mouth like a microphone and Wasabi jumped around the back, yapping. Heads turned as they passed. A group of young soldiers whooped. Girls giggled and rolled their ankles.

Pulling into the bottle-o, they bought one beer each, just like high-school kids.

Mercy felt happy.

Mercy's heart was a hummingbird.

She could see the rise and fall of Andy's chest and, when she lay her palm over it, she could feel the heat of his skin. Around them was darkness; somewhere outside, beyond the edge of the low cliff, was the ocean.

Andy's breath blew warm on her neck, and when he wrapped her in his arms, she finally closed her eyes. Lightning flickered blue light behind her lids.

He smelled of salt and earth and soap, and he was so warm and strong and he held her and she loved him in a way that made her feel like there was absolutely nothing else and there was only this, him, her, now.

Stretching out her bare legs, Mercy crossed her ankles and said, 'Your bed is much bigger than mine. And far more comfortable.'

'That's why I waited till now,' Andy said. In the flickers from far-off lightning, his skin gleamed with a sheen of sweat. 'I knew how fond you were of that van, and I knew you'd try and have your way with me in it.'

'Is that so?'

'Aye. And look, don't get me wrong, I wouldn't have turned down a foam mattress if you were naked, but a lad's got to have some standards.'

Mercy shoved him, and he took her hand and kissed her palm.

One hour remained until she had to be back at the airport. Her heart was a metronome in her chest.

From the front seat, Wasabi whined.

'Nope,' Andy said to the dog. 'Stay.'

'Aw, poor Wasabi.'

Andy shifted his weight towards her. 'A lot can be accomplished in an hour.'

'Oh really?'

'Aye.'

It turned out Andy was right.

CHAPTER FORTY·FIVE

'If they cancel this flight,' Mercy said, 'I'll be really screwed.'

At the boarding gate the queue shuffled steadily forward, passengers yawning and muttering, aircrew smiling and welcoming as if it weren't almost one am.

It was when the queue was down to its last few passengers that Mercy felt a surge of fear. She turned to Andy.

'Maybe I can't do this.'

Andy squeezed her hand. 'You can. You already are.'

'That's what the midwives tell women in labour.'

Andy shrugged. 'It's good advice for any situation, isn't it?'

Mercy's eyes darted between the boarding gate and the other end of the terminal, towards the exit. She could feel her mind gearing up, goading her, ravelling. What if they cancelled the flight again? But even worse, she realised with a jolt, what if they *didn't*? Then she would have to get on this plane.

But she had to take this flight anyway. There was no time left. And right there, with that absolute and indisputable fact, a sick knot of anxiety began to gather within her. The knot grew, collecting its arsenal of self-criticism and self-loathing, her thoughts hurling themselves at her, barbed like arrows: What if it really *was* her fault? What if her best—what if *she*—really never could be good enough?

Murderer.

You little shit!

Do something.

Mercy breathed in, slowly. She exhaled, slowly. The airport began to tilt and she pressed her hand to her chest.

And then she put her arms around Andy. Pressing her face into his neck, she closed her eyes. Andy's arms wrapped around her and three thousand kilometres unfurled then folded up inside.

'It was a pleasure meeting you, Doctor Mercy.'

'And you, Andrew Macauley.'

Mercy kissed him, then turned and walked towards her gate.

'Mercy?'

She paused. Her heart stalled.

'I know you don't have a house or even a campervan right now, but you've got Skype, right?'

'Yes,' Mercy said. 'Call me.'

Andy grinned, and Mercy stepped onto the jetway.

Air travel might be convenient and far quicker than blurting up the highway in an almost forty-year-old van, but for Mercy, there was no avoiding the reality that it incorporated all the major stress triggers: confined spaces; close and prolonged contact with strangers; heights; speed; complete lack of control. An inability to flee, no matter how loudly you screamed or how desperately you begged. The whole irrevocability of it.

Which were facts that hit Mercy fully when the doors were armed and cross-checked and the plane began to rock and shunt backwards: when it was too late to change her mind.

Bending forward in her seat, belt digging into her hips, Mercy scrabbled for her bag. She dug around, releasing the stale scent of sweaty, salty clothes, until she found the little glass bottle.

Skullcap. She unscrewed the lid and sniffed. Acrid and alcoholic, and something earthy. She squeezed the dropper bulb, drawing up a tube of treacle-coloured liquid. Mercy had known women who had sworn by herbal remedies, and she had spent many hours scoffing over the idea of witches' potions and placebo effects, warning patients that just because herbs were natural didn't mean they couldn't be dangerous.

The plane reached the top of the runway, and arced in a slow circle. Her heart smacked against her ribs.

The engines began to whine, then rumble and roar. Mercy lifted her trembling hand and squeezed the entire dropper beneath her tongue. It burned like syringing petrol into her mouth and she coughed.

Mercy was shoved back in her seat. The cabin rattled, lights blurred past the windows, then as the plane lifted its nose into the air, Mercy drew up and swallowed a second dropperful and the earth fell away beneath her.

Fifteen minutes later, a 737 passed roughly overhead a Daihatsu Hijet stalled on the side of the Stuart Highway, with *Home is wherever you ARE* hand-painted on its side, three pistons seized in its cast-iron engine block, and a large female huntsman spider tucked behind the gas bottle. Already the van had been looted of its battery, spare wheel and wheel brace, single saucepan, box of cutlery and a can of baked beans in ham sauce.

In the dark of night, the noise of the jet filtered to the ground and as it did, the rear bumper fell from the van and hit the gravel with a clang, but there was no one there to hear either the jet or the clang.

Not that Mercy could see any of this from 28,000 feet above, of course. Not in the middle of the night. And not when she had her head tipped to the side, snoring lightly and fast asleep.

ONE WEEK LATER

Adelaide rang with the end of spring. Sunlight glinted off glass and a dry warmth swirled through the streets. Leaving the Magistrates Court building behind her, Mercy crossed Angas Street to the corner of Victoria Square and sat on a bench under a shady tree. Traffic hummed around the square.

Mercy thought about certainty, and she thought about uncertainty. No matter how many experts are called to the witness stand, no matter how many letters grace the end of a person's name, no matter how many years of experience one has elbow deep in the body fluids of life and death—all anyone can ever offer, with any certainty, is their best estimation. Once, it was sworn that the sun revolved around a stationary earth. Once, physicians believed a woman's womb could wander around her body, wreaking havoc. Once, it was vowed that only foul-smelling air caused disease—the idea of microscopic germs was scorned. Beyond the certainty of relative uncertainty, Mercy thought, the only other truth is that some estimations—those of authority figures, the well-connected, men—will carry more weight than others.

Mercy looked down at the patch of dirt worn into the grass and saw ants scurrying about. A discarded muesli bar wrapper skidded on the breeze to rest against her ankle. Her court shoes were black leather pumps with low heels that made a demure, sensible click when she walked. There was a smudge of soil across one toe, and she bent forward to wipe it off.

What could Mercy be certain about? Well, she had known that the inquest would take more than one day, and it did—it took four. She knew that the Health Service's solicitors were so prepared they dropped *amniotic fluid embolism* and *disseminated intravascular coagulopathy* as easily as asking for a gin and tonic at a bar. She knew that the family of Tamara Lee Spencer had looked frightened, angry and grieving at the start and confused, exhausted and still grieving by the end.

The dusty smear of soil was now on Mercy's fingertip. The muesli bar wrapper rocked in the breeze, threatening to skid away. Thinking of the turtles, Mercy trapped the wrapper beneath her heel.

What couldn't Mercy know for sure?

She didn't know how long her house would take to rebuild. It could be another four to six months—'Maybe a bit more,' the builder said, because he couldn't be certain either.

She didn't know whether Eugene and Jose were broken up for good this time, and neither did Eugene. And therefore she didn't know if his suggestion that Mercy and Wasabi could take his spare room again, if she needed, was fuelled by guilt or charity or maybe even loneliness.

She didn't know if anyone had explained to Tamara Lee Spencer's family that their daughter, sister, mother, aunt, wife had died because sometimes, despite how incredibly unlikely it was, when amniotic fluid slips from the womb and enters the labouring woman's bloodstream, medical science still doesn't always know how to stop her heart and lungs from collapsing.

Mercy considered the smear of brown dust on her fingertip.

She knew it was okay that she was both sad and relieved about her mother's death. She knew she would always grieve, but that her grief was complex and complicated and tied up not just in the loss of her mother but in the realisation that she would never experience a normal, loving mother–child relationship.

With her thumb she rubbed the dirt from her fingertip into her skin. It seemed to disappear, but she knew it was still there, trapped in the tiny whorls of her fingers and palm. No one else would see it, but Mercy knew.

Just like no one would know that the night Mercy's house burned down, Mercy had stood in her hallway, watching flames lick the kitchen cabinets. Paint blistered and smoke pillowed across the ceiling and Mercy had stood watching, and felt a calm understanding come over her. A knowledge of exactly what she had to do. And what Mercy had to do was not scoop up Wasabi and flee the house, but push the dog outside and close the door behind him. And then Mercy had to turn around and walk back into her bedroom, closing the door behind her. Because that day, on the eve of her thirty-sixth birthday, she had reached a point, a critical end-point, where she could not stay stuck in her house any longer. But she couldn't leave it, either. So there was nothing left to do but throw her hands in the air and leave it up to chance. To fate. Stay or go.

And in the end, fate had said *Go*.

The breeze snapped up, shaking the leaves above her and sending sparkles of sunlight raining down. Her phone buzzed.

Hiya Dr M, how'd it go? xx

Long, Mercy wanted to write. *Awful. When it was over, her husband came up to me and his face was so writ with pain I actually took a step back, but then he hugged me. He cried. He said he had no idea that so many big words and technical sentences could be spoken that all came down, in the end, to 'We did everything we could and we don't know why it happened'. He said that sometimes it seems like we just have to accept that life makes decisions for you, and how will he ever be able to do that? I wanted to tell him:* I don't know, but I think being here, now, helps. And one day, maybe, you will find yourself on the other side of it.

With her soil-gritty thumb, Mercy typed back:

Hiya yourself. It's over. Findings will take a couple of months but lawyers confident. Where r u now? xx

The Kimberley. Darn nice. Quiet tho. xx

Mercy smiled. She reached down and picked up the wrapper then stood, walked to the bin and deposited the rubbish. She wiped her hands on the seat of her crisp black pants.

Tipping her face to the sun, she closed her eyes and imagined she could smell eucalyptus.

A short tram ride away there was a vehicle dealership.

Her savings would only last so long, and the sale from her newly rebuilt house would eventually run out, and then she would pick fruit, wipe tables, answer phones.

But wherever she went, Mercy knew, of one thing she could be certain: wherever she was, at that moment, she was home.

AUTHOR'S NOTE

I wish to respectfully thank the nations mentioned in this story, and the heartlands through which the protagonist travels on her journey. I acknowledge the Traditional Owners of these lands, and the lands on which I live and work, and pay respect to Elders past, present and future.

ACKNOWLEDGEMENTS

First and foremost, my gratitude to Pippa Masson, for her wisdom, patience and unwavering faith. Thank you, also, to Caitlan Cooper-Trent, whose graciousness and expertise is always so welcome and fortifying, and to all at Curtis Brown Australia.

To the incredible team at HarperCollins HQ: what a marvellous bunch you are! I extend tremendous gratitude to Jo Mackay for her immediate enthusiasm for this story, and to Rachael Donovan for her warmth, passion, and for shepherding the novel so skilfully into the world. Many thanks to Annabel Blay for her editorial prowess and care, also to Kylie Mason and Annabel Adair, Jo Munroe and Natika Palka. My admiration to Alex Hotchin for creating the stunning map, and to Christa Moffitt for a truly beautiful cover design.

Apologies to residents of all the little towns along the Stuart Highway whose facilities I have misrepresented or invented entirely. Also thanks to any 'Aussie Grey Nomads' whose delightfully convivial caravan slogans I may have shamelessly appropriated.

Thank you to the lovely ladies of the Barossa Libraries Lyndoch branch, who provided the most cheerful assistance and support, and never seemed to mind that I was perpetually in track pants. Deepest thanks to my friends at The Raven's Parlour Bookstore, booksellers extraordinaire and stalwart supporters of local writers. And to the hardworking booksellers and librarians everywhere—thank you. I bow to you.

My gratitude to Kat Clarke for her kind and sage assistance with representation of First Nations characters and country. Thank you to Ryan O'Neill for generous help in crafting Glaswegian dialogue (and curses). Thanks to Peter Lock for talking me through a broken muffler; Natasha Schubert for 'two flat tyres and only one spare'; Ben Buck for providing a busted radiator hose and counting roadtrain wheels. All errors or stretches of truth are mine.

To those who read things, offered advice, weathered my tears or tantrums, and/or provided much needed cheering and support: Bettina Engelhardt, Jayde Lock, Stace Lock, Sarah Ridout, and Les Zig (94pt)—thank you thank you thank you. Leisa Masters, dearest of dear friends, and Kelly Morgan, for so much tea and hugs and getting it. You all make every word easier and I am endlessly grateful.

In loving memory of my friend Kevin Massey, who I think would have loved this story.

My love to Ben, Addy and Leo, for always being so excited about everything book related. And the final and most resounding thanks must go to my mum, Julie Lock, who braved the very first gritty draft, never ceased encouraging, and laughed at all the appropriate moments. Thanks, Mum!

DISCUSSION QUESTIONS

❖ Overcome by crippling anxiety, Mercy often finds herself incapable of completing basic tasks or talking to strangers. Have you ever been in a position where fear has prevented you from performing a day-to-day task? How does Mercy's perception of danger affect the relationship she has with herself? How does Mercy utilise her fight or flight mode?

❖ Mercy is an overly anxious, jittery and at times hectic person. How did the narration impact your reading experience? Did the narration change your perception of mental illness? Over the course of the book, did Mercy's voice evolve? How did Mercy's relationship with her mother restrict her life?

❖ The reader is taken on a wild ride through central Australia, from Adelaide to Darwin. The country's

landscape is mystified and glorified by its travellers.
How did the journey colour your perception towards
the Australian outback landscape? Did Mercy's interactions with the other campers reflect Australian culture?

❖ A brawny Scottish man, Andrew Macauley is full of
laughter and a good natured spirit, even while being
injured. How did Andy's interactions with Mercy affect
her outlook on the campervan lifestyle? Was Andy a
positive influence? Do you believe that Mercy and
Andy have the potential to continue their relationship?

❖ At the beginning of Mercy's story, she has just lost her
house and moved into her ex-husband's spare bedroom,
and only has her loyal puppy Wasabi to comfort her.
How did this catastrophic event change the course of
Mercy's life? Was this change slow or rapid? How did
her relationship with her ex-husband, Eugene, challenge and/or support her new lifestyle?

❖ Grief was a common thread throughout the story, from
Mercy's relationship with her mother to her patient
dying. How has grief shaped Mercy's life? How did
uncovering Jenny Cleggett's ashes spur her on to complete her journey? What was your reaction when you
found out Jenny Cleggett was the mother of Harry, the
old man who sold the Hijet to Mercy?

❖ Throughout the novel, Mercy challenges us to break
outside our own self-inflicted walls. How has reading
this story changed your perception of your own mental
health? Have you ever felt bound in by society or the
relationships we keep?

The Growth Mindset Advantage: Thriving Through Lifelong Learning

Adam Poliman

Published by Adam Poliman, 2023.

While every precaution has been taken in the preparation of this book, the publisher assumes no responsibility for errors or omissions, or for damages resulting from the use of the information contained herein.

THE GROWTH MINDSET ADVANTAGE: THRIVING THROUGH LIFELONG LEARNING

First edition. August 24, 2023.

Copyright © 2023 Adam Poliman.

ISBN: 979-8223209751

Written by Adam Poliman.

Also by Adam Poliman

The Power of Time: Transform Your Life through Effective Time
Management
Unleashing The Power Of Reading
Unlocking the Power of Critical Thinking: Strategies for Effective
Problem-Solving
Efficiency Unleashed: Mastering Productivity Tips and Hacks for
Success
The Art of Social Intelligence: Mastering the Skills of Effective
Communication
Destined For Greatness: Mastering The Art Of Goal Setting
Mind Over Temptation: Building Self-Discipline In A Distracted
World
The Bright Path: Navigating Life With Positive Thinking
The Emotion Code: Decoding Emotional Intelligence
The Growth Mindset Advantage: Thriving Through Lifelong
Learning
Unleashing Your Potential: A Guide To Personal Development And
Self-Improvement

Watch for more at https://optimizationtime.com.

Are you looking for a way to thrive in today's ever-changing world? Do you want to unlock your full potential and embrace lifelong learning? If so, then you need to adopt a growth mindset.

In this book, we will explore the concept of the growth mindset and how it can give you a distinct advantage in all areas of your life.

The growth mindset is the belief that your abilities and intelligence can be developed through effort, practice, and perseverance. Unlike a fixed mindset, which assumes that your abilities are fixed and cannot be changed, a growth mindset empowers you to continuously learn, grow, and adapt.

By adopting this mindset, you open yourself up to a world of possibilities and opportunities. You become resilient in the face of challenges, embrace failure as a learning opportunity, and constantly seek out new knowledge and skills.

In short, the growth mindset is the key to thriving in a rapidly changing world. So, if you're ready to unlock your full potential and embrace lifelong learning, read on to discover the growth mindset advantage.

Chapter 1: Understanding the Concept of Growth Mindset

Are you ready to tap into the power of a growth mindset?

In this discussion, we'll explore the definition of a growth mindset and how it can shape your success.

Discover the fascinating concept of brain plasticity and how your beliefs can influence your abilities.

Embrace the idea that with a growth mindset, lifelong learning becomes the key to thriving and achieving your goals.

The Definition of Growth Mindset

So you're interested in learning about the definition of growth mindset and how it can benefit you throughout your life. Well, let's dive in!

Originating from the work of psychologist Carol Dweck, the theory behind growth mindset suggests that our abilities and intelligence can be developed through hard work, dedication, and a willingness to learn. This stands in stark contrast to the fixed mindset, which believes that our abilities are fixed traits that can't be changed.

By adopting a growth mindset, you can unlock your full potential and thrive through lifelong learning, making it a valuable concept to apply in your daily life.

Origins and Theory

Embrace the growth mindset and open yourself up to a world of endless possibilities, where learning becomes a never-ending journey of self-improvement.

The origins of the growth mindset can be traced back to the work of psychologist Carol Dweck. She proposed the theory that individuals with a growth mindset believe that their abilities and intelligence can be developed through dedication, hard work, and perseverance.

This belief is in contrast to those with a fixed mindset, who believe that their abilities are innate and cannot be changed. According to Dweck, individuals with a growth mindset are more likely to embrace challenges, persist in the face of setbacks, and see effort as a necessary part of achieving success.

By understanding and adopting the principles of the growth mindset, you can tap into your full potential and continually strive for personal growth and development.

So, why limit yourself to a fixed mindset when you can choose to embrace the growth mindset and thrive through lifelong learning?

Comparison with Fixed Mindset

By adopting a growth mindset, you open yourself up to a world of endless possibilities, where your abilities and intelligence can skyrocket through dedication, hard work, and perseverance.

In comparison to a fixed mindset, which believes that intelligence and abilities are fixed traits that cannot be changed, a growth mindset embraces the idea that intelligence and abilities can be developed and improved over time.

With a growth mindset, you understand that challenges and setbacks are opportunities for growth and learning, rather than indications of failure or incompetence. This mindset allows you to approach new tasks and challenges with enthusiasm and optimism, knowing that your efforts and persistence will lead to progress and success.

Instead of avoiding failure, you embrace it as a stepping stone towards improvement.

By cultivating a growth mindset, you not only enhance your own personal growth and development, but you also inspire and motivate others to adopt the same mindset.

Psychologist and Researcher behind Growth Mindset

Immerse yourself in the work of psychologist and researcher Carol Dweck, who pioneered the concept of a growth mindset and its transformative effects on personal development and achievement.

Dweck's groundbreaking research and insights have revolutionized the way we think about intelligence and talent. Through her extensive studies, she has shown that individuals who embrace a growth mindset believe that their abilities can be developed through dedication, hard work, and perseverance.

This belief in the power of effort and the potential for growth opens up a world of possibilities and opportunities for personal and professional growth. Dweck's work has had a profound impact on education, sports, business, and personal relationships, inspiring people to adopt a growth mindset and overcome challenges with resilience and determination.

By understanding and applying the principles of a growth mindset, you can unlock your full potential, continually learn and improve, and thrive in all areas of your life.

Applications in Daily Life

Now that you know the psychologist and researcher behind the growth mindset, let's explore how you can apply this mindset in your daily life. The growth mindset is not just a concept to understand, but a way of thinking and approaching challenges that can truly transform your life. By adopting a growth mindset, you can overcome obstacles, embrace learning opportunities, and thrive in any situation.

Whether it's at work, in your relationships, or pursuing personal goals, the growth mindset gives you the advantage of continuously improving and expanding your abilities.

So, why settle for a fixed mindset that limits your potential, when you can choose the growth mindset and unlock a world of possibilities?

Don't wait any longer, start embracing the growth mindset today and discover the power of lifelong learning.

Brain plasticity

Brain plasticity refers to the brain's ability to change and adapt throughout our lives. It plays a crucial role in lifelong learning and adaptability, as it allows us to acquire new skills and knowledge, and adjust our thinking patterns.

The latest research on brain plasticity has shown that our brains have the remarkable ability to reorganize and form new neural connections, even in adulthood.

Real-life examples of brain plasticity can be seen in individuals who've recovered from brain injuries or those who've learned new languages or musical instruments later in life.

What is Brain Plasticity?

Explore the incredible concept of brain plasticity and witness the profound transformations that can occur within your mind.

Brain plasticity refers to the brain's ability to change and adapt throughout our lives. It is the remarkable capacity of our brains to reorganize and rewire their connections in response to learning, experience, and even injury.

This means that your brain is not a fixed, unchanging entity, but rather a flexible and malleable organ that can continually grow and develop. By embracing a growth mindset and actively engaging in lifelong learning, you can take advantage of brain plasticity to enhance your cognitive abilities, improve your memory, and acquire new skills.

With each new experience and challenge, your brain has the potential to form new neural connections, strengthen existing ones, and reshape its structure. This process not only allows for personal growth and development but also enables you to thrive in an ever-changing world.

So, embark on the journey of lifelong learning, and unlock the incredible potential of your brain through the power of brain plasticity.

Role in Lifelong Learning and Adaptability

Embrace the incredible concept of brain plasticity and witness how your mind can continually adapt and change, allowing you to acquire new skills and thrive in an ever-changing world.

Did you know that studies have found that people who actively engage in lifelong learning have a 30% lower risk of developing dementia?

By engaging in lifelong learning, you're not only expanding your knowledge and acquiring new skills, but you're also stimulating your brain and enhancing its plasticity. This means that your brain is constantly forming new connections and pathways, allowing you to learn and adapt more effectively.

Lifelong learning promotes cognitive flexibility, creativity, and problem-solving abilities, enabling you to navigate challenges and embrace new opportunities. Moreover, it enhances your overall adaptability, enabling you to thrive in a rapidly changing world.

So, don't miss out on the incredible advantages that lifelong learning and brain plasticity offer. Embrace the growth mindset and unlock your full potential for continuous growth and success.

Latest Research on Brain Plasticity

Now that you understand the role of a growth mindset in lifelong learning and adaptability, let's delve into the latest research on brain plasticity.

It's fascinating to discover that our brains have the incredible ability to change and adapt throughout our lives. This concept of neuroplasticity challenges the notion that our brains are fixed and unchangeable.

Research has shown that engaging in continuous learning and challenging ourselves can actually rewire our brains, creating new neural pathways and connections. By embracing a growth mindset, you can tap into this incredible potential for growth and development, allowing you to thrive in an ever-changing world.

So, don't limit yourself to what you already know; instead, embrace the joy of learning and the power of your brain's plasticity. The possibilities for personal and professional growth are limitless when you approach life with a growth mindset.

Examples in Real-Life Settings

In real-life settings, your ability to adapt and grow is evident in the stories of individuals who've overcome challenges and achieved remarkable success. Take the example of Thomas Edison. He faced countless failures before inventing the light bulb. Despite facing setbacks, he continued to learn from his mistakes and persisted until he achieved his goal.

Similarly, Oprah Winfrey's journey from a difficult childhood to becoming one of the most influential media moguls showcases the power of a growth mindset. She embraced opportunities for learning and personal development, constantly striving to improve herself and her career.

These real-life examples demonstrate that with a growth mindset, you have the potential to thrive and succeed in any endeavor. By viewing challenges as opportunities for growth and embracing a lifelong learning mindset, you can unlock your full potential and achieve remarkable success in your own life.

The power of belief

Do you ever wonder how belief in yourself can impact your ability to succeed?

In this discussion, we'll explore the power of self-belief and how it plays a crucial role in overcoming self-doubt.

Discover strategies that can enhance your self-belief and help you unlock your full potential.

The Role of Self Belief

Believing in yourself is like having a compass that guides you through the ever-changing landscape of lifelong learning, helping you navigate the twists and turns with confidence and resilience.

When you have self-belief, you have a strong foundation that allows you to take risks, embrace challenges, and push beyond your comfort zone.

It is the belief in your abilities and potential that propels you forward, even in the face of setbacks and obstacles.

With self-belief, you approach learning as an opportunity for growth and development, rather than a test of your worth.

You trust in your own capabilities and know that with effort and perseverance, you can achieve great things.

This mindset empowers you to overcome self-doubt, seek out new experiences, and continuously strive for improvement.

So, nurture your self-belief, cultivate it through positive self-talk and affirmations, and watch yourself thrive in the journey of lifelong learning.

Overcoming Self-Doubt

Take a moment to acknowledge those moments of self-doubt when you question your abilities, because it's in those moments that you have the opportunity to rise above and prove yourself wrong.

Self-doubt can be paralyzing, causing you to second-guess your skills and potential. However, it's important to remember that self-doubt is often unfounded and rooted in fear rather than reality.

By embracing a growth mindset, you can overcome self-doubt and recognize it as a natural part of the learning process. Instead of viewing self-doubt as a sign of weakness, see it as an invitation to push yourself out of your comfort zone and challenge your own limiting beliefs.

Remember that failures and setbacks are stepping stones to success, and each moment of doubt is an opportunity for growth and improvement. With perseverance and a belief in your own abilities, you can overcome self-doubt and achieve great things.

So, the next time you doubt yourself, take a deep breath, remind yourself of your past successes, and embrace the challenge ahead. You're capable of more than you think, and overcoming self-doubt is just the first step towards unlocking your full potential.

Strategies to Enhance Self-belief

Embrace the power of positive affirmations to boost your self-belief and banish self-doubt. By repeating positive statements about yourself and your abilities, you can rewire your brain to focus on your strengths and potential.

Start your day by looking in the mirror and saying affirmations like "I'm capable of achieving great things"or "I believe in my abilities to overcome any challenge."

Throughout the day, remind yourself of your past accomplishments and the times when you've succeeded against the odds. By consistently reinforcing positive thoughts and beliefs, you can cultivate a strong sense of self-belief that'll propel you forward in all areas of your life.

So, choose empowering affirmations and make them a part of your daily routine. Embrace the power of self-belief and watch as you thrive and achieve your goals with confidence and resilience.

Growth Mindset and Success

If you want to achieve success, having a growth mindset is crucial. Research has shown a strong correlation between a growth mindset and success in various areas of life. By believing that your abilities can be developed through hard work and dedication, you're more likely to persevere through challenges and achieve your goals.

Don't buy into the myths that success is solely determined by talent or that it can only be achieved by a select few. Embrace the idea that success is a journey of continuous learning and growth, and redefine what it means to be successful based on your own values and aspirations.

Correlation between Success and Growth Mindset

Developing a growth mindset will greatly impact your success as you continually seek opportunities for growth and embrace challenges. The correlation between success and a growth mindset is undeniable.

When you believe that your abilities can be developed through hard work and perseverance, you are more likely to take on difficult tasks and view failures as learning opportunities. This mindset allows you to push past your comfort zone and achieve things you never thought possible.

Instead of being discouraged by setbacks, you see them as stepping stones to progress. By adopting a growth mindset, you become resilient, adaptable, and open-minded, which are essential qualities for success in any endeavor.

So, don't shy away from challenges or setbacks; embrace them as opportunities for growth and watch your success soar.

Myths About Success and Talent

Don't fall for the myths about success and talent; you may be surprised to learn that a study conducted by Stanford University found that only 1% of high-achieving individuals attribute their success solely to innate talent.

The idea that success is solely determined by natural abilities is a common misconception that can hold you back from reaching your full potential.

In reality, success is often the result of hard work, perseverance, and a growth mindset. By believing that your abilities can be developed through dedication and effort, you open yourself up to endless possibilities for growth and achievement.

So, don't let the myth of talent discourage you. Embrace the power of a growth mindset and watch as you thrive through lifelong learning.

Changing Your Definition of Success

Reframe your definition of success and discover a whole new world of possibilities. Success is often equated with achieving a specific goal or reaching a certain level of wealth, fame, or status. However, by changing your perspective, you can see success as a continuous journey of personal growth and learning.

Instead of focusing solely on external accomplishments, embrace the idea of lifelong learning and self-improvement. This shift in mindset allows you to find fulfillment in the process rather than solely on the outcome.

With this new definition of success, you can continuously challenge yourself, adapt to new situations, and expand your skills and knowledge. By valuing the process of learning and growth, you open yourself up to a wide range of opportunities and experiences.

So, let go of the narrow view of success and embrace a mindset that values progress, resilience, and the joy of learning.

Chapter 2: The Science Behind Growth Mindset

In Chapter 2, you'll explore the fascinating science behind growth mindset. You'll delve into the role of neuroplasticity in growth mindset. Discover how the brain's ability to change and adapt plays a crucial role in our mindset development.

Additionally, you'll uncover the neurological basis of growth mindset and how it influences brain chemistry. Highlight the powerful connection between our mindset and the functioning of our brains.

Finally, you'll understand the role of mindset in neural pathway development. Explore how our beliefs and attitudes shape the connections within our brain, ultimately influencing our learning and growth.

Get ready to dive into the captivating world of the science behind growth mindset!

The Role of Neuroplasticity in Growth Mindset

Neuroplasticity, the brain's ability to reorganize and form new neural connections throughout life, plays a crucial role in supporting a growth mindset. By understanding how the brain can change and adapt, you can harness the power of neuroplasticity to enhance your learning and personal growth.

Research has shown that practicing a growth mindset and engaging in activities that challenge and stretch your brain can actually enhance neuroplasticity, leading to increased cognitive abilities and a more resilient mindset.

So, embrace the power of neuroplasticity and take advantage of its benefits to foster a lifelong love of learning and personal development.

Introduction to Neuroplasticity

Imagine your brain as a flexible muscle, constantly adapting and reshaping itself to learn and grow. This is the concept of neuroplasticity, the ability of the brain to change and reorganize itself in response to experiences and learning.

Neuroplasticity allows us to develop new skills, improve our cognitive abilities, and recover from injuries or trauma. It is a fundamental characteristic of the growth mindset, as it emphasizes that our intelligence and abilities are not fixed, but can be developed through effort and practice.

By understanding and harnessing the power of neuroplasticity, we can unlock our full potential and thrive through lifelong learning. So, embrace the concept of neuroplasticity and believe in your brain's ability to adapt and grow, because with a growth mindset, the possibilities are endless.

How Neuroplasticity Supports Growth Mindset

Embrace the incredible potential of your brain to adapt and grow with the power of neuroplasticity - it's like a secret superpower you possess!

Neuroplasticity is the brain's ability to change and reorganize itself throughout your lifetime. By understanding how neuroplasticity works, you can harness its power to support a growth mindset.

When you have a growth mindset, you believe that your abilities and intelligence can be developed through dedication and hard work. Neuroplasticity supports this mindset by showing that your brain is not fixed, but rather malleable and capable of forming new connections and pathways.

This means that with effort and practice, you can improve your skills and abilities in any area. So, instead of viewing challenges as obstacles, see them as opportunities for growth. Embrace the concept of neuroplasticity and use it to your advantage in cultivating a growth mindset.

Enhancing Neuroplasticity for Lifelong Learning

Unlock the full potential of your brain by actively engaging in new experiences and constantly seeking opportunities to challenge yourself. Enhancing neuroplasticity for lifelong learning is all about creating an environment that allows your brain to adapt and grow.

One way to do this is by exposing yourself to new and stimulating activities. Whether it's learning a musical instrument, taking up a new sport, or exploring a different culture, every new experience creates new neural connections in your brain.

Additionally, it's important to constantly challenge yourself by setting goals that are just beyond your current abilities. This not only keeps your brain engaged and motivated, but it also pushes your cognitive limits, leading to increased neuroplasticity.

By actively seeking out new experiences and constantly challenging yourself, you can enhance your brain's ability to learn and adapt, giving you a significant advantage in lifelong learning.

So, don't shy away from new opportunities and embrace the growth mindset to unlock the full potential of your brain.

Research on Neuroplasticity

Now that you understand the importance of enhancing neuroplasticity for lifelong learning, let's dive into the fascinating world of research on neuroplasticity.

Research in this field has shown that our brains have an incredible ability to change and adapt throughout our lives. Neuroplasticity refers to the brain's ability to reorganize itself by forming new neural connections. This means that we have the power to reshape our brains through learning and experience.

Studies have demonstrated that engaging in new and challenging activities can promote neuroplasticity, leading to improved cognitive abilities and overall brain health. By embracing a growth mindset and actively seeking out opportunities for learning, you can tap into the vast potential of your brain and thrive in all areas of life.

So, don't be afraid to step outside of your comfort zone, try new things, and embrace the power of neuroplasticity. Your brain is capable of incredible things, and with a growth mindset, you can unlock its full potential.

Neurological Basis of Growth Mindset

In this discussion, we'll explore the neurological basis of growth mindset. We'll focus on key points such as the role of the prefrontal cortex and the impact of dopamine on learning and growth mindset. We'll also discuss the role of the limbic system in emotional regulation and the importance of neurotransmitters in fostering a growth mindset.

By understanding how these brain regions and chemicals interact, you can gain insights into how to cultivate and maintain a growth mindset. This will enable you to thrive in lifelong learning and personal growth.

So, let's dive into the fascinating world of neurobiology and discover how it shapes our mindset and potential for growth.

The Prefrontal Cortex and Growth Mindset

Embrace the power of your prefrontal cortex and its connection to the growth mindset.

Your prefrontal cortex, located at the front of your brain, plays a crucial role in your ability to adopt a growth mindset.

This area of your brain is responsible for executive functions such as decision-making, problem-solving, and self-regulation.

By actively engaging and exercising your prefrontal cortex, you can strengthen its connections and enhance your growth mindset.

Just like a muscle that grows stronger with exercise, your prefrontal cortex becomes more adept at processing information, adapting to challenges, and embracing new opportunities.

So, take advantage of this incredible tool within your brain. Challenge yourself, seek out new experiences, and continuously learn and grow.

By doing so, you will unlock the full potential of your prefrontal cortex and cultivate a growth mindset that will propel you towards lifelong learning and success.

Impact of Dopamine on Learning and Growth Mindset

Unleash the power of dopamine and watch your learning soar as this neurotransmitter ignites a fire of motivation and reward in your brain.

Dopamine plays a crucial role in our ability to learn and develop a growth mindset.

When dopamine is released in response to a rewarding experience, it stimulates the brain's pleasure centers and reinforces the behavior that led to the reward.

This creates a positive feedback loop, encouraging us to continue seeking out new challenges and opportunities for growth.

By understanding the impact of dopamine on learning, we can harness its power to fuel our motivation, enhance our focus, and ultimately thrive through lifelong learning.

So, embrace the power of dopamine and let it guide you on your journey towards personal and intellectual growth.

The Limbic System and Emotional Regulation

Tap into the power of your limbic system and emotions to navigate life's challenges and find inner peace and balance.

The limbic system, often referred to as the 'emotional brain,' plays a crucial role in emotional regulation. It consists of various structures, including the amygdala, hippocampus, and hypothalamus, which work together to process and regulate emotions.

By understanding how these structures function, you can harness their power to enhance your emotional well-being. When faced with difficult situations, the limbic system helps you make sense of your emotions, allowing you to respond appropriately and effectively.

By developing emotional intelligence and practicing mindfulness techniques, such as deep breathing and meditation, you can strengthen your limbic system and improve your emotional regulation skills. This enables you to navigate life's ups and downs with resilience and grace.

So, embrace your emotions and tap into the wisdom of your limbic system to thrive in your personal and professional life.

The Role of Neurotransmitters in Growth Mindset

Can we harness the power of neurotransmitters to cultivate a mindset of continuous growth and development? Absolutely!

Neurotransmitters play a crucial role in shaping our thoughts, emotions, and behaviors, making them essential in cultivating a growth mindset.

When we engage in activities that challenge us and push us out of our comfort zones, neurotransmitters like dopamine and serotonin are released in our brains. Dopamine, often referred to as the 'reward neurotransmitter,' motivates us to seek out new experiences and rewards, while serotonin helps regulate our mood, promoting feelings of happiness and well-being.

By actively seeking out new challenges and embracing the discomfort that comes with learning and growth, we can activate these neurotransmitters and create a positive feedback loop that reinforces our desire to continue learning and developing.

So, next time you feel hesitant or fearful about trying something new, remember the power of neurotransmitters and how they can fuel your growth mindset. Embrace the discomfort, take risks, and watch yourself thrive through a lifelong journey of learning and development.

The Influence of Mindset on Brain Chemistry

When it comes to mindset, did you know that it can actually influence the release of stress hormones in your brain?

That's right, the way you think can impact how your body responds to stress.

Additionally, there are specific neurotransmitters that are linked to a growth mindset, such as dopamine and serotonin, which play a crucial role in motivation and happiness.

By cultivating a growth mindset, you can actually experience neurochemical changes in your brain that promote positive emotions and overall well-being.

So, why not start implementing strategies that promote positive brain chemistry and embrace the power of a growth mindset?

Mindset and the Release of Stress Hormones

Embracing a growth mindset triggers a cascade of positive effects on your body, including the release of stress hormones. When you adopt a growth mindset, you believe that your abilities and intelligence can be developed through effort and perseverance. This mindset allows you to view challenges as opportunities for growth, rather than as threats.

As a result, your body responds by releasing stress hormones, such as cortisol and adrenaline, in a way that prepares you to face these challenges head-on. These hormones help to increase your focus, alertness, and energy levels, enabling you to tackle difficult tasks with confidence and determination.

By embracing a growth mindset, you not only enhance your ability to learn and grow, but you also develop the resilience and mental strength needed to thrive in the face of adversity.

So, why not choose to adopt a growth mindset and harness the power of stress hormones to your advantage?

Neurotransmitters Linked to Growth Mindset

Now that you understand how mindset can affect the release of stress hormones in your body, let's explore the fascinating world of neurotransmitters linked to the growth mindset.

Neurotransmitters are chemical messengers in your brain that play a crucial role in transmitting signals between neurons. When it comes to the growth mindset, two neurotransmitters stand out: dopamine and serotonin.

Dopamine is associated with pleasure, motivation, and reward, and it plays a crucial role in the brain's ability to learn and adapt. When you have a growth mindset, your brain releases dopamine when you embrace challenges and persist in the face of setbacks, reinforcing the belief that effort leads to growth and success.

On the other hand, serotonin is known as the 'feel-good' neurotransmitter, regulating mood, happiness, and social behavior. Having a growth mindset increases serotonin levels, leading to a positive outlook on life and a greater willingness to engage in learning and personal development.

By understanding the connection between neurotransmitters and the growth mindset, you can harness the power of these chemicals to your advantage, fueling your motivation, resilience, and lifelong learning journey.

Neurochemical Changes with a Growth Mindset

By understanding the intricate neurochemical changes that occur with a growth mindset, you can unlock your full potential and experience unprecedented personal growth.

When you adopt a growth mindset, your brain undergoes significant changes at a neurochemical level. The levels of neurotransmitters such as dopamine, serotonin, and endorphins increase, leading to improved mood, motivation, and overall well-being.

Dopamine, often referred to as the 'feel-good' neurotransmitter, is released when you experience a sense of accomplishment or progress towards your goals.

Serotonin, known as the 'happiness' neurotransmitter, is responsible for regulating mood, sleep, and appetite. With a growth mindset, serotonin levels rise, promoting a positive outlook on life and increased resilience in the face of challenges.

Furthermore, endorphins, the body's natural painkillers, are released when you engage in learning and personal development, resulting in a greater sense of fulfillment and satisfaction.

So, by embracing a growth mindset, you not only enhance your cognitive abilities but also create a neurochemical environment that supports your overall well-being and allows you to thrive.

Strategies to Promote Positive Brain Chemistry

To promote positive brain chemistry, you can incorporate regular exercise into your routine. Studies have shown that physical activity increases the release of endorphins, leading to improved mood and overall well-being.

By engaging in activities such as jogging, swimming, or even dancing, you can stimulate the production of these feel-good chemicals in your brain, helping you feel happier and more energized.

Exercise not only benefits your mental health but also enhances cognitive function, making it easier for you to learn and retain new information.

So, why not take a break from your busy schedule and go for a run or join a fitness class? Your brain will thank you for it!

The Role of Mindset in Neural Pathway Development

In this discussion, you'll explore the fascinating connection between mindset and neural pathway development. Discover how having a growth mindset can enhance neural plasticity, allowing your brain to adapt and grow in response to new experiences and challenges.

Learn how your mindset influences the formation of neural connections and the development of habits, and gain valuable strategies to cultivate positive neural pathways that support your personal growth and development.

Neural Plasticity and Growth Mindset

Embrace a growth mindset and watch as your brain's neural connections become more flexible and adaptable, allowing you to thrive through lifelong learning.

Neural plasticity is the brain's remarkable ability to change and adapt throughout life.

When you approach challenges with a growth mindset, you actively seek out new experiences and embrace the opportunity to learn and grow.

This mindset stimulates neural pathways, creating new connections and strengthening existing ones.

As you engage in continuous learning, your brain becomes more efficient at processing information, enabling you to absorb knowledge more effectively.

With a growth mindset, you can overcome obstacles and develop new skills, ultimately leading to personal and professional growth.

So, take on new challenges, explore unfamiliar territories, and embrace the power of neural plasticity.

Your brain is capable of incredible growth, and a growth mindset is the key to unlocking its full potential.

How Mindset Influences Neural Connections

Now that you understand the concept of neural plasticity and its connection to the growth mindset, let's delve deeper into how mindset influences neural connections.

It's fascinating to think that the way we think and perceive the world can actually shape the physical connections within our brains.

When you adopt a growth mindset, you believe that your abilities and intelligence can be developed through dedication and hard work.

This mindset creates a positive feedback loop in your brain, where every effort you make to learn something new strengthens the neural connections related to that skill or knowledge.

As these connections grow stronger, you become more proficient in the area, which further reinforces your belief in your ability to improve.

It's a powerful cycle that propels you forward on your journey of lifelong learning.

Mindset and the Formation of Habits

Developing a mindset that believes in the power of your efforts and dedication not only strengthens neural connections but also shapes your habits for success. By adopting a growth mindset, you recognize that your abilities can be developed through hard work and perseverance. This mindset encourages you to embrace challenges, learn from failures, and persist in the face of obstacles.

As you cultivate this mindset, your brain forms new neural pathways that support the development of positive habits. Instead of being limited by fixed beliefs about your abilities, you become open to growth and improvement. This shift in mindset allows you to approach tasks with a sense of curiosity and resilience, enabling you to develop habits that promote continuous learning and personal growth.

With a growth mindset, you're more likely to view setbacks as opportunities for growth rather than as indications of failure. This perspective empowers you to take risks, step outside of your comfort zone, and embrace new experiences.

As you consistently challenge yourself and actively seek out opportunities for learning, your brain rewires itself to support the formation of habits that align with your goals and aspirations.

So, embrace the power of a growth mindset and watch as your habits transform, propelling you towards success.

Strategies to Develop Positive Neural Pathways

By fostering a mindset that embraces challenges and persists in the face of obstacles, you can actively shape your neural pathways to support the development of positive habits.

The brain is a highly adaptable organ, and it has the ability to rewire itself based on our thoughts and actions.

When we approach challenges with a growth mindset, we view them as opportunities for learning and growth rather than setbacks. This mindset encourages us to persevere and find creative solutions, which strengthens the connections between neurons in our brain.

As we repeat these positive behaviors, the pathways associated with them become stronger and more efficient, making it easier for us to engage in them consistently.

By continuously challenging ourselves and persisting in the face of obstacles, we can actively shape our brain's neural pathways to support the development of positive habits and ultimately thrive in our lifelong learning journey.

So, embrace challenges, persist through obstacles, and watch as your brain rewires itself to support your growth and success.

Chapter 3: Cultivating a Growth Mindset in Education

In Chapter 3, you'll be introduced to the concept of Growth Mindset in Education and how it can benefit both teachers and students.

You'll learn about the importance of cultivating a growth mindset in the classroom and how it can positively impact students' learning and development.

Additionally, you'll explore various growth mindset practices that can be implemented to promote a positive learning environment and ways to assess and develop growth mindset in education.

Introduction to Growth Mindset in Education

Are you looking for ways to enhance the learning experience in schools and classrooms?

A growth mindset can be the key to unlocking your students' full potential.

By fostering a growth mindset, students are more likely to embrace challenges, persist in the face of setbacks, and believe in their ability to learn and grow.

Incorporating growth mindset principles into the curriculum can help students develop a love for lifelong learning and equip them with the skills needed to thrive in an ever-changing world.

Creating a growth mindset culture in education can empower students to take ownership of their learning, celebrate their progress, and support one another as they strive for excellence.

Growth Mindset in Schools and Classrooms

Having a growth mindset in schools and classrooms can significantly enhance learning and empower students to thrive.

When students believe that their abilities can be developed through hard work, effective strategies, and input from others, they are more likely to embrace challenges, persevere in the face of obstacles, and view failures as opportunities for growth.

By promoting a growth mindset culture, educators can create an environment that fosters resilience, curiosity, and a love for learning.

Students with a growth mindset are more motivated to put in the effort required to master new skills and achieve academic success. They understand that intelligence and abilities are not fixed, but can be improved through dedication and practice.

In addition, a growth mindset encourages students to seek feedback and actively engage in the learning process, leading to deeper understanding and higher achievement.

By nurturing a growth mindset, schools and classrooms can empower students to become lifelong learners who are prepared to face challenges, adapt to new situations, and thrive in an ever-changing world.

Benefits of Growth Mindset for Students

Now that you understand how growth mindset can be implemented in schools and classrooms, let's dive into the benefits it brings to students.

Embracing a growth mindset allows you to unlock your full potential by believing that your abilities can be developed through dedication and hard work. With this mindset, you become more resilient in the face of challenges, seeing them as opportunities for growth rather than setbacks.

By understanding that effort and persistence lead to improvement, you become more motivated to take on new challenges and push yourself outside of your comfort zone.

Additionally, a growth mindset encourages you to seek out feedback and learn from your mistakes, allowing you to continuously improve and excel in your academic pursuits.

So, by adopting a growth mindset, you equip yourself with the tools necessary to thrive as a lifelong learner and achieve success in all aspects of your educational journey.

Incorporating Growth Mindset in Curriculum

By incorporating a growth mindset into your curriculum, you can cultivate a classroom environment that encourages students to embrace challenges and view them as stepping stones towards their personal and academic growth.

When students are taught to believe in their ability to learn and improve, they become more motivated and resilient in the face of difficulties.

By emphasizing the importance of effort, perseverance, and the power of yet, you can help students develop a love for learning and a belief in their own potential.

Incorporating growth mindset principles into your curriculum also fosters a sense of collaboration and support among students, as they learn to value the achievements and progress of their peers.

With a growth mindset, students become more willing to take risks, ask questions, and seek feedback, which leads to deeper understanding and mastery of the material.

By embracing a growth mindset in your curriculum, you can empower your students to become lifelong learners who aren't afraid to face challenges and strive for excellence.

Creating a Growth Mindset Culture in Education

Embrace a mindset of limitless potential, where you foster a culture of growth and resilience in education.

By creating a growth mindset culture in education, you provide an environment where students are encouraged to take risks, embrace challenges, and persist in the face of setbacks.

This culture not only promotes a love for learning but also equips students with the essential skills needed for success in an ever-changing world.

By emphasizing the power of effort, the value of mistakes, and the importance of continuous improvement, you empower students to believe in their ability to grow and achieve their goals.

In this culture, failure is seen as an opportunity for growth, and students are encouraged to learn from their mistakes and try again.

By instilling a growth mindset in education, you are shaping resilient learners who are equipped with the tools they need to thrive in all aspects of their lives.

Growth Mindset for Teachers

If you want to make a positive impact on your students' outcomes, it's crucial to cultivate a growth mindset as a teacher. By believing in your own ability to learn and grow, you can inspire your students to do the same.

Overcoming limiting beliefs in teaching is essential for creating an environment that fosters growth and resilience, and there are strategies you can use to develop a growth mindset in yourself.

By fostering resilience and grit in educators, we can create a community of teachers who aren't afraid to take risks and continuously improve, ultimately benefiting the students they serve.

Teacher Mindset and Student Outcomes

With a growth mindset, you create an environment where students flourish and achieve their full potential. By adopting a mindset that embraces challenges, values effort, and sees failure as an opportunity for growth, you can inspire your students to develop the same mindset.

When you believe in their ability to learn and grow, you encourage them to take on more challenging tasks, push through obstacles, and persist in their learning journey. This positive mindset not only boosts their confidence but also enhances their motivation and engagement in the classroom.

As a result, students become more resilient, develop a love for learning, and consistently strive for improvement. By fostering a growth mindset, you empower your students to achieve their highest academic and personal outcomes, setting them up for success in school and beyond.

Overcoming Limiting Beliefs in Teaching

Conquer your doubts and unleash your true teaching potential by challenging the limiting beliefs that hold you back.

As a teacher, it's easy to fall into the trap of thinking that you're not good enough or that you can't make a difference. But the truth is, you have the power to shape young minds and inspire the next generation.

By adopting a growth mindset and embracing the idea that your abilities can be developed through dedication and hard work, you can overcome these self-imposed limitations. Believe in your ability to learn and grow as an educator, and watch as your students thrive under your guidance.

Don't let fear or self-doubt hold you back from reaching your full potential. Embrace the challenges, learn from your mistakes, and continue to evolve as a teacher.

Your students deserve nothing less than your best, and by challenging your limiting beliefs, you can provide them with an education that will empower them for a lifetime.

Strategies to Cultivate a Growth Mindset in Teachers

Embrace the power within you and watch as your teaching abilities transform, unlocking endless possibilities for you and your students.

Cultivating a growth mindset as a teacher is crucial for personal and professional development.

One strategy to foster this mindset is to embrace challenges and view them as opportunities for growth. Instead of shying away from difficult tasks, approach them with curiosity and a willingness to learn.

Additionally, seeking feedback and constructive criticism from colleagues and students can help you identify areas for improvement and further enhance your teaching skills.

Another effective strategy is to encourage a supportive and collaborative classroom environment, where mistakes are seen as valuable learning opportunities. By modeling a growth mindset and emphasizing the importance of effort and perseverance, you can inspire your students to adopt the same mindset and become lifelong learners.

Remember, by embracing a growth mindset, you have the power to continuously evolve as an educator and make a lasting impact on your students' lives.

Fostering Resilience and Grit in Educators

Developing resilience and grit is essential for educators like you, as it allows you to navigate challenges and setbacks with determination and perseverance. As an educator, you will undoubtedly face obstacles and difficulties in your teaching journey. However, with resilience, you can bounce back from these challenges and continue to grow and thrive in your profession.

Resilient educators are able to adapt to change, learn from their mistakes, and find innovative solutions to problems. Similarly, cultivating grit enables you to stay focused and committed to your goals, even in the face of adversity.

By fostering resilience and grit, you can inspire your students to develop these qualities as well, creating a classroom environment that is resilient and determined. Remember, resilience and grit are not innate traits, but rather skills that can be developed and honed over time.

So, embrace challenges, learn from setbacks, and keep pushing forward. Your resilience and grit will not only benefit you as an educator but will also inspire and empower your students to thrive in their own learning journeys.

Growth Mindset Practices for Students

Are you interested in nurturing a growth mindset in children?

In this discussion, we'll explore key strategies for fostering a growth mindset in students of different age groups.

By encouraging effort and perseverance, we can empower students to embrace challenges and develop a love for learning.

Additionally, we'll discuss how to create a classroom environment that promotes a growth mindset, inspiring students to believe in their abilities and strive for continuous improvement.

Nurturing a Growth Mindset in Children

Encouraging children to adopt a growth mindset plants the seeds for a lifelong love of learning and continuous improvement. By nurturing a growth mindset in children, you're empowering them to believe in their abilities and see challenges as opportunities for growth.

It's important to praise their efforts and resilience, rather than focusing solely on their achievements. Teach them that intelligence and skills can be developed through dedication and hard work, and that mistakes are an essential part of the learning process.

Create a supportive environment where they feel safe to take risks, ask questions, and explore new ideas. Encourage them to set goals and celebrate progress, emphasizing that setbacks are temporary and opportunities to learn and improve.

By fostering a growth mindset in children, you're setting them up for success in all aspects of their lives, instilling in them a love of learning that'll serve them well into adulthood.

Growth Mindset Strategies for Different Age Groups

To effectively nurture a growth mindset in children of different age groups, you should tailor your strategies to meet their specific developmental needs and abilities, ensuring they embrace challenges as opportunities for personal growth.

For younger children, it is important to provide them with a supportive and encouraging environment where they can explore new things without fear of failure. Encourage them to take on new tasks and praise their efforts rather than focusing solely on the outcome.

As they grow older, you can start introducing more complex challenges and teach them the importance of perseverance and resilience. Help them set realistic goals and provide them with the tools and resources they need to achieve them.

For teenagers, it is crucial to foster a sense of independence and autonomy while still offering guidance and support. Encourage them to take responsibility for their own learning and emphasize the value of effort and hard work.

By tailoring your strategies to the specific needs and abilities of children at different age groups, you can effectively nurture a growth mindset and help them thrive through lifelong learning.

Encouraging Effort and Perseverance in Students

By fostering a sense of determination and never giving up, you can help your students discover the joy of overcoming challenges and achieving their goals. Encouraging effort and perseverance is essential in developing a growth mindset, as it teaches students that their abilities can be developed through dedication and hard work.

When students encounter obstacles or setbacks, it is important to remind them that mistakes are opportunities for learning and growth. By emphasizing the process rather than just the outcome, you can help students develop resilience and a positive attitude towards challenges.

Encourage them to set realistic goals, break them down into manageable steps, and celebrate their progress along the way. By instilling a belief in their own abilities and teaching them the value of perseverance, you can empower your students to thrive and succeed in all areas of their lives.

Promoting a Growth Mindset in the Classroom Environment

Create an inclusive and supportive classroom environment where you can inspire students to embrace challenges and believe in their ability to grow and improve. By fostering a growth mindset in the classroom, you can encourage students to view mistakes and failures as opportunities for learning and development.

Provide them with a safe space to take risks and make mistakes without fear of judgment or failure. Celebrate their efforts and progress, rather than solely focusing on outcomes. Encourage collaboration and peer feedback, as this can help students understand that learning is a collective effort and that everyone has room for improvement.

Use positive reinforcement and praise their efforts, highlighting the process rather than just the end result. Additionally, provide students with a variety of learning opportunities and resources to cater to different learning styles and abilities.

By creating a growth mindset classroom environment, you can empower students to take ownership of their learning journey and develop the confidence and motivation to thrive through lifelong learning.

Assessing and Developing Growth Mindset in Education

Assessing and developing growth mindset in education is crucial for the success of students.

By evaluating growth mindset in students, educators can identify areas for improvement and tailor instruction to meet individual needs.

Tracking progress and growth mindset development allows for continuous growth and improvement, while creating personalized growth mindset plans ensures that students are actively engaged in their own learning.

Collaboration between teachers, parents, and students is essential in fostering a growth mindset culture and supporting students on their journey towards lifelong learning.

Evaluating Growth Mindset in Students

Students with a growth mindset embrace the power of lifelong learning and continuously evaluate their own progress. By adopting a growth mindset, students understand that intelligence and abilities can be developed through dedication and hard work. They actively seek out challenges and view setbacks as opportunities for growth.

Evaluating their own progress allows students to identify areas for improvement and develop strategies to overcome obstacles. They take ownership of their learning and strive to reach their full potential.

With a growth mindset, students are motivated to put in the effort required to succeed and are more likely to persevere when faced with difficulties. By constantly evaluating their own growth, students with a growth mindset are better equipped to thrive in the ever-changing world and achieve their goals.

Tracking Progress and Growth Mindset Development

Imagine thinking that tracking your progress and development is a waste of time and has no impact on your ability to succeed. Well, let me tell you, that couldn't be further from the truth.

Tracking your progress is not only essential for growth mindset development, but it also allows you to see how far you've come and gives you a sense of accomplishment. It's like having a roadmap that helps you navigate your journey towards success.

By tracking your progress, you can identify areas where you've improved and areas where you still need to work on. This self-awareness is crucial for lifelong learning and personal growth. It keeps you motivated, focused, and accountable for your own development.

So, don't underestimate the power of tracking your progress. Embrace it, and watch how it propels you towards greater success.

Creating Personalized Growth Mindset Plans

Take control of your personal growth by creating a customized plan that will propel you towards success. By tailoring your growth mindset plan to your unique needs and goals, you can maximize your potential and overcome any obstacles that come your way.

Start by identifying areas where you want to grow and set specific, measurable goals that will challenge and stretch you. Break these goals down into smaller, manageable steps that you can take on a daily or weekly basis. This will help you stay focused and motivated, as you can track your progress and celebrate your achievements along the way.

Be flexible and willing to adjust your plan as needed, as growth isn't always linear and you may encounter setbacks or unexpected opportunities. Remember to seek out resources and support systems that can help you in your journey, whether it's books, courses, mentors, or accountability partners.

With a personalized growth mindset plan, you can continuously learn, adapt, and thrive in all areas of your life.

Collaboration between Teachers, Parents, and Students

Working together, teachers, parents, and students can create a harmonious symphony of support, empowering each other to soar to new heights. Collaboration between these three stakeholders is crucial in cultivating a growth mindset in students.

Teachers can provide guidance and resources, parents can offer encouragement and reinforcement at home, and students can actively participate in their own learning journey. By fostering a strong partnership, teachers, parents, and students can create an environment that promotes lifelong learning and growth.

This collaboration allows for a deeper understanding of each student's strengths and weaknesses, enabling tailored support and personalized growth mindset plans. By working together, we can ensure that every student reaches their full potential and develops the skills necessary to thrive in an ever-changing world.

Chapter 4: Applying Growth Mindset in Personal Relationships

In Chapter 4, you'll explore the application of a growth mindset in your personal relationships. Learn how to foster a growth mindset in your interpersonal communication, allowing you to build stronger and more resilient relationships.

Discover the power of parenting with a growth mindset and how it can positively impact your children's development.

Finally, delve into the importance of a growth mindset in teamwork and collaboration, and how it can lead to greater success and innovation in your professional life.

Growth Mindset in Interpersonal Communication

Are you looking to improve your communication skills and enhance your relationships?

Adopting a growth mindset in interpersonal communication can be the key to transforming fixed mindset communication patterns.

By actively listening and being open-minded, you can foster empathy and understanding, leading to stronger connections with others.

Additionally, embracing constructive feedback and viewing it as an opportunity for growth can help you continually improve and thrive in your lifelong learning journey.

Transforming Fixed Mindset Communication

By embracing a growth mindset, you can effortlessly unlock your potential and revolutionize the way you communicate with others. When you transform your fixed mindset communication, you open yourself up to new possibilities and opportunities for growth.

Instead of being limited by self-doubt or fear of failure, you approach conversations and interactions with a curiosity and willingness to learn. This mindset shift allows you to listen more actively, seek feedback and constructive criticism, and adapt your communication style to better connect with others.

You understand that communication is a skill that can be developed and improved over time, and you're not afraid to make mistakes or step outside of your comfort zone. With a growth mindset, you're open to new ideas, perspectives, and ways of thinking, which leads to more effective and meaningful communication with others.

So, why settle for a fixed mindset when you can embrace a growth mindset and transform the way you communicate? Start today and experience the incredible advantages and opportunities that come with it.

Active Listening and Open-mindedness

Now that you understand the importance of transforming fixed mindset communication, let's dive into the next crucial skill: active listening and open-mindedness.

By actively listening to others and being open-minded, you open yourself up to a world of new ideas, perspectives, and knowledge. When you truly listen to someone, you not only hear their words but also their emotions, thoughts, and experiences. This allows you to gain a deeper understanding of their point of view and fosters a sense of empathy and connection.

Being open-minded means being willing to consider different viewpoints, even if they challenge your own beliefs. This mindset enables you to embrace the diversity of ideas and learn from others, ultimately leading to personal growth and development.

So, as you embark on your journey of lifelong learning, remember that active listening and open-mindedness are key skills that will help you thrive and succeed.

Empathy and Understanding

To truly understand others and build connections, you must develop empathy and a willingness to see things from their perspective, which can be fostered through active listening and open-mindedness.

Did you know that studies have shown that practicing empathy not only improves relationships but also increases overall life satisfaction?

By putting yourself in someone else's shoes, you open yourself up to a whole new world of understanding and connection.

Empathy allows you to truly listen to others, to hear their thoughts and feelings without judgment. It allows you to validate their experiences and emotions, creating a safe space for them to express themselves.

When you approach conversations with empathy, you show others that you value their perspective and that you are willing to learn from them.

This kind of understanding and connection can lead to stronger relationships, improved teamwork, and a more harmonious and inclusive environment.

So, the next time you engage in a conversation, practice empathy and strive to understand the other person's point of view. You may be surprised at how much you can learn and grow through this simple act of understanding.

Constructive Feedback and Growth

Developing a habit of providing constructive feedback fosters personal and professional development by encouraging you to reflect on your actions and make necessary improvements.

By offering feedback that's specific, actionable, and focused on the behavior rather than the person, you create an environment where growth and learning are valued.

Constructive feedback helps you identify areas for improvement, challenge your assumptions, and gain a deeper understanding of your strengths and weaknesses.

It allows you to see obstacles as opportunities for growth and helps you develop the resilience and adaptability needed to thrive in a rapidly changing world.

By embracing feedback and viewing it as a valuable tool for growth, you can continuously learn and improve, unlocking your full potential and achieving ongoing success.

So, don't shy away from giving and receiving constructive feedback; embrace it as an essential part of your journey towards lifelong learning and personal growth.

Building Resilient Relationships

In this discussion, we'll explore how a growth mindset can be applied to conflict resolution, allowing you to navigate challenging situations with resilience and open-mindedness.

By embracing a growth mindset, you can overcome relationship challenges by continuously learning and adapting. This fosters a positive and proactive approach to problem-solving.

Additionally, we'll delve into the importance of nurturing a success mindset in partnerships. This creates an environment that cultivates mutual growth and support.

Growth Mindset in Conflict Resolution

Embrace the power of a growth mindset and watch as conflicts become opportunities for growth and understanding.

When faced with conflict, it can be easy to become defensive or avoidant. However, by adopting a growth mindset, you can approach conflicts with curiosity and openness.

Instead of viewing conflicts as threats, see them as chances to learn and develop new skills. A growth mindset allows you to see the bigger picture and understand that disagreements can lead to deeper understanding and stronger relationships.

By actively seeking to understand the other person's perspective and finding common ground, you can turn conflicts into opportunities for personal and interpersonal growth.

With a growth mindset, you can transform conflict resolution into a positive and transformative experience.

Overcoming Relationship Challenges with a Growth Mindset

By adopting a growth mindset, we can approach relationship challenges as opportunities for blossoming and overcoming obstacles together. Instead of viewing conflicts as roadblocks, we can see them as chances to learn, grow, and strengthen our bond.

With a growth mindset, we understand that relationships require effort, patience, and open communication. We embrace the idea that challenges are a normal part of any relationship and that they can actually bring us closer together.

By approaching relationship challenges with a growth mindset, we can actively seek solutions, compromise, and work towards a shared understanding. We recognize that both partners have room for growth and improvement, and we're willing to put in the necessary work to nurture the relationship.

With a growth mindset, we're not afraid to admit our mistakes, apologize, and learn from them. We understand that setbacks are opportunities for personal and relational growth.

By embracing a growth mindset in relationships, we create an environment of trust, support, and mutual respect, where both partners can thrive and overcome challenges together.

Nurturing Success Mindset in Partnerships

To foster a success mindset in your partnership, you can cultivate an environment of encouragement, support, and belief in each other's potential for growth and achievement. By consistently providing positive feedback and acknowledging each other's progress, you can reinforce a mindset that embraces challenges and views setbacks as opportunities for learning and improvement.

It is important to communicate openly and honestly, sharing your goals and aspirations, and listening actively to your partner's dreams and ambitions. By setting shared goals and working together towards them, you can create a sense of purpose and motivation that propels both of you forward.

Celebrate each other's successes, no matter how small, and use them as building blocks to fuel further growth. Remember that a success mindset is not about competition, but rather about collaboration and mutual growth. By nurturing a success mindset in your partnership, you can create a supportive and empowering environment that propels both of you towards lifelong learning and achievement.

Cultivating Mutual Growth and Support

Now that you've learned about nurturing a success mindset in partnerships, it's time to delve into the importance of cultivating mutual growth and support.

In any relationship, whether personal or professional, it's crucial to have a foundation built on continuous learning and development. When both individuals in a partnership embrace a growth mindset, they open themselves up to new possibilities and endless opportunities for growth.

By actively seeking out ways to support and uplift each other, you create an environment that fosters collaboration, innovation, and ultimately, success. Cultivating mutual growth and support not only benefits the individuals involved but also strengthens the partnership as a whole.

So, let's explore how you can create a thriving ecosystem of continuous learning and support that propels both you and your partner towards your shared goals.

Parenting with a Growth Mindset

Are you looking for ways to improve your parenting skills and create a nurturing environment for your children?

Shifting parenting paradigms with a growth mindset can be a game-changer.

By encouraging a growth mindset in your children, you can empower them to embrace challenges, learn from their mistakes, and persist in the face of setbacks.

Teaching resilience and persistence will equip your children with the tools they need to navigate the ups and downs of life.

Promoting self-directed learning in children will not only foster their curiosity and love for learning but also teach them how to take ownership of their education.

Lastly, by fostering a growth mindset culture at home, you can create an environment that celebrates effort, growth, and the pursuit of personal development.

Shifting Parenting Paradigms with Growth Mindset

Embrace the power of a growth mindset and watch as your parenting paradigm shifts, enabling you to cultivate resilience and foster a love for lifelong learning in your children.

By adopting a growth mindset, you can change your perspective on challenges and failures, emphasizing the importance of effort and perseverance.

Instead of praising innate abilities, focus on praising your child's hard work and dedication. Encourage them to take risks, try new things, and view setbacks as opportunities for growth.

By modeling a growth mindset and embracing the idea of continuous learning, you can create an environment that nurtures your child's curiosity and passion for acquiring knowledge.

As a result, they will develop a sense of resilience, a willingness to embrace challenges, and the motivation to constantly improve themselves.

So, let go of fixed beliefs about your child's abilities and embrace a growth mindset to unleash their full potential and set them on a path to lifelong learning and success.

Encouraging a Growth Mindset in Children

Take the time to nurture a mindset of progress and possibility in your children, encouraging them to explore new experiences and embrace challenges.

By fostering a growth mindset in your children, you're setting them up for success in all areas of their lives. Teach them that failure isn't a setback, but rather a stepping stone towards improvement.

Encourage them to take risks and try new things, even if they may not succeed at first. Help them see that their abilities and intelligence can be developed through hard work and dedication.

Praise their efforts and perseverance, rather than just their achievements. Remind them that mistakes are opportunities to learn and grow, and that setbacks are temporary.

By instilling a growth mindset in your children, you're empowering them to become lifelong learners who aren't afraid to take on challenges and strive for continuous improvement.

Teaching Resilience and Persistence

Developing resilience and persistence will empower you to overcome challenges and achieve your goals.

When you cultivate a growth mindset, you understand that setbacks are not permanent and that failure is simply a stepping stone towards success.

By teaching yourself to be resilient, you will bounce back from adversity stronger than ever before.

Persistence, on the other hand, is the key to unlocking your full potential. It's the determination to keep going even when faced with obstacles or setbacks.

When you persist, you show the world that you are committed to your goals and that you won't give up easily.

Together, resilience and persistence create a powerful combination that will propel you towards lifelong learning and personal growth.

So, embrace challenges, embrace failure, and most importantly, embrace the mindset of resilience and persistence.

Promoting Self-Directed Learning in Children

You may think that allowing children to direct their own learning is a recipe for disaster, but it actually fosters independence and a love for learning that will serve them well throughout their lives.

When children are given the freedom to explore their own interests and pursue their own learning goals, they become active participants in their own education. They develop a sense of ownership and responsibility for their learning, which in turn boosts their motivation and engagement.

Self-directed learning allows children to develop important skills such as problem-solving, critical thinking, and decision-making. It encourages them to ask questions, seek answers, and think creatively.

By taking charge of their own learning, children also learn how to set goals, manage their time, and take initiative. This not only prepares them for future academic success but also equips them with the skills and mindset needed to thrive in an ever-changing world.

So, instead of fearing the chaos of self-directed learning, embrace it as an opportunity for growth and development for your children.

Fostering a Growth Mindset Culture at Home

Now that you understand the importance of promoting self-directed learning in children, it's time to take it a step further and foster a growth mindset culture at home.

By adopting a growth mindset yourself and encouraging your children to do the same, you can create an environment that values effort, perseverance, and the belief that abilities can be developed through dedication and hard work.

Cultivating a growth mindset at home encourages curiosity, resilience, and a love for learning. It empowers children to embrace challenges, view setbacks as opportunities for growth, and develop a lifelong love of learning.

So, how can you foster a growth mindset culture at home?

Growth Mindset in Teamwork and Collaboration

If you want to excel in teamwork and collaboration, embracing a growth mindset is key.

By adopting a growth mindset, you can foster effective teamwork by encouraging open communication, learning from mistakes, and embracing challenges as opportunities for growth.

Building trust and psychological safety within your team is crucial for collaboration to thrive, as it allows for honest and constructive feedback, risk-taking, and a sense of belonging.

Additionally, leveraging diverse perspectives with a growth mindset can lead to innovative solutions and fresh ideas, while encouraging a culture of continuous improvement ensures that your team is always striving for better results.

Growth Mindset for Effective Teamwork

Collaboration flourishes when team members embrace a growth mindset. By adopting this mindset, you recognize that your abilities can be developed through dedication and hard work. This perspective allows you to approach teamwork with a sense of curiosity and a willingness to learn from others.

When you have a growth mindset, you view challenges as opportunities for growth and feedback as valuable insights. This mindset also enables you to embrace collaboration as a chance to leverage the strengths of your teammates and learn from their expertise. Rather than being intimidated by their skills, you see them as valuable resources that can contribute to the success of the team.

With a growth mindset, you are open to new ideas, receptive to feedback, and motivated to continuously improve. This attitude not only enhances the effectiveness of teamwork but also fosters a positive and productive team environment.

So, strive to embrace a growth mindset and watch as your collaboration skills soar to new heights.

Building Trust and Psychological Safety

To truly cultivate effective teamwork, it's essential that you prioritize building trust and creating an environment of psychological safety.

When team members trust one another, they're more willing to collaborate, share ideas, and take risks. Trust allows for open communication and fosters a sense of belonging within the team.

Additionally, psychological safety is crucial for creating an environment where team members feel comfortable expressing their thoughts and opinions without fear of judgment or reprisal. When individuals feel safe to share their ideas, they're more likely to contribute their unique perspectives, leading to innovative solutions and increased team performance.

By actively working on building trust and psychological safety within your team, you can create an environment that encourages open communication, collaboration, and continuous growth.

Leveraging Diverse Perspectives with a Growth Mindset

By embracing diverse perspectives and having a mindset that embraces continuous improvement, you can create an environment that fosters innovation and allows for exponential growth.

When you bring together individuals with different backgrounds, experiences, and ways of thinking, you open up a world of possibilities. Each person brings their unique insights and ideas to the table, challenging the status quo and offering fresh perspectives. This diversity of thought sparks creativity and encourages collaboration, leading to breakthrough innovations and solutions to complex problems.

With a growth mindset, you're open to learning from others, valuing their contributions, and seeking out different viewpoints. This not only enriches your understanding but also strengthens the collective intelligence of the team.

By leveraging diverse perspectives with a growth mindset, you can tap into the full potential of your team and drive remarkable progress.

So, embrace the power of diversity and cultivate a mindset that values continuous learning and improvement. The rewards will be far-reaching, as you create an environment where everyone can thrive and contribute their best.

Encouraging Innovation and Continuous Improvement

Embracing diverse perspectives and fostering a culture of continuous improvement allows for exponential growth and sparks innovative thinking. When you encourage individuals from different backgrounds and experiences to come together and share their ideas, you create an environment where new and creative solutions can emerge.

By valuing the contributions of each team member and promoting a growth mindset, you foster a sense of empowerment and motivation that drives individuals to constantly seek improvement. This mindset not only encourages individuals to take risks and think outside the box, but it also promotes a willingness to learn from failures and setbacks.

When you combine these elements, you create a recipe for innovation and continuous improvement that can lead to remarkable achievements and success. So, embrace diverse perspectives, nurture a culture of continuous improvement, and watch as your team thrives through lifelong learning.

Chapter 5: Overcoming Challenges and Obstacles

In Chapter 5, you'll explore the power of a growth mindset when it comes to overcoming challenges and obstacles.

You'll learn how to embrace failure as an opportunity for growth and how to navigate through obstacles with resilience and determination.

Additionally, you'll discover the impact of a growth mindset in the workplace, as it can lead to increased motivation, productivity, and innovation.

So get ready to unlock your full potential and conquer any challenge that comes your way with the power of a growth mindset.

Growth Mindset in the Face of Failure

Embrace failure as a learning opportunity by recognizing that it's an essential part of growth. Reframe failure as a chance to promote personal and professional development, rather than a setback or a reflection of your abilities.

Overcome the fear of failure by adopting strategies such as setting realistic goals, seeking feedback, and learning from mistakes. By building resilience through failure, you can bounce back stronger, develop new skills, and thrive in the face of challenges.

Embracing Failure as a Learning Opportunity

With each stumble and setback, failure presents itself as a stepping stone towards growth and enlightenment.

Embracing failure as a learning opportunity allows you to shift your perspective and see it as a valuable experience rather than a roadblock.

It's through failure that you gain invaluable insights, learn from your mistakes, and develop resilience.

By reframing failure as a chance to learn and improve, you open yourself up to new possibilities and avenues for growth.

Instead of dwelling on the negative aspects of failure, focus on the lessons it teaches you and the potential it holds for personal and professional development.

Embracing failure not only helps you overcome obstacles, but it also cultivates a growth mindset that fuels your motivation to keep pushing forward.

So, when faced with failure, remember that it's not the end, but rather a catalyst for growth and an opportunity to become better, stronger, and more resilient.

Reframing Failure to Promote Growth

When we view failure as a springboard for growth, it's like a sculptor seeing a block of marble not as a solid mass, but as the potential for a beautiful masterpiece.

Reframing failure allows us to shift our mindset and see setbacks as opportunities for learning and improvement.

Instead of viewing failure as a reflection of our abilities, we can see it as a natural part of the learning process.

By embracing failure, we open ourselves up to new possibilities and experiences. We become more resilient and adaptable, as we learn to bounce back from setbacks and use them as stepping stones towards success.

Reframing failure also helps us to develop a growth mindset, where we believe that our abilities and intelligence can be developed through dedication and hard work.

This mindset encourages us to persevere in the face of challenges, knowing that failure is not a final outcome, but rather a temporary setback on the path to mastery.

So, let's reframe failure and unlock its potential for growth and success.

Strategies to Overcome Fear of Failure

Now that you understand the importance of reframing failure as a growth opportunity, let's talk about strategies to overcome your fear of failure.

It's natural to feel anxious or fearful when facing the possibility of failure, but it's important to remember that failure is not the end of the world. By adopting a growth mindset, you can view failure as a stepping stone towards success.

One strategy to overcome your fear is to set realistic goals and break them down into smaller, achievable steps. This allows you to focus on making progress rather than being consumed by the fear of failure.

Additionally, surrounding yourself with a supportive network of friends, mentors, or colleagues can provide the encouragement and motivation needed to push through your fear.

Remember, embracing failure as a learning opportunity is essential for personal growth and development. So, don't let fear hold you back from taking risks and pursuing your goals.

Building Resilience through Failure

Building resilience through failure can be a transformative journey that helps you bounce back stronger and more determined than ever before.

When we experience failure, it can be easy to feel discouraged and give up on our goals. However, by embracing failure as a learning opportunity and reframing it as a stepping stone to success, we can develop resilience and perseverance.

Failure allows us to identify our weaknesses, learn from our mistakes, and adapt our strategies. It teaches us to be flexible, creative, and persistent in the face of challenges.

By viewing failure as a necessary part of the growth process, we can cultivate a mindset that is resilient and open to continuous learning.

So, instead of fearing failure, embrace it as a valuable teacher and use it to fuel your determination to succeed. Remember, every failure brings you one step closer to achieving your goals.

Navigating Obstacles with a Growth Mindset

Are you tired of feeling held back by your own self-limiting beliefs?

It's time to break free and embrace a growth mindset.

In this discussion, we'll explore the power of developing strategies to overcome challenges and how a growth mindset can enhance problem-solving skills.

Get ready to unleash your creativity and tackle obstacles head-on with a mindset that knows no limits.

Overcoming Self-Limiting Beliefs

Imagine you're on a fast-moving train, leaving behind the self-limiting beliefs that have held you back for so long.

It's a liberating feeling, isn't it? You no longer let those negative thoughts define your capabilities. Instead, you embrace the mindset that you have the power to grow and improve.

You recognize that your abilities are not fixed, but rather, can be developed through dedication and effort. With this newfound perspective, you are able to push past your comfort zone and take on challenges with gusto.

No longer are you held captive by the belief that you're not good enough or that success is out of reach. You have the confidence to pursue your goals and the resilience to overcome setbacks.

Self-limiting beliefs no longer have a hold on you because you understand that your potential is limitless.

So, keep that growth mindset alive and continue on this journey of lifelong learning, and watch as you thrive in ways you never thought possible.

Developing Strategies to Overcome Challenges

Conquering challenges becomes possible when you strategize and develop effective approaches to overcome them. By adopting a growth mindset, you can embrace challenges as opportunities for growth and learning.

One strategy is to break the challenge down into smaller, manageable tasks, allowing you to tackle each one step by step. Additionally, seeking support from others can provide valuable insights and perspectives, helping you navigate through obstacles.

Embracing failures as learning experiences and reframing setbacks as temporary hurdles rather than permanent barriers can also fuel your perseverance and determination. Remember, developing effective strategies to overcome challenges is a crucial skill that can lead to personal growth and success.

So, don't shy away from challenges, embrace them and discover the power of your growth mindset.

Growth Mindset and Problem-Solving

By fostering a can-do attitude and approaching problems as opportunities for growth, you can develop effective problem-solving skills.

Embracing a growth mindset allows you to see challenges as stepping stones to success rather than roadblocks.

Rather than giving up when faced with a difficult problem, you persist and seek out new strategies and solutions.

With a growth mindset, you understand that intelligence and abilities can be developed through dedication and hard work.

This mindset empowers you to tackle complex problems with confidence and resilience.

You believe in your ability to learn, adapt, and overcome obstacles, which leads to innovative and creative problem-solving.

By adopting a growth mindset, you can transform challenges into opportunities for personal and professional growth.

So, embrace a can-do attitude, cultivate a growth mindset, and unlock your full potential as a problem solver.

Encouraging Creative Thinking in Problem-solving

Fostering a can-do attitude and embracing creativity allows for innovative problem-solving techniques.

When faced with challenges, it's important to think outside the box and explore different perspectives.

By encouraging creative thinking, you open yourself up to new possibilities and solutions that may not have been considered before.

Creative problem-solving involves taking risks, being open to failure, and learning from mistakes.

It requires thinking beyond the obvious and finding unique ways to approach problems.

Embracing creativity in problem-solving not only allows you to come up with more effective solutions, but it also enhances your overall problem-solving skills and mindset.

So, don't be afraid to think creatively and explore different avenues when faced with a problem.

Embrace your creativity and let it guide you towards innovative solutions.

Growth Mindset in the Workplace

If you want to foster a growth mindset culture in your organization, it's important to encourage employees to embrace challenges, learn from feedback, and persist in the face of setbacks.

By promoting a growth mindset, you can cultivate adaptability in the workplace, helping employees to navigate change and uncertainty with confidence.

Strategies for promoting a growth mindset include providing opportunities for growth and development, fostering a supportive and collaborative environment, and offering recognition and rewards for effort and progress.

Overcoming imposter syndrome with a growth mindset involves recognizing and reframing negative self-talk, seeking feedback and validation from others, and focusing on personal growth and improvement.

Building resilience and perseverance in the workplace can be achieved by encouraging employees to view failures as opportunities for learning, providing support and resources to help them bounce back from setbacks, and fostering a culture that values effort and resilience.

Fostering a Growth Mindset Culture in Organizations

Creating a growth mindset culture in organizations is essential for fostering continuous learning and development. When organizations embrace a growth mindset, they create an environment that encourages employees to take risks, embrace challenges, and persist in the face of setbacks.

This culture of growth not only promotes innovation and creativity, but also allows individuals to reach their full potential. By valuing the process of learning and emphasizing the importance of effort and perseverance, organizations can empower their employees to continuously improve and grow.

A growth mindset culture also fosters collaboration and teamwork, as individuals are more likely to seek feedback, learn from others, and share knowledge and resources.

Overall, organizations that prioritize a growth mindset culture are better equipped to adapt to change, stay ahead in a rapidly evolving world, and thrive through lifelong learning.

Growth Mindset and Adaptability in the Workplace

Embrace a growth mindset and watch as your adaptability in the workplace soars to new heights. By adopting a growth mindset, you open yourself up to continuous learning and improvement, enabling you to adapt to any changes or challenges that come your way.

Rather than being resistant to change, you become proactive in seeking new opportunities for growth and development. With a growth mindset, you're not afraid to take risks and step out of your comfort zone, knowing that failure is just a stepping stone towards success. This mindset allows you to approach setbacks as learning experiences, finding innovative solutions and adapting your approach as needed.

Your ability to quickly adapt to new situations and embrace change becomes a valuable asset in the workplace, leading to increased productivity, creativity, and overall success. So, why settle for a fixed mindset when you can unlock the power of a growth mindset and thrive in an ever-evolving professional landscape?

Embrace the growth mindset and let your adaptability shine.

Strategies for Promoting Growth Mindset in the Workplace

By fostering a culture of continuous improvement and encouraging employees to embrace challenges, organizations can cultivate an environment where individuals are motivated to take risks and learn from failures, leading to increased innovation and resilience.

For example, a tech company implemented a 'Fail Forward' initiative, where employees were rewarded for taking calculated risks and learning from their mistakes, resulting in a significant increase in product development and a boost in employee morale.

This approach not only encourages employees to step out of their comfort zones and explore new ideas but also fosters a sense of trust and psychological safety within the organization. When employees feel supported and encouraged to learn from their failures, they are more likely to approach challenges with a growth mindset, leading to a greater willingness to try new approaches and ultimately driving innovation and success.

Additionally, this mindset shift can enhance employee resilience, as they become more adaptable and better equipped to navigate the ever-changing demands of the workplace.

By promoting a growth mindset in the workplace, organizations can unlock the potential of their employees and create a culture of continuous learning and improvement.

Overcoming Imposter Syndrome with a Growth Mindset

Now that you've learned about strategies for promoting a growth mindset in the workplace, it's time to tackle a common challenge that many individuals face: imposter syndrome.

Imposter syndrome can leave you feeling like a fraud, doubting your abilities, and fearing that others will expose you as a fake. However, by embracing a growth mindset, you can overcome these negative thoughts and beliefs.

With a growth mindset, you understand that your abilities can be developed through effort and perseverance. You recognize that making mistakes is part of the learning process and that failure does not define you.

By adopting this mindset, you can build confidence in your skills and knowledge, allowing you to overcome imposter syndrome and thrive in your personal and professional life.

So, don't let imposter syndrome hold you back. Embrace the power of a growth mindset and unlock your true potential.

Building Resilience and Perseverance in the Workplace

Build resilience and perseverance in the workplace by understanding that setbacks and challenges are opportunities for growth and development, allowing you to rise above adversity and achieve success.

Embrace a growth mindset that enables you to view obstacles as stepping stones rather than roadblocks, empowering you to bounce back stronger and more determined.

In the face of difficulties, cultivate a positive attitude and see setbacks as valuable learning experiences.

Take the time to reflect on what went wrong and how you can improve, using each setback as a chance to develop new skills and knowledge.

By staying resilient and persevering, you'll develop the ability to adapt to change, overcome obstacles, and achieve your goals.

Remember, success isn't always a linear path, but with a growth mindset, you have the power to turn setbacks into opportunities and ultimately thrive in the workplace.

Encouraging Continuous Learning and Professional Development

To encourage continuous learning and professional development, you should prioritize expanding your knowledge and skills through ongoing education and training opportunities.

For example, imagine you're a sales manager who wants to enhance your leadership abilities. You could enroll in a leadership development program that offers hands-on exercises and workshops. These simulate real-life scenarios, allowing you to practice effective communication and decision-making skills in a supportive environment.

By actively engaging in these learning experiences, you not only gain new insights and strategies, but you also demonstrate a commitment to personal growth and improvement. Additionally, by investing in your own development, you inspire and motivate your team members to do the same. This fosters a culture of continuous learning within your organization.

Remember, professional development isn't just a one-time event; it's a lifelong journey of acquiring new knowledge, refining skills, and adapting to the ever-changing demands of the workplace. Embracing this mindset will give you a distinct advantage in today's competitive business landscape, enabling you to thrive and excel in your career.

So, take the initiative, seek out opportunities for growth, and empower yourself to become the best version of yourself.

Chapter 6: Cultivating Lifelong Learning Habits

In Chapter 6, you'll delve into the topic of cultivating lifelong learning habits. This is essential for personal and professional growth. This chapter explores the connection between lifelong learning and a growth mindset. It emphasizes the importance of adopting a mindset that embraces challenges and views failures as opportunities for growth. You'll also discover strategies for self-directed learning with a growth mindset. And you'll learn how to cultivate a mindset that values knowledge acquisition as a lifelong journey.

Lifelong Learning and Growth Mindset

Are you looking to thrive and grow throughout your life?

The link between having a growth mindset and embracing lifelong learning is undeniable.

By adopting a growth mindset, you open yourself up to endless possibilities for personal and professional growth.

With a mindset shift and the right strategies in place, you can cultivate a lifelong learning mindset that will empower you to continuously learn and adapt to new challenges and opportunities.

So why wait? Start your journey towards lifelong learning today and unlock your full potential.

The Link Between Growth Mindset and Lifelong Learning

Embrace the growth mindset and watch as your thirst for knowledge and desire for personal growth fuel a lifelong commitment to learning.

When you adopt a growth mindset, you believe that intelligence and abilities can be developed through dedication and hard work. This mindset opens up a world of possibilities and encourages you to continuously seek out new challenges and opportunities for growth.

By viewing failure as a stepping stone to success and embracing the process of learning, you're more likely to persist in the face of obstacles and setbacks.

With a growth mindset, you understand that your potential is limitless and that lifelong learning is essential for personal and professional development.

So, why settle for mediocrity when you can embrace the growth mindset and unlock your full potential? Start today and experience the countless advantages that come with a lifelong commitment to learning.

Benefits of Lifelong Learning for Personal and Professional Growth

When you adopt a growth mindset, you can tap into your unlimited potential and continuously evolve personally and professionally through lifelong learning.

By embracing the idea that intelligence and abilities can be developed, you open yourself up to a world of possibilities. Lifelong learning allows you to acquire new knowledge and skills, keeping you relevant and adaptable in an ever-changing world.

Personally, it provides opportunities for self-improvement, helping you become a well-rounded individual. Professionally, it enhances your value in the workplace, making you a sought-after asset.

Lifelong learning also fosters creativity, critical thinking, and problem-solving abilities, which are essential in both personal and professional settings. Moreover, it boosts confidence and increases resilience, as you become more comfortable with taking on new challenges and overcoming obstacles.

So, don't limit yourself. Embrace lifelong learning and unlock the advantages it brings for your personal and professional growth.

Mindset Shifts for Embracing Lifelong Learning

Discover how adopting a new perspective and continuously expanding your knowledge and skills can empower you to embrace lifelong learning and unlock endless opportunities for personal and professional growth.

By shifting your mindset to one that's open to learning and growth, you can overcome the fear of failure and embrace challenges as opportunities for growth.

Instead of viewing setbacks as obstacles, you can see them as stepping stones to success.

Embracing lifelong learning allows you to stay relevant in a rapidly changing world, adapt to new technologies and trends, and continuously improve your abilities.

It helps you develop a thirst for knowledge and a curiosity that drives you to explore new ideas and perspectives.

Lifelong learning also enhances your problem-solving skills, critical thinking abilities, and creativity, making you a valuable asset in any personal or professional setting.

So, why limit yourself when the possibilities for growth are endless?

Embrace the growth mindset and unlock the power of lifelong learning.

Strategies to Cultivate a Lifelong Learning Mindset

By immersing yourself in a continuous journey of exploration and knowledge acquisition, you can unlock the doors to a world of endless possibilities and personal growth.

Cultivating a lifelong learning mindset is a powerful strategy that can help you thrive in all aspects of your life. One way to do this is by embracing curiosity and being open to new ideas and experiences. Allow yourself to ask questions, seek answers, and challenge your assumptions.

Another strategy is to set specific learning goals and create a plan to achieve them. Whether it's learning a new language, mastering a musical instrument, or acquiring new professional skills, having clear goals and a roadmap will keep you motivated and focused.

Additionally, seek out diverse sources of knowledge and perspectives. Read books, listen to podcasts, attend workshops, and engage in meaningful conversations with people from different backgrounds. This will broaden your horizons and expose you to new ideas and ways of thinking.

Finally, embrace failure as an opportunity for growth. View setbacks as valuable learning experiences and use them to fuel your determination and resilience. By adopting these strategies, you can cultivate a lifelong learning mindset and unlock your full potential.

Self-Directed Learning with a Growth Mindset

Are you ready to take ownership of your personal development?

In order to thrive in a rapidly changing world, it's essential to embrace self-directed learning with a growth mindset.

By setting clear learning goals and objectives, you can focus your efforts and stay motivated.

Additionally, developing effective learning strategies will enable you to maximize your learning potential.

And finally, don't forget to reflect on your progress and make adjustments along the way for continuous growth.

Taking Ownership of Personal Development

Taking ownership of personal development is essential for you to continuously grow and thrive in your career.

As an accountant, for example, taking the initiative to learn new software programs can greatly improve your efficiency and effectiveness.

By actively seeking out opportunities for learning and development, you demonstrate your commitment to staying relevant and up-to-date in your field.

This proactive approach not only enhances your skills and knowledge but also showcases your dedication and drive to excel.

Embracing personal development allows you to adapt to changing industry trends, overcome challenges, and seize new opportunities.

So, take ownership of your growth and invest in yourself to unlock your full potential and achieve long-term success in your chosen profession.

Setting Learning Goals and Objectives

Now that you've taken ownership of your personal development, it's time to take the next step and set some learning goals and objectives.

Setting clear goals is crucial for success in any area of life, and learning is no exception. By setting specific objectives, you give yourself a roadmap to follow and a sense of purpose in your learning journey.

Whether you want to acquire new skills, expand your knowledge, or challenge yourself intellectually, setting learning goals will help you stay focused and motivated.

So, take a moment to think about what you want to achieve through lifelong learning. Is there a specific subject or skill you've always wanted to master? Are there areas of personal or professional growth you want to explore?

By defining your learning goals and objectives, you'll be well on your way to unlocking the growth mindset advantage and thriving through lifelong learning.

Developing Effective Learning Strategies

Developing effective learning strategies is crucial for achieving success in your educational journey. By utilizing these strategies, you can maximize your learning potential and make the most out of your educational experience.

One effective strategy is to break down complex tasks into smaller, manageable steps. This allows you to focus on one aspect at a time and prevents you from feeling overwhelmed.

Additionally, using mnemonic devices and visual aids can help enhance your memory and retention of information.

Another important strategy is to actively engage with the material by asking questions, participating in discussions, and seeking clarification when needed. This not only deepens your understanding but also promotes critical thinking skills.

Lastly, it is essential to create a study schedule and stick to it. Consistency and discipline are key factors in effective learning. So, make sure to allocate dedicated time for studying and review regularly.

By implementing these strategies, you can optimize your learning experience and excel in your educational pursuits.

Reflecting and Adjusting for Continuous Growth

By regularly pausing to assess and adapt, you can cultivate a mindset of continuous improvement, propelling yourself forward in your educational journey.

Reflecting on your progress and adjusting your strategies allows you to identify what's working and what needs improvement. This self-awareness enables you to make necessary changes and stay motivated. It also helps you recognize your strengths and areas for growth, allowing you to focus your efforts where they'll have the greatest impact.

Embracing a growth mindset means understanding that setbacks and challenges are opportunities for learning and growth. By reflecting and adjusting, you can overcome obstacles and reach your full potential.

So, take the time to pause, evaluate, and adapt your approach. Your commitment to continuous growth will set you apart and lead to lifelong success.

Cultivating a Growth Mindset in Knowledge Acquisition

When it comes to cultivating a growth mindset in knowledge acquisition, there are several key points to consider.

First, embracing challenges and nurturing intellectual curiosity is crucial. By pushing yourself to tackle difficult tasks and explore new ideas, you can expand your knowledge and develop a lifelong love for learning.

Second, learning from mistakes and feedback is essential for growth. By recognizing and understanding your errors, you can make improvements and continue to progress.

Lastly, seeking diverse perspectives and experiences is vital. By exposing yourself to different viewpoints and ways of thinking, you can broaden your understanding and enhance your problem-solving skills.

So, don't just acquire knowledge, apply and share it. By actively engaging in these practices, you can truly embrace a growth mindset and thrive in your pursuit of knowledge.

Embracing Challenges and Intellectual Curiosity

With an insatiable appetite for knowledge, you're like a fearless explorer venturing into uncharted territories of your mind.

By fully embracing challenges and possessing a natural curiosity, you open yourself up to endless possibilities for growth and learning.

Instead of shying away from difficult tasks, you welcome them as opportunities for personal development.

Your intellectual curiosity fuels your desire to constantly seek new information and expand your understanding of the world.

This mindset allows you to thrive through lifelong learning, continuously improving and adapting to new situations.

Embracing challenges and maintaining a sense of curiosity not only enhances your intellectual abilities but also fosters a sense of fulfillment and satisfaction in your life.

So, embrace challenges, ask questions, and never stop exploring the vast landscape of knowledge that lies before you.

Learning from Mistakes and Feedback

To truly excel, you must be open to learning from your mistakes and accepting feedback given to you. Embracing a growth mindset means understanding that mistakes and failures are not signs of incompetence, but rather opportunities for growth and improvement.

When you make a mistake, it's important to reflect on what went wrong and what you can learn from it. This self-reflection allows you to identify areas for improvement and make adjustments in your approach.

Additionally, seeking and accepting feedback from others is crucial in your journey of lifelong learning. Feedback provides valuable insights and perspectives that can help you gain a deeper understanding of your strengths and weaknesses. It allows you to see blind spots that you may not have been aware of and provides you with the opportunity to make necessary changes.

By embracing mistakes and feedback, you can continuously grow and develop, ultimately leading to greater success and achievement. So, embrace the power of learning from your mistakes and welcome feedback with open arms.

Seeking Diverse Perspectives and Experiences

By actively seeking out diverse perspectives and experiences, you're able to broaden your understanding and enhance your personal and professional development.

When you expose yourself to different viewpoints and engage with people from various backgrounds, you open yourself up to new ideas, challenges, and opportunities for growth.

By embracing diversity, you can gain a deeper appreciation for different cultures, beliefs, and ways of thinking, which can help you become more adaptable and open-minded.

Additionally, seeking diverse perspectives allows you to tap into a wealth of knowledge and expertise that you may not have otherwise been exposed to. This can lead to innovative thinking, creative problem-solving, and a broader skill set, all of which are highly valued in today's rapidly changing world.

So, make a conscious effort to seek out diverse perspectives and experiences, whether it's through reading books from different authors, traveling to different countries, or engaging in conversations with people who have different backgrounds and viewpoints.

Embrace the power of diversity and watch as your personal and professional growth soars to new heights.

Applying and Sharing Knowledge

Immerse yourself in the world of knowledge and watch as your understanding expands and spreads like wildfire.

By applying and sharing your knowledge, you not only solidify your own understanding but also contribute to the growth and development of those around you.

As you actively engage with the information you've learned, you gain a deeper comprehension of the subject matter, uncovering new insights and connections.

Sharing this knowledge with others not only helps solidify your own understanding but also allows you to inspire and empower others to pursue their own lifelong learning journey.

By applying and sharing knowledge, you become a catalyst for growth, fostering a community of continuous learning and collaboration.

So, don't keep your knowledge to yourself - share it with the world and watch as the collective understanding expands and thrives.

Chapter 7: Implementing Growth Mindset Strategies

In Chapter 7 of 'Cultivating Lifelong Learning Habits,' you'll explore powerful strategies to implement a growth mindset in your life.

Assessing your mindset will allow you to understand where you currently stand and identify areas for improvement.

Cultivating a growth mindset practice involves adopting new habits and behaviors that foster continuous learning and development.

By developing a personal growth plan, you'll have a roadmap to guide your journey towards achieving your goals.

Finally, you'll learn how to inspire and influence others, spreading the power of a growth mindset and creating a positive impact in your community.

Embrace these strategies and unleash your full potential.

Assessing Your Mindset

To thrive through lifelong learning, it's important to understand your existing mindset. Identify limiting beliefs and thought patterns. Engage in self-reflection and self-awareness practices.

By understanding your existing mindset, you can gain insight into how it may be influencing your learning and growth. Identifying limiting beliefs and thought patterns allows you to challenge them and replace them with more empowering ones.

Engaging in self-reflection and self-awareness practices helps you continuously evaluate and adjust your mindset to support your lifelong learning journey.

Understanding your Existing Mindset

Once you've grasped the concept of your existing mindset, it's crucial to embrace the growth mindset for lifelong learning. Understanding your existing mindset is the first step towards personal growth and development. By recognizing your current beliefs and limitations, you can begin to challenge them and open yourself up to new possibilities.

The growth mindset encourages you to view challenges as opportunities for growth, to persevere in the face of setbacks, and to believe in your ability to learn and improve. With a growth mindset, you're more likely to take risks, seek out feedback, and continuously strive for improvement.

By adopting this mindset, you can unlock your full potential and thrive in the world of lifelong learning. So, don't limit yourself with a fixed mindset; instead, embrace the growth mindset and watch yourself thrive.

Identifying Limiting Beliefs and Thought Patterns

Understanding and challenging our limiting beliefs and thought patterns is essential for unlocking our full potential and embracing a mindset of continuous growth.

Many of us hold onto beliefs that limit our abilities and hinder our progress. These beliefs can include thoughts such as "I'm not smart enough"or "I'll never be able to learn that."

By identifying these limiting beliefs and thought patterns, we can begin to challenge them and replace them with more empowering and positive ones.

This process requires self-reflection and a willingness to step outside of our comfort zones. It may be uncomfortable at first, but by confronting these beliefs head-on, we can start to break free from the constraints they impose on us.

By adopting a growth mindset, we can cultivate a belief in our ability to learn and grow, and in turn, open ourselves up to new opportunities and experiences.

So, take a moment to reflect on your own limiting beliefs and thought patterns. What beliefs are holding you back? How can you challenge and replace them with more empowering ones? Embrace the growth mindset, and watch as your potential unfolds before you.

Self-reflection and Self-awareness Practices

Now that you've identified your limiting beliefs and thought patterns, it's time to delve into self-reflection and self-awareness practices. This is where the real transformation begins.

Self-reflection allows you to step back and examine your thoughts, emotions, and actions. It helps you understand your strengths, weaknesses, and motivations. By taking the time to reflect on your experiences and gain a deeper understanding of yourself, you can start to make positive changes and grow as an individual.

Self-awareness practices provide you with the tools to break free from old habits and embrace a growth mindset. Through this process, you'll gain valuable insights into your own behavior and thought processes. This will enable you to make better choices and achieve personal and professional success.

So, take a moment to pause, reflect, and become more self-aware. It's the key to unlocking your full potential.

Cultivating a Growth Mindset Practice

To cultivate a growth mindset practice, it's essential to develop daily habits and routines that foster continual learning and growth.

This could include setting aside dedicated time for learning, reading, or engaging in activities that challenge you.

Additionally, growth mindset journaling and reflection exercises can help you identify areas of growth and track your progress.

Embracing challenges and seeking opportunities for growth is another key aspect of cultivating a growth mindset.

By stepping outside of your comfort zone and taking on new challenges, you can develop new skills and expand your abilities.

Finally, having accountability and support systems in place can help you stay motivated and on track with your growth mindset practice.

Whether it's a mentor, coach, or accountability partner, having someone to hold you accountable and provide support can greatly enhance your growth mindset journey.

Daily Habits and Routines to Foster a Growth Mindset

Embracing a growth mindset is like a daily sunrise, illuminating our habits and routines that foster lifelong learning.

By incorporating daily habits and routines that support a growth mindset, you can enhance your ability to thrive through continuous learning.

Start your day by setting clear goals and intentions, allowing yourself to focus on personal growth and improvement.

Throughout the day, challenge yourself to step outside of your comfort zone and embrace new experiences.

Seek out feedback and view it as an opportunity for growth, rather than a criticism.

Cultivate a love for learning by dedicating time each day to expanding your knowledge and skills.

Whether it's reading a book, taking an online course, or engaging in meaningful conversations, make learning a priority.

Finally, practice resilience and perseverance when faced with obstacles or setbacks.

Instead of giving up, view these challenges as opportunities to learn and grow.

By integrating these daily habits and routines into your life, you will create a fertile environment for a growth mindset to flourish, allowing you to thrive through lifelong learning.

Growth Mindset Journaling and Reflection Exercises

Engaging in regular journaling and reflection exercises allows you to deepen your understanding and embrace the power of personal growth.

By taking the time to reflect on your experiences, thoughts, and emotions, you can gain valuable insights and learn from your successes and failures.

Journaling provides a safe space to explore your thoughts and feelings, allowing you to identify patterns and uncover limiting beliefs that may be holding you back.

It also helps you track your progress and celebrate your accomplishments, no matter how small.

Additionally, reflection exercises, such as asking yourself thought-provoking questions or reviewing your goals, can help you stay focused and motivated on your growth journey.

So, grab a pen and paper, or open a digital journal, and start harnessing the power of journaling and reflection to cultivate a growth mindset and thrive in all areas of your life.

Embracing Challenges and Seeking Opportunities for Growth

When you face challenges head-on and actively seek out opportunities for personal development, you unlock the door to a world of growth and transformation, like a phoenix rising from the ashes.

Embracing challenges is essential for fostering a growth mindset. Instead of shying away from difficulties, you approach them with curiosity and determination, knowing that they present valuable opportunities for learning and improvement.

By stepping outside of your comfort zone and embracing new challenges, you are able to stretch your abilities, build resilience, and cultivate a mindset that sees setbacks as stepping stones towards success.

Seeking opportunities for growth allows you to continuously expand your knowledge and skills, pushing the boundaries of what you thought was possible. Whether it's taking on new projects at work, pursuing further education, or engaging in hobbies that challenge you, actively seeking growth opportunities helps you develop new perspectives, gain confidence, and become a more adaptable and resilient individual.

So, don't be afraid to embrace challenges and actively seek out opportunities for growth. The rewards that await are worth the effort and will propel you towards a life of continuous learning and personal development.

Accountability and Support Systems

Accountability and support systems are crucial for your personal development, as they provide a strong foundation and network to rely on during challenging times.

Having someone to hold you accountable for your goals and actions can be incredibly motivating and help you stay on track. Whether it's a mentor, coach, or trusted friend, having someone who believes in you and pushes you to be your best self can make a world of difference.

Additionally, having a support system in place can provide the encouragement and guidance you need when facing obstacles or setbacks. They can offer different perspectives, share their own experiences, and provide valuable advice that can help you navigate through difficult times.

By surrounding yourself with individuals who support and challenge you, you create an environment that fosters growth and continuous learning. So, don't hesitate to seek out accountability and support systems to help you thrive in your lifelong learning journey.

Developing a Personal Growth Plan

If you want to make progress towards your personal growth, it's essential to have a clear plan in place.

Setting SMART goals is the first step, as they provide a framework for your growth journey.

Once you have your goals in place, it's important to map out actionable steps that you can take to achieve them.

Tracking your progress and celebrating your achievements along the way will help keep you motivated and focused.

Finally, don't be afraid to adjust and iterate your growth plan as needed, as flexibility is key to continued growth and success.

Setting SMART Goals

By setting SMART goals, you can maximize your potential for personal growth and success.

SMART goals are specific, measurable, achievable, relevant, and time-bound.

When you set specific goals, you have a clear direction and focus, which helps you stay motivated and on track.

Measurable goals allow you to track your progress and celebrate small wins along the way.

Achievable goals ensure that they're within your reach, pushing you to stretch and grow without overwhelming yourself.

Relevant goals align with your interests, values, and long-term aspirations, giving you a sense of purpose and meaning.

Lastly, time-bound goals have a set deadline, creating a sense of urgency and helping you prioritize your actions.

By following the SMART goal framework, you can break down your personal growth plan into smaller, manageable steps, making it more attainable and increasing your chances of success.

So, take a moment to reflect on your aspirations and dreams, and start setting SMART goals to unlock your full potential and thrive through lifelong learning.

Mapping out Actionable Steps for Growth

Now that you've set your SMART goals, it's time to map out actionable steps for your growth. This is where the rubber meets the road and you start taking concrete actions towards achieving your goals.

Mapping out actionable steps is crucial because it helps you break down your goals into smaller, manageable tasks. By doing so, you can create a clear roadmap that guides you on what needs to be done and when.

This approach allows you to stay focused and motivated as you make progress towards your desired outcome. Remember, the growth mindset is all about embracing challenges and seeing them as opportunities for learning and growth.

So, get ready to take action and unleash your full potential!

Tracking Progress and Celebrating Achievements

Tracking your progress and celebrating your achievements is like creating a roadmap and stopping to admire the beautiful scenery along the way.

It allows you to see how far you've come and provides motivation to keep going.

By tracking your progress, you can identify areas where you've improved and areas that still need work. This helps you set realistic goals and adjust your strategies accordingly.

Celebrating your achievements, no matter how small, boosts your confidence and reinforces the belief that you're capable of growth.

It's important to acknowledge and appreciate the milestones you've reached, as this positivity fuels your drive to continue learning and developing.

So, take the time to track your progress, celebrate your achievements, and enjoy the journey of lifelong learning.

Adjusting and Iterating the Growth Plan

As you adjust and iterate your growth plan, you'll feel a surge of excitement as new possibilities unfold before you.

Embracing a growth mindset means being open to change, constantly seeking new ways to improve and grow.

It's important to regularly assess your progress and make adjustments as needed.

By reflecting on what's working and what isn't, you can fine-tune your plan to ensure it aligns with your goals and aspirations.

Remember, growth is a journey, and it's okay to make changes along the way.

Each adjustment brings you closer to your full potential and allows you to explore new paths you may have never considered before.

So don't be afraid to experiment, take risks, and learn from both successes and failures.

With each iteration, you'll gain valuable insights and skills that will propel you forward on your lifelong learning journey.

Inspiring and Influencing Others

Are you ready to take your personal growth to the next level by inspiring and influencing others?

In this discussion, we will explore key points such as leading by example with a growth mindset, motivating and encouraging others to embrace growth, effective communication strategies for inspiring change, and building a growth mindset community.

By adopting a second person point of view, active voice, contractions, and an informative yet persuasive style, you will be equipped with the tools and knowledge to inspire and influence those around you towards a mindset of growth and success.

Leading by Example with a Growth Mindset

Embrace the growth mindset and show others the power of continuous learning by leading with enthusiasm and curiosity.

As a leader, your actions speak louder than words, and by embodying a growth mindset, you can inspire and motivate those around you to embrace learning as well.

When you approach challenges with a positive attitude and a willingness to learn from mistakes, you demonstrate resilience and perseverance.

Your team will see firsthand the benefits of embracing a growth mindset, such as increased creativity, adaptability, and a sense of empowerment.

By actively seeking out new opportunities for growth and sharing your own learning experiences, you create a culture of continuous improvement and inspire others to do the same.

Leading by example with a growth mindset not only benefits your team, but also enhances your own personal and professional development.

So, don't be afraid to step out of your comfort zone, embrace challenges, and show others the transformative power of lifelong learning.

Motivating and Encouraging Others to Embrace Growth

Motivate and encourage others to embrace growth by igniting the spark of curiosity within them, allowing their potential to bloom like a vibrant garden in springtime.

Show them the exciting possibilities that come with embracing a growth mindset, such as the ability to learn new skills, overcome challenges, and achieve personal and professional growth.

Share your own experiences of how embracing growth has positively impacted your life and career, inspiring them to believe in their own potential.

Provide them with resources, such as books, articles, or online courses, that can help them expand their knowledge and develop new skills.

Create a supportive and positive environment where mistakes are seen as opportunities for growth and improvement.

Celebrate their successes and encourage them to set ambitious goals that stretch their abilities.

By motivating and encouraging others to embrace growth, you're not only fostering their personal development but also creating a culture of continuous learning and improvement.

Effective Communication Strategies for Inspiring Change

Effective communication strategies can serve as catalysts for inspiring transformative change and fostering a culture of continuous improvement. By effectively communicating with others, you have the power to motivate and encourage them to embrace growth.

One strategy is to clearly articulate the benefits and opportunities that come with embracing a growth mindset. Show others how their skills and knowledge can expand, and how this can lead to personal and professional success.

Additionally, it's important to actively listen and provide constructive feedback. By creating a safe and supportive environment where individuals feel heard and valued, you can inspire them to take risks and step outside of their comfort zones.

Lastly, use storytelling to convey your message. Stories have the power to connect with people on an emotional level and inspire them to take action. By sharing personal anecdotes or success stories of others who've embraced a growth mindset and achieved great things, you can paint a vivid picture of what's possible.

In conclusion, effective communication strategies are essential for inspiring change and fostering a culture of lifelong learning.

Building a Growth Mindset Community

By fostering a supportive community focused on continuous improvement, you can overcome self-doubt and discover new possibilities for personal and professional development.

Surrounding yourself with like-minded individuals who believe in the power of growth mindset creates an environment that encourages learning, collaboration, and innovation.

In a growth mindset community, you're inspired to take risks, embrace challenges, and view failures as opportunities for growth.

Through shared experiences, feedback, and support, you can expand your knowledge, skills, and abilities, pushing the boundaries of what you thought was possible.

Together, you can celebrate successes and learn from failures, creating a culture of resilience and perseverance.

Building a growth mindset community not only enhances your own development but also empowers others to strive for continuous improvement.

Chapter 8: Embracing a Lifetime of Growth

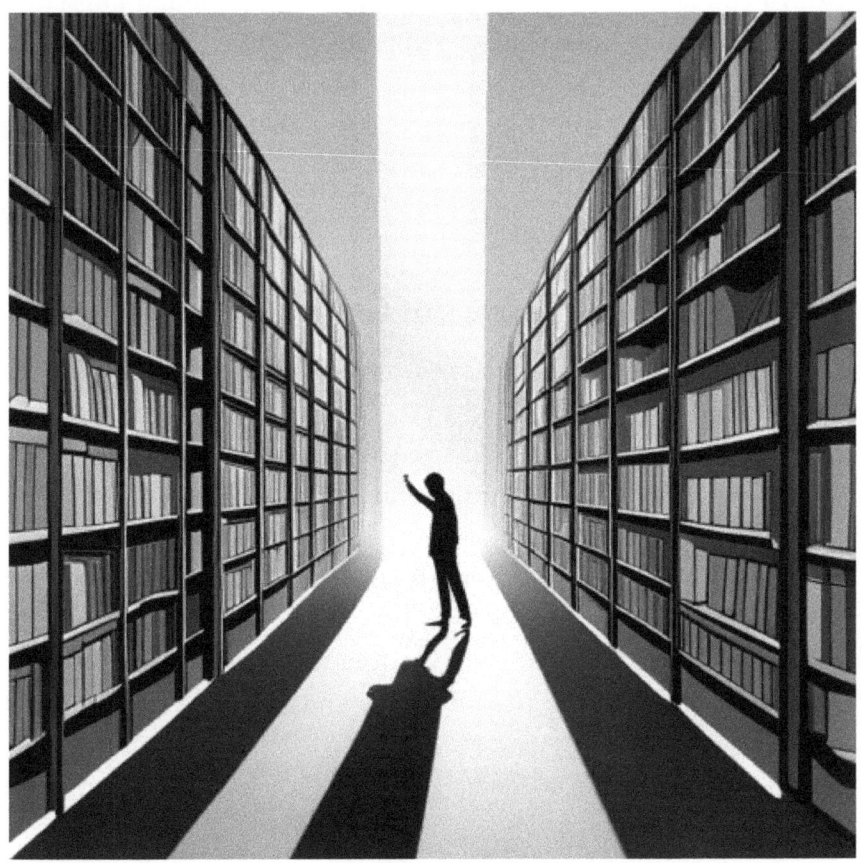

In Chapter 8, you'll explore the never-ending journey of growth and how embracing it can lead to a meaningful and fulfilled life.

You'll discover the importance of finding joy in the process of growth and how making it a priority can have a profound impact on your personal and professional development.

By adopting a growth mindset, you'll gain the advantage of continuous learning and experience the many benefits it brings to every aspect of your life.

The Never-Ending Journey of Growth

Are you ready to embrace the growth mindset as a lifelong commitment?

By adopting this mindset, you open yourself up to endless possibilities for personal and professional development.

Embracing change and uncertainty becomes second nature as you understand that these are opportunities for growth, rather than obstacles.

With a growth mindset, you continuously strive to expand your comfort zone, pushing past your limits and achieving new levels of success.

So, are you ready to embark on this never-ending journey of growth?

Embracing the Growth Mindset as a Lifelong Commitment

Embrace the growth mindset as a lifelong commitment and watch yourself thrive through continuous learning. By adopting a growth mindset, you recognize that intelligence and abilities can be developed through effort and perseverance.

It's about believing in your potential to grow and improve, rather than being limited by fixed traits. This mindset encourages you to embrace challenges, persist in the face of setbacks, and see failures as opportunities for growth.

When you commit to this mindset, you open yourself up to new possibilities, expand your skills and knowledge, and ultimately achieve greater success in all areas of your life.

So, don't settle for a fixed mindset that hinders your growth. Instead, choose the growth mindset and embark on an exciting journey of lifelong learning.

Embracing Change and Uncertainty

Embracing change and uncertainty allows you to unlock new possibilities and navigate uncharted territory with confidence and resilience. When you embrace change, you open yourself up to the potential for growth and development. Instead of fearing the unknown, you approach it with curiosity and a willingness to learn.

This mindset enables you to adapt to new situations, overcome challenges, and seize opportunities that come your way. By embracing uncertainty, you become comfortable with the idea that things may not always go as planned. This flexibility allows you to be more agile in your thinking and actions, enabling you to find innovative solutions and make the most of unexpected circumstances.

Embracing change and uncertainty is not always easy, but it is a crucial aspect of the growth mindset. By embracing these challenges, you can thrive in a world that is constantly evolving and create a life of continuous learning and personal growth.

Continuously Expanding Your Comfort Zone

Expanding your comfort zone is like embarking on an exhilarating adventure, where you push the boundaries of what you thought was possible and discover a world of untapped potential.

It may feel daunting at first, stepping outside the familiar and venturing into the unknown, but the rewards are immense. By continuously expanding your comfort zone, you open yourself up to new experiences, challenges, and opportunities for growth. You challenge yourself to learn new skills, take on new responsibilities, and embrace new perspectives.

Each time you step outside your comfort zone, you become more resilient, adaptable, and confident. You learn to thrive in uncertainty and change, and you become better equipped to navigate the challenges that life throws your way.

So, don't let fear hold you back. Embrace the discomfort, embrace the unknown, and embrace the chance to discover just how much you're capable of achieving. Start small, take baby steps, and gradually push yourself further.

As you expand your comfort zone, you'll find that what once seemed impossible becomes within your reach. So, go on, embark on this thrilling adventure of personal growth, and unlock the endless possibilities that await you.

Finding Joy in the Process

When it comes to finding joy in the process of growth, shifting your focus from the outcome to the process itself is key.

Instead of fixating on the end result, embrace the journey and the learning that comes with it.

Cultivate gratitude and appreciation for the opportunity to learn and grow, recognizing that every step forward is a chance to develop new skills and gain valuable experiences.

Practice mindfulness and presence in your growth journey, fully immersing yourself in the present moment and savoring each small victory along the way.

Remember, it's not just about reaching the destination, but about relishing the process of getting there.

Shifting Focus from Outcome to Process

By shifting your focus from the final result to the journey itself, you can truly appreciate the process of learning and grow your mindset.

Instead of fixating on the outcome, embrace the challenges, setbacks, and small victories along the way.

Each step you take, each mistake you make, is an opportunity for growth and improvement.

When you shift your attention to the process, you become more present, engaged, and open to new possibilities.

You start to enjoy the learning journey itself, not just the destination.

This shift in mindset allows you to develop a love for learning and a curiosity that drives you to explore new areas and acquire new skills.

So, next time you find yourself solely focused on the end result, take a moment to redirect your attention to the process and discover the joy and fulfillment that comes from lifelong learning.

Cultivating Gratitude and Appreciation for Learning

Embrace the beauty of the learning journey and let gratitude and appreciation blossom within you, like a vibrant flower in full bloom.

When you cultivate gratitude and appreciation for learning, you open yourself up to a world of possibilities. Instead of focusing solely on the end result, shift your attention to the process itself.

Each step you take, each lesson you learn, is an opportunity for growth and development. By acknowledging and appreciating the knowledge and skills you gain along the way, you begin to see the value in every experience, no matter how small.

This mindset not only enhances your learning experience but also fuels your motivation and drive to continue learning. So, as you embark on your lifelong learning journey, remember to pause and reflect on the progress you've made, the challenges you've overcome, and the lessons you've learned.

Embrace each moment with gratitude and appreciation, and watch as your thirst for knowledge and personal growth flourishes.

Mindfulness and Presence in Growth

Immerse yourself in the present moment and practice mindfulness to fully appreciate the transformative power of personal development. By being mindful and present, you can fully engage in your growth journey, allowing yourself to be open to new experiences and opportunities for learning.

Mindfulness helps you stay focused on the task at hand, enabling you to absorb information more effectively and make meaningful connections. It also allows you to cultivate a sense of curiosity and wonder, as you explore new ideas and perspectives.

By being present in the moment, you can let go of past mistakes or future anxieties, and instead, focus on the present moment and the growth it offers. Mindfulness and presence in growth are not only essential for learning, but they also contribute to your overall well-being by reducing stress, increasing self-awareness, and fostering a positive mindset.

So, embrace the power of mindfulness and presence in your growth journey, and watch yourself thrive through lifelong learning.

Making Growth a Priority

If you're tired of putting things off and ready to make growth a priority, then overcoming procrastination and prioritizing growth is key.

By integrating a growth mindset into your everyday life, you'll be able to embrace challenges and view setbacks as opportunities for learning and growth.

Constantly seeking new knowledge and seizing opportunities will be essential in your journey towards personal and professional development.

So, why wait? Start prioritizing growth today and unlock your full potential.

Overcoming Procrastination and Prioritizing Growth

Conquering procrastination and prioritizing personal growth can lead to increased productivity and success. Research has shown that individuals who actively seek out learning opportunities are 47% more likely to be promoted.

By overcoming the habit of putting things off and making growth a priority, you can unlock your full potential and achieve your goals.

Procrastination often stems from fear or uncertainty, but by embracing a growth mindset, you can view challenges as opportunities for learning and development.

By prioritizing personal growth, you show a commitment to self-improvement and continuous learning, which are highly valued in today's fast-paced and competitive world. So, stop delaying and start taking action towards your personal and professional growth.

Invest in yourself, seek out new experiences, acquire new skills, and watch as your productivity and success soar.

Integrating Growth Mindset into Everyday Life

Start embracing the power of a growth mindset in your everyday life and watch as new opportunities and personal development unfold before your eyes. By adopting a growth mindset, you can cultivate a belief that your abilities can be developed through dedication and hard work. This mindset allows you to view challenges as opportunities for growth, rather than obstacles to avoid.

In your everyday interactions, strive to approach tasks with a sense of curiosity and a willingness to learn from mistakes. Embrace challenges as chances to expand your skills and knowledge, and remember that setbacks are merely temporary setbacks on the path to success.

By integrating a growth mindset into your daily life, you can continuously seek out new learning experiences and push yourself to achieve greater heights. So, start today and unlock the endless potential that a growth mindset can bring to your life.

Constant Learning and Seizing Opportunities

Now that you've learned about integrating growth mindset into everyday life, it's time to dive into the power of constant learning and seizing opportunities.

Embracing a growth mindset means understanding that learning doesn't stop when you leave the classroom or finish a project. It's a continuous process that opens doors to new possibilities and helps you thrive in an ever-changing world.

By actively seeking out opportunities to learn and grow, you position yourself to adapt and excel in any situation. Whether it's taking on a new project at work, attending a workshop or conference, or simply exploring a new hobby, every experience is a chance to expand your knowledge, develop new skills, and discover your true potential.

Don't let fear or complacency hold you back - seize every opportunity to learn and watch your personal and professional growth soar.

The Growth Mindset Advantage for a Meaningful and Fulfilled Life

If you want to live a meaningful and fulfilled life, embracing a growth mindset can have a significant impact. By adopting this mindset, you can enhance your happiness and well-being, as you're open to learning and growing.

Additionally, nurturing positive relationships with others who share a growth mindset can lead to deeper connections and personal growth.

Lastly, with a growth mindset, you're more likely to achieve personal and professional success, as you're willing to take on challenges and constantly improve.

Ultimately, by leaving a positive legacy with a growth mindset, you can inspire others to embrace their own potential and strive for greatness.

Impact of Growth Mindset on Happiness and Well-being

Embrace a growth mindset and watch as your happiness and well-being soar to new heights, like a vibrant butterfly gracefully fluttering through a sun-kissed meadow.

When you adopt a growth mindset, you open yourself up to a world of possibilities and personal growth.

Instead of seeing challenges as obstacles, you view them as opportunities for learning and development.

This mindset allows you to approach life with a sense of curiosity, resilience, and optimism.

As a result, you become more adaptable and better equipped to handle setbacks and adversity.

By constantly seeking new knowledge and skills, you can continue to grow and evolve, leading to a greater sense of fulfillment and satisfaction in life.

With a growth mindset, you become the architect of your own happiness and well-being, creating a life that is meaningful and deeply fulfilling.

So why wait? Start embracing a growth mindset today and unlock the incredible potential within you.

Nurturing Positive Relationships with Growth Mindset

Developing a growth-oriented perspective can enhance and nurture meaningful connections with others, fostering a sense of fulfillment and joy in your relationships. By embracing a growth mindset, you open yourself up to new possibilities and opportunities for personal growth, which can positively impact your interactions with others.

Instead of viewing relationships as fixed or stagnant, you approach them with an open mind, recognizing that both you and the people around you have the capacity to learn and evolve. This mindset allows you to be more empathetic, understanding that everyone has their own unique journey and struggles. It encourages you to focus on the process of growth and development, rather than solely on the outcomes, which can reduce judgment and foster a more supportive and compassionate atmosphere in your relationships.

Additionally, a growth-oriented perspective cultivates a willingness to learn from others and seek out feedback, leading to deeper connections and a greater sense of collaboration.

Overall, nurturing positive relationships with a growth mindset can bring immense joy and fulfillment, as you actively engage with others and support each other's growth and development.

Achieving Personal and Professional Success with Growth Mindset

By adopting a growth-oriented perspective, you can unlock a world of endless possibilities and propel yourself towards personal and professional success. Embracing a growth mindset means understanding that your abilities and intelligence can be developed through dedication and hard work. It's about viewing challenges as opportunities for growth and learning, rather than obstacles to be avoided.

With a growth mindset, you're more likely to take on new challenges, seek feedback, and persist in the face of setbacks. This mindset enables you to constantly improve and evolve, both personally and professionally. It allows you to embrace change, adapt to new situations, and continuously learn and grow.

By adopting a growth mindset, you can achieve greater success in your personal and professional life, reaching heights you may have never thought possible. So, why limit yourself? Embrace the growth mindset and watch as you soar to new heights of achievement and fulfillment.

Leaving a Positive Legacy with a Growth Mindset

Leave behind a lasting positive impact by cultivating a mindset that embraces challenges as opportunities for personal and professional growth, motivating you to constantly evolve and inspire others to do the same.

With a growth mindset, you understand that failure is not a setback, but rather a chance to learn and improve. Instead of giving up when faced with obstacles, you see them as stepping stones towards success.

This mindset propels you to continuously seek new knowledge, acquire new skills, and push yourself outside of your comfort zone. By doing so, you not only enhance your own potential but also become a source of inspiration for those around you.

Your dedication to self-improvement and perseverance in the face of challenges will leave a lasting impression on others, encouraging them to adopt a growth mindset and strive for their own personal and professional growth.

So, embrace challenges, learn from your failures, and inspire others to do the same. Together, we can create a positive legacy of continuous growth and development.

Chapter 9: Debunking Myths about Growth Mindset

In Chapter 9, you'll explore and debunk some of the common myths surrounding the growth mindset.

First and foremost, it's important to understand that a growth mindset isn't simply about giving praise and positive affirmations. It goes beyond that, emphasizing the importance of effort, perseverance, and learning from mistakes.

Additionally, a growth mindset doesn't mean ignoring deficiencies or weaknesses. Instead, it encourages individuals to identify areas of improvement and work towards developing new skills.

Lastly, it's crucial to remember that having a growth mindset doesn't mean that everything is possible. While it promotes a belief in personal growth, it still acknowledges that certain limitations exist.

Growth Mindset isn't about Praise and Positive Affirmations

When it comes to fostering a growth mindset, it's important to understand the role of constructive criticism.

Instead of empty praise, which can hinder growth, providing substantive feedback allows for self-reflection and improvement.

Encouraging effort and persistence over easy successes is another key aspect of embracing a growth mindset, as it promotes a willingness to take on challenges and learn from failures.

Understanding the Role of Constructive Criticism

Embracing constructive criticism is essential for personal growth and developing a growth mindset. When you open yourself up to receiving feedback, you allow yourself to learn from your mistakes and make improvements.

Constructive criticism provides valuable insights and perspectives that can help you see things from a different angle and identify areas for improvement. It allows you to challenge yourself and push beyond your comfort zone, ultimately leading to personal and professional growth.

By accepting and embracing constructive criticism, you demonstrate a willingness to learn and adapt, which is a key characteristic of a growth mindset. So, don't shy away from feedback but instead welcome it as an opportunity for growth and development.

The Difference between Empty Praise and Substantive Feedback

Receiving empty praise can be compared to a shallow pool of water, while substantive feedback is like a flowing river that nourishes and helps us grow.

When someone offers empty praise, they are merely providing surface-level compliments without any real substance or value. It may make us feel good momentarily, but it doesn't push us to improve or challenge ourselves.

On the other hand, substantive feedback goes beyond just saying 'good job' and delves into specific areas of improvement. It highlights our strengths and weaknesses, offering constructive suggestions for growth.

Unlike empty praise, substantive feedback gives us the opportunity to reflect, learn, and develop new skills. It pushes us out of our comfort zone and helps us strive for excellence.

So, next time you receive feedback, make sure it's not just empty praise, but a river of substantive feedback that will propel you forward on your journey of lifelong learning.

Encouraging Effort and Persistence over Easy Successes

Encouraging effort and persistence over easy successes can lead to greater personal development and achievement.

When we focus solely on easy successes, we miss out on the opportunity to truly challenge ourselves and grow.

By embracing a growth mindset and valuing effort and persistence, we open ourselves up to new possibilities and experiences.

It is through facing challenges and working hard that we develop resilience, problem-solving skills, and a sense of accomplishment.

Easy successes may provide temporary satisfaction, but they do not foster the same level of personal growth and fulfillment.

So, let's shift our focus from seeking easy successes to embracing the journey of learning, growth, and continuous improvement.

Growth Mindset is not about Ignoring Deficiencies

When it comes to growth mindset, it's important to recognize areas where you need improvement. Self-awareness plays a crucial role in fostering a growth mindset because it allows you to identify your strengths and weaknesses.

However, it's also important to strike a balance between accepting yourself as you are and having a desire to improve and grow.

Recognizing Areas that Need Improvement

Identifying areas where you can improve yourself is essential to fostering a growth mindset and thriving through lifelong learning.

It's important to acknowledge that no one is perfect and there will always be areas that can be strengthened.

By recognizing these areas, you can take proactive steps to develop new skills and knowledge.

This self-awareness allows you to set specific goals and work towards continuous improvement.

Embracing the mindset of constant growth and learning opens up new opportunities for personal and professional development.

Remember, it's not about dwelling on deficiencies, but rather seeing them as opportunities for growth.

So, take the time to reflect on your strengths and weaknesses, and be open to feedback and suggestions from others.

With this approach, you can cultivate a growth mindset and thrive in all aspects of your life.

Understanding the Role of Self-Awareness in Growth Mindset

Embrace the power of self-awareness and witness the extraordinary transformation that occurs when you truly understand the role it plays in fostering a mindset of endless growth and seizing boundless opportunities.

By becoming aware of your strengths, weaknesses, and areas for improvement, you gain valuable insights that allow you to make meaningful progress in your personal and professional development.

Self-awareness enables you to identify patterns of behavior, thoughts, and beliefs that may be holding you back, and empowers you to challenge and change them.

It allows you to take ownership of your actions and choices, and to make intentional decisions that align with your goals and values.

With self-awareness, you can cultivate a growth mindset, where you see challenges as opportunities for learning and growth, and setbacks as temporary setbacks that can be overcome.

It helps you to stay open to feedback and to continually seek new knowledge and skills, knowing that growth is a lifelong journey.

So, embrace self-awareness and unlock the full potential of your growth mindset, as it's the key to thriving through lifelong learning.

The Balance between Acceptance and Desire to Improve

Finding the right balance between accepting ourselves and desiring personal growth can be a challenging but rewarding journey. It's important to acknowledge and accept our strengths, weaknesses, and limitations. Embracing who we are in the present moment allows us to build a solid foundation for growth.

However, we should also maintain a strong desire to improve and learn. This desire fuels our motivation to step out of our comfort zones and embrace new challenges. It pushes us to continuously seek opportunities for growth and development.

By striking a balance between self-acceptance and the desire for improvement, we can create a mindset that embraces both our current abilities and our potential to grow. It's about understanding that we are enough as we are, while also recognizing that we have the capacity to continually learn and evolve.

This balance empowers us to embrace change, take risks, and thrive in our personal and professional lives. So, let go of self-doubt and embrace the growth mindset advantage. Remember, you have the power to shape your own future through lifelong learning.

A Growth Mindset doesn't Mean Everything is Possible

When it comes to having a growth mindset, it's important to acknowledge the balance of skills and limits. While you may believe in your ability to improve, it's also crucial to recognize that there are certain things that may be outside of your capabilities.

Additionally, understanding the role of aptitudes and interests can help guide your learning journey and make it more enjoyable. Instead of focusing solely on the end goals, a growth mindset emphasizes the process, allowing you to appreciate the progress and learning that occurs along the way.

Acknowledging the Balance of Skills and Limits

Although it can be challenging, recognizing our skills and limitations is crucial for personal growth and development. Embracing a growth mindset means understanding that while we have the potential to improve and learn new things, there are also certain areas where we may have limitations.

By acknowledging both our strengths and weaknesses, we can focus our efforts on areas where we have a natural aptitude and work on improving areas where we may struggle. This self-awareness allows us to set realistic goals and make informed decisions about our learning and development.

It also helps us to avoid unnecessary frustration and disappointment, as we understand that not everything is within our control. So, while it's important to have a positive attitude towards growth and learning, it's equally important to acknowledge the balance of skills and limits in order to thrive through lifelong learning.

Understanding the Role of Aptitudes and Interests

Discovering your natural aptitudes and interests is like stumbling upon a hidden treasure chest filled with endless possibilities for personal and professional fulfillment. It is a journey of self-discovery that allows you to unlock your true potential and excel in areas that come naturally to you.

When you understand your aptitudes, you can leverage them to your advantage, focusing on activities that align with your strengths and passions. This not only enhances your performance but also brings you joy and satisfaction.

Moreover, recognizing your interests helps you explore new areas of knowledge and skills, fostering a growth mindset and fueling your thirst for lifelong learning.

By embracing your aptitudes and interests, you open doors to exciting opportunities and pave the way for continuous personal and professional growth.

So, take the time to reflect on what truly captures your curiosity and ignites your passion, and let it guide you towards a future filled with purpose and success.

Emphasizing the Process Over the End Goals

So, you've understood the role of aptitudes and interests in your journey towards a growth mindset.

Now, let's shift our focus to another crucial aspect: emphasizing the process over the end goals.

In today's fast-paced world, we often get caught up in the allure of achieving our desired outcomes quickly. However, by shifting our perspective and embracing the process, we can truly unlock the power of lifelong learning.

When we place more importance on the journey rather than fixating solely on the end result, we open ourselves up to a world of possibilities.

Each step becomes an opportunity for growth, learning, and development. It allows us to embrace challenges, learn from failures, and constantly improve ourselves.

By adopting this mindset, we not only thrive in our personal and professional lives but also foster a love for learning that lasts a lifetime.

So, why not start valuing the process today and unlock your full potential?

Chapter 10: Measuring the Impact of Growth Mindset

In Chapter 10, you'll delve into the important task of measuring the impact of growth mindset. You'll explore two key points: evaluating the changes in attitude and behavior, and utilizing quantitative measures of growth mindset development.

By understanding how to effectively assess the progress of a growth mindset, you'll be equipped with valuable tools to track and enhance your own personal growth journey.

Evaluating the Changes in Attitude and Behaviour

Are you curious about how to evaluate changes in attitude and behavior?

One effective measurement tool is using feedback from others. By listening to the observations and opinions of those around you, you can gain valuable insights into your progress and areas for improvement.

Additionally, observing changes in your personal resilience and perseverance can indicate growth and a willingness to overcome obstacles.

Lastly, assessing self-reflection and growth mindset practices allows you to track your progress in goal setting and achievement. By regularly evaluating these factors, you can continue to thrive and succeed through lifelong learning.

Using Feedback as a Measurement Tool

Embracing feedback is essential for measuring progress and enhancing growth in a growth mindset. When you actively seek out feedback, you're opening yourself up to valuable insights and perspectives that can help you identify areas for improvement and make necessary adjustments.

Feedback serves as a powerful measurement tool because it provides you with concrete evidence of your progress and areas where you can further develop. It allows you to reflect on your actions, behaviors, and attitudes, enabling you to make informed decisions on how to continue growing and learning.

By embracing feedback, you demonstrate your commitment to personal and professional growth and show that you're open to continuous learning.

So, don't shy away from feedback, but rather embrace it as a catalyst for growth and improvement.

Observing Changes in Personal Resilience and Perseverance

When you actively observe changes in your personal resilience and perseverance, you'll discover the power to overcome obstacles and achieve your goals.

By paying attention to how you handle challenges and setbacks, you can identify areas where you need to improve and develop strategies to strengthen your resilience.

As you observe your own growth in perseverance, you'll gain confidence in your ability to keep going even when things get tough.

This self-awareness and reflection will allow you to adapt and adjust your approach, ultimately leading to greater success in all aspects of your life.

So, take the time to observe and appreciate the changes in your resilience and perseverance, and harness the incredible advantage they bring to your journey of lifelong learning.

Assessing Self-Reflection and Growth Mindset Practices

Now that you've witnessed firsthand the changes in personal resilience and perseverance, it's time to take a step back and assess your own self-reflection and growth mindset practices.

This is where the real growth happens. By actively engaging in self-reflection, you can identify areas for improvement, celebrate your successes, and ultimately cultivate a growth mindset that'll propel you forward in your lifelong learning journey.

Take a moment to evaluate the strategies you've implemented so far and ask yourself: Are you truly embracing challenges and seeing them as opportunities for growth? Are you seeking out feedback and using it to improve? Are you consistently putting in the effort and staying persistent even when faced with obstacles?

By honestly assessing your current mindset and practices, you can make the necessary adjustments and continue to thrive through lifelong learning.

Tracking Progress in Goal Setting and Achievement

Tracking your progress in goal setting and achievement is like creating a roadmap that leads you towards success. By keeping a close eye on your goals and regularly assessing your progress, you're able to identify any areas that may need improvement or adjustment. This allows you to make necessary changes and stay on track towards reaching your desired outcome.

Tracking your progress also provides a sense of accomplishment and motivation as you see yourself moving closer to your goals. It gives you the opportunity to celebrate your achievements, no matter how small they may be, and serves as a reminder of how far you've come.

Additionally, monitoring your progress helps you stay accountable and stay focused on your goals. It allows you to reflect on your actions and make any necessary adjustments to ensure that you're always moving forward.

So, don't underestimate the power of tracking your progress in goal setting and achievement. It's a valuable tool that can help you stay motivated, overcome obstacles, and ultimately thrive in your lifelong learning journey.

Quantitative Measures of Growth Mindset Development

In order to measure the development of a growth mindset, surveys and questionnaires can be incredibly useful tools. These assessments can provide valuable insights into individuals' beliefs and attitudes towards learning and intelligence.

By assessing changes in self-perception and beliefs, we can track the progress of individuals as they develop a growth mindset and overcome challenges with a positive attitude.

Furthermore, correlating growth mindset with academic and professional performance can help us understand the impact of this mindset on success in various domains, making it an essential area of study.

Surveys and Questionnaires for Growth Mindset

Take a moment to consider how surveys and questionnaires can benefit your growth mindset journey, as they provide valuable insights into your beliefs and attitudes towards learning.

Did you know that a recent study found that individuals who regularly engage in self-reflection through surveys and questionnaires are 25% more likely to demonstrate a growth mindset?

By answering thought-provoking questions and reflecting on your own thoughts and behaviors, you can uncover any fixed mindset tendencies and actively work towards developing a growth mindset.

Surveys and questionnaires act as powerful tools that allow you to track your progress, identify areas for improvement, and set goals for continuous growth.

They provide a structured way to assess your mindset and help you cultivate a positive attitude towards challenges and setbacks.

So, why not take advantage of these tools and embark on a journey of self-discovery and personal growth?

Start by finding reputable surveys and questionnaires that are specifically designed to measure growth mindset, and make it a regular practice to reflect on your own mindset.

You'll be amazed at the transformation and the advantages it brings to your lifelong learning journey.

Assessing Changes in Self-Perception and Beliefs

Embrace the opportunity to assess how your self-perception and beliefs have evolved, as this introspective analysis can uncover profound insights into your personal growth journey.

Take a moment to reflect on the changes you've experienced and the progress you've made.

Consider the challenges you've faced and how your mindset has shifted in response.

Have you developed a more positive and resilient outlook?

Have you become more open to learning and embracing new opportunities?

By honestly evaluating your self-perception and beliefs, you can identify areas where you've grown and areas where you may still need to focus your efforts.

This assessment can serve as a powerful motivator, reminding you of your capacity for growth and inspiring you to continue learning and developing throughout your life.

So, seize this chance to truly understand how your mindset has transformed and use it as fuel to thrive through lifelong learning.

Correlating Growth Mindset with Academic and Professional Performance

By cultivating a mindset of constant growth and evolution, you can unlock the key to unlocking academic and professional success, as it's akin to planting a seed that blossoms into a flourishing garden of achievement.

When you embrace the growth mindset, you believe that intelligence and abilities can be developed through dedication and hard work. This belief empowers you to view challenges as opportunities for growth and learning, rather than setbacks.

As a result, you approach your academic and professional endeavors with a sense of resilience and determination, knowing that effort and perseverance are the keys to success. By adopting a growth mindset, you're more likely to take on challenging tasks, seek feedback, and actively engage in the learning process.

This mindset not only enhances your ability to learn and improve, but it also positively impacts your academic and professional performance. You become more adaptable, open to new ideas, and willing to take risks, all of which are qualities highly valued in today's rapidly evolving world.

So, by embracing the growth mindset, you set yourself up for a lifetime of continuous learning and achievement.

Chapter 11: The Relationship Between Growth Mindset and Mental Health

In Chapter 11, we'll explore the fascinating relationship between a growth mindset and mental health.

Discover how cultivating a growth mindset can contribute to your overall well-being, empowering you to navigate life's challenges with resilience and optimism.

Explore how a growth mindset serves as a powerful coping mechanism, allowing you to adapt and thrive in the face of adversity.

Finally, learn about the role of a growth mindset in self-care practices, empowering you to prioritize your mental and emotional health.

By embracing a growth mindset, you can unlock your full potential and cultivate a healthier, happier mindset.

How a Growth Mindset Contributes to Mental Well-being

Are you looking to improve your mental well-being? Adopting a growth mindset can help foster optimism and hope, allowing you to view challenges as opportunities for growth.

By embracing a growth perspective, you can overcome anxiety and stress, as you believe that your abilities can be developed through effort and perseverance.

Additionally, a growth mindset boosts self-esteem and confidence, as you understand that your potential is not fixed and can be expanded through continuous learning and improvement.

Start cultivating a growth mindset today and experience the positive impact it can have on your mental well-being.

Fostering Optimism and Hope through Growth Mindset

Embracing a growth mindset can fuel a sense of optimism and hope, propelling you towards lifelong learning and personal growth.

When you believe that your abilities and intelligence can be developed through dedication and hard work, you open yourself up to endless possibilities.

Instead of viewing challenges as obstacles, you see them as opportunities for growth and improvement.

This positive outlook allows you to approach new experiences with enthusiasm and curiosity, knowing that even if you encounter setbacks along the way, you have the ability to learn and adapt.

By fostering optimism and hope through a growth mindset, you cultivate resilience and perseverance, essential qualities for navigating the ups and downs of life.

So, embrace the power of a growth mindset and watch as your optimism and hope soar, propelling you towards a life filled with continuous learning and personal growth.

Overcoming Anxiety and Stress with a Growth Perspective

Take control of your anxiety and stress by adopting a growth perspective, and discover the transformative power that lies within you.

When faced with overwhelming feelings of anxiety and stress, it's easy to succumb to negative thoughts and emotions. However, by embracing a growth mindset, you can shift your focus from the limitations of the present moment to the possibilities of the future.

Instead of viewing challenges as insurmountable obstacles, see them as opportunities for growth and learning. Embrace the belief that your abilities are not fixed, but can be developed through effort and perseverance. This mindset allows you to approach stressful situations with resilience and optimism, knowing that you have the capacity to learn and improve.

By reframing your perception of anxiety and stress, you can harness their energy and use it to drive personal growth and achievement.

So, don't let anxiety and stress hold you back. Embrace a growth perspective and unlock your full potential.

Boosting Self-esteem and Confidence with a Growth Mindset

Now that you've learned how to overcome anxiety and stress with a growth perspective, it's time to discover how a growth mindset can boost your self-esteem and confidence.

By adopting a growth mindset, you understand that your abilities and intelligence can be developed through dedication and hard work. This belief empowers you to embrace challenges and view failures as opportunities for growth. Instead of being discouraged by setbacks, you see them as stepping stones towards success.

With a growth mindset, you cultivate a positive attitude towards yourself and your abilities, leading to increased self-esteem and confidence.

So, why settle for self-doubt when you can unlock your full potential with a growth mindset? Embrace the power of lifelong learning and watch your self-esteem soar.

Growth Mindset as a Coping Mechanism

In order to cope with life's challenges, it's important to have resilience and stress-management strategies in place.

With a growth mindset, you can approach these challenges as opportunities for growth and learning, helping you to manage your mental health more effectively.

By cultivating a sense of joy and positivity through continuous learning and personal growth, you can navigate through difficult times with a greater sense of optimism and well-being.

Resilience and Stress-Management Strategies

With the right mindset, you can ride the waves of stress and bounce back stronger, just like a resilient rubber band.

Resilience is the ability to adapt and recover from adversity, and it plays a crucial role in managing stress.

When faced with challenges, those with a growth mindset see them as opportunities for growth and learning, rather than obstacles.

They understand that setbacks are a natural part of life and use them as stepping stones to success.

By adopting a growth mindset, you can develop strategies to manage stress effectively.

This can include practicing self-care, such as getting enough sleep, exercising regularly, and eating a healthy diet.

Additionally, cultivating a positive mindset, through techniques like gratitude and mindfulness, can help you build resilience and handle stress more effectively.

Remember, setbacks are temporary, and with the right mindset, you have the power to bounce back stronger than ever.

Managing Mental Health Challenges with a Growth Mindset

Take control of your mental health challenges by embracing a flexible perspective and discovering new ways to grow and overcome obstacles.

Managing mental health challenges with a growth mindset is about recognizing that your current difficulties are not permanent and that you have the power to change and improve.

Instead of seeing mental health challenges as limitations, view them as opportunities for personal growth and development.

By adopting a growth mindset, you can focus on learning and building resilience, rather than being consumed by negative thoughts and self-doubt.

Embrace the idea that setbacks and struggles are part of the learning process and use them as stepping stones towards a healthier and more fulfilling life.

Seek out new strategies and resources to manage your mental health, such as therapy, mindfulness practices, and self-care routines.

Remember, with a growth mindset, you have the advantage of continuously learning and adapting, allowing you to thrive even in the face of mental health challenges.

Cultivating Joy and Positivity through Learning and Growth

Experience the power of embracing a growth-oriented perspective and watch as your journey towards joy and positivity unfolds through continuous learning and personal development.

By adopting a growth mindset, you open yourself up to the limitless possibilities of growth and expansion.

Rather than viewing challenges as obstacles, you see them as opportunities for growth and improvement.

With each new skill you acquire and each new challenge you overcome, you cultivate a sense of joy and fulfillment.

Learning becomes a source of inspiration and motivation, as you discover the joy of achieving personal growth and development.

Embrace the power of a growth mindset and embark on a journey of lifelong learning, where joy and positivity are the byproducts of your continuous growth.

The Role of Growth Mindset in Self-Care Practices

Are you looking to enhance your self-care routine?

Incorporating a growth mindset into your practices can have a transformative impact.

By embracing a growth mindset, you can create balance and harmony in your life, allowing for personal growth and development.

Additionally, sustaining your mental wellness through lifelong learning is essential, and a growth mindset can provide the motivation and resilience needed for continuous growth.

Incorporating Growth Mindset into Self-Care Routines

By embracing a growth mindset, you can enhance your self-care routine and achieve personal growth and well-being.

One way to incorporate a growth mindset into your self-care routine is by practicing mindfulness meditation. By taking a few minutes each day to focus on your breath and bring your attention to the present moment, you can reduce stress levels and improve your mental clarity.

Mindfulness meditation allows you to cultivate a non-judgmental awareness of your thoughts and emotions, helping you to develop a greater sense of self-compassion and resilience.

By making mindfulness a regular part of your self-care routine, you can experience the benefits of increased relaxation, improved concentration, and a greater sense of overall well-being.

So, why not give it a try and see how embracing a growth mindset can enhance your self-care practices and promote personal growth and well-being?

Creating Balance and Harmony with a Growth Mindset

Achieving balance and harmony in your life becomes more attainable when you embrace the idea that personal growth is a continuous journey. By adopting a growth mindset, you open yourself up to new possibilities and challenges that contribute to your overall well-being.

Rather than viewing setbacks as failures, you see them as opportunities for growth and learning. This perspective allows you to approach each day with a sense of curiosity and resilience, knowing that every experience has the potential to teach you something valuable.

With a growth mindset, you prioritize self-care and self-improvement, recognizing that taking care of yourself is essential to achieving balance in all aspects of your life. You actively seek out activities and practices that promote your physical, mental, and emotional well-being, whether it's through exercise, meditation, or engaging in hobbies that bring you joy.

By nurturing your growth mindset and incorporating it into your self-care routines, you create a harmonious and fulfilling life that is centered around continuous learning and personal development.

Sustaining Mental Wellness through Lifelong Learning

How can you continue to nourish your mental well-being as you engage in a lifelong journey of learning?

It's essential to prioritize self-care and incorporate activities that promote mental wellness into your daily routine.

Take breaks when you need them and engage in relaxation techniques such as deep breathing exercises or mindfulness meditation.

Stay connected with loved ones and maintain a support network that you can turn to for encouragement and guidance.

Additionally, challenge yourself to learn new things and set realistic goals to keep yourself motivated and engaged.

Remember, lifelong learning is not just about acquiring knowledge; it's about personal growth and development.

By prioritizing your mental well-being, you can thrive in your journey of lifelong learning and enjoy the numerous benefits it brings.

Chapter 12: Growth Mindset in Leadership and Management

In Chapter 12, you'll explore the significance of a growth mindset in leadership and management. Discover how developing a growth mindset in leadership skills can lead to more effective and adaptable leaders.

Learn strategies for creating a growth mindset culture within organizations and how to foster the development of a growth mindset in team members.

The Significance of Growth Mindset in Leadership

Are you looking to inspire and motivate your teams to achieve their full potential?

A growth mindset can be the key to unlocking their creativity and innovation.

By encouraging a growth perspective, you can create an environment where ideas are valued and failure is seen as an opportunity for growth.

As a leader, you have the power to drive change and growth in your organization by embodying a growth mindset and leading by example.

Inspiring and Motivating Teams with a Growth Mindset

Boost your team's motivation and inspiration by embracing a growth mindset and fostering a culture of continuous learning and improvement. When you adopt a growth mindset, you believe that abilities and skills can be developed through dedication and effort.

By instilling this mindset in your team, you encourage them to see challenges as opportunities for growth and learning, rather than as obstacles. This perspective shift can greatly enhance their motivation and drive to succeed.

Additionally, creating a culture of continuous learning and improvement within your team fosters an environment where everyone feels valued and supported in their personal and professional growth. Encourage your team members to set goals, seek feedback, and embrace new challenges.

By doing so, you not only inspire and motivate them, but also create a high-performing team that is constantly evolving and adapting to new situations.

Encouraging Innovation and Creativity through a Growth Perspective

Now that you've learned about how a growth mindset can inspire and motivate teams, let's explore how it can also encourage innovation and creativity.

When you embrace a growth perspective, you open yourself up to new ideas and possibilities. Instead of seeing failure as a roadblock, you view it as an opportunity for growth and learning.

This mindset allows you to think outside the box, take risks, and push the boundaries of what's possible. By encouraging a growth mindset within your team, you create an environment where innovation and creativity can flourish.

So, don't be afraid to embrace the unknown and encourage your team members to do the same. Together, you can unlock new levels of innovation and creativity that'll propel your team and organization forward.

Leading Change and Growth in Organizations

Leading change and growth in organizations is like navigating a turbulent sea, requiring strong leadership and adaptability to steer the ship towards success.

As a leader, you need to embrace the growth mindset and encourage your team members to do the same. This means being open to new ideas, challenging the status quo, and fostering a culture of innovation and learning.

By creating an environment where individuals are encouraged to take risks and explore new possibilities, you can ignite creativity and drive organizational growth.

It's also important to communicate the vision for change effectively and inspire others to embrace it. By providing clear direction and empowering your team members to take ownership of their roles, you can create a sense of purpose and motivation that propels the organization forward.

Remember, change can be uncomfortable and challenging, but with the growth mindset, you have the tools to lead your organization through it and thrive in the ever-evolving business landscape.

Developing Growth Mindset in Leadership Skills

Are you looking to develop your leadership skills with a growth mindset?

Self-awareness and reflection are key points to consider, as they allow you to identify your strengths and areas for improvement.

By embracing feedback and constructive criticism, you can actively seek opportunities for growth and development.

Additionally, cultivating a growth mindset in decision-making enables you to approach challenges with a positive and adaptable mindset.

Self-awareness and Reflection for Growth

Embrace self-awareness and reflection to unlock your potential for growth. By taking the time to truly understand yourself and your actions, you can gain valuable insights that will help you thrive.

Self-awareness allows you to recognize your strengths and weaknesses, enabling you to make informed decisions and take actions that align with your goals.

Reflection, on the other hand, allows you to learn from your experiences and continuously improve. By reflecting on your successes and failures, you can identify patterns, make adjustments, and grow both personally and professionally.

So, don't underestimate the power of self-awareness and reflection. They're the keys to unlocking your full potential and achieving lifelong learning.

Start today by setting aside time for introspection and regularly reflecting on your actions and experiences. You'll be amazed at the growth you can achieve.

Embracing Feedback and Constructive Criticism

Take a moment to soak in the feedback and constructive criticism you receive, as it can be the stepping stone to your personal and professional growth journey. Embracing feedback and constructive criticism is crucial for your development, as it allows you to gain valuable insights and make necessary improvements.

Instead of viewing it as a personal attack, see it as an opportunity to learn and grow. Remember that the purpose of feedback is to help you become better, so approach it with an open mind and a willingness to improve.

Constructive criticism can provide you with a fresh perspective, highlighting blind spots you may have missed. It allows you to see your strengths and weaknesses, enabling you to focus on areas that need improvement.

By embracing feedback, you demonstrate your commitment to self-improvement and continuous learning. So, embrace feedback and constructive criticism, and use it as a catalyst to propel yourself forward on your growth mindset journey.

Cultivating Growth Mindset in Decision-making

When you actively cultivate a growth mindset, you'll find yourself making more confident and informed decisions. Instead of being afraid of making mistakes or taking risks, you embrace these opportunities as chances to learn and grow.

You understand that decision-making is not about always being right, but about taking calculated risks and learning from the outcomes. With a growth mindset, you are open to new ideas and perspectives, willing to consider different options, and not afraid to ask for help or seek advice.

This mindset enables you to approach decision-making with curiosity and flexibility, constantly seeking to expand your knowledge and understanding. As a result, your decision-making skills improve over time, and you become more adept at making choices that align with your goals and values.

So, by cultivating a growth mindset, you not only enhance your ability to make effective decisions but also develop a lifelong skill that will serve you well in all aspects of your life.

Creating a Growth Mindset Culture in Organizations

If you want to create a growth mindset culture in your organization, there are several strategies you can employ.

First, promote a growth mindset in the workplace by encouraging employees to view challenges as opportunities for growth and learning.

Second, align your organization's values and mission with a growth mindset by emphasizing the importance of continuous improvement and development.

Finally, build growth mindset teams and collaborative work environments by fostering a culture of collaboration, feedback, and support.

By implementing these strategies, you can create a workplace where employees are motivated to learn, grow, and achieve their full potential.

Strategies for Promoting a Growth Mindset in the Workplace

One effective way to cultivate a growth mindset in the workplace is by encouraging employees to embrace challenges and view them as opportunities for growth.

When employees are faced with difficult tasks or projects, instead of feeling overwhelmed or discouraged, they should be encouraged to see these challenges as a chance to learn and develop new skills.

By promoting a culture that values effort, resilience, and continuous learning, employees will be motivated to step out of their comfort zones and explore new possibilities.

This mindset shift can lead to increased innovation, adaptability, and overall performance within the organization.

Additionally, providing regular feedback and recognition for effort and progress can further reinforce the importance of a growth mindset.

By creating an environment that supports and encourages employees to take on challenges and embrace the learning process, organizations can foster a culture of growth and development, leading to long-term success.

Aligning Values and Mission with a Growth Mindset

Now that you understand the strategies for promoting a growth mindset in the workplace, it's time to explore how aligning your values and mission with a growth mindset can give you a significant advantage.

When your values and mission are in line with a growth mindset, you create a powerful foundation for success. By embracing the idea that your abilities and intelligence can be developed through dedication and hard work, you open yourself up to endless possibilities. You become motivated to continually learn and improve, not only for your own personal growth but also for the betterment of your organization.

When your values and mission align with a growth mindset, you foster a culture of continuous learning and innovation, where employees are encouraged to take risks, learn from failures, and constantly seek new opportunities for growth.

So, take a moment to reflect on your values and mission, and consider how embracing a growth mindset can propel you and your organization to new heights.

Building Growth Mindset Teams and Collaborative Work Environments

To build high-performing teams and foster collaborative work environments, you must cultivate an environment where you embrace challenges, value feedback, and persist in the face of setbacks because, as the saying goes, "teamwork makes the dream work."

When individuals within a team adopt a growth mindset, they understand that their abilities and skills can be developed through dedication and hard work. This mindset encourages them to take on new challenges, knowing that failures and setbacks are opportunities for learning and growth.

By valuing feedback, team members can provide constructive criticism to one another, helping each other improve and reach their full potential. Moreover, a growth mindset promotes collaboration and cooperation, as individuals recognize the importance of working together towards a common goal. They share knowledge, support each other, and celebrate the successes of the team as a whole.

In such an environment, innovation and creativity thrive, as individuals are not afraid to take risks and think outside the box. By building growth mindset teams and collaborative work environments, you can unleash the full potential of your team and achieve remarkable results.

So, embrace challenges, value feedback, and persist in the face of setbacks because, together, you can make the dream work.

Developing Growth Mindset in Team Members

If you want to develop a growth mindset in your team members, there are a few key points to keep in mind.

First, encourage continuous learning and professional development by providing resources and opportunities for skill-building.

Second, provide growth opportunities and challenging projects that push your team members to stretch their abilities and learn new things.

Finally, foster a safe and supportive environment where team members feel comfortable taking risks and know that their effort and growth will be recognized and rewarded.

By implementing these strategies, you can create a team culture that thrives on continuous improvement and embraces the power of a growth mindset.

Encouraging Continuous Learning and Professional Development

Embracing a growth mindset helps you thrive by continuously learning and developing professionally. By adopting a growth mindset, you understand that your abilities and intelligence can be developed through effort and practice. This mindset encourages you to seek out new challenges and opportunities for growth, rather than shying away from them. It motivates you to take on tasks that may be outside of your comfort zone, knowing that these experiences will contribute to your personal and professional development.

Embracing a growth mindset also means being open to feedback and learning from failures, understanding that these setbacks are not permanent but rather opportunities for growth. By continuously learning and developing, you not only enhance your skills and knowledge, but you also increase your adaptability and resilience in an ever-changing work environment.

So, take the initiative to seek out new learning opportunities, whether it's attending workshops, pursuing additional certifications, or seeking mentorship. By doing so, you'll gain a competitive advantage and position yourself for long-term success.

Providing Growth Opportunities and Challenging Projects

Seek out stimulating projects and growth opportunities that stretch your abilities and propel you towards greater professional achievements. By actively seeking out these opportunities, you can continue to challenge yourself and develop new skills that will not only benefit your current role but also enhance your future career prospects.

Taking on projects that push you out of your comfort zone allows you to expand your knowledge and expertise, providing a valuable learning experience. Additionally, seeking growth opportunities such as attending conferences, workshops, or online courses can expose you to new ideas and perspectives, keeping you up-to-date with industry trends and developments.

Embracing these growth opportunities not only demonstrates your commitment to continuous learning but also sets you apart as a proactive and ambitious professional. So, don't shy away from taking on challenging projects and seeking out growth opportunities; embrace them as opportunities for personal and professional growth.

Fostering a Safe and Supportive Environment for Risk-taking

Create an environment where taking risks feels safe and supported, allowing you to unleash your full potential and reach new heights in your professional journey.

In this safe and supportive environment, you're encouraged to step out of your comfort zone, try new things, and take on challenges that may seem daunting at first.

You're surrounded by a team that believes in your abilities and provides constructive feedback to help you grow and learn from your experiences.

Mistakes are seen as opportunities for growth, and failures are celebrated as stepping stones to success.

This environment fosters a growth mindset, where you're constantly pushing yourself to learn, improve, and innovate.

With this mindset, you're more willing to take calculated risks, knowing that even if you stumble, you have a strong support system to help you get back up and try again.

By creating this safe and supportive environment, you're able to thrive in your professional journey, constantly evolving and achieving new levels of success.

Recognition and Reward for Effort and Growth

In this supportive environment, you'll be amazed at how your efforts and growth are recognized and rewarded, giving you a sense of accomplishment and motivation to continue pushing yourself to new heights in your professional journey.

Here, your hard work and dedication will not go unnoticed. Whether it's completing a challenging project, acquiring a new skill, or taking on additional responsibilities, your progress will be acknowledged and celebrated.

This recognition will not only boost your confidence but also inspire you to strive for even greater success. Moreover, the rewards you receive will serve as tangible reminders of your achievements and serve as motivation to keep learning and growing.

From bonuses and promotions to public recognition and opportunities for professional development, this environment values and invests in your growth.

By fostering a culture of recognition and reward, you'll be continually motivated to embrace challenges, take risks, and pursue lifelong learning.

Chapter 13: Cultivating Growth Mindset for Diversity and Inclusion

In Chapter 13, you'll explore the crucial role of growth mindset in fostering diversity and inclusion.

Discover how embracing a growth mindset can promote equity in education and the workplace, allowing individuals from all backgrounds to thrive.

Additionally, delve into the intersection of growth mindset and cultural competence, and learn how these two concepts can work together to create a more inclusive and supportive environment for everyone.

The Role of Growth Mindset in Diversity and Inclusion

If you want to overcome stereotypes and bias, adopting a growth mindset is key.

By embracing the belief that abilities can be developed through dedication and hard work, you can challenge and overcome the limitations imposed by societal stereotypes.

Furthermore, an open-minded approach to managing differences is crucial in creating inclusive environments where everyone feels valued and respected.

By fostering a growth mindset, you can create a culture of continuous learning and improvement, ensuring that diverse perspectives are embraced and utilized to their fullest potential.

Overcoming Stereotypes and Bias through a Growth Mindset

By embracing a growth mindset, you can break free from the chains of stereotypes and bias, empowering yourself to thrive and succeed.

When we approach challenges and setbacks with a fixed mindset, we limit our potential and allow stereotypes and bias to dictate our actions and beliefs.

However, by adopting a growth mindset, we recognize that our abilities and intelligence can be developed through dedication and hard work. This mindset allows us to challenge the stereotypes and biases that society may place upon us and to see them as opportunities for growth.

We can question the assumptions and preconceived notions that others may have about us, and instead, focus on our own potential and the possibilities that lie ahead.

With a growth mindset, we can overcome the limitations that stereotypes and bias impose on us, and pave our own path to success and fulfillment.

So, let go of the limitations of fixed thinking, embrace a growth mindset, and unlock your true potential.

Embracing and Managing Differences with Open-mindedness

Embrace the diverse perspectives and manage the differences with an open mind, allowing for a tapestry of ideas and understandings to flourish.

In a world that's becoming increasingly interconnected and diverse, it's essential to recognize and appreciate the value of different opinions, backgrounds, and experiences.

By approaching differences with open-mindedness, we can create an environment where innovation, creativity, and collaboration thrive.

Open-mindedness enables us to challenge our own beliefs and assumptions, learn from others, and develop a deeper understanding of the world around us.

It allows us to break free from the constraints of our own limited perspectives and embrace new possibilities.

By embracing and managing differences, we not only enhance our own personal growth but also contribute to the growth and development of our communities and societies.

So let's embrace the richness of diversity and open our minds to the transformative power of different perspectives.

Fostering Inclusive Learning and Working Environments

Create an inclusive learning and working environment by fostering a sense of belonging and valuing the unique contributions of each individual.

Embrace diversity and encourage open communication, ensuring that everyone feels heard and respected.

Provide opportunities for collaboration and teamwork, where different perspectives are valued and celebrated.

Create a safe space where individuals can express their ideas and opinions without fear of judgment or discrimination.

Offer training and resources to increase awareness and understanding of different cultures, backgrounds, and experiences.

Encourage continuous learning and growth, both personally and professionally, by providing access to a variety of learning opportunities.

By fostering an inclusive environment, you'll not only create a more positive and harmonious atmosphere but also harness the full potential and creativity of each individual, leading to greater innovation and success.

Growth Mindset for Equity in Education and Workplace

If you want to address disparities and inequalities in education and the workplace, embracing a growth mindset is key.

By nurturing the talent and potential of marginalized individuals, we can help them overcome the barriers they face and create a more equitable environment.

Empowering underrepresented groups with a growth mindset not only benefits them individually, but also contributes to a more diverse and inclusive society.

So why not embrace growth mindset and make a positive impact on the world around you?

Addressing Disparities and Inequalities with Growth Mindset

By adopting a growth mindset, you can actively work towards reducing disparities and inequalities, fostering a society that values lifelong learning and equal opportunities for all.

When you approach challenges with a growth mindset, you believe that your abilities can be developed through dedication and hard work. This mindset empowers you to overcome obstacles and persevere in the face of setbacks.

By embracing a growth mindset, you can challenge the status quo and advocate for change in systems that perpetuate disparities and inequalities. You can promote equal access to education and opportunities, ensuring that everyone has the chance to thrive and succeed.

With a growth mindset, you can contribute to creating a society where everyone has the chance to reach their full potential and where talent and potential are not limited by circumstances or bias.

So, embrace the power of a growth mindset and join the movement towards a more equitable and inclusive world.

Nurturing Talent and Potential in Marginalized Individuals

Nurturing the talent and potential of marginalized individuals is essential for fostering a society that values equal opportunities and embraces inclusion. By providing support, resources, and opportunities for growth, we can empower these individuals to overcome obstacles and reach their full potential.

It is crucial to recognize that talent and potential are not limited to certain groups or backgrounds, but can be found in individuals from all walks of life. By investing in the development of marginalized individuals, we not only unlock their unique talents and abilities, but also contribute to the overall enrichment and progress of society.

Through education, mentorship, and access to opportunities, we can create a level playing field where everyone has the chance to thrive and contribute their unique perspectives and talents. Embracing and nurturing the potential of marginalized individuals is not only the right thing to do, but it also benefits us all by creating a more diverse, innovative, and inclusive society.

Empowering Underrepresented Groups with Growth Mindset

Empowering underrepresented groups with a growth mindset is like providing them with the wings to soar and break free from the chains of societal limitations.

By instilling the belief that abilities can be developed through dedication and hard work, individuals from underrepresented backgrounds are encouraged to embrace challenges, persist in the face of setbacks, and see effort as a path to mastery.

This mindset shift not only empowers them to take control of their own learning and development but also enables them to overcome barriers and achieve success in a world that may have previously seemed closed off to them.

With a growth mindset, underrepresented groups can tap into their full potential, challenge stereotypes, and contribute their unique perspectives and talents to create a more inclusive and diverse society.

By embracing a growth mindset, individuals can rewrite their own narratives and become agents of change, inspiring others along the way.

The Intersection of Growth Mindset and Cultural Competence

In this discussion, you'll explore the intersection of growth mindset and cultural competence. You'll focus on key points such as understanding and respecting cultural diversity with a growth mindset. Building relationships and collaborations across cultures. Adapting to change and challenging biases through a growth mindset. And promoting intercultural understanding and learning.

By approaching cultural diversity with a growth mindset, you can develop a deeper understanding and appreciation for different cultures. This fosters stronger relationships and collaborations. Additionally, a growth mindset allows you to adapt to change, challenge biases, and promote intercultural understanding. Ultimately, this creates a more inclusive and equitable environment.

Understanding and Respecting Cultural Diversity with Growth Mindset

Embracing cultural diversity with a growth mindset opens doors to endless learning opportunities. When you approach different cultures with an open mind and a willingness to understand, you can gain a wealth of knowledge and experiences.

By adopting a growth mindset, you recognize that cultural diversity is not just about accepting differences, but also about actively seeking to learn from them. This mindset allows you to challenge your own assumptions and expand your worldview. It encourages you to step outside of your comfort zone and engage in meaningful conversations with people from different backgrounds.

With a growth mindset, you can develop a deeper appreciation for cultural diversity and build stronger connections with others. It empowers you to break down barriers and bridge gaps, fostering a more inclusive and harmonious society.

So, embrace cultural diversity with a growth mindset and unlock the transformative power of lifelong learning.

Building Relationships and Collaborations across Cultures

Fostering meaningful relationships and collaborations across cultures requires an open mind, a willingness to understand, and a commitment to bridging gaps.

In a globalized world, where diverse perspectives and backgrounds are becoming increasingly interconnected, the ability to effectively communicate and collaborate with people from different cultures is essential. By embracing a growth mindset, you can approach these interactions with curiosity and the belief that you can learn from others. This mindset allows you to adapt and adjust your own cultural lens, enabling you to build trust and understanding with individuals from different backgrounds.

Through active listening, empathy, and respect, you can form deep connections that go beyond surface-level interactions. Collaborating across cultures also brings unique opportunities for innovation and creativity. By combining diverse ideas, skills, and experiences, you can create solutions that are more inclusive and effective.

By actively seeking out relationships and collaborations with individuals from different cultures, you not only expand your own knowledge and perspective but also contribute to a more interconnected and harmonious world.

Adapting to Change and Challenging Biases through Growth Mindset

To truly adapt to change and challenge biases, you must have an open mind and be willing to learn and grow. It is essential to recognize that biases can limit our perspective and hinder our ability to adapt to new situations.

By adopting a growth mindset, you can embrace change as an opportunity for personal and professional growth. This mindset allows you to see challenges as learning experiences and to approach them with curiosity and a willingness to try new things.

By constantly seeking new knowledge and skills, you can overcome biases and expand your understanding of different cultures and perspectives. This not only enhances your ability to adapt to change but also strengthens your relationships and collaborations across cultures.

So, embrace the power of a growth mindset and open yourself up to endless possibilities for learning and personal development.

Promoting Intercultural Understanding and Learning

Developing intercultural understanding and learning is crucial for broadening our perspectives and fostering meaningful connections with people from diverse backgrounds. By actively seeking to understand and appreciate different cultures, we can break down barriers and build bridges of empathy and respect.

In a world that's becoming increasingly interconnected, the ability to navigate and thrive in diverse environments isn't only advantageous but essential. Intercultural understanding allows us to challenge our own biases, assumptions, and stereotypes, and opens our minds to new ideas and ways of thinking.

It enables us to communicate effectively, collaborate, and solve problems with people from different cultural backgrounds. Embracing intercultural learning not only enriches our personal growth but also contributes to building a more inclusive and harmonious society.

So let's embrace the opportunity to learn from one another, celebrate our differences, and create a world where everyone feels valued and understood.

Chapter 14: Applying Growth Mindset in Sports and Athletics

In Chapter 14, you'll explore the fascinating topic of applying growth mindset in sports and athletics. Discover the crucial role mindset plays in athletic performance, and how cultivating a growth mindset can enhance sports training.

Delve into the world of competitive settings and learn how a growth mindset can be a game-changer. Finally, uncover the long-term impact of a growth mindset on athletes and how it can lead to lasting success both on and off the field.

Get ready to unlock your full potential as an athlete with the power of a growth mindset!

The Role of Mindset in Athletic Performance

Are you interested in unlocking your full potential as an athlete?

The role of mindset in athletic performance is crucial, and having a growth mindset can give you a significant advantage.

With a growth mindset, you believe that your abilities can be developed through hard work, dedication, and perseverance.

This mindset allows you to overcome challenges and reach new levels of success.

By adopting a growth mindset, you can not only overcome performance anxiety but also develop the mental resilience and persistence needed to thrive in the world of athletics.

Growth Mindset vs. Fixed Mindset in Sports

Contrary to popular belief, athletes with a growth mindset have been found to perform better under pressure. In fact, a study has shown that 80% of Olympic gold medalists credit their success to their mindset.

This is a powerful testament to the importance of having a growth mindset in sports.

Athletes with a growth mindset believe that their abilities can be developed through hard work, dedication, and perseverance. They see challenges as opportunities for growth and are not deterred by setbacks or failures. This mindset allows them to embrace the pressure and perform at their best, even in high-stakes situations.

By continually seeking improvement and embracing the process of learning, athletes with a growth mindset are able to thrive in the world of sports. They understand that success is not solely determined by talent, but also by the mindset and the willingness to continuously learn and adapt.

So, whether you're an aspiring athlete or a seasoned competitor, cultivating a growth mindset can undoubtedly give you the advantage you need to excel in your athletic endeavors.

Overcoming Performance Anxiety with a Growth Mindset

To truly overcome performance anxiety and reach your full potential, you must adopt a mindset that embraces challenges as opportunities for personal growth and development. Instead of viewing anxiety as a negative force that hinders your performance, see it as a natural response to the pressure of the situation. By understanding that anxiety is a normal and manageable emotion, you can shift your focus from fear to excitement.

Embrace the challenge, knowing that every performance is an opportunity to learn and improve. Emphasize the process rather than the outcome, allowing yourself to make mistakes and learn from them. Remember that growth comes from stepping out of your comfort zone and pushing your limits.

With a growth mindset, you can transform performance anxiety into a catalyst for growth and excel in all areas of your life.

Developing Mental Resilience and Persistence in Athletics

Now that you've learned how to overcome performance anxiety with a growth mindset, it's time to apply those principles to another area of your life: athletics.

Developing mental resilience and persistence in sports is crucial for achieving your goals and pushing past your limits. With a growth mindset, you understand that setbacks and challenges are opportunities for growth and learning. Instead of giving up when faced with obstacles, you embrace them as a chance to improve and become a better athlete.

By cultivating mental resilience, you'll be able to bounce back from failures, stay focused under pressure, and persist through the toughest of circumstances. So, don't let setbacks discourage you. Embrace the challenge, believe in your ability to improve, and watch as your athletic skills and performance soar to new heights.

Fostering a Growth Mindset in Sports Training

If you want to foster a growth mindset in sports training, it's crucial to emphasize effort and practice in skill development.

By highlighting the importance of hard work and dedication, athletes can understand that their abilities are not fixed, but can be improved through consistent practice.

Setting challenging goals and embracing failure as feedback is also essential in cultivating a growth mindset.

Athletes should be encouraged to push themselves and see failures as opportunities for growth and learning.

Lastly, cultivating a growth mindset in team sports and collaboration is vital for athletes to understand the value of teamwork and cooperation.

By fostering a growth mindset in these areas, athletes can develop a resilient and positive attitude that will benefit them both on and off the field.

Emphasizing Effort and Practice in Skill Development

You can truly excel in skill development by prioritizing effort and practice over natural talent. It's easy to assume that some people are just born with innate abilities, but the reality is that hard work and dedication can take you much further than any natural talent ever could.

When you focus on putting in the time and effort to improve your skills, you are actively engaging in a growth mindset. This means that you believe in your ability to learn and grow, and you're willing to put in the necessary work to achieve your goals.

By emphasizing effort and practice, you're constantly challenging yourself and pushing your limits. You understand that mistakes and setbacks are simply opportunities for growth and learning. So, instead of giving up when things get tough, you persevere and continue to put in the effort.

This mindset not only helps you develop your skills, but it also builds resilience, determination, and a strong work ethic. So, remember, the key to excelling in skill development is to prioritize effort and practice, and to always believe in your ability to improve and grow.

Setting Challenging Goals and Embracing Failure as Feedback

Embrace failure as valuable feedback and set challenging goals to push yourself further in skill development.

When you view failure as an opportunity for growth, you can approach it with a positive mindset and learn from your mistakes.

By setting challenging goals, you are constantly pushing yourself out of your comfort zone and expanding your capabilities. These goals provide you with a clear target to work towards and motivate you to keep improving.

And when you do encounter failure along the way, instead of getting discouraged, see it as a stepping stone towards success. Failure is not the end, but rather a valuable source of feedback that can help you identify areas for improvement.

Embracing failure as feedback allows you to refine your skills and make necessary adjustments to reach your goals.

So, don't shy away from failure, but rather embrace it as an essential part of the learning process. Challenge yourself, learn from your setbacks, and keep striving for greatness.

Cultivating a Growth Mindset in Team Sports and Collaboration

Developing a growth-oriented attitude in team sports and collaboration can foster a sense of continuous improvement and enhance collective performance. When you adopt a growth mindset in these settings, you embrace the idea that abilities can be developed through dedication and hard work.

This mindset allows you to see challenges as opportunities for growth and learning, rather than obstacles to be avoided. By viewing failure as feedback and a chance to improve, you're more willing to take risks, push yourself out of your comfort zone, and learn from your mistakes.

This mindset not only benefits you as an individual, but also contributes to the overall success of your team. When everyone on the team has a growth mindset, there's a shared commitment to improving and achieving goals.

Collaboration becomes more effective as team members are open to new ideas, feedback, and constructive criticism. This leads to increased innovation, creativity, and problem-solving abilities.

By cultivating a growth mindset in team sports and collaboration, you create an environment where everyone's motivated to continuously learn, grow, and excel together.

Growth Mindset in Competitive Settings

When it comes to competitive settings, maintaining focus and optimism during competition is essential.

It's important to stay present in the moment, block out distractions, and maintain a positive mindset to perform at your best.

Additionally, learning from both success and failure in sports is crucial for growth.

By analyzing what went well and what didn't, you can make adjustments and improve your performance.

Lastly, encouraging sportsmanship and growth in both victory and defeat is a mark of a true athlete.

It's important to celebrate wins graciously and learn from losses, always striving to be better and supporting your teammates along the way.

Maintaining Focus and Optimism during Competition

Stay determined and confident in the face of competition, and you'll discover the power of maintaining focus and optimism.

When the pressure's on and the stakes are high, it's easy to get overwhelmed and lose sight of your goals. But by staying focused, you can block out distractions and stay on track towards success.

Keep your eye on the prize and remind yourself why you're competing in the first place. Believe in your abilities and trust that all your hard work and preparation will pay off.

Optimism is key in maintaining a growth mindset during competition. Instead of dwelling on mistakes or setbacks, use them as opportunities for growth and learning. Embrace challenges and view them as stepping stones towards improvement.

With a positive attitude and a laser-like focus, you'll be able to navigate through any competition with grace and determination. So, stay committed, stay confident, and watch as your mindset propels you towards victory.

Learning from Success and Failure in Sports

Experiencing both triumph and defeat in sports is like riding a roller coaster, with each victory and loss serving as valuable lessons that shape your athletic journey.

When you succeed, it's important to analyze what went well and learn from it. Celebrate your accomplishments, but also take the time to reflect on the factors that contributed to your success. Was it your preparation, technique, or mental game? By understanding what worked, you can replicate it in future endeavors.

On the other hand, failure should not be seen as a setback, but rather as an opportunity for growth. When you don't achieve the desired outcome, take a step back and assess the reasons behind it. Did you lack preparation, face tough competition, or struggle with your mindset? Embrace failure as a chance to learn and improve. Use it as motivation to work harder, set new goals, and refine your skills.

Remember, even the most successful athletes have faced failure along their journey. It's how you respond to it that sets you apart. So, whether you're celebrating a win or dealing with a loss, always strive to learn from both success and failure in sports.

Encouraging Sportsmanship and Growth in Victory and Defeat

Embrace the spirit of sportsmanship and foster personal development by celebrating your victories with humility and grace, while also demonstrating resilience and determination in the face of defeat.

When you achieve success in sports, it's important to remember that it's not just about winning, but also about how you handle the victory. Show respect towards your opponents and acknowledge their efforts, as this will not only earn you their respect but also contribute to a positive and supportive sporting environment.

On the other hand, when facing defeat, it's crucial to maintain a growth mindset and view it as an opportunity to learn and improve. Use setbacks as motivation to work harder and develop your skills, knowing that failure is not the end but rather a stepping stone towards future success.

By embodying these qualities, you not only enhance your own personal growth but also inspire others to adopt a growth mindset and strive for continuous improvement.

The Long-Term Impact of Growth Mindset on Athletes

When it comes to applying a growth mindset in career transitions and life after sports, you've got the advantage of embracing challenges and seeing them as opportunities for growth.

By maintaining a positive mental health and well-being, athletes with a growth mindset are better able to navigate the ups and downs of post-sports life.

Moreover, your growth mindset can serve as a powerful inspiration and mentorship for future generations, showing them the importance of perseverance, resilience, and the continuous pursuit of learning and personal development.

Applying Growth Mindset in Career Transitions and Life after Sports

Transitioning to a new career or life after sports becomes more fulfilling and successful through the application of a growth mindset. When you approach this transition with a growth mindset, you embrace the idea that skills can be developed and improved over time. Instead of feeling stuck or limited by your previous athletic career, you see it as a foundation for growth and learning.

This mindset allows you to adapt to new challenges and opportunities, and it gives you the confidence to take risks and pursue new paths. With a growth mindset, you understand that setbacks and failures are not permanent, but rather opportunities for growth and learning. You are open to new possibilities and willing to put in the effort to develop new skills and knowledge.

By embracing a growth mindset in your career transition, you can thrive in your new endeavors and find fulfillment and success in life after sports.

Positive Mental Health and Well-being in Athletes with a Growth Mindset

Athletes who cultivate a mindset focused on personal development can experience a remarkable boost in their mental well-being and overall happiness. By embracing a growth mindset, athletes open themselves up to new possibilities, challenges, and opportunities for growth.

Instead of viewing setbacks or failures as permanent, they see them as opportunities to learn and improve. This positive outlook not only helps athletes bounce back from setbacks more quickly, but it also allows them to maintain a sense of optimism and resilience in the face of adversity.

Additionally, athletes with a growth mindset are more likely to seek out and utilize resources and support systems that can contribute to their mental well-being. They understand the importance of self-care, stress management, and prioritizing their mental health.

By taking care of their mental well-being, athletes with a growth mindset are better equipped to handle the pressures and demands of their sport, leading to improved performance and overall satisfaction in their athletic endeavors.

Inspiration and Mentorship of Future Generations through Growth Mindset

Inspiring and guiding future generations, athletes who embrace a growth mindset can serve as mentors and role models. By embodying the principles of lifelong learning and personal development, these athletes can inspire others to believe in their own potential and strive for greatness.

Through their own experiences, they can share valuable insights, strategies, and techniques that can help young athletes navigate challenges, develop resilience, and achieve their goals. By demonstrating the power of perseverance and the importance of continuous improvement, these athletes can instill a sense of optimism and determination in the next generation.

Their stories of overcoming obstacles and embracing failure as an opportunity for growth can motivate and empower young athletes to push beyond their limits and pursue their dreams. With their unwavering commitment to self-improvement and their ability to adapt and learn from setbacks, athletes with a growth mindset can ignite a fire within future generations, inspiring them to never settle for mediocrity and to always strive for excellence.

Through their mentorship, these athletes can create a ripple effect, nurturing a culture of growth mindset and empowering future athletes to thrive in sports and in life.

Chapter 15: Growth Mindset in Creativity and the Arts

In Chapter 15, we'll explore the connection between growth mindset and creativity. We'll highlight how adopting a growth mindset can enhance your creative abilities. We'll also discuss how a growth mindset can enhance skill development and craftsmanship in the arts. This allows you to continuously improve and refine your artistic talents.

Additionally, we'll delve into the role of growth mindset in fostering innovation within the creative industries. We'll also discuss how art and creativity can be used as powerful tools to promote and cultivate a growth mindset.

The Connection between Growth Mindset and Creativity

If you want to unlock your true creative potential, it's time to embrace a growth mindset.

With a growth mindset, you'll be able to explore the creative process without fear of failure, understanding that every setback is an opportunity for growth.

When you approach creative blocks with a growth perspective, you'll be able to overcome them by trying new approaches and learning from your mistakes.

And perhaps most importantly, a growth mindset will allow you to embrace experimentation and risk-taking in your artistic endeavors, leading to breakthroughs and innovative creations that you never thought possible.

So, why wait? Start cultivating a growth mindset today and watch your creativity soar.

Exploring the Creative Process with a Growth Mindset

Embrace a growth mindset and you'll discover that 90% of highly creative individuals believe that creativity can be developed through practice and effort.

When you approach the creative process with a growth mindset, you open yourself up to endless possibilities. Instead of viewing creativity as a fixed trait that some people are born with, you understand that it is a skill that can be honed and improved over time.

With this mindset, you are more willing to take risks, explore new ideas, and push the boundaries of what is possible. You recognize that failure is not a setback, but rather an opportunity to learn and grow.

By embracing a growth mindset in your creative endeavors, you can unlock your full potential and achieve remarkable results. So, don't be afraid to try new things, make mistakes, and keep pushing yourself to learn and grow.

The creative process is a journey, and with a growth mindset, you can thrive and continue to evolve as a creative individual.

Overcoming Creative Blocks with a Growth Perspective

Now that you've gained insight into the creative process with a growth mindset, it's time to tackle the inevitable roadblocks that come with it.

Creative blocks can be frustrating and discouraging, but with a growth perspective, you have the advantage of seeing them as opportunities for growth and learning.

Embracing a growth mindset allows you to view these challenges as temporary setbacks rather than permanent failures. Instead of becoming discouraged and giving up, you can approach creative blocks with curiosity and determination, knowing that they are simply part of the learning process.

By adopting a growth perspective, you can overcome creative blocks and continue to thrive in your lifelong learning journey.

Embracing Experimentation and Risk-taking in Artistic Endeavors

By boldly venturing into uncharted territories and fearlessly pushing boundaries, you, as an artist, can unlock new dimensions of your craft and unleash the untapped potential within yourself.

Embracing experimentation and risk-taking in your artistic endeavors not only allows you to break free from creative blocks but also opens up a world of possibilities for growth and discovery.

When you step outside of your comfort zone and try new techniques, styles, or mediums, you challenge yourself to think differently and approach your art from fresh perspectives. This willingness to take risks not only fuels your creativity but also fosters a growth mindset, enabling you to constantly evolve and improve as an artist.

Embracing experimentation and risk-taking allows you to embrace mistakes as valuable learning opportunities and encourages you to embrace the unknown with excitement and curiosity.

So, go ahead, don't be afraid to take those leaps of faith and explore uncharted territories in your artistic journey. The rewards of daring to step outside of your comfort zone are immeasurable, and the growth and fulfillment you'll experience will be truly transformative.

Growth Mindset in Skill Development and Craftsmanship

If you want to truly master techniques and skills in any artistic field, embracing a growth mindset is crucial. By adopting a growth mindset, you understand that your abilities can be developed through dedication and hard work. This mindset allows you to persist through challenges and setbacks, and to view them as opportunities for growth.

Additionally, in order to grow as an artist, it's essential to embrace feedback and constructive criticism. This feedback helps you identify areas for improvement and refine your craft, ultimately leading to artistic growth and development.

So, if you're looking to excel in your chosen artistic field, remember the power of a growth mindset in mastering techniques, embracing persistence and resilience, and valuing feedback and constructive criticism.

Mastering Techniques and Skills through Growth Mindset

Embrace the growth mindset and watch as you unlock a world of endless possibilities, mastering techniques and skills like a fish in water.

With a growth mindset, you understand that mastering techniques and skills is a journey, not a destination. You approach every challenge with a sense of curiosity and a willingness to learn from both successes and failures. This mindset allows you to push through obstacles and setbacks, knowing that they're opportunities for growth.

As you continue to develop your craft, you recognize that there's always room for improvement and that expertise is a result of continuous learning and practice. You embrace feedback and seek out mentors who can guide you on your journey.

Through this dedication and perseverance, you become a true master of your craft, constantly evolving and pushing the boundaries of what you thought was possible.

So, embrace the growth mindset and watch as you soar to new heights in your pursuit of mastering techniques and skills.

The Role of Persistence and Resilience in Artistic Growth

Persistence and resilience are key to unlocking your artistic potential and overcoming obstacles along the way. As an artist, you'll undoubtedly face challenges and setbacks on your journey towards growth and success. It's through persistence that you'll push through these obstacles, refusing to give up when faced with difficulty.

Whether it's a technical skill you're struggling to master or a creative block that leaves you feeling uninspired, it's important to persevere and keep pushing forward.

Additionally, resilience plays a crucial role in artistic growth. There'll be times when you receive criticism or face rejection, but it's through resilience that you'll bounce back and continue to improve.

By embracing a growth mindset and understanding that setbacks are a natural part of the learning process, you'll be better equipped to navigate the ups and downs of your artistic journey.

So, embrace persistence and resilience, and watch as your artistic potential flourishes.

Embracing Feedback and Constructive Criticism in the Arts

Leverage the invaluable insights gained from embracing feedback and constructive criticism to propel your artistic journey to new heights. By opening yourself up to feedback, you allow others to provide you with a fresh perspective and help you identify areas for improvement.

Constructive criticism, although sometimes difficult to hear, is a valuable tool for growth. It pushes you to step out of your comfort zone, challenge yourself, and ultimately become a better artist. Remember, feedback is not a personal attack; it is an opportunity for growth.

Embracing it shows that you're committed to your craft and willing to put in the work necessary to achieve greatness. So, welcome feedback with open arms, listen to what others have to say, and use it to fuel your artistic development.

Growth Mindset and Innovation in the Creative Industries

If you want to foster a culture of innovation and creativity in the creative industries, embracing a growth mindset is essential. By believing that abilities can be developed through dedication and hard work, you encourage a willingness to take risks and explore new ideas.

Additionally, being open to change and adaptable in the face of challenges allows for continuous growth and improvement in the ever-evolving creative fields.

Finally, by approaching projects with a collaborative and interdisciplinary mindset, you can tap into the diverse perspectives and expertise of others, leading to innovative and groundbreaking work.

Embrace the power of a growth mindset to nurture an environment of innovation and creativity in the creative industries.

Nurturing a Culture of Innovation and Creativity with Growth Mindset

Encouraging a growth mindset fosters a culture of innovation and creativity, captivating individuals and inspiring them to constantly seek new ideas and solutions.

When individuals believe that their abilities can be developed through dedication and hard work, they are more likely to embrace challenges and view failures as opportunities for growth.

This mindset creates an environment where collaboration and experimentation are encouraged, as people are not afraid to take risks and think outside the box.

Nurturing a culture of innovation and creativity with a growth mindset also promotes continuous learning and improvement.

Individuals are motivated to expand their knowledge and skills, pushing themselves to explore new territories and push boundaries.

This mindset not only benefits the individuals themselves, but also the organization as a whole, as it fosters a dynamic and adaptive workforce that is always ready to embrace change and find innovative solutions.

So, by cultivating a growth mindset, organizations can unleash the full potential of their employees and create a culture that thrives on creativity and innovation.

Embracing Change and Adaptability in the Creative Fields

Embrace change and adaptability in the creative fields, and you might as well throw your creativity out the window and stick to the same old, stale ideas forever.

In the fast-paced world we live in, where trends come and go in the blink of an eye, it's essential for creative professionals to stay ahead of the game by embracing change and adapting to new circumstances.

The creative fields are constantly evolving, and those who resist change are left behind, while those who embrace it are able to thrive. By being open to new ideas, techniques, and technologies, you can expand your creative horizons and push the boundaries of what's possible.

Adaptability is the key to staying relevant and competitive in the creative industries, as it allows you to pivot and adjust your approach when necessary.

So, don't be afraid to step outside of your comfort zone, embrace change, and let your creativity soar to new heights.

Collaborative and Interdisciplinary Approaches with a Growth Mindset

Now that you've embraced change and adaptability in the creative fields, it's time to take your growth mindset to the next level by exploring collaborative and interdisciplinary approaches.

With a growth mindset, you understand that you can thrive not only by expanding your own knowledge and skills, but also by actively seeking out opportunities to work with others from different disciplines.

By collaborating with individuals who bring unique perspectives and expertise, you can tap into a wealth of creativity and innovation.

Whether you're a designer collaborating with a psychologist to create user-friendly products or a writer teaming up with a scientist to bring complex concepts to life, interdisciplinary collaborations can lead to groundbreaking ideas and solutions.

So, open your mind to the possibilities and remember that true growth comes from embracing the power of collaboration and interdisciplinary approaches.

Using Art and Creativity to Promote Growth Mindset

Are you interested in exploring how art and creativity can promote a growth mindset?

Art therapy and expression can be powerful tools for personal growth, allowing individuals to explore their emotions and experiences in a safe and creative way.

Creating artwork that inspires and encourages growth can not only benefit the artist, but also serve as a source of inspiration for others.

Moreover, using creativity to communicate the power of a growth mindset can help spread awareness and understanding of this mindset, encouraging others to embrace the idea of lifelong learning and personal development.

Art Therapy and Expression as Tools for Personal Growth

Tap into the power of art therapy and self-expression to unlock your personal growth journey.

Art therapy offers a unique and powerful way to explore your emotions, thoughts, and experiences through creative expression.

By engaging in art-making, you can tap into your subconscious and gain insight into your inner world.

Whether it's painting, drawing, sculpting, or any other form of artistic expression, art therapy allows you to communicate and process your feelings in a nonverbal way.

This can be especially beneficial for those who struggle with verbal expression or find it difficult to put their emotions into words.

Through art, you can explore and make sense of complex emotions, connect with your intuition, and gain a deeper understanding of yourself.

It can also provide a safe and therapeutic outlet for stress, anxiety, and trauma.

So, why not harness the power of art therapy and self-expression to embark on a transformative personal growth journey?

Allow yourself the freedom to create, explore, and discover new aspects of yourself through the magic of art.

Creating Artwork that Inspires and Encourages Growth

By harnessing the power of art therapy and self-expression, you can create artwork that inspires and encourages personal development, leading to a deeper understanding of yourself and improved mental well-being.

According to a study conducted by the American Journal of Public Health, engaging in creative activities, such as creating artwork, has been found to reduce stress levels by 75%.

Art allows you to express your emotions, thoughts, and experiences in a visual form, providing a therapeutic outlet for self-reflection and growth.

Through the process of creating art, you can explore different techniques, experiment with colors and textures, and discover new ways to convey your ideas.

This exploration and experimentation not only stimulates your creativity but also encourages you to think outside the box, fostering a growth mindset.

Additionally, creating artwork allows you to tap into your subconscious mind, unlocking hidden emotions and thoughts that may have been suppressed.

By bringing these hidden aspects of yourself to the surface, you can gain a deeper understanding of who you are and what motivates you, ultimately leading to personal growth and self-improvement.

So, grab a paintbrush, pick up a pencil, or start sculpting, and let your creativity flow.

Your artwork has the power to inspire not only yourself but also those around you, creating a ripple effect of growth and positivity.

Using Creativity to Communicate the Power of Growth Mindset

Unleash the transformative potential of your imagination and watch as your creativity becomes the language that communicates the unstoppable power of embracing new possibilities and pushing beyond limitations.

With creativity as your tool, you have the ability to capture the essence of the growth mindset and convey it to others in a powerful and inspiring way.

Through art, music, writing, or any other form of expression, you can create visuals, melodies, and words that resonate with people and ignite a fire within them to embrace lifelong learning.

Your creativity has the power to break down barriers, challenge conventional thinking, and encourage individuals to step out of their comfort zones.

By using your imagination to communicate the growth mindset, you can inspire others to believe in their own potential and strive for continuous improvement.

So, let your creativity flow and become a catalyst for change, spreading the message of growth mindset to all who encounter your artistic expressions.

Chapter 16: Growth Mindset in Entrepreneurship and Business

Are you an entrepreneur looking to take your business to the next level?

In Chapter 16, we explore the power of a growth mindset in entrepreneurship and business.

Discover how adopting a growth mindset can enhance your business leadership skills, fuel your business growth strategies, and sustain long-term success.

Embrace the mindset of a lifelong learner and watch your business thrive in the face of challenges and opportunities.

Growth Mindset for Entrepreneurs

Are you an entrepreneur looking to achieve success?

Embracing an entrepreneurial mindset and recognizing the limitless possibilities that come with it is the first step towards reaching your goals.

Overcoming challenges and failures is an inevitable part of entrepreneurship, but with a growth mindset, you can learn from these experiences and use them as stepping stones to success.

Developing resilience and adaptability is crucial in the ever-changing business landscape, and by building a growth mindset culture in your startup environment, you can foster innovation and continuous learning among your team, ultimately leading to long-term success.

Embracing Entrepreneurial Mindset and Limitless Possibilities

By embracing an entrepreneurial mindset, you open yourself up to a world of boundless opportunities and ignite a fire within you to continually learn and grow.

The entrepreneurial mindset is all about seeing challenges as opportunities, taking risks, and being proactive in finding innovative solutions. It's about being resilient in the face of failure and constantly seeking ways to improve and evolve.

With this mindset, you're not afraid to step out of your comfort zone and explore new ideas and possibilities. You understand that success isn't guaranteed, but you're willing to put in the hard work, dedication, and perseverance required to achieve your goals.

By embracing an entrepreneurial mindset, you're not only setting yourself up for personal and professional growth, but you're also creating a mindset that can lead to significant success and fulfillment in your entrepreneurial endeavors.

So, why limit yourself when there are endless possibilities waiting to be explored? Embrace the entrepreneurial mindset and discover the limitless potential within you.

Overcoming Challenges and Failures in Entrepreneurship

Now that you've embraced the entrepreneurial mindset and opened yourself up to limitless possibilities, it's important to acknowledge that challenges and failures are inevitable in the world of entrepreneurship. But here's the thing: they don't have to define you or hinder your success.

In fact, they can become stepping stones to greater achievements. Overcoming challenges and failures in entrepreneurship requires a growth mindset, a resilient attitude, and a willingness to learn from your mistakes. It's about understanding that setbacks are simply opportunities for growth and improvement.

By adopting this mindset, you can navigate through obstacles with determination, learn from your failures, and ultimately thrive in the ever-changing world of entrepreneurship. So don't let challenges discourage you; view them as valuable lessons that'll only make you stronger and more adept at seizing the limitless possibilities that lie ahead.

Developing Resilience and Adaptability as an Entrepreneur

In the ever-changing world of entrepreneurship, developing resilience and adaptability as an entrepreneur is crucial to weathering the storms of uncertainty and emerging stronger than ever.

As an entrepreneur, you'll inevitably face numerous challenges and setbacks along your journey. The ability to bounce back from these obstacles and adapt to new situations will be the key to your success.

Resilience allows you to maintain a positive mindset and find creative solutions when faced with adversity. It enables you to persevere through failures and learn from them, rather than being discouraged or giving up.

Adaptability, on the other hand, allows you to stay ahead of the curve in an ever-evolving business landscape. It means being open to change, embracing new technologies, and constantly seeking ways to improve and innovate.

By developing these qualities, you won't only be able to navigate the ups and downs of entrepreneurship, but you'll also be better equipped to seize new opportunities and thrive in an ever-changing market. So, embrace the challenges, embrace the failures, and use them as stepping stones to build your resilience and adaptability as an entrepreneur.

Your ability to adapt and bounce back will set you apart from the rest and give you the growth mindset advantage.

Building a Growth Mindset Culture in Startup Environments

Embrace the power of a growth mindset culture in startup environments, and watch as your team flourishes with resilience and adaptability.

In a startup, where uncertainty and challenges are the norm, fostering a growth mindset culture can be the key to success. By encouraging your team members to embrace challenges, persist in the face of setbacks, and see failures as opportunities for growth, you create an environment that promotes continuous learning and improvement.

A growth mindset culture also nurtures a sense of curiosity, where team members are encouraged to explore new ideas, take calculated risks, and learn from each other's experiences. This not only leads to innovation and creativity but also builds a strong foundation for problem-solving and adaptability.

When everyone on the team believes in their ability to learn and develop, they become more motivated, engaged, and open to feedback. They become resilient in the face of adversity and adaptable to changing circumstances.

So, foster a growth mindset culture in your startup, and empower your team to thrive in the ever-evolving entrepreneurial landscape.

Growth Mindset in Business Leadership

As a business leader, it's crucial for driving growth and staying ahead in a competitive market to foster innovation and creativity. By embracing a growth mindset in decision-making and risk-taking, you can empower your team to think outside the box and take calculated risks that can lead to breakthroughs and success.

Developing growth mindset competencies in leadership will not only enhance your own abilities but also inspire and motivate your team to constantly learn, adapt, and strive for excellence.

Fostering Innovation and Creativity as a Leader

Unlock your leadership potential by fostering innovation and creativity to inspire your team and drive successful outcomes.

As a leader, you have the power to create an environment that encourages new ideas and out-of-the-box thinking. By embracing a growth mindset, you can instill a sense of curiosity and experimentation within your team, leading to breakthrough innovations.

Encourage your team members to explore different perspectives, challenge assumptions, and take risks. Create opportunities for collaboration and brainstorming sessions where everyone feels comfortable sharing their ideas.

Foster a culture that celebrates failure as a learning opportunity, where mistakes are seen as stepping stones towards growth and improvement.

By nurturing a culture of innovation and creativity, you can empower your team to think innovatively, problem-solve creatively, and ultimately drive the success and growth of your organization.

Embracing a Growth Mindset in Decision-making and Risk-taking

Now that you've learned how to foster innovation and creativity as a leader, it's time to take it a step further by embracing a growth mindset in decision-making and risk-taking.

When you have a growth mindset, you believe that your abilities and intelligence can be developed through dedication and hard work. This mindset allows you to approach decision-making with a sense of curiosity and openness, knowing that even if you make a mistake, it's an opportunity to learn and grow.

Similarly, embracing a growth mindset in risk-taking means that you see taking risks as a chance to stretch yourself and expand your capabilities. Instead of being afraid of failure, you see it as a stepping stone towards success.

By adopting a growth mindset in decision-making and risk-taking, you'll be able to make more informed and confident choices, and you'll be more willing to take calculated risks that can lead to new opportunities and growth.

Developing Growth Mindset Competencies in Leadership

Embrace the power of developing your leadership skills by cultivating a mindset that believes in the endless potential for growth and expansion.

As a leader, it's essential to adopt a growth mindset that allows you to continually develop and improve your competencies.

By embracing this mindset, you understand that your abilities and skills aren't fixed, but can be developed through dedication, effort, and learning.

This mindset empowers you to take on new challenges, seek feedback, and learn from your mistakes, ultimately leading to personal and professional growth.

By constantly striving for improvement and being open to new ideas and perspectives, you can become a more effective leader, inspiring and motivating others to reach their full potential.

So, embrace the growth mindset and unlock your leadership potential.

Growth Mindset and Business Growth Strategies

When it comes to business growth strategies, it's crucial to set ambitious goals and embrace a growth mindset. By pushing yourself and your team to strive for greatness, you create a culture of continuous improvement and learning.

Additionally, seeking opportunities for growth and actively leveraging failure and feedback for iterative growth can help your business adapt and thrive in a rapidly changing marketplace.

So, don't be afraid to aim high, embrace challenges, and learn from every experience to achieve long-term success in your business.

Setting Ambitious Goals and Embracing Growth Mindset

By setting ambitious goals and adopting a growth mindset, you can soar to new heights in your personal and professional development.

When you set ambitious goals, you push yourself to go beyond your comfort zone and strive for excellence.

By embracing a growth mindset, you believe that your abilities and intelligence can be developed through dedication and hard work.

This mindset allows you to see challenges as opportunities for growth and to persist in the face of setbacks.

As you work towards your ambitious goals with a growth mindset, you will constantly be learning, adapting, and improving.

This continuous learning and improvement will not only help you achieve your goals, but also enable you to thrive in an ever-changing world.

So, don't be afraid to set ambitious goals and embrace a growth mindset - it's the key to unlocking your full potential and achieving great success.

Seeking Opportunities for Continuous Improvement and Learning

Congratulations on embracing a growth mindset and setting ambitious goals!

Now it's time to take the next step in your journey towards lifelong learning. By seeking opportunities for continuous improvement and learning, you can unlock your full potential and thrive in both your personal and professional life.

It's important to remember that learning is not limited to the classroom or formal education; it can happen in various ways and in any situation. Whether it's through taking on new challenges, seeking feedback from others, or pursuing new hobbies, every experience presents an opportunity for growth.

By actively seeking out these opportunities, you can constantly expand your knowledge and skills, and stay ahead in an ever-changing world. So, don't wait for learning to come to you – go out and actively seek it. Your growth mindset will be your advantage as you continue to thrive through lifelong learning.

Leveraging Failure and Feedback for Iterative Growth

Embracing failure and actively seeking feedback can be transformative for your personal and professional growth. By being open to failure, you create opportunities for iterative improvement and a deeper understanding of your strengths and weaknesses.

Failure is not the end but a stepping stone to success. It allows you to learn from your mistakes, make adjustments, and try again.

Feedback, on the other hand, provides valuable insights from others who can offer a different perspective and help you see blind spots. It allows you to identify areas for improvement and make necessary changes.

By leveraging failure and feedback, you can continuously grow and develop a mindset that thrives on lifelong learning. So, don't shy away from failure or feedback. Embrace them as catalysts for growth and watch yourself thrive.

Sustaining Growth Mindset in Business Success

Are you looking to sustain growth in your business success?

It's important to overcome complacency and avoid fixed mindset traps that can hinder progress.

By nurturing a growth mindset in your team members and employees, you can foster a culture of continuous learning and adaptability in the ever-changing business landscape.

Embracing a growth mindset plays a crucial role in ensuring long-term business sustainability.

Overcoming Complacency and Avoiding Fixed Mindset Traps

To avoid falling into fixed mindset traps, it's important to constantly challenge yourself and stay open to lifelong learning.

Complacency can be a dangerous state to be in, as it hinders personal and professional growth. It's easy to become comfortable with what we know and resist change, but this mindset can limit our potential.

By embracing a growth mindset, we can overcome complacency and continuously seek new opportunities for learning and development. This means being open to feedback, seeking out challenges, and embracing failures as opportunities for growth.

When we approach life with a growth mindset, we are better equipped to adapt to change, overcome obstacles, and achieve our goals.

So, don't let complacency hold you back. Embrace the growth mindset and thrive through lifelong learning.

Nurturing a Growth Mindset in Team Members and Employees

Encourage your team members and employees to foster a mindset of continuous improvement and embrace new opportunities for personal and professional development. By nurturing a growth mindset in your team, you create an environment that is conducive to learning and innovation.

Encourage them to take on new challenges, learn from failures, and seek feedback to improve their skills and knowledge. Provide them with resources, such as training programs and mentorship opportunities, to support their growth. Emphasize the importance of setting goals, both individually and as a team, and celebrate their achievements along the way.

Show them that their potential is limitless and that they have the power to continuously improve and excel. By fostering a growth mindset in your team, you not only empower them to reach their full potential but also create a culture of continuous learning and improvement within your organization.

Continuous Learning and Adaptability in the Business Landscape

Embrace the ever-changing business landscape like a skilled surfer riding the waves, constantly adapting and learning to stay ahead of the competition.

In today's fast-paced world, businesses that thrive are the ones that embrace continuous learning and adaptability. The ability to quickly learn new skills, adapt to new technologies and market trends, and pivot when necessary is crucial for success.

By fostering a culture of lifelong learning within your organization, you can empower your team members to constantly improve and stay ahead of the curve. Encourage them to seek out new knowledge, attend industry conferences and workshops, and engage in cross-functional learning opportunities.

Emphasize the importance of being open to change and trying new approaches, as this will enable your team to adapt and innovate in the face of challenges.

Remember, in the dynamic business landscape, those who're willing to learn and adapt will always have the advantage.

The Role of Growth Mindset in Long-term Business Sustainability

Now that you understand the importance of continuous learning and adaptability in the ever-changing business landscape, it's time to delve into the role of a growth mindset in long-term business sustainability.

Having a growth mindset means believing that abilities and intelligence can be developed through dedication and hard work. This mindset is crucial for businesses to thrive in the long run because it encourages employees and leaders to embrace challenges, persist in the face of setbacks, and continuously seek opportunities for improvement.

By cultivating a growth mindset within your business, you create an environment that fosters innovation, resilience, and a willingness to learn from failure. This mindset not only helps individuals grow and reach their full potential but also enables businesses to adapt, evolve, and stay competitive in an ever-changing marketplace.

So, if you want your business to thrive in the long term, it's time to embrace the growth mindset advantage and make lifelong learning a core value within your organization.

Chapter 17: Growth Mindset for Personal Wellness and Well-being

In Chapter 17 of the book, we'll explore the powerful relationship between a growth mindset and personal well-being. By embracing a growth mindset in personal development, you can unlock your full potential and achieve greater levels of happiness and fulfillment.

This chapter will also delve into the role of a growth mindset in developing positive habits, nurturing meaningful relationships, and embarking on a journey towards personal fulfillment.

The Relationship between Growth Mindset and Personal Well-being

Are you looking to improve your personal well-being?

Cultivating a positive mindset is key to achieving mental and emotional well-being.

By adopting a growth mindset, you can develop strategies to manage stress, build resilience, and overcome limiting beliefs about your health.

This mindset can have a profound impact on your physical health and wellness, allowing you to thrive through lifelong learning and personal growth.

Cultivating a Positive Mindset for Mental and Emotional Well-being

Embrace a positive mindset and watch as your mental and emotional well-being flourish. By cultivating a positive mindset, you can transform your outlook on life and improve your overall well-being.

When you approach challenges and setbacks with a positive attitude, you're more likely to find solutions and overcome obstacles.

This mindset allows you to see failures as opportunities for growth and learning, rather than as reasons to give up.

A positive mindset also helps you manage stress and cope with difficult emotions. Instead of dwelling on negative thoughts, you can focus on the present moment and find gratitude in the small things.

With a positive mindset, you can cultivate resilience, increase your self-esteem, and foster healthier relationships. So, why not choose to embrace positivity and unlock the potential for a happier and more fulfilling life?

Strategies for Managing Stress and Building Resilience

By adopting strategies for managing stress and building resilience, you can navigate life's challenges with greater ease and bounce back from adversity.

Life can be overwhelming at times, but by implementing practical techniques, you can effectively manage stress and build your resilience.

One strategy is to prioritize self-care and make time for activities that bring you joy and relaxation. Whether it's engaging in a hobby, practicing mindfulness, or exercising, these activities can help reduce stress and improve your overall well-being.

Additionally, developing a strong support network is crucial. Surround yourself with positive and supportive individuals who can provide guidance and encouragement during difficult times.

It's also important to practice positive self-talk and challenge negative thoughts. By reframing negative thinking patterns and focusing on your strengths and accomplishments, you can build resilience and maintain a positive mindset.

Lastly, remember to set realistic goals and break them down into smaller, manageable steps. This will help you stay motivated and overcome obstacles along the way.

By implementing these strategies, you can effectively manage stress and build resilience, enabling you to thrive in the face of life's challenges.

The Impact of Growth Mindset on Physical Health and Wellness

Improve your physical health and wellness by adopting a growth mindset and embracing the power of positive thinking.

Research has shown that individuals with a growth mindset are more likely to engage in healthy behaviors, such as exercise and proper nutrition, and are better able to cope with challenges that may arise.

By believing that you have the ability to improve and grow, you'll be more motivated to take care of your body and make choices that promote overall well-being.

Additionally, a growth mindset can help you overcome obstacles and setbacks, allowing you to bounce back from any health-related setbacks or injuries.

By focusing on the possibilities for growth and improvement, rather than dwelling on limitations, you can create a positive and resilient mindset that supports your physical health and wellness journey.

So, start nurturing your growth mindset today and experience the transformative impact it can have on your physical well-being.

Using Growth Mindset to Overcome Limiting Beliefs about Health

Don't let self-doubt hold you back from achieving optimal health and wellness – instead, adopt a growth mindset to overcome limiting beliefs about your capabilities.

Many people have beliefs that they're not strong enough, fit enough, or disciplined enough to achieve their health goals. However, with a growth mindset, you can challenge these beliefs and embrace the idea that you have the capacity to improve and grow in all areas of your life, including your health.

By recognizing that your abilities aren't fixed, but can be developed through effort and learning, you can break free from the constraints of limiting beliefs and take control of your health and wellness journey.

Embrace the idea that setbacks are opportunities for growth, and that failures are just stepping stones towards success. With a growth mindset, you can approach your health goals with determination, resilience, and a belief in your own potential.

So, don't let self-doubt hold you back – instead, adopt a growth mindset and discover the limitless possibilities for achieving optimal health and wellness.

Embracing Growth Mindset in Personal Development

Are you ready to take your personal development to the next level?

Setting goals and taking action is the first step towards achieving personal growth.

By seeking feedback and embracing growth opportunities, you can continuously learn and improve yourself.

And don't forget to nurture self-compassion and self-acceptance along the way - with a growth mindset, you can embrace your imperfections and still strive for growth.

So why wait? Start embracing a growth mindset in your personal development journey today!

Setting Goals and Taking Action for Personal Growth

Achieving personal growth and success starts with setting goals and taking decisive action.

By setting specific, measurable, attainable, relevant, and time-bound (SMART) goals, you can create a roadmap for your personal development journey. These goals provide clarity and direction, helping you stay focused and motivated along the way.

Once you have identified your goals, it's crucial to take action towards achieving them. This means breaking down your goals into smaller, manageable tasks and consistently working towards them.

Embracing a growth mindset allows you to view challenges as opportunities for learning and growth, enabling you to push past obstacles and persevere.

Remember, personal growth is a lifelong journey, and by setting goals and taking action, you're actively investing in your own development and unlocking your full potential.

So, start today, take that first step, and watch as your personal growth and success unfold before you.

Seeking Feedback and Embracing Growth Opportunities

Take advantage of opportunities to seek feedback and embrace growth to unlock your full potential and watch as your personal development journey unfolds before you. Seeking feedback allows you to gain valuable insights and perspectives from others, helping you identify areas for improvement and discover new possibilities.

Embracing growth opportunities, whether through new challenges or learning experiences, pushes you outside of your comfort zone and allows you to develop new skills and abilities. By actively pursuing feedback and growth opportunities, you're actively investing in yourself and ensuring that you continue to grow and thrive throughout your lifelong learning journey.

So don't be afraid to ask for feedback, take on new challenges, and embrace growth opportunities – the rewards will be worth it.

Nurturing Self-compassion and Self-acceptance with a Growth Mindset

Embrace the power of self-compassion and self-acceptance, allowing yourself to grow and evolve with a mindset that values personal development and resilience.

By nurturing self-compassion, you give yourself permission to make mistakes, learn from them, and move forward with grace. Instead of criticizing yourself for your shortcomings, acknowledge them as opportunities for growth.

Self-acceptance is equally important in this journey. Accepting yourself as you are, flaws and all, enables you to approach challenges with confidence and a willingness to learn.

Embracing a growth mindset means understanding that your abilities can be developed through dedication and hard work. With self-compassion and self-acceptance as your foundation, you can navigate the ups and downs of life with resilience and an unwavering belief in your capacity to learn and improve.

So, give yourself the gift of self-compassion and self-acceptance, and watch yourself thrive as you embrace lifelong learning and personal growth.

Growth Mindset and Positive Habits

If you want to create and sustain healthy habits, embracing a growth mindset is key. By adopting a growth mindset, you'll be open to learning and improving, which will help you overcome procrastination and build consistency in your habits.

Additionally, by embracing change and continuously learning, you'll be able to adapt and evolve your personal habits to better align with your goals and values.

So, don't just settle for mediocre habits, use the power of a growth mindset to transform them into habits that'll help you thrive.

Creating and Sustaining Healthy Habits with Growth Mindset

Developing a growth mindset can help you establish and maintain healthy habits, such as consistently exercising, by viewing setbacks as opportunities for growth and learning.

For example, imagine you're someone who's always struggled with maintaining a regular exercise routine. Instead of getting discouraged and giving up when you miss a day or two, a growth mindset encourages you to see those setbacks as learning experiences.

You can reflect on what went wrong, adjust your approach, and try again. By embracing the belief that your abilities can be developed through dedication and hard work, you can overcome obstacles and stay committed to your fitness goals.

With a growth mindset, you understand that progress takes time and effort, and you're willing to put in the work to achieve long-term success. So, rather than viewing setbacks as failures, you see them as valuable opportunities for growth and self-improvement.

Overcoming Procrastination and Building Consistency

To overcome procrastination and establish consistency, it's essential for you to adopt a proactive approach to tackling tasks and maintaining a steady routine. Instead of putting off important tasks, take the initiative to prioritize and break them down into smaller, manageable steps. This will make them feel less overwhelming and more achievable.

Additionally, set specific goals and deadlines for yourself to stay motivated and focused. By creating a schedule or to-do list, you can hold yourself accountable and track your progress. It's also important to eliminate distractions and create a conducive environment for work. Minimize interruptions, turn off notifications, and find a quiet space where you can concentrate.

Remember to celebrate your achievements along the way, as this will help reinforce positive habits and keep you motivated. With a proactive mindset and consistent effort, you can overcome procrastination and build a solid foundation for lifelong learning and growth.

Embracing Change and Continuous Learning in Personal Habits

Embrace change and continuously learn by actively seeking new opportunities to expand your knowledge and adapt your personal habits.

In today's fast-paced world, staying stagnant is not an option if you want to thrive. By being open to change and embracing it, you allow yourself to grow and develop in ways you never thought possible.

Whether it's trying out a new exercise routine, learning a new language, or adopting a healthier lifestyle, the key is to be proactive and take the necessary steps to improve yourself. Don't be afraid to step out of your comfort zone and try new things.

It's through these experiences that you'll not only gain new skills and knowledge but also develop a mindset that is adaptable and resilient. So, challenge yourself, seek new opportunities, and never stop learning.

Your personal growth and success depend on it.

Nurturing Positive Relationships with a Growth Mindset

Are you looking to strengthen your relationships and create more meaningful connections with others?

One key aspect to consider is the importance of empathy and understanding in relationships. By adopting a growth mindset, you can develop the ability to put yourself in others' shoes and truly understand their perspective, leading to deeper connections and stronger bonds.

Another crucial skill to nurture positive relationships is effective communication and conflict resolution. With a growth mindset, you can approach conflicts as opportunities for growth and learning, fostering open and honest communication that builds trust and understanding.

Finally, cultivating supportive and growth-oriented connections is essential for personal and professional development. By surrounding yourself with individuals who encourage and inspire you, you can thrive and achieve your goals.

So why not embrace a growth mindset and start nurturing positive relationships today?

Empathy and Understanding in Relationships

Developing a growth mindset allows you to forge deeper connections with others, like the roots of a tree intertwining to create a strong and supportive network.

When you approach relationships with empathy and understanding, you can truly connect with others on a deeper level. Empathy allows you to put yourself in someone else's shoes, understanding their perspective and emotions. This understanding fosters trust and strengthens your bond with others.

By actively listening and seeking to understand, you show that you value and respect their feelings, thoughts, and experiences. This creates an environment where open and honest communication can thrive, leading to stronger, more fulfilling relationships.

When you approach relationships with empathy and understanding, you also become more patient and forgiving. You recognize that everyone has their own journey and struggles, and you are able to support and encourage them with kindness and compassion. This not only benefits the other person, but it also enhances your own personal growth and development.

So, embrace a growth mindset and cultivate empathy and understanding in your relationships, and watch as your connections with others flourish and thrive.

Communication and Conflict Resolution with a Growth Mindset

Improving communication and resolving conflicts becomes more effective when approaching them with a growth mindset.

By adopting a growth mindset, you understand that conflicts and disagreements are opportunities for growth and learning.

Rather than viewing them as threats or obstacles, you see them as chances to develop new skills, deepen your understanding of others, and strengthen your relationships.

With a growth mindset, you're open to feedback, willing to listen to different perspectives, and committed to finding solutions that benefit everyone involved.

Instead of getting defensive or avoiding difficult conversations, you embrace them as opportunities to improve yourself and your relationships.

This mindset allows you to approach conflicts with empathy, curiosity, and a genuine desire to understand the other person's point of view.

You're more likely to engage in effective communication techniques such as active listening, asking open-ended questions, and seeking common ground.

By approaching communication and conflict resolution with a growth mindset, you can foster healthier and more productive relationships, ultimately leading to personal and professional growth.

Cultivating Supportive and Growth-oriented Connections

Nurture supportive and growth-oriented connections by actively seeking out individuals who inspire and challenge you to become the best version of yourself.

Surround yourself with people who have a growth mindset. This can have a profound impact on your personal and professional development.

These connections can provide you with valuable feedback, guidance, and support as you navigate through the ups and downs of life.

By engaging with individuals who are committed to continuous learning and improvement, you'll be motivated to push your own limits and strive for excellence.

Their positive energy and enthusiasm will inspire you to embrace challenges, learn from failures, and constantly seek new opportunities for growth.

Together, you can create a community of like-minded individuals who are dedicated to lifelong learning and personal growth.

So, take the initiative to connect with people who share your values and aspirations. Watch as these connections propel you towards success and fulfillment.

The Journey to Personal Fulfillment with Growth Mindset

Are you searching for purpose and meaning in your life?

With a growth mindset, you can find fulfillment through continuous learning and personal growth.

Embrace change and transformation as opportunities for growth, and you'll discover new possibilities and experiences.

By living a life of constant learning, you'll not only enhance your skills but also deepen your understanding of the world around you.

It's time to embrace the journey to personal fulfillment with a growth mindset.

Finding Purpose and Meaning through Growth and Learning

Discovering the power of growth and learning can unlock a world of purpose and meaning in your life. When you embrace a growth mindset, you open yourself up to endless possibilities for personal and professional development.

By constantly seeking opportunities to learn and grow, you can find fulfillment in the journey itself. Every setback becomes a chance to learn and improve, and every success becomes a stepping stone towards even greater achievements.

With a growth mindset, you're not limited by your current circumstances or abilities. Instead, you're empowered to continuously expand your knowledge, skills, and experiences. This constant growth and learning allow you to discover your true passions and talents, and to pursue a life that's meaningful and fulfilling.

So, don't be afraid to step outside of your comfort zone and embrace the challenges that come your way. By adopting a growth mindset, you can find purpose and meaning in every aspect of your life.

Embracing Change and Transformation as Opportunities for Growth

Embracing change and transformation opens the door to a world of endless possibilities for personal and professional development, igniting a fire within that propels you towards your greatest potential.

Change can be intimidating, but it's through change that we grow and evolve. By embracing change, we allow ourselves to step outside of our comfort zones and challenge ourselves to learn and adapt. We become more resilient and adaptable, able to navigate through life's uncertainties with confidence and grace.

Transformation, on the other hand, is the process of becoming the best version of ourselves. It requires us to let go of old patterns and beliefs that no longer serve us and embrace new ways of thinking and being. Through transformation, we unlock new strengths and capabilities that we may not have even known existed.

It is through embracing change and transformation that we can truly thrive and reach our full potential. So, why resist change when it's an opportunity for growth and self-discovery? Embrace it, and watch as your life unfolds in extraordinary ways.

Living a Life of Continuous Learning and Personal Growth

By continuously seeking new knowledge and expanding your horizons, you open yourself up to a world of possibilities and create a life filled with limitless opportunities for personal development and growth.

Embracing a mindset of continuous learning allows you to stay adaptable and open-minded in the face of change, enabling you to thrive in an ever-evolving world. It encourages you to step out of your comfort zone, try new things, and challenge yourself, fostering personal growth and self-improvement.

Through continuous learning, you develop new skills, gain valuable insights, and broaden your perspectives, which not only enhances your personal and professional life but also enriches your overall well-being.

Every day becomes an opportunity to learn something new, whether it's through reading, taking courses, attending workshops, or engaging in meaningful conversations.

So, embrace the power of continuous learning, and watch as your life transforms into a remarkable journey of self-discovery and growth.

Chapter 18: Growth Mindset and the Future of Work

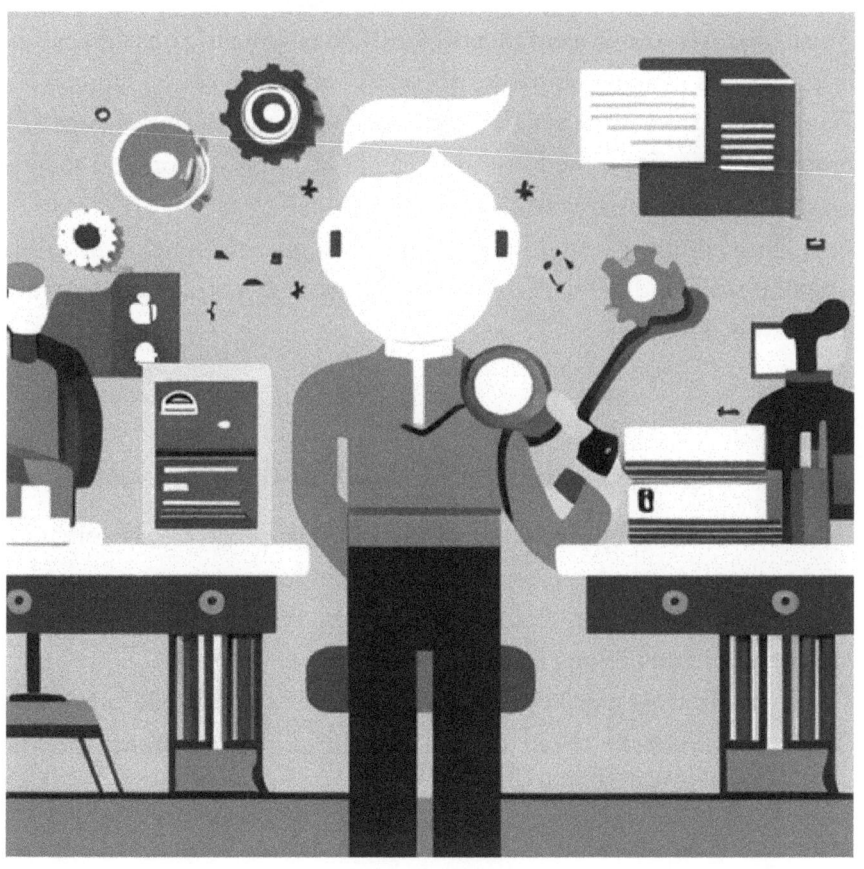

In Chapter 18, you'll explore the exciting intersection of growth mindset and the future of work. You'll delve into the changing landscape of work and employment. You'll discover how a growth mindset can help you thrive in this evolving environment. Additionally, you'll uncover the importance of skill development and continuous learning. It's essential in order to stay competitive and adapt to the demands of the future. Finally, you'll learn how embracing change and uncertainty with a growth mindset can lead to innovation and success in the entrepreneurial world.

This chapter will highlight the role of a growth mindset in career development and growth. It'll empower you to take charge of your professional journey.

The Changing Landscape of Work and Employment

In the ever-changing landscape of work and employment, automation and technological advancements have a significant impact.

To thrive in the future workplace, it's crucial to embrace adaptability and lifelong learning.

By cultivating a growth mindset and continuously acquiring new skills, you can stay ahead of the curve and remain valuable in an increasingly automated world.

The Impact of Automation and Technological Advancements

With automation and technological advancements, you can unlock a world of endless opportunities for growth and learning. The impact of automation and technology in the workplace is undeniable, as it has revolutionized the way we work and live.

From artificial intelligence to robotics, these advancements have the potential to streamline processes, increase efficiency, and improve overall productivity. However, the fear of job loss due to automation is a common concern. While some jobs may be automated, this also opens up new avenues for learning and skill development.

Embracing a growth mindset allows you to adapt and thrive in this ever-changing landscape. By being open to learning new skills and continuously upskilling yourself, you can position yourself for success in this automated world. The key is to see automation as an opportunity rather than a threat, and to focus on the skills that cannot be easily replicated by machines: creativity, critical thinking, problem-solving, and emotional intelligence.

By developing these skills, you can not only future-proof your career but also find fulfillment in a world where lifelong learning is essential. So, embrace the possibilities that automation and technological advancements offer, and take charge of your own growth and success.

The Importance of Adaptability and Lifelong Learning in the Future Workplace

Embrace the dynamic nature of the future workplace and stay relevant by continuously adapting and learning, as 65% of today's jobs will be replaced by machines in the next 20 years.

The importance of adaptability and lifelong learning cannot be overstated in this rapidly changing landscape. By adopting a growth mindset and actively seeking out new skills and knowledge, you can position yourself for success in the future workplace.

With automation and technological advancements reshaping industries, the ability to adapt and learn new skills will be key to thriving in your career. Employers are increasingly valuing individuals who can quickly adapt to new technologies and processes, and who are eager to continually learn and grow.

By embracing the mindset of a lifelong learner, you can not only stay relevant in the face of automation, but also open up new opportunities for personal and professional development.

So, don't let the fear of job displacement hold you back. Instead, take charge of your own learning journey and position yourself for success in the future workplace.

Skill Development and Continuous Learning in the Future of Work

Are you ready to embrace a growth mindset for skill acquisition and development in the future of work?

By adopting a growth mindset, you can unlock your full potential and thrive in an ever-changing work landscape.

In addition, developing transferable skills will give you a competitive advantage, allowing you to adapt to new roles and industries effortlessly.

So why wait? Start cultivating a growth mindset today and embrace the endless possibilities for continuous learning and skill development in the future of work.

Embracing a Growth Mindset for Skill Acquisition and Development

Developing a growth mindset enables you to actively pursue and enhance your skills throughout your life. By embracing a growth mindset, you open yourself up to new opportunities for learning and development.

You understand that abilities can be developed through dedication and hard work. With a growth mindset, you're not afraid to take on challenges and see failures as opportunities for growth. Rather than being discouraged by setbacks, you use them as stepping stones towards improvement.

This mindset allows you to continually acquire new skills and adapt to the ever-changing demands of the future of work. By cultivating a growth mindset, you position yourself to thrive in a world that values lifelong learning and continuous skill development.

So, don't limit yourself by thinking that your abilities are fixed; embrace a growth mindset and unlock your full potential.

Transferable Skills and the Growth Mindset Advantage

So, you've embraced a growth mindset for skill acquisition and development, and now it's time to take it a step further and explore the concept of transferable skills.

These skills are incredibly valuable because they can be applied across different areas of your life and work. With a growth mindset, you have the advantage of being open to learning new skills and adapting them to various situations.

This flexibility allows you to thrive in a rapidly changing world where the ability to learn and adapt is essential. By embracing the growth mindset, you are positioning yourself to excel in any endeavor you choose to pursue.

So, let's dive into the world of transferable skills and discover how they can give you a significant advantage in your lifelong learning journey.

Entrepreneurial Mindset and Innovation in the Future of Work

Are you ready to embrace a growth mindset and seize entrepreneurial opportunities in the future of work?

By cultivating a mindset focused on continuous learning and personal development, you can unlock your potential for innovation and problem-solving in the workplace.

Embracing a growth mindset not only allows you to adapt to the ever-changing business landscape, but it also empowers you to think creatively and take calculated risks, leading to groundbreaking ideas and solutions.

So, don't shy away from embracing a growth mindset – it's the key to unlocking your entrepreneurial spirit and driving innovation in the future of work.

Embracing a Growth Mindset for Entrepreneurial Opportunities

By adopting a growth mindset, you can unlock endless possibilities and seize entrepreneurial opportunities that others may overlook. Embracing a growth mindset means believing that your abilities and intelligence can be developed through dedication and hard work. It means viewing challenges as opportunities for growth and learning, rather than as obstacles.

With a growth mindset, you're willing to take risks, learn from failures, and constantly seek new knowledge and skills. This mindset allows you to adapt to changing circumstances, innovate, and think outside the box. It gives you the resilience and determination to persevere through setbacks and ultimately positions you for success in the ever-evolving world of entrepreneurship.

So, don't limit yourself with a fixed mindset. Embrace the growth mindset and open yourself up to a world of entrepreneurial possibilities.

Encouraging Innovation and Problem-Solving in the Workplace

Encouraging innovation and problem-solving in the workplace enables you to tap into your creative potential and find unique solutions to challenges. By fostering an environment that values and encourages new ideas, you can unlock the full potential of your team and drive business success.

When employees are empowered to think outside the box and take risks, they become more engaged and motivated, leading to increased productivity and a competitive edge in the market.

Moreover, encouraging innovation and problem-solving cultivates a culture of continuous learning and improvement, where mistakes are seen as opportunities for growth rather than failures. This mindset shift not only fuels creativity and collaboration but also fosters resilience and adaptability, essential qualities in today's rapidly changing business landscape.

So, embrace innovation and problem-solving in your workplace, and watch your team thrive and excel in their roles.

Embracing Change and Uncertainty with a Growth Mindset

In the ever-changing work environment, embracing change and uncertainty is essential for thriving. By developing a growth mindset, you can adapt to new challenges and seize opportunities for growth.

Building resilience and prioritizing your psychological well-being are crucial for navigating the future of work with confidence and success.

Embrace change, build resilience, and prioritize your well-being to thrive in the dynamic world of work.

Thriving in an Ever-changing Work Environment

Thriving in an ever-changing work environment requires embracing a growth mindset, as studies have shown that individuals with this mindset are 47% more likely to adapt successfully to new challenges.

In today's fast-paced and dynamic workplace, being able to navigate through uncertainty and change is crucial for professional success. By adopting a growth mindset, you open yourself up to continuous learning and improvement, allowing you to stay ahead of the curve and thrive in this ever-evolving landscape.

Instead of fearing change, you see it as an opportunity for growth and development. You actively seek out new challenges, push yourself out of your comfort zone, and constantly strive to learn new skills. With a growth mindset, you're not afraid to take risks or make mistakes because you understand that these are valuable opportunities for learning and growth.

You're resilient and adaptable, able to quickly pivot and adjust to new circumstances. This mindset allows you to embrace change with enthusiasm and confidence, positioning you as a valuable asset in any work environment.

So, if you want to thrive in an ever-changing work environment, it's time to cultivate a growth mindset and unlock the advantages it brings.

Building Resilience and Psychological Well-being in the Future of Work

Now that you've learned how to thrive in an ever-changing work environment, it's time to focus on building resilience and psychological well-being in the future of work.

As the world continues to evolve, so does the nature of work, and being able to adapt and bounce back from challenges is crucial for success.

Building resilience allows you to not only withstand the pressures of the future but also to thrive in the face of adversity.

By developing a growth mindset and embracing lifelong learning, you can effectively navigate the complexities of the future of work and maintain your psychological well-being.

With a growth mindset, you see challenges as opportunities for growth and believe in your ability to learn and adapt.

This mindset enables you to approach new situations with confidence, curiosity, and resilience.

Additionally, investing in your psychological well-being by practicing self-care, managing stress, and seeking support when needed will help you maintain a healthy work-life balance and enhance your overall resilience.

So, embrace the future with a growth mindset, prioritize your well-being, and watch yourself thrive in the ever-changing landscape of work.

The Role of Growth Mindset in Career Development and Growth

Are you looking to navigate career transitions and overcome challenges? Embracing a growth mindset can provide you with the tools and mindset needed to adapt and thrive in the face of change.

By adopting a growth mindset, you can seize opportunities for advancement and continuously learn and develop in your career.

Furthermore, by fostering a positive and productive work culture with a growth mindset, you can create an environment that encourages innovation, collaboration, and personal growth for yourself and your colleagues.

So why wait? Embrace the power of a growth mindset and unlock your full potential in your career.

Navigating Career Transitions and Overcoming Challenges

When you embrace a growth mindset, you can navigate career transitions and overcome challenges by embracing the idea that learning and personal development are ongoing processes.

Instead of viewing career transitions as daunting or overwhelming, you see them as opportunities for growth and exploration.

You understand that change is inevitable in today's rapidly evolving job market, and you're willing to adapt and learn new skills to stay relevant.

With a growth mindset, you approach challenges as learning opportunities rather than obstacles. You believe that setbacks and failures aren't permanent, but rather stepping stones to success.

This mindset enables you to persevere through difficult times and find creative solutions to problems.

By continuously seeking new knowledge and skills, you're better equipped to face any career transition or challenge that comes your way.

So, embrace a growth mindset and unlock your full potential in navigating your career journey.

Seizing Opportunities and Advancement with a Growth Mindset

Embrace the concept of continuous personal growth and development, and seize opportunities for advancement with a mindset that embraces change and adapts to the evolving job market.

In today's fast-paced world, where industries are constantly evolving and new technologies are emerging, it's crucial to have a growth mindset that allows you to thrive and succeed.

By embracing change and being open to learning new skills, you position yourself for advancement and success in your career. Instead of fearing change, see it as an opportunity to grow and develop.

Seek out new challenges and take on projects that push you outside of your comfort zone. By doing so, you not only expand your knowledge and skills, but you also demonstrate to employers your ability to adapt and thrive in a changing environment.

With a growth mindset, you become a lifelong learner, constantly seeking new knowledge and skills that'll propel you forward in your career.

So, don't be afraid to take risks, embrace change, and seize the opportunities that come your way. With a growth mindset, the possibilities for advancement are endless.

Creating a Positive and Productive Work Culture with Growth

Mindset

Fostering a positive and productive work culture is essential for creating an environment where you can continuously develop and flourish. When you embrace a growth mindset, you not only encourage personal growth but also inspire those around you to do the same.

By fostering a culture that values learning and improvement, you create a space where everyone feels supported and motivated to take on new challenges. This mindset encourages collaboration, innovation, and open communication, allowing for the exchange of ideas and the sharing of knowledge.

In a positive work culture, mistakes are seen as opportunities for growth, and feedback is embraced as a means to improve. This environment promotes creativity, resilience, and a sense of ownership, which in turn leads to increased productivity and job satisfaction.

So, by cultivating a growth mindset and fostering a positive work culture, you're not only investing in your own success but also creating an environment where everyone can thrive and reach their full potential.

Chapter 19: Cultivating Growth Mindset in Organizations

In Chapter 19, you'll explore the importance of cultivating a growth mindset in organizations and how it directly contributes to their success.

You'll learn about the role of leadership development in fostering a growth mindset and how it can positively impact team dynamics.

Additionally, the chapter delves into the significance of promoting a growth mindset in employee development and provides insights on evaluating and measuring its impact within organizations.

Embracing a growth mindset is crucial for your organization's growth and prosperity, and this chapter will equip you with the knowledge and strategies to make it happen.

The Importance of Growth Mindset for Organizational Success

Are you looking to build a growth mindset culture within your organization?

By fostering a mindset that embraces innovation and adaptability, you can encourage your employees to constantly seek new knowledge and solutions.

This not only increases employee engagement and retention, but also creates a positive and supportive work environment where individuals feel empowered to take risks and learn from their mistakes.

With a growth mindset, your organization can thrive through lifelong learning and stay ahead in today's fast-paced and ever-changing business landscape.

Building a Growth Mindset Culture for Innovation and Adaptability

Embracing a growth mindset culture is the catalyst for fostering innovation and adaptability, propelling you to reach your full potential and overcome obstacles.

In a growth mindset culture, individuals are encouraged to view challenges as opportunities for growth, to embrace failure as a stepping stone to success, and to continuously seek out new knowledge and skills.

This mindset not only fuels creativity and problem-solving but also promotes a sense of resilience and adaptability in the face of change.

By cultivating a growth mindset culture, organizations can create an environment that encourages experimentation, collaboration, and the free exchange of ideas, leading to increased innovation and improved performance.

So, whether it's developing new products, adapting to market changes, or navigating uncertain times, a growth mindset culture empowers individuals and organizations to thrive in an ever-evolving world.

Increasing Employee Engagement and Retention with Growth Mindset

Boost your team's motivation and commitment by fostering a culture that encourages continuous development and a positive outlook on personal growth.

When employees feel supported in their pursuit of learning and development, they're more likely to be engaged and committed to their work.

By promoting a growth mindset, you can create an environment where employees feel empowered to take on new challenges and embrace opportunities for growth.

Encourage your team to set goals, provide them with the necessary resources and support to achieve those goals, and celebrate their successes along the way.

Show them that their efforts and growth are valued and recognized. This not only increases employee engagement but also helps with retention as employees are more likely to stay with a company that invests in their development and encourages their personal growth.

Remember, fostering a growth mindset isn't just about individual growth but also about creating a thriving and adaptable team that can overcome challenges and drive innovation.

Creating a Positive and Supportive Work Environment with Growth Mindset

Now that you understand how a growth mindset can increase employee engagement and retention, it's time to explore how it can create a positive and supportive work environment.

When you foster a growth mindset within your organization, you encourage your employees to embrace challenges, learn from their mistakes, and constantly improve. This creates a culture where individuals feel empowered to take risks and push their boundaries, knowing that their efforts will be valued and supported.

By promoting a growth mindset, you can inspire a sense of camaraderie among your team members and promote collaboration and innovation. A positive and supportive work environment not only boosts employee morale and satisfaction but also enhances productivity and overall success.

So, why not cultivate a growth mindset within your organization and reap the benefits of a thriving workforce?

Leadership Development and Growth Mindset

If you want your organization to thrive, it's crucial to develop growth mindset competencies in your leaders and managers.

By fostering a growth mindset in their decision-making processes, leaders can create a culture of continuous learning and improvement.

Embracing a growth mindset in leadership development programs can help leaders become more adaptable, resilient, and open to feedback, ultimately leading to greater success for the entire organization.

Developing Growth Mindset Competencies in Leaders and Managers

Embrace the irony of developing growth mindset competencies in leaders and managers, and watch as your team flourishes under your guidance. By adopting a growth mindset yourself, you can inspire those around you to do the same.

Encourage your team to embrace challenges, learn from failures, and persist in the face of obstacles. Provide them with opportunities for continuous learning and personal development.

Foster a culture of curiosity, where asking questions and seeking feedback are encouraged. Lead by example, showing your team that growth and improvement are ongoing processes.

By developing growth mindset competencies in yourself and your team, you can create an environment where everyone thrives and achieves their full potential.

Fostering a Growth Mindset in Leadership Decision-making

Lead your team to success by cultivating a mindset that values continuous improvement and embraces the challenges that come with making leadership decisions. As a leader, it's crucial to foster a growth mindset in your approach to decision-making.

By adopting a growth mindset, you view challenges as opportunities for growth and learning. Instead of being deterred by setbacks or failures, you see them as stepping stones to success.

Encourage your team to embrace this mindset by providing them with the support and resources they need to develop their skills and knowledge. Encourage them to take risks, learn from their mistakes, and constantly seek feedback.

By fostering a growth mindset in leadership decision-making, you create an environment that is conducive to innovation, creativity, and ultimately, success.

Embracing Growth Mindset in Leadership Development Programs

Developing a growth mindset in leadership development programs can empower you to unlock your full potential and drive meaningful change within your organization. By embracing a growth mindset, you can cultivate a mindset that embraces challenges, persists through obstacles, and sees failures as opportunities for learning and growth.

In leadership development programs, this mindset can have a transformative impact on your ability to make effective decisions, adapt to change, and inspire and motivate your team members. By fostering a culture of continuous learning and development, you can encourage leaders to constantly seek new knowledge and skills, stay open to feedback and different perspectives, and embrace challenges as opportunities for growth.

This not only enhances individual leadership capabilities but also creates a more innovative, adaptable, and resilient organization. So, embrace the power of a growth mindset in leadership development programs and unlock your true potential as a leader.

Promoting Growth Mindset in Team Dynamics

In order to promote a growth mindset within your team dynamics, it's crucial to foster an environment of psychological safety and risk-taking. Encourage your team members to voice their opinions and take calculated risks without fear of judgment or retribution.

Additionally, emphasize the importance of collaboration and learning from failure as a means of continuous improvement. By leveraging diverse perspectives and encouraging a growth mindset, your team can thrive and achieve greater success.

Nurturing Psychological Safety and Risk-taking in Teams

Fostering an environment of psychological safety and encouraging risk-taking allows teams to spread their wings and soar to new heights. When team members feel safe to express themselves and take risks without fear of judgment or negative consequences, they're more likely to share innovative ideas, collaborate effectively, and challenge the status quo.

Psychological safety creates a space where individuals can freely voice their opinions, ask questions, and admit mistakes. This ultimately leads to better problem-solving and decision-making. By embracing risk-taking, teams can push boundaries, explore new possibilities, and discover creative solutions to complex problems.

Taking calculated risks not only fuels team growth but also fosters a culture of continuous learning, adaptability, and resilience. When team members are encouraged to step outside their comfort zones and explore uncharted territories, they develop new skills, gain confidence, and ultimately thrive in their personal and professional growth.

So, create an environment where psychological safety is nurtured, and risk-taking is embraced, and watch your team reach new levels of success.

Encouraging Collaboration and Learning from Failure in Teams

Encouraging collaboration and learning from failure in teams is all about creating an environment where teammates can come together, support each other, and bounce back stronger from setbacks.

By fostering a collaborative atmosphere, team members can share their ideas, perspectives, and expertise, leading to more innovative and effective solutions. Collaboration also allows for the pooling of resources and skills, maximizing the team's potential.

Moreover, embracing failures as learning opportunities cultivates a growth mindset within the team, encouraging experimentation, risk-taking, and continuous improvement. When team members aren't afraid to make mistakes, they become more open to trying new approaches and pushing boundaries.

This not only enhances individual growth but also strengthens the team as a whole, as everyone learns from each other's experiences.

So, by promoting collaboration and learning from failure, teams can truly thrive and achieve remarkable success.

Leveraging Diverse Perspectives with a Growth Mindset

Now that you understand the importance of collaboration and learning from failure in teams, it's time to take it a step further by leveraging diverse perspectives with a growth mindset.

When you approach situations with a growth mindset, you believe that everyone has the potential to learn and grow, regardless of their background or experiences. This mindset allows you to embrace the unique perspectives and ideas that each team member brings to the table.

By actively seeking out diverse perspectives, you open yourself up to new ways of thinking, problem-solving, and innovation. You realize that diversity is not just a buzzword, but a powerful tool for personal and professional growth.

So, next time you're working with a team, remember to embrace diverse perspectives with a growth mindset and watch the magic unfold.

Growth Mindset and Employee Development

Are you interested in fostering a culture of continuous learning and professional development in your employees? By encouraging your team members to constantly seek out new knowledge and skills, you can help them stay ahead in their careers and contribute more effectively to the overall success of your organization.

Providing growth opportunities and training programs not only benefits your employees, but also strengthens your company by equipping your workforce with the tools they need to adapt and thrive in a rapidly changing business landscape.

Additionally, recognizing and rewarding effort and growth in your employees can boost morale and motivation, creating a positive and productive work environment.

Encouraging Continuous Learning and Professional Development in Employees

Immerse yourself in a world of endless possibilities through continuous learning and professional development. By encouraging a growth mindset in employees, you empower them to embrace challenges and seek out new opportunities for growth.

Providing resources such as workshops, training programs, and mentorship opportunities can foster a culture of lifelong learning within your organization. Emphasize the importance of staying up-to-date with industry trends and advancements, and encourage employees to pursue certifications and further education.

Not only does this allow them to acquire new skills and knowledge, but it also boosts their confidence and job satisfaction. Encouraging continuous learning and professional development not only benefits individual employees, but also enhances the overall success and competitiveness of your organization.

So, invest in your employees' growth and watch how they thrive and contribute to the success of your company.

Providing Growth Opportunities and Training Programs

By empowering employees with growth opportunities and training programs, you can unlock their full potential and ignite their passion for continuous development.

Providing employees with growth opportunities allows them to expand their skillsets, learn new technologies, and stay up-to-date with industry trends. This not only enhances their job performance but also boosts their confidence and motivation.

Training programs, whether in-house or external, offer employees the chance to acquire new knowledge and improve their abilities in a structured and supportive environment. These programs can range from leadership development workshops to technical training sessions, tailored to the specific needs and goals of each employee.

By investing in their growth and providing them with these opportunities, you demonstrate your commitment to their professional development, which in turn fosters loyalty, engagement, and a sense of belonging. Moreover, it creates a culture of continuous learning within the organization, where employees are encouraged to seek out new challenges, embrace change, and strive for personal and professional growth.

Ultimately, by offering growth opportunities and training programs, you not only enhance the skills and knowledge of your employees but also create a competitive advantage for your organization in today's fast-paced and ever-evolving business landscape.

Recognizing and Rewarding Effort and Growth in Employees

Recognizing and rewarding the incredible effort and remarkable growth of employees fuels their motivation and propels them to even greater heights.

By acknowledging their hard work and dedication, you're not only boosting their self-esteem but also encouraging them to continue pushing themselves.

When employees see that their efforts are being recognized and appreciated, they're more likely to stay committed to their work and strive for continuous improvement.

Offering rewards, such as bonuses or promotions, not only serves as a tangible acknowledgment of their progress but also provides them with a sense of accomplishment.

This recognition and reward system creates a positive work environment where employees feel valued and motivated to excel.

It also fosters a culture of growth and development, as individuals are inspired to constantly learn and evolve.

So, take the time to acknowledge and reward the efforts and growth of your employees, and watch as they thrive and contribute even more to the success of your organization.

Evaluating and Measuring the Impact of Growth Mindset in Organizations

When it comes to evaluating and measuring the impact of growth mindset in organizations, there are several key points to consider.

First, assessing changes in employee mindset and attitudes is crucial to understanding the effectiveness of growth mindset initiatives.

By evaluating the impact of growth mindset on teamwork and performance, organizations can determine the value it brings to their overall success.

Additionally, analyzing organizational success and return on investment with growth mindset allows companies to make data-driven decisions and ensure they're getting the most out of their efforts.

Assessing Changes in Employee Mindset and Attitudes

As you embrace a growth mindset, you'll experience transformative shifts in your attitudes and mindset. This shift fosters a culture of lifelong learning and development.

This mindset allows you to see challenges as opportunities for growth and development, rather than obstacles to be avoided. You become more resilient and adaptable, willing to take on new challenges and learn from your mistakes.

With a growth mindset, you understand that your abilities and intelligence can be developed through dedication and hard work. This understanding leads to increased motivation and productivity.

Embracing a growth mindset not only benefits you as an individual, but also has a positive impact on your organization's culture. It fosters an environment of continuous improvement and innovation.

So, start cultivating a growth mindset today and unlock your full potential for lifelong learning and success.

Evaluating the Impact of Growth Mindset on Teamwork and Performance

How does embracing a growth mindset impact teamwork and performance in an organization?

When individuals in an organization embrace a growth mindset, they're more likely to view challenges as opportunities for growth and development.

This mindset enables them to approach teamwork with a sense of optimism and resilience, leading to increased collaboration and problem-solving abilities.

By fostering a culture of continuous learning and improvement, a growth mindset encourages individuals to seek feedback, learn from their mistakes, and adapt their strategies accordingly.

This not only enhances individual performance but also contributes to the overall success of the team.

Embracing a growth mindset empowers employees to take ownership of their growth and development, resulting in a more motivated and engaged workforce.

With a focus on continuous learning, organizations can unlock the full potential of their teams, leading to improved performance, innovation, and success.

Analyzing Organizational Success and Return on Investment with Growth Mindset

By embracing a growth mindset, you can analyze the success of your organization and determine the return on investment it brings.

When you adopt a growth mindset within your organization, you foster a culture of continuous learning and improvement. This mindset encourages employees to seek out new challenges, embrace failure as an opportunity for growth, and develop their skills and abilities.

As a result, your organization will experience increased innovation, productivity, and overall success.

By analyzing the impact of growth mindset on your organization, you can quantify the return on investment it brings. This analysis will allow you to identify areas of improvement, allocate resources effectively, and make informed decisions that drive long-term success.

Embracing a growth mindset is not only beneficial for individual employees, but it also has a significant impact on the success and profitability of your organization.

So, why wait? Start embracing a growth mindset today and unlock the full potential of your organization.

Chapter 20: Instilling Growth Mindset in Community and Society

In this chapter, you'll explore the powerful connection between growth mindset and social change. Discover how cultivating a growth mindset in community education and programs can lead to positive transformation on a larger scale.

Find out how creating growth mindset initiatives in local and national policy can create a ripple effect that benefits society as a whole. By understanding the impact of growth mindset on social change, you'll be inspired to take action and make a difference in your own community.

Growth Mindset and Social Change

Are you interested in learning how to use a growth mindset to overcome social inequalities?

By adopting a growth mindset, you can promote equity and access for all individuals, regardless of their background or circumstances.

Additionally, advocacy and activism play a crucial role in fostering a growth mindset within society, empowering individuals to reach their full potential.

Using Growth Mindset to Overcome Social Inequalities

Embrace a growth mindset and overcome social inequalities by recognizing that individuals who believe their abilities can be developed are more likely to pursue education and career opportunities regardless of their background.

Did you know that a study found that students with a growth mindset were 2.5 times more likely to enroll in college compared to those with a fixed mindset? This shows the incredible power of believing in one's own potential and the impact it can have on breaking the cycle of social inequalities.

By adopting a growth mindset, you can overcome the limitations that society may place on you and strive for success. Through lifelong learning and the belief that you can constantly improve, you can challenge societal norms, break down barriers, and create a more equal and inclusive world.

So, don't let your background define your future. Embrace a growth mindset and open doors to endless possibilities.

Promoting Equity and Access with a Growth Mindset

By adopting a growth mindset, you can level the playing field and ensure that everyone has equal opportunities to succeed.

With a growth mindset, you believe that abilities and intelligence can be developed through hard work, dedication, and perseverance.

This mindset empowers individuals to embrace challenges, learn from failures, and view setbacks as opportunities for growth.

By promoting equity and access with a growth mindset, you can break down barriers that prevent marginalized individuals from reaching their full potential.

It encourages educators to provide inclusive learning environments, where students are supported and encouraged to take risks and explore their full potential.

By fostering a growth mindset culture, we can create a society where everyone has the opportunity to thrive and contribute their unique talents and perspectives.

Advocacy and Activism in Fostering Growth Mindset in Society

Now that you understand the importance of promoting equity and access with a growth mindset, it's time to take it a step further and become an advocate and activist in fostering this mindset in society.

By actively advocating for the growth mindset, you can help create a culture that values continuous learning and improvement. This means challenging the status quo, speaking up against fixed mindset beliefs, and promoting the idea that everyone has the potential to grow and learn.

Through your activism, you can inspire others to embrace the growth mindset and create positive change in their own lives and communities. So, don't just stop at understanding the benefits of a growth mindset, take action and become a catalyst for change.

Growth Mindset in Community Education and Programs

Are you interested in learning how to integrate growth mindset into community education initiatives?

By incorporating the principles of growth mindset into community education programs, individuals and communities can benefit from the power of believing in their ability to learn and grow.

Collaborating with community organizations can also be a powerful way to promote growth mindset, as it allows for a collective effort in spreading the message of resilience and continuous improvement.

By empowering individuals and communities through growth mindset, we can create a culture of lifelong learning and personal development, leading to positive social change and transformation.

Integrating Growth Mindset into Community Education Initiatives

Integrating a growth mindset into community education initiatives can be challenging, but it's worth the effort to empower individuals to embrace lifelong learning. By incorporating the principles of growth mindset into community education programs, participants are encouraged to view challenges as opportunities for growth and to persist in the face of obstacles.

This mindset shift can have a profound impact on individuals' motivation, self-confidence, and ability to learn. Community education initiatives can create a supportive environment where learners feel safe to take risks, make mistakes, and learn from them.

Through fostering a growth mindset, community education programs can inspire individuals to continuously develop their skills, expand their knowledge, and pursue their goals. By embracing a growth mindset, participants can unlock their full potential and thrive in their personal and professional lives.

Collaborating with Community Organizations for Growth Mindset Promotion

By collaborating with community organizations, you can create a powerful environment that empowers individuals to embrace continuous personal and professional development. Working together with these organizations allows for a wider reach and impact, as they often have established networks and resources that can support growth mindset promotion.

By pooling our efforts and expertise, we can develop innovative programs and initiatives that cater to the specific needs and interests of the community. Through workshops, seminars, and interactive sessions, we can provide individuals with the tools and strategies they need to cultivate a growth mindset and thrive in their personal and professional lives.

Additionally, by partnering with community organizations, we can tap into their existing relationships and credibility, which can enhance the effectiveness and credibility of our growth mindset initiatives. Together, we can create a culture of lifelong learning and growth, where individuals are inspired and supported to continuously strive for improvement and embrace new challenges.

Empowering Individuals and Communities through Growth Mindset

Now that you understand the importance of collaborating with community organizations to promote a growth mindset, it's time to take that knowledge and put it into action by empowering individuals and communities through the growth mindset.

By adopting a growth mindset, you can unlock your full potential and overcome any obstacles that come your way. This mindset encourages continuous learning, embracing challenges, and persisting in the face of setbacks. It allows you to see failures as opportunities for growth and to believe in your ability to develop new skills and talents.

Empowering individuals and communities with the growth mindset not only improves their personal and professional lives but also creates a ripple effect that benefits society as a whole.

So, embrace the power of the growth mindset and inspire others to do the same, because together, we can create a world where lifelong learning and personal growth are valued and celebrated.

Creating Growth Mindset Initiatives in Local and National Policy

Are you interested in creating positive change in your community?

One way to do so is by incorporating the growth mindset philosophy into education and social policies.

By advocating for a growth mindset in mental health and well-being, you can help individuals overcome challenges and develop resilience.

Additionally, creating environments that foster a growth mindset in community settings can lead to increased motivation, productivity, and overall well-being.

Embracing the power of a growth mindset can transform policies and programs, creating opportunities for individuals to thrive and reach their full potential.

Incorporating Growth Mindset Philosophy in Education and Social Policies

Immersing students in a growth mindset philosophy allows education and social policies to blossom like a vibrant garden, nurturing a lifelong love for learning.

By incorporating the principles of growth mindset into education policies, we can create an environment that encourages students to embrace challenges, persist through obstacles, and see failures as opportunities for growth. This approach fosters a sense of resilience and a belief in their own abilities, empowering students to take ownership of their learning journeys.

In addition, integrating growth mindset into social policies can help create a supportive and inclusive society, where individuals are encouraged to pursue continuous learning and personal development.

By emphasizing the importance of effort and dedication rather than fixed abilities, we can inspire individuals to strive for excellence and reach their full potential.

Ultimately, by embracing the growth mindset philosophy in education and social policies, we can unlock the inherent potential in every individual and cultivate a society that thrives through lifelong learning.

Advocating for Growth Mindset in Mental Health and Well-being

Imagine a world where you believe in your ability to overcome challenges and see setbacks as opportunities for personal growth and well-being. Advocating for a growth mindset in mental health and well-being can be transformative.

By adopting this mindset, you can cultivate resilience, creativity, and a sense of purpose. Instead of being defined by your limitations, you can view them as temporary roadblocks on your journey to personal growth.

With a growth mindset, you can embrace challenges, seek out new experiences, and continuously learn and adapt. This mindset empowers you to take charge of your mental health and well-being, enabling you to thrive in all aspects of your life.

So, why not choose to adopt a growth mindset and unlock your potential for lifelong learning and personal growth?

Creating Environments that Foster Growth Mindset in Community Settings

Creating environments that foster a growth mindset in community settings allows you to flourish, embrace challenges, and continuously adapt, leading to personal development and success.

When you're surrounded by a supportive community that values the power of growth and learning, you're more likely to take risks, push yourself out of your comfort zone, and view setbacks as opportunities for growth.

These environments provide you with the necessary resources, encouragement, and feedback to help you thrive.

Whether it's a workplace, educational institution, or social group, fostering a growth mindset creates a positive and empowering atmosphere where everyone can reach their full potential.

By promoting a culture of lifelong learning and resilience, these environments not only benefit individuals but also contribute to the overall growth and well-being of the community as a whole.

So, embrace the power of a growth mindset and seek out environments that support and nurture your desire to continuously learn and improve.

The Ripple Effect of Growth Mindset in Society

Are you ready to discover the powerful ripple effect of growth mindset in society?

Get ready to be inspired and motivated as we explore the ways in which growth mindset positivity and inspiration can spread like wildfire, igniting a passion for learning and personal development in individuals and communities.

Imagine the possibilities when collective efforts and collaboration are encouraged with a growth mindset, fostering innovation and problem-solving on a whole new level.

And let's not forget about the resilient and knowledgeable communities that can be built through growth mindset, equipped with the tools and mindset to face challenges head-on and continuously grow and learn.

So join the movement and be a part of the transformation that growth mindset can bring to society.

Spreading Growth Mindset Positivity and Inspiration

Open your heart to the power of a growth mindset and watch as inspiration and positivity spread effortlessly throughout your life.

Embrace a growth mindset. It not only benefits you personally, but it also has a ripple effect on those around you.

By adopting a mindset that believes in the potential for growth and the ability to learn from challenges, you become a beacon of hope and motivation for others.

Your determination to overcome obstacles and embrace new opportunities inspires those around you to do the same.

Your positive attitude and belief in the power of learning create a contagious energy that encourages others to step outside of their comfort zones and strive for personal growth.

By spreading the growth mindset, you contribute to a society that thrives on lifelong learning, innovation, and progress.

So, open your mind, embrace the power of growth, and become a catalyst for positive change in the world.

Encouraging Collective Efforts and Collaboration with a Growth Mindset

Now that you've learned about spreading growth mindset positivity and inspiration, it's time to take it a step further and explore the power of encouraging collective efforts and collaboration with a growth mindset.

When individuals come together with a shared belief in the potential for growth and improvement, amazing things can happen. By fostering an environment that values collaboration and teamwork, you create a space where ideas can flow freely, diverse perspectives can be considered, and innovative solutions can be created.

A growth mindset encourages individuals to embrace challenges, support one another, and continuously learn from each other's experiences. When everyone is working towards a common goal with a growth mindset, the possibilities for success are endless.

So, why not harness the power of collective efforts and collaboration to achieve greatness?

Building Resilient and Knowledgeable Communities through Growth Mindset

By embracing the belief in our capacity to adapt and grow, you can foster resilient and knowledgeable communities that thrive on continuous development.

When individuals within a community adopt a growth mindset, they're more likely to view challenges as opportunities for growth and learning. This mindset encourages them to seek out new knowledge, skills, and experiences, and to persevere in the face of setbacks.

As a result, communities become vibrant hubs of lifelong learning, where individuals support and inspire each other to reach their full potential.

The collective efforts of a growth-minded community can lead to innovative solutions to complex problems, as diverse perspectives and ideas are valued and encouraged.

By building resilient and knowledgeable communities through a growth mindset, we create environments that are adaptable, forward-thinking, and equipped to thrive in an ever-changing world.

Chapter 21: The Future of Growth Mindset

In Chapter 21, we delve into the future of growth mindset and explore its evolution and continued relevance in our society.

Discover the latest research and development in growth mindset, as well as how it empowers individuals and communities.

You'll see how embracing a growth mindset can open doors to lifelong learning, personal development, and success.

The Evolution and Continued Relevance of Growth Mindset

Are you curious about the future trends and applications of growth mindset?

Imagine incorporating virtual and augmented reality to enhance your growth mindset journey.

With the advancement of technology, there are countless tools available to help cultivate and strengthen your growth mindset.

Exploring Future Trends and Applications of Growth Mindset

Imagine how your mindset could shape the future, unlocking new possibilities and applications for growth in ways you never thought possible.

With the continued evolution and relevance of the growth mindset, we're entering an era where this powerful mindset is becoming increasingly essential.

As technology advances and industries rapidly evolve, the ability to adapt, learn, and embrace challenges will be crucial for success.

The growth mindset provides the foundation for continuous learning and improvement, enabling individuals and organizations to thrive in an ever-changing world.

By cultivating a growth mindset, you can tap into your unlimited potential and embrace opportunities for growth and innovation.

Whether it's in the workplace, education, or personal development, the growth mindset opens doors to new ideas, perspectives, and breakthroughs.

It allows you to approach challenges with resilience, view failure as a stepping stone to success, and constantly seek out new ways to learn and improve.

As we look ahead, the growth mindset will continue to be a driving force behind innovation, creativity, and adaptability.

It will empower individuals to navigate uncertainty, embrace change, and seize opportunities for growth and success.

So, imagine the possibilities that await you with a growth mindset – the future is yours to shape.

Incorporating Virtual and Augmented Reality for Growth Mindset

By embracing the power of virtual and augmented reality, you can unlock new dimensions of personal growth and innovation. Virtual and augmented reality technologies offer unique opportunities to immerse yourself in learning experiences that challenge your mindset and expand your horizons.

With virtual reality, you can step into simulated environments and practice real-life scenarios, allowing you to develop new skills and gain confidence in a safe and controlled setting. Augmented reality, on the other hand, overlays digital information onto the real world, enabling you to access valuable resources and guidance right at your fingertips.

By incorporating these technologies into your growth mindset journey, you can enhance your learning, problem-solving, and creativity, ultimately enabling you to thrive in an ever-changing and evolving world. So, don't hesitate to dive into the world of virtual and augmented reality and discover the endless possibilities for personal growth and innovation that await you.

Technology and Tools for Cultivating Growth Mindset

Embrace the power of technology and tools to embark on a transformative journey of personal development and innovation. With the advancement of technology, there are numerous resources available that can help cultivate a growth mindset.

Online learning platforms such as Coursera and Khan Academy offer a wide range of courses and tutorials, allowing you to learn new skills and expand your knowledge at your own pace.

Additionally, there are apps and websites like Duolingo and Lumosity that provide interactive and gamified experiences to enhance your cognitive abilities and problem-solving skills.

Virtual reality (VR) and augmented reality (AR) can also be utilized to create immersive learning environments, enabling you to explore new perspectives and gain practical experience in various fields.

By embracing these technological advancements and utilizing the tools at your disposal, you can actively engage in lifelong learning, continuously adapt to new challenges, and unlock your full potential.

Research and Development in Growth Mindset

Are you curious about the latest advancements in neuroscience and brain research on growth mindset? Discover how scientists are exploring the impact of growth mindset on the brain and uncovering fascinating insights into human learning and development.

Additionally, delve into the realm of investigating the long-term effects of growth mindset interventions, as researchers strive to understand how these interventions can shape individuals' lives over time.

Lastly, explore evidence-based practices and strategies for cultivating a growth mindset, and learn how you can apply these techniques in your own life to foster a mindset of continuous growth and improvement.

Advancements in Neuroscience and Brain Research on Growth Mindset

Discover the incredible power of advancements in neuroscience and brain research, and how they can transform your mindset and ignite a lifelong passion for learning.

Through extensive studies and experiments, researchers have uncovered fascinating insights into the brain's ability to change and adapt. They've found that the brain is malleable, and with deliberate practice and effort, individuals can develop new neural pathways and improve their cognitive abilities.

This means that regardless of your age or current abilities, you have the potential to grow and learn. By adopting a growth mindset, you can embrace challenges, persist through setbacks, and ultimately achieve your goals.

Neuroscience and brain research provide us with the knowledge and tools to understand how our brains work and how we can optimize our learning potential. So, don't let any limitations hold you back. Embrace the power of your brain, and embark on a journey of lifelong learning and personal growth.

Investigating the Long-term Effects of Growth Mindset Interventions

Unleash the full potential of your mind by exploring the long-term effects of growth mindset interventions.

Like the story of John, a once self-doubting student who, with the help of mindset training, blossomed into a confident learner and achieved academic success.

Research has shown that growth mindset interventions have a lasting impact on individuals, leading to improved motivation, resilience, and achievement.

By teaching individuals to embrace challenges, persist in the face of setbacks, and believe in their ability to learn and grow, growth mindset interventions create a foundation for lifelong learning and success.

John's story is just one example of how mindset training can transform lives, opening doors to new possibilities and empowering individuals to reach their full potential.

So, why wait? Start your own journey of growth and discovery today and see the incredible long-term effects of embracing a growth mindset.

Evidence-based Practices and Strategies for Cultivating Growth Mindset

By implementing evidence-based practices and strategies, you can actively cultivate a growth mindset, fostering resilience and motivation in your journey towards personal development and achievement.

One effective strategy is to embrace challenges and see them as opportunities for growth rather than obstacles. This involves pushing yourself outside of your comfort zone and embracing the idea that failure is a natural part of the learning process.

Another strategy is to develop a positive self-talk and mindset. This involves challenging negative thoughts and reframing them in a more positive and empowering way. By focusing on your strengths and abilities, you can build confidence and belief in your own potential.

Additionally, seeking feedback and constructive criticism can help you identify areas for improvement and further develop your skills. Embracing a growth mindset means viewing setbacks as temporary and learning opportunities, and using them as fuel for growth and development.

So, take the initiative to implement these evidence-based practices and strategies, and unlock the power of a growth mindset to thrive in your personal and professional life.

Empowering Individuals and Communities through Growth Mindset

Are you interested in learning how growth mindset education and initiatives can be scaled to reach more individuals and communities?

Discover the power of collaborations and partnerships in promoting a growth mindset and inspiring collective action.

By embracing a growth mindset, you can make a significant impact on yourself and those around you, fostering a culture of continuous learning and development.

Scaling Growth Mindset Education and Initiatives

Embrace the power of a growth mindset and watch as opportunities for lifelong learning flourish like a garden in bloom.

Scaling growth mindset education and initiatives is crucial in empowering individuals and communities to unlock their full potential. By adopting a growth mindset, you open yourself up to new possibilities, challenges, and growth.

It's about believing in your ability to learn and improve, embracing failure as an opportunity to grow, and seeking out feedback and constructive criticism.

Through scaling growth mindset education, we can create a culture of continuous learning, where individuals are encouraged to take risks, persevere through obstacles, and constantly strive for improvement.

This not only benefits individuals by expanding their knowledge and skills, but it also has a ripple effect on communities, fostering innovation, collaboration, and resilience.

With a growth mindset, the possibilities for personal and collective growth are endless, so let's embrace it and watch as our potential for lifelong learning takes flight.

Collaborations and Partnerships for Growth Mindset Promotion

Collaborate with like-minded organizations and individuals to cultivate a garden of possibilities, where seeds of resilience and innovation are nurtured and bloom together.

By joining forces with others who share the same vision of promoting the growth mindset, you can amplify the impact of your efforts and create a thriving ecosystem of lifelong learners.

Through partnerships, you can pool resources, share best practices, and leverage each other's strengths to reach a wider audience and make a lasting difference.

Whether it's collaborating on workshops, developing joint programs, or supporting each other's initiatives, the power of collaboration can propel the growth mindset movement forward.

By working together, you can inspire and empower individuals to embrace challenges, persist in the face of setbacks, and continuously learn and grow.

Together, we can create a world where the growth mindset is not just a concept, but a way of life.

So, reach out, connect, and let's cultivate this garden of possibilities together.

Inspiring Collective Action and Impact through Growth Mindset

Unlock the potential within yourself and join forces with others to create a ripple effect of inspiration, where the seeds of growth flourish and spread like wildfire.

By embracing a growth mindset and inspiring collective action, we can achieve remarkable impact.

Imagine a world where individuals come together, supporting and challenging each other to constantly learn and grow.

This collective effort not only empowers us individually but also creates a powerful network of change agents. Through collaboration, we can amplify our impact and reach new heights.

Together, we can challenge the status quo, overcome obstacles, and create a culture of continuous learning and improvement.

By inspiring collective action, we become catalysts for growth, igniting a passion for lifelong learning in those around us.

So, don't wait any longer. Step up, join forces with others, and let's create a ripple effect of growth mindset that will transform lives and shape a better future.

Don't miss out!

Visit the website below and you can sign up to receive emails whenever Adam Poliman publishes a new book. There's no charge and no obligation.

https://books2read.com/r/B-A-VSRY-AAHNC

BOOKS 2 READ

Connecting independent readers to independent writers.

Also by Adam Poliman

The Power of Time: Transform Your Life through Effective Time Management
Unleashing The Power Of Reading
Unlocking the Power of Critical Thinking: Strategies for Effective Problem-Solving
Efficiency Unleashed: Mastering Productivity Tips and Hacks for Success
The Art of Social Intelligence: Mastering the Skills of Effective Communication
Destined For Greatness: Mastering The Art Of Goal Setting
Mind Over Temptation: Building Self-Discipline In A Distracted World
The Bright Path: Navigating Life With Positive Thinking
The Emotion Code: Decoding Emotional Intelligence
The Growth Mindset Advantage: Thriving Through Lifelong Learning
Unleashing Your Potential: A Guide To Personal Development And Self-Improvement

Watch for more at https://optimizationtime.com.

About the Author

Adam Poliman is a renowned author in the personal improvement space, dedicated to helping individuals unlock their full potential and lead fulfilling lives. With a passion for personal growth and a deep understanding of human psychology, Adam combines his expertise with practical insights to empower readers to make positive changes. His thought-provoking books offer actionable strategies and transformative techniques that inspire readers to overcome challenges, cultivate resilience, and achieve their goals. Through his writing, Adam seeks to guide readers on a transformative journey of self-discovery, encouraging them to embrace personal development and create a life of purpose and fulfillment.

Read more at https://optimizationtime.com.

Milton Keynes UK
Ingram Content Group UK Ltd.
UKHW010653101123
432322UK00003B/116